NORSEMAN'S DESIRE

"Thank you for caring for me this morning," Erik said softly.

"It is my duty to care for my master," Lenora replied, not meeting his eyes. "You need not thank me."

He tilted her chin up until she was forced to look straight into his eyes. His fingers wove themselves through her chestnut curls, playing with the ends. His eyes were bottomless green pools, in which she would gladly drown.

"You are a beautiful young woman, Lenora. Do you know how difficult it has been to lie beside you all these nights and not touch you?"

"I am your slave," she answered with false meekness. "You may do what you want with me and I must obey."

"I do not want a woman who only obeys."

Still his eyes held her. She fought against feelings that threatened to burst out of control and overwhelm her. She wanted to put her arms around him, wanted his arms around her. Most of all, she wanted the touch of his wide, burning mouth on her lips.

Other *Leisure Books* by Flora Speer:

BY HONOR BOUND
VENUS RISING
MUCH ADO ABOUT LOVE
DESTINY'S LOVERS

FLORA SPEER

VIKING PASSION

LEISURE BOOKS NEW YORK CITY

*For my agent, Adele Leone,
and my editor, Alicia Condon.
My thanks to both of you
for your advice and
positive criticism,
and for believing in me.*

A LEISURE BOOK®

March 1992

Published by

Dorchester Publishing Co., Inc.
276 Fifth Avenue
New York, NY 10001

Printed in the United States of America.

Prologue

The skalds, those poetic makers of Viking legends and sagas, tell the story of Ragnar Lodbrok, Ragnar Hairy-breeches, who in the middle years of the ninth century harried the northeastern coast of Britain until he was finally captured by King AElle of Northumbria. He was condemned to death and cast into a pit of vipers.

Though Ragnar would have much preferred to live, he was not afraid to die, and so as the venomous snakes writhed about his body he cheerfully sang his Viking death-song. He cried out only once during his ordeal. It was not a plea for mercy, but a threat.

"Ah," he called to those watching him, "if only my little pigs knew how it fares with their old boar."

His "little pigs," his four sons, soon learned the

manner of their father's death. The legend says Ragnar's oldest son, Bjorn Ironside, when he heard the news, gripped the shaft of his spear so tightly that his fingerprints were permanently impressed upon it. Sigurd Snake-eye, the second son, was told of his father's fate as he pared his nails with a knife. He kept on cutting until he reached bone. The third son, Hvitserk, sat at his chessboard when the news was brought to him. The skalds say he clenched the ivory pawn so hard it crumbled into dust in his fingers. The fourth son, Ivar the Boneless, said nothing. His expression did not change, but his face became red, and then blue, and then white.

It was Ivar who gathered a powerful army and, with two of his brothers, sailed to England seeking vengeance. In autumn of the Year of Our Lord 866, Ivar landed in East Anglia. He spent the winter consolidating his forces and acquiring horses and supplies from the cowed Saxons who lived there. In the spring of 867, Ivar marched north to lay siege to AElle's capital at York. Thus began the Viking invasions that soon overpowered most of England.

In Ivar's wake sailed Snorri Thorkellsson of Denmark, Snorri the Late-comer, who, having been abroad on a voyage of plunder and trade, arrived home to learn of these events from his father. There was some discussion as to what Snorri should do. Should he offer his services to Ivar, who was a distant cousin on his mother's side?

"It is too late for that, Snorri, almost a year

too late," his father told him.

Old Thorkell gazed with affection upon the robust blond man before him. A valiant warrior, this oldest of his children, a son to make a father proud. Would that Snorri's half-brother Erik had also remained strong and battle-worthy. More damage than the injury to Erik's leg had been done by those soft Greeks, with their silken ways and strange learning. The old man sighed. Luck, that was it. Erik's luck was bad. He forced his attention back to what his older son was saying.

Snorri was a clever man. He loved bloodshed and battle as much as any Viking, but he loved the gleam of gold and silver even more. His cunning mind had devised a scheme.

"There will still be loot to take," Snorri said. "I will discover exactly where Ivar's army landed, and then I will sail to settlements on the coast or along the rivers, where he and his men have not been. A rapid series of raids, with easy plunder. The young men of East Anglia will surely have marched north to join the Northumbrians opposing Ivar's army. There will be only old men and boys left to fight us. There will be gold and silver in the churches and the thegn's halls, and there will be female slaves for the taking."

Snorri remembered well the lovely, rosy-gold maidens he had met on his last raid in England. They screamed and clawed and fought. Snorri grinned. He liked spirited women. And Saxon girls sold easily in the slave market of Hedeby.

"Would you like some soft, plump Anglian

women, Father? A few new slaves to warm your bed?"

Father and son smiled at each other in complete understanding.

With the resources of his wealthy father behind him, Snorri moved quickly. Thorkell had more than enough food and ale and extra weapons in the storerooms of Thorkellshavn to supply such an expedition.

Snorri paused in Denmark only long enough to reprovision his longship, the *Sea Dragon*, and ravish half a dozen or so slave girls before collecting his eager men once more and setting off on his mission.

Part One

East Anglia
Mid-June, A.D. 867

Chapter One

"Hurry, Lenora, we don't have much time."

"I'm coming. There is so much to do, and it's all in your honor, my dear."

Lenora came running, her long, unbound chestnut curls bouncing. She embraced her friend with an enthusiasm that left poor Edwina breathless and clutching at the gatepost of the log stockade surrounding the tun.

"What a beautiful day," Lenora exclaimed, taking in the midsummer green of the East Anglian landscape. "It's perfect for a wedding."

The rich, flat farmlands stretched away beyond the tiny Saxon settlement, bounded to the north and west by thick forest and on the south and east by a lazy, shimmering river that meandered slowly out to the North Sea. All the land as far as the girls could see belonged to Lenora's half-brother, Wilfred. Like his father before him, Wilfred was thegn to Edmund, King of East Anglia. His home, a large wooden hall with a thatched roof, stood within the stockade fence, as did the women's quarters, a tiny wooden church, the barn, and the small cottages of those who worked Wilfred's land. Although the farmers were free men, they had pledged their loyalty to him and dwelt within the safety of Wilfred's tun.

The appearance of early morning drowsiness that surrounded the dwellings was deceptive, for inside the great hall buzzed with activity as preparations were made for the wedding later that day.

Lenora's older half-sister Matilda was supervising the servants, an arrangement for which Lenora, never very domestic, was extremely grateful. Matilda had arrived two days earlier with her husband, Athelstan, and her children, and had at once set about cleaning the hall, directing the hanging of the fine tapestries that were saved for festive occasions, and cooking vast quantities of food for the wedding feast.

The wedding might be a small one, lacking the pomp a noble family would have enjoyed in less troubled times, and done a bit hastily during the short time when both Wilfred and Athelstan were free from their duties to King Edmund at his court at Rendlesham, but Matilda would see to it that her brother's nuptials were properly celebrated.

Lenora, her spirits bubbling high, her dark

14

gray eyes sparkling with excitement, hugged Edwina again.

"I'm so glad you are marrying Wilfred. You will manage this household much better than I do. And we will all live together. It will be wonderful!"

Edwina smoothed down her honey-blond braids, in disarray after her friend's affectionate attacks.

"You will marry soon yourself," she said in her quiet, cool voice. "Then you will have your own household to manage."

"No. I think I shall never marry. I was not meant to be a matron with a ring of keys at my girdle."

"You were never meant to be a nun, Lenora."

Edwina knew her beloved Wilfred's young sister was too proud and, yes, too undisciplined, for the humble vocation of nun. Lenora must marry. It was inevitable, although so far she had rejected the few suitors who had steeled themselves to ask for her hand, and her kind-hearted brother could not bring himself to press her to make an unwilling choice.

"I should have been a man," Lenora said. "Then I could sail away to the land of the Franks as my father did. Or I could ride north to York and fight the Northmen."

"The Northmen." Edwina shivered, her thin shoulders hunching beneath her fine woolen gown. The heavy gold bracelet Wilfred had given her glittered as she wrapped her arms around herself. "I cannot bear to think of them. Father

Egbert says they are wicked, heathen beasts. I hope they never come here."

"They got all the horses they wanted and now they have marched northward. They won't bother us," Lenora told her confidently. "We have better things to think of. Let's go before Matilda tries to stop us."

She caught Edwina's hand and pulled her away from the tun. A short distance from the settlement, close to the encroaching forest, was a hill, an ancient mound of earth that, some said, had been raised on the flat Anglian plain by the people who had lived in this land before the Saxons came. No one knew its purpose. Most avoided it, fearing evil spirits, but Lenora loved to climb to the very top. From its modest height she could look down on her home and the fields surrounding it. The hill was her special place. There, she knew, she and Edwina would find what they sought.

"Wait. Edwina, Alienor, please wait."

"Oh, no." Lenora glanced back and sighed. There was nothing to do but wait until the fat little priest had caught up with them.

"Oh, dear," he panted. "Oh, my dear young women, what are you doing?" Father Egbert's shiny face and tonsured head gleamed, his dark robe flapping about his stubby legs as he hurried forward. "What are you thinking of? You dare not wander about unescorted. Your brother will be angry, Alienor."

"Nonsense. He won't know unless you tell him."

Lenora regarded the priest with haughty distaste. His constant disapproval of her independent ways irritated her. She noticed that his feet, thrust into well-worn sandals, were very dirty. Lenora was not overly fastidious herself, but the sight of Father Egbert's grubby toes only increased her dislike for the man.

"We are going to pick flowers for my bridal wreath," Edwina explained. "We won't be gone long."

"Does Matilda know of this?" the priest inquired.

"There is no need to tell her. She is busy and we don't want to disturb her," Lenora told him coldly.

"It is dangerous to go out unattended," Father Egbert insisted.

"We won't be out of sight of the tun," Lenora argued. "We will be perfectly safe. Come along, Edwina." She took Edwina's hand again and turned toward the hill, where midsummer flowers bloomed among the grasses, in soft white and yellow and blue.

"Oh, dear, oh, dear. If you insist on going, then I must accompany you." Father Egbert puffed after them. "It is my duty. You need protection. We never know when the Northmen will appear."

Lenora stifled her annoyance. She longed to tell Father Egbert there was nothing he could do to protect them in the event of danger, but she bit her tongue and said nothing.

She had wanted this last hour alone with Edwina before the marriage ceremony. By this time tomorrow, her dear friend, a wealthy orphan who had been first her father Cedric's ward and then, after his death, her brother Wilfred's ward, would be her sister-in-law. Edwina would be privy to those mysteries of the marriage bed about which, of late, Lenora was unable to stop thinking. She knew the bare facts of human mating. No one growing up as she had, running free about her father's farmlands, could long remain innocent of such knowledge. It was the emotional content of such a relationship, the desire for one man above all others, that had so far eluded her. At sixteen, Lenora was intensely curious, but still unawakened.

She had planned to question Edwina, to obtain from her friend some information about her feelings toward Wilfred as their bridal night approached. There was no doubt in Lenora's mind that Edwina cared deeply for Wilfred, and although she, Lenora, could not comprehend why her older brother should inspire such passion, she wanted to understand its causes.

Now Father Egbert had spoiled her plan. There could be no question of a discussion of earthly love with the priest listening to every word. Lenora wanted to shake him until his rosary beads rattled, and then give him a good, swift kick that would send him scurrying back to the church, where he belonged. She dismissed the priest from her mind as Edwina called out in delight.

"Look up here, there is a clump of beautiful buttercups. They are like gold. Help me, Lenora. We must hurry. After we gather them, we still have to weave the wreath.''

The two girls bent to their task, smooth honey-gold braids and burnished chestnut curls close together, as they whispered and talked.

Father Egbert watched them, thinking what a pretty picture they made. They were clothed in the brilliant colors all Saxons loved, Edwina's slender form in a bright green wool kirtle, Lenora's fuller figure in deep blue.

If only Lenora—Alienor—could absorb some of her friend's more placid disposition. Father Egbert did not dislike Lenora, but he worried about her. She was different from other women he knew, adventurous and impulsive and full of pride. Before he had died four years ago her father had even taught her to read and write a little Latin. It was most unseemly. Father Egbert feared Lenora would never find a husband, for what man would want a wife more learned than himself? Cedric should have been wiser about his daughter's future.

Cedric had been an unusual man. Like Lenora, the daughter of his middle age, Cedric was proud of the long line of Saxon nobles from whom he was descended, and like her, he, too, was adventurous. Braving the treacherous waters of the Narrow Seas, he had traveled to distant lands after the death of his first wife, returning with a strange, beautiful Frankish woman as his second wife. Father Egbert could not understand the violent passion with which Cedric had loved his dark-eyed Alienor, or his grief when she died in childbirth. Cedric had insisted on calling the

19

baby Alienor for her mother, instead of a good Saxon name, although in time the more gentle sound of Lenora had replaced the outlandish foreign name.

Little Alienor had been cared for by her older halfsister Matilda, now married to a neighboring land-holder, and by Wilfred, the other child of Cedric's first marriage. Lenora and the gentle orphan Edwina, who was the same age, had grown up together, as close as sisters.

A loud burst of laughter from Lenora made the priest shake his head sadly. The girl was incorrigible. Her demeanor was definitely not that of a modest maiden. She sat on the grass, skirts crumpled up about her shapely calves, a pile of flowers in her lap, their bright colors contrasting with the blue of her gown. The priest looked away quickly.

Ashamed of his unkind thoughts toward an innocent young girl, however difficult she might be, Father Egbert grasped his rosary and began to tell his beads. He became so engrossed that he did not see the ship.

Chapter Two

It was the shouting that drew his attention. Father Egbert looked up from his rosary. He gasped, his eyes nearly starting out of his head in terror.

A ship lay at the river's edge near the open entrance to the tun. How it had come so quickly and so silently he did not know, but there was no mistaking that graceful form. It was the stuff of nightmares to all decent men and women. Long and low and sleek, it rose at each end to a slender, tapered shape. A fierce, grinning beast, some heathen demon-god carved in wood, adorned the bow. A square sail lay furled across the yard at the base of the single mast.

Out of the ship poured tall, hard-muscled men. Their leader's rounded metal helmet gleamed dully in the early morning sun. The others were bareheaded. Blond or red hair, light brown hair, bushy beards, a few clean-shaven faces, brightly painted wooden shields held against taut bodies, drawn broadswords ready for action, spears and sharp-edged battleaxes, all swam before Father Egbert's appalled eyes. The Vikings had come.

Lenora heard Father Egbert's gasp and followed his gaze. For a moment she froze. Then, always quick to react, she rose, pulling Edwina with her. The flowers scattered out of her skirt, falling in bruised profusion into the grass at her feet.

"We must flee," she said. "Run, Edwina. They haven't seen us yet. We can get away. We can hide in the forest."

"No." Edwina did not hesitate. "I must go to Wilfred. Whatever happens, I will be at his side."

Edwina headed for the stockade gate, through which they could see the Viking warriors rushing in a terrifying wave. Lenora clutched at her friend's arm. Edwina, though fragile in appearance, was surprisingly strong. She dragged Lenora after her as she ran down the hill.

"You can't go in there," Lenora screamed at her. "Look." She pointed with her free hand as flames ran up one side of the barn and caught the thatched roof. The shrieks and cries and the clatter of battle now coming from within the enclosure were deafening, although the high fence blocked their view of what was happening.

"I don't care," Edwina cried hysterically. "Wilfred! Wilfred!"

"Help me," Lenora called to the priest, as she

struggled to stop Edwina.

Father Egbert caught Edwina's other arm.

"You must run away," he gasped, his voice trembling with fright. "Oh, what they will do to you, what those heathens do to Christian women. Oh, Edwina, I beseech you, run, run for your life."

Together Lenora and the priest struggled to turn Edwina from her headlong flight toward the little village. It was already too late to escape detection. The sound of their voices had attracted the attention of one of the Vikings left at the river's edge to guard the ship. He began to move toward them, a wicked-looking sword held in one large hand.

"Please," Father Egbert moaned, "please, Edwina, I beg you, run."

Edwina did not seem to hear him.

"I must go to Wilfred," she insisted wildly.

"You can't help Wilfred now," Lenora cried, still tugging at Edwina's arm, "but we can save ourselves."

"I will try to delay that man," Father Egbert told Lenora. "Get her away from here. God bless and protect you both."

He dropped Edwina's arm and moved to place himself between the Viking and the women. Lenora continued to pull at Edwina's arm, Edwina pulling in the opposite direction with the same effort. The two girls stood balanced in their tug-of-war as Father Egbert met the Viking.

Lenora felt a flash of admiration for the fat little man, and remorse for her earlier dislike of him as he bravely faced the Norse giant.

23

Father Egbert spread his arms wide. His black robe billowed in the summer breeze as he looked up at the Viking, who regarded him with a cruel smile.

"I implore you," Father Egbert began.

He got no further. With a harsh laugh, the Viking lifted a fist and punched Father Egbert squarely on the jaw. The Norseman caught the priest as he crumpled, and laid him gently on the ground, carefully straightening the black robe about his ankles. Then he turned to face the two girls.

Lenora, caught in horror, could not move. She was dimly aware, as she clutched Edwina's arm, that her friend had gone limp. The Viking said something Lenora did not understand, and reached for the fainting Edwina.

A red mist was forming before Lenora's eyes. Released at last from the paralysis that had held her immobilized, she flew at the man, fingernails raking his face, screaming her fury and her fear. The Viking laughed again, and then the world went black.

Snorri stood in the space between the stockade and the river, feet planted firmly apart, hands on hips, enjoying a feeling of power. His two friends, Bjarni and Hrolf, stood at his right and left shoulders. Sentries had been posted to guard against any surprise attempt at rescue of his Saxon victims, although that was not very likely. The raid, like the others on this voyage, had been stealthy and lightning quick and very successful.

As the flames roared and crackled in the wooden buildings behind them, consuming Wilfred's tun until it was only ashes, Snorri's men carried out the treasures they had found there. They had spread cloths and tapestries upon the ground and were busily piling onto them all the loot they had taken from the great hall and its surrounding buildings. There were silver plates, Snorri noted, and a large silver drinking cup in a style made by the Franks, and a silver crucifix and chalice from the church, as well as the priest's embroidered vestments. A small casket filled with silver coins brought an appreciative grunt from Snorri.

His attention strayed to the women. They were a sorry lot, huddled together on the ground just outside the stockade. No need to guard them. They were too frightened to do anything more than weep or faint. He knew what they feared, but Snorri, unlike most Norse leaders, held his men under firm discipline, and allowed nothing to be done to captives that might lower the price he could get for them in the slave markets. What his men did with their personal slaves once the plunder was divided was no concern of his, but until they reached the shelter of Thorkellshavn the women would remain untouched.

So far, they had not taken any prisoners, preferring to load the *Sea Dragon* with the goods gotten in their raids. It was easier that way. Gold and silver did not require food and water, did not attempt to escape, did not make noises at inconvenient times. But Snorri had promised his father Saxon slave girls, and this was the last stop of the voyage. He had better choose two or three to set aside for Thorkell, and then his men could divide the rest among themselves when they got home.

Snorri moved forward, Hrolf and Bjarni close beside him as always. He stopped when he reached a pair of women a little apart from the rest. One, chestnut curls in disarray, blue gown torn and dirty, lay unconscious on the ground.

"What happened to her?" Snorri asked.

"That's a wild woman. She tried to scratch my eyes out," Hrolf informed him. "I would have killed her, but I remembered you wanted a few wenches for Thorkell, and I thought he might have an evening's entertainment taming her."

"My father is a bit too old for that sort of thing." Snorri laughed. "But she appears to be a noblewoman and that should please him. Will she live, do you think?"

"The hilt of my sword barely grazed the back of her head," Hrolf assured him. "And I did not harm the priest, either. The last time I killed one of those holy men, their White Christ sent a terrible storm on the voyage home to punish us, and we nearly sank. The ship is so heavily laden with treasure I did not want to chance that happening again. I left him there, on that mound. He will wake up soon."

Snorri nodded, not really listening, his blue eyes now fixed on the pale girl sitting beside the one he had been considering. His huge, heavy-knuckled hand caught Edwina's chin and lifted her face. She stared back at him with a blank expression. Snorri was accustomed to seeing that look of hopelessness in his victim's eyes. It never disturbed him.

"So," he mused, "another noblewoman, and this one is the quiet type. She is too thin for my taste, but Thorkell likes blondes. She'll be just the thing for him, if she doesn't die on the voyage back to Denmark. She can sooth his wounds after the other has exhausted him." His companions guffawed at Snorri's wit.

"You missed this," Snorri called to the men still piling up the plunder. He grabbed at the heavy gold bracelet on Edwina's wrist.

"You can't have it!" Edwina jerked her arm away. Snorri, paying no attention to her words, pulled the bracelet roughly off her arm, leaving a red mark along the side of her thumb where the metal had scratched.

"Wilfred, Wilfred," Edwina moaned, rocking back and forth, her arms now crossed over her chest, tears trickling down her pale cheeks. "Oh, Wilfred, my dearest, my love."

"Women." Snorri shook his head in disgust and tossed the bracelet onto the last heap of loot, watching as two of his men wrapped and tied the cloth it lay on, and then struggled to lift it so they could carry it onto the ship. "Hurry up with that. We have stayed here too long. Our luck has been too good. I don't want to spoil it. Hrolf, Bjarni, get the women on board. We sail at once."

Chapter Three

Lenora could not remember where she was. When she opened her eyes the sky directly above her was a blue so bright it hurt her to look at it. She closed her eyes again and lay still, feeling the odd motion beneath her. It was a gentle rocking sensation, so soothing she nearly drifted off again into the velvety blackness that had held her since—since what? As memory returned, she gave a strangled cry and sat up. Dull pain throbbed at the base of her skull. She put a hand to the spot and felt a lump under her thick hair.

"Edwina?" She touched her friend's arm. Edwina sat beside Lenora, staring fixedly ahead, apparently seeing nothing.

"Edwina!" Still Lenora got no response.

"She has been like that since before we came aboard," said a voice.

Lenora turned to face the speaker, wincing at the pain in her head. She recognized the woman as the wife of one of her brother's farmers.

"Maud, what happened? Where are we?"

"On the longship. Don't you remember? The Norsemen came. They burned everything and killed—killed—" Maud gave way to loud sobs.

Lenora caught at the woman's shoulders and shook her. She was certain the gesture hurt her more than it hurt Maud, for her head was still throbbing, and a wave of queasiness threatened to overcome her.

"Maud, tell me everything." Lenora had to know, however much it hurt to hear the truth, no matter if Maud's words confirmed the fear now searing her heart. "Why can't Edwina see me? What did they do to her?"

After a while Maud regained some self-control and began to speak.

"There was a battle. Our men fought bravely but they were all killed. Only a few women were left alive."

"Where is my sister Matilda?" Lenora, looking around her, now saw a group of miserable women sitting dejectedly together on an oak plank floor. No, not a floor. It was a deck. They were on a ship, and there were Vikings all about them, engaged in sailing it. "Matilda?"

"She is gone, Lenora," Maud said quietly.

"Gone?"

"I have been trying to tell you. These murderers killed everyone but the ten of us who are here on this ship. All of them. All gone." She began to cry again.

"*NO!*" Lenora leapt to her feet, forgetting the pain in her head. "*NO!* It's not true, I won't let it be true. It can't be. Matilda! Wilfred!"

A heavy hand clapped her on the shoulder. Lenora spun around, nearly falling from a combination of dizziness and the motion of the ship. She looked up into the sunburned face of the Viking leader.

"Snorri," he said, grinning at her. "Lenora. Edwina." He gestured toward the silent girl still sitting on the deck of his ship.

He was tall, a heavily muscled, bulky man, with a thick blond beard and matted shoulder-length blond hair. He wore the same kind of rough wool jerkin and narrow breeches as his men did, with a heavy leather belt with a battleaxe thrust through it and a large broadsword hanging on the left side. Snorri did not look much different from the other Vikings on the ship, but there was about him an air of authority that made it clear that among this rough band, he was in charge. Lenora regarded him with loathing.

"What have you done to my family?" she demanded. "What is wrong with Edwina?"

"Edwina." Snorri laughed, tapping his forehead and making a face.

"What did you do to her, you Norse murderer?" Lenora's rage was clear in her burning cheeks and flashing gray eyes. Snorri poked a thick finger toward her chest.

30

"Down," he said in a loud voice. "Sit."

"Lenora, for heaven's sake." Maud pulled at Lenora's torn blue skirts. "Do as he says or he'll kill you. They kill so easily. Just sit down and be quiet."

Lenora sat. Snorri grinned triumphantly, standing over her.

"Thrall," he said in his harsh, heavily accented voice, opening his arms as if to embrace the entire group of captive women. "All are Snorri's thralls." He walked away, calling out cheerfully to one of his men.

Thrall. Lenora shuddered. She knew what the word meant. Slave. She was now that murdering monster's slave, to do with as he wished. She put her aching head down on her knees and sat that way for a long, long time.

"Lenora." Maud touched her elbow lightly and Lenora lifted her head. "They've given us cloaks. They must want to keep us warm and healthy for—for whatever they plan for us." She wrapped a gray woolen garment about Lenora's shoulders.

"Edwina?"

"Still the same. She hasn't moved."

Lenora could see that for herself. She and Maud wrapped Edwina's silent form in a dark green cloak. When Lenora pulled the girl into her arms, Edwina gave no sign that she recognized her friend.

"Why is she like this?" Lenora asked.

"I think it is because she knows what happened. You were unconscious, but Edwina saw

31

it all. It was horrible, Lenora." Maud choked back tears. "She hasn't spoken since Snorri took her bracelet. Look." Maud pointed to the long scratch on Edwina's hand.

"That filthy Norse beast. I have never hated anyone so much," Lenora told her, indicating Snorri by the barest movement of her head. He stood toward the bow of the ship, a hulking mass of finely tuned muscle. His back was turned to them as he discussed something with his two companions. "If I had a dagger, I would kill him now," Lenora added. "And his friends."

"His men would kill you first."

"Not if I were quick. I could do it."

"Don't think of such a thing, Lenora. You are no longer free. If you want to live, you must do as you are told. You must submit to your new master. That is what I am going to do."

"Never!" All of Lenora's fierce pride was in that one word. "I want revenge for what they have done to us."

Maud was possessed of a good deal more common sense than pride.

"It is impossible for a slave to get revenge. The first time you raise your hand to try, you will be killed." When Lenora made an impatient movement, Maud leaned forward, her voice tense. "Hear me, Lenora. Don't turn your head away and close your ears to reason. It is foolishness to die unnecessarily. It is always preferable to live, because while you yet live, there is hope. You might regain your freedom one day, and then you can think of revenge, but for now you cannot fight

32

them. They are too strong, and you can see there are too many of them. Don't let them destroy you." Maud paused to take a deep breath before adding her final argument. "And if you continue to live, you will be able to help Edwina. She has always depended on you. What will happen to her if you are dead?"

Lenora did not answer, but her arms tightened protectively about Edwina. She bent her head and felt Edwina's smooth hair beneath her cheek. She thought of the lovely, happy beginning of that day. Now everyone and everything she cared for had been taken from her, lost forever. All were gone except for herself and poor, senseless Edwina, and the eight other women who sat weeping or moaning behind her.

Throughout the long midsummer twilight that never seemed to turn into real night, the *Sea Dragon* smoothly sailed on, its great square blue and yellow sail taut with wind, and Lenora sat holding Edwina and staring at Snorri's tall form, feeding her hatred and thinking of revenge. In her heart she knew Maud was right. But even as she admitted her own helplessness, something in Lenora, some undefeated corner of her being, cried out against the enormity of Snorri's crimes against her family.

I will be patient for now, she thought, *but someday if I have the chance, even for a moment, to pay you back, Snorri the Viking, then beware of me....*

Part Two

Denmark
June, A.D. 867

–

March, A.D. 868

Chapter Four

Thorkell the Viking chieftain had been given his lands and made a king's jarl 20 years earlier, in return for his services to King Horik. He had been charged with protecting the flat, marshy wastes of western Jutland against invasion from the sea, and from the incursions by land of the Franks and Slavs who lived south of Denmark. His prowess as a warrior and his skill as a negotiator during the civil strife that had wracked Denmark after Horik's murder in the year 854 were legendary. Now, in his fifth decade, Thorkell ruled a strong, peaceful earldom that was almost an independent domain.

Thorkellshavn, his home, was securely situated behind wide tidal marshes and sand dunes. It lay on a gentle rise above the river, the only elevated land for miles around. More than a farm, less than a village, it consisted of a great hall built of wood, with a thatched roof that had a hole in the center to let light in and smoke out. The gable ends of the roof were finished with double carved wood representations of legendary beasts similar to those on the prows of Norse ships that were intended to frighten off demons and to protect the household.

Behind the hall, well protected from the constant westerly winds, was a cluster of outbuildings for storage of foodstuffs and the merchandise obtained on raids, and the small buildings that served Thorkell and his family as private quarters and bedchambers, for Thorkell was wealthy enough to indulge his family in the almost unheard-of luxury of privacy. The other household members—the free servants, the slaves, and Thorkell's hird—slept on the platforms that ran down both sides of the great hall, or in the women's quarters off the kitchen.

Spread out beyond the hall and its outbuildings were the homes of the farmers who worked Thorkell's lands. These men and women were more fortunate than peasants in other parts of Europe, for they were not bound either to Thorkell or the land. They owed him allegiance, but they were free to come and go as they pleased, and many were the young men who went off a-viking after the spring planting was done, to return before harvest with the loot that made their lives more comfortable. Thorkell's older son, Snorri, was a popular leader; his luck was known to be good.

Nearly everyone who lived in or near Thorkellshavn was in the great hall on this day to enjoy the spectacle presented by the display of plunder from Snorri's latest voyage, and to eye the new slaves who had just been brought in from the *Sea Dragon*.

"Where are we, Lenora? What is this place?"

"I don't know, Edwina."

They stood in a huge wood-paneled, tapestry-hung hall. Its high roof was supported by a long double row of carved and brightly painted wooden posts, each as large as a tree trunk. Torches flared, providing light in the shadowy building. The hall smelled of wood smoke and charred fat, of boiled vegetables and damp wool, and of the unwashed bodies of Snorri's men and their captives.

Lenora shivered. In spite of the fire burning in a stone-lined oblong pit in the center of the hall, it was nearly as cold and damp inside as it had been out of doors. Snorri's crew had rowed through thick fog and drizzle for most of the day, bringing the longship at last to this mist-wrapped place at the edge of a peaceful river. Everyone who had been aboard the ship was thoroughly wet. The Vikings did not seem to mind.

Raising both hands, Lenora brushed back the sodden curls hanging over her forehead, feeling the water dripping off her hair and running down her back. She straightened her shoulders and stood proudly. She would not let these Norsemen see her discomfort or her fear.

At least Edwina had begun to speak again. That was the only spark of hope in a miserable world.

Upon the beaten earth floor of the hall the Vikings were spreading the plunder obtained in their raids on East Anglia. There was a lot of it tumbling out of cloth bundles and leather sacks.

Lenora recognized a few items from her own home as clothing, weapons, dishes, coins, jewelry, and gold and silver ornaments from dozens of churches and houses were displayed.

The slaves stood to one side, dirty, bedraggled, and hopeless, eight of them, including Maud, tied together by hide ropes. Lenora and Edwina, unbound, but no less dirty and no more hopeful than their comrades, had been separated from the others.

Now the Vikings were dividing their loot, each member of the ship's crew claiming his share. There was much discussion, and some noisy argument among the sailors, as to who got which prize, but Lenora could not understand what was being said. Only a word here and there was intelligible to her.

Unable to decipher the conversation of the Vikings, Lenora continued her examination of her surroundings. In the center of the hall, set between two pillars and close to the firepit, was an ornately carved wooden settle, big enough to hold two people. Its intricate interlacing patterns were highlighted by paint applied in gaudy shades of red, blue, green, and yellow. In this wide chair sat an old man. He was tall, still well muscled and strong, but his hair and his luxuriant beard were almost completely white. Fine lines radiated from his pale blue eyes. He wore a robe of wine red made of a fabric such as Lenora had never seen before. The embroidered gold bands at its hem and the edges of its wide sleeves glittered and the dark wine cloth shimmered as he leaned to one side to speak to the man standing next to him.

This second man was very tall, muscular but slender, lacking the heavy, bulky appearance of many of the Northmen. He was dark. Tanned skin stretched smoothly over high cheek bones, over a firm, clean-shaven jaw and a long straight nose. His wide mouth turned up at the corners, as though he knew some private joke. There was a thin scar running from the outer edge of his left eyebrow straight up until it ended in a streak of pure white hair, startling against the inky blackness of the rest of his mane. His shoulder-length hair was confined by a gold-embroidered ribbon wrapped across his forehead and tied behind his head. He wore a knee-length blue jerkin of fine Frisian wool and tight brown breeches. A heavy gold chain lay close about his throat. His leather belt was decorated with gold bosses and his sword hilt was jeweled. On it one long, tapering hand rested gracefully, a gold ring on his little finger winking in the torchlight.

He stood at an odd angle. Something about his tense stance struck Lenora as not quite normal. He watched the proceedings intently as the goods were divided. Once, Lenora had the sensation that he was looking at her closely, but then he bent over and said something to the old man in the chair, and she decided she was mistaken.

At last the plunder was divided to everyone's satisfaction. One by one the captured women were freed of their bonds and handed over to Snorri's crew in exchange for a portion of each man's share of the loot. Finally a pile of the best goods was placed before the old man, who nodded his approval and said something to Snorri. Lenora decided it must have been a compliment, for Snorri grinned broadly and his friends, Bjarni and Hrolf, clapped him on the back.

"Thorkell," Snorri said, and continued to speak in a language tantalizingly similar to her own, but in her distressed condition, not intelligible to Lenora. Snorri motioned to Lenora and Edwina, and a crew member who had been standing beside the two young women pushed them forward.

They stood before Thorkell, their arms about each other, eyes wide with fear. When Snorri finished speaking, Thorkell looked them over, one gnarled hand stroking his beard. Then he spoke.

At first Snorri looked angry. Then he burst into laughter, stained teeth showing behind his blond beard and mustache. He nodded vigorously and replied in a scornful tone.

Lenora heard the other Vikings laugh behind her. She saw the dark man beside Thorkell flush, his hand tightening on the hilt of his sword, before he relaxed, lifted his head to meet Snorri's eyes, and responded in a quiet, low-pitched voice. There was a murmur of approval throughout the hall, and in that moment Lenora understood that Snorri and the dark man were enemies.

Snorri took Edwina by the elbow and led her to Thorkell's side.

"Lenora," Edwina cried, looking around anxiously.

Confused, uncertain what was happening, Lenora followed her friend closely. Snorri pushed her back with his free hand, snarling something in his harsh voice.

Lenora started to protest. Snorri ignored her. He was speaking to Thorkell again. It was now clear to Lenora that Snorri was giving Edwina to Thorkell. She could see Edwina trembling as Thorkell's hand ran lightly up and down her bare arm.

"No," Lenora exclaimed, again moving toward her friend.

She was stopped by the voice of the dark man. His tone was low and urgent. It took a moment for his words to sink into her mind.

"Be still," he said. "Do not interfere, or you both die."

Lenora stared at him in amazement. He had spoken Latin, the language her father had once attempted to teach her, which since his death she had heard only in Father Egbert's church services. How could this Viking know Latin?

As she met the full intensity of his gaze, Lenora caught her breath. His eyes were a clear, beautiful green fringed by thick dark lashes. Like two emeralds set in his tanned face, they bore into her, seeming to reach into her very soul. Stunned, she looked back at him in silent wonder.

"Your friend will be treated kindly by Thorkell," the dark man said. "She is safer with him than with Snorri."

At that moment Snorri caught Lenora's shoulder and pushed her at the dark man.

"Erik," Snorri said, and then continued in a rush of words Lenora did not comprehend.

Again there was laughter in the hall. The dark man's eyes narrowed, becoming cold green pools, but he made no response to what was obviously another insult from Snorri. He looked down at Lenora.

"You also were intended for Thorkell, but at

43

his order you have been given to me," he said, still speaking in Latin, "along with a few suggestions as to what I should do with you."

There was no doubt about it this time; he was examining her. His eyes filled with admiration and something else that made Lenora go hot and then cold under her tattered gown as he looked her over, beginning with her tangled and none-too-clean curls and her dirt-smudged face. His glance slowed for a leisurely inspection of her full, rounded breasts. One dark eyebrow arched upward; a corner of his mouth tilted in a half smile. Lenora felt her face flaming. He seemed not to notice. He was too busy visually measuring the slenderness of her waist and then proceeding to a cool appraisal of her well-rounded hips and the curves of long, slender legs, just visible where the seam of her skirt had split. At last he raised his eyes to her face again, contemplating her features with a bemused expression.

"For once," he said softly, "I agree with my brother."

"Snorri is your brother?" Lenora, shaking with helpless anger at being subjected to such close scrutiny, spoke in her own language, which this strange man seemed to understand, although he replied once more in Latin.

"I am Erik, called the Far-traveler," he said. "Snorri and I are both the sons of Thorkell the Fair-speaker." He indicated the white-haired man who had now risen from his chair.

Thorkell spoke, and two men came forward to carry away his share of the goods from Snorri's voyage. Thorkell took Edwina by the arm and said something to Snorri, who gave a wolfish grin in response. Still holding Edwina, Thorkell moved toward a door at one side of the hall. Edwina cast a pleading glance backward at Lenora.

"No." Lenora started forward again. Erik's hand grasped hers.

"You cannot stop that. Don't even try," he said.

"She is my best friend. She was to marry my brother. What will he do to her?"

Erik's expression did not soften. "He will take her to his bed," he said. "You must understand, your friend belongs to Thorkell, and you belong to me now."

Once more his sea-green eyes lingered on her trembling lips and slid lower, along the slender column of her throat, to dwell on the full swell of her breasts, heaving in agitation beneath the blue wool gown.

Lenora glared up at him. This man was undoubtedly as cruel and heartless as his brother, and already she hated him almost as much as she hated Snorri, but she would not let him see how frightened she was.

"And will you take me to your bed?" she asked, her vioce quavering in spite of her best efforts to control it.

A glint of humor softened the expression of those remarkable eyes.

"You may be certain of it," he told her.

Chapter Five

Erik made her sit on a bench opposite Thorkell's chair. He sat beside her, the length of his thigh pressed firmly against her own. When she tried to move away, he put one arm about her waist and pulled her back against him.

"Stay here," he commanded, "or I will give you back to Snorri."

Outraged and furious, Lenora dared not defy him.

Snorri sat next to Erik on a carved and painted seat similar to Thorkell's chair directly across the firepit. A dark-haired woman sat at Snorri's side, his great coarse hand fondling one of her heavy breasts. Snorri disgusted Lenora. She could not bear to look at him. She vowed again that she would never forget what he had done to her family. She wished with all her heart it was not necessary to eat at the same table with him.

Trestle tables were quickly set up before them as Snorri's homecoming feast began. Lenora and Erik shared a wooden plate and a silver cup. The serving women handed around huge wooden platters of boiled meat or fish, cabbage and turnips, and dark rye bread. Ale and mead were poured freely.

"Here." Erik handed her their cup.

"No," she said.

"Drink it," he ordered.

She put her lips to the cup and swallowed, Erik watching her closely. She swallowed again, greedily. On the voyage from Anglia the Vikings had given food to their captives, but Lenora, sick at heart, had been unable to do more than take a few bites. Nor had she been able to sleep. Now the sweet, fiery warmth of the mead went quickly to her head, enveloping her in misty lassitude. She was too exhausted, too drained of energy to fight against her fate any longer. Meekly she ate and drank as Erik told her to do. Her weary mind could not think beyond the immediate moment.

Erik sliced off a piece of meat from a nearby platter, picked it up on the tip of his dagger, and handed it to her. She took it in her fingers, noticing as she did so that the knife had a finely wrought gold handle inlaid with blue and green enamel, and a thin, sharp blade of some shiny blue-gray metal. She wondered how Erik had come to possess such a strange, beautiful instrument. She had never seen one like it before.

She glanced up at him. He was talking to a

brawny, brown-haired man who had sat down on Lenora's other side. She studied her new owner, noticing the crinkled skin about his eyes, the tight lines from nose to mouth. The scar above his left eyebrow was a thin red line, the swath of white hair beyond it an eye-catching contrast to the man's general darkness.

She had learned one important thing about him. When he had left his position beside Thorkell's chair, Lenora had learned the reason for his odd posture. Erik limped. It was not a pronounced defect, but it was clear there was something wrong with his left leg. She wondered if the same injury that had scarred his handsome face had also wounded his leg.

He looked down at her, seeing her still holding the piece of greasy boiled meat in her fingers.

"Eat it," he said.

She bit off a piece and began to chew. He handed her the silver cup again, and once more she drank deeply of the mead, tasting the honey from which it had been made. The room began to swim around her, and she blinked to keep her eyes open. Erik was speaking to her again.

"I do not know your name."

"Alienor."

"That is not a Saxon name."

"My mother was Frankish. My father named me for her. He loved her very much."

Erik looked faintly surprised.

"So was my mother Frankish," he said, "But my father loved her not at all. And Snorri's mother saw to it that she did not live long."

Chilled, she stared at him, not knowing what to say. In spite of her hatred of all the Norse, she felt a thin, tenuous thread of circumstance beginning to bind them together. This man had also suffered because of Snorri, or at least because of Snorri's mother, which was close enough for Lenora.

"She was a slave," Erik went on, "and Thorkell was too proud of me. Snorri's mother was jealous."

"Where is Snorri's mother now?" Lenora asked.

"She died while I was away in Miklagard. Let Odin be thanked for that." He drained his cup and motioned a serving woman to refill it. "Your friend called you something other than Alienor," he remarked.

"I am called Lenora."

"Lenora." He said the name softly, bending his dark head toward her. His leg pressed more closely against hers, and his left hand stroked her thigh in a sensuous rhythm.

Exhausted, her head reeling from the mead, Lenora had begun to relax. She was startled by the pleasant sensation of his hand on her. She could feel its warmth through her woolen skirt. She tilted her head up to look at him again and met his clear green eyes. For just a moment her fate did not seem as horrible as it had when she had first come into Thorkell's hall.

Then Snorri laughed, and she remembered all that had happened to her recently. Straightening her back, she pushed Erik's hand away. He

grinned with a self-confident air that told her
more clearly than threats or violence could have
done that when he was ready to take her she
would have no choice in the matter.

I hate them, she thought despairingly. *I hate
them all.*

The Viking feast ground slowly on. Vast quantities of food, mead, and ale were consumed. The
noise level increased rapidly. A fight or two broke
out, the participants leaving to settle their differences elsewhere. Several serving girls were
despoiled on the benches or on the raised earthen
platform that ran down both sides of the hall,
depending on the preferences of the men involved. No one paid much attention. Placing bets
on the wrestling match going on beside the firepit
was more interesting.

Among the women sitting at the feast Lenora
saw Maud and two others who had been with her
on Snorri's ship.

"What will happen to them?" she asked Erik.

"After the feast is over most of them will go
home. Some, like that fellow," he indicated the
man with Maud, "live several days' journey from
here. If the women please their owners, the men
might keep them. Otherwise, they will probably
be sold in the slave market at Hedeby."

"Where is Hedeby?"

"It is east of here, near the Baltic Sea," he replied shortly, and then ignored her as he ate and
drank.

Thorkell returned to the hall, laughing at the
boisterous welcome he was given and the shouted

jokes directed at him. He was alone.

"Where is Edwina?" Lenora asked Erik.

"Probably asleep," he replied, with no sign of concern.

She decided she hated him more than she hated his brother.

Shortly after Thorkell's return, a woman appeared and seated herself next to him on the carved settle. She was not much older than Lenora, but taller, and big-boned. She had silver-blond hair and dark blue eyes that seemed to be fixed on Lenora. It was not until she heard a sigh from the brown-haired man seated on her left that Lenora realized the newcomer was staring at him, not at her. She turned to look at this man more closely. She was surprised to find he was extremely handsome. He wore no beard, but an enormous brown mustache curled almost to his chin on either side of a firm mouth. Blue eyes twinkled and white teeth flashed as he smiled at her. It was an expression of pure friendliness, with not the slightest tinge of the lecherous looks with which nearly all the other Vikings had met her. Lenora felt her own mouth curving into a smile in response to his warmth.

The Viking touched his chest.

"Halfdan," he said. "Erik's friend."

"Lenora," she replied, indicating herself.

Halfdan nodded, and then began talking over her head to Erik. Lenora noticed that his eyes frequently strayed across the firepit to the blond woman, who, in spite of her cool demeanor, often returned his looks.

51

Now a skald, the traditional entertainer at Viking feasts, took up his harp and began to sing, a long, strange-sounding song Lenora could not begin to understand. Listening to the music, Snorri wept into his cup of mead and then fell asleep, his head resting on the table. Lenora looked at him with contempt.

Finally, much later, when Lenora thought she would collapse with weariness, Erik rose.

"Come," he said quietly.

She nearly fell trying to rise from the bench, and he swept her up into his arms as though she weighed nothing. He held her close to him, his eyes entrancing her, his mouth heart–stoppingly close. Then he stood her on her feet beside him.

He had not had as much to drink as the other men. Despite his lameness, he moved easily beside Lenora, guiding her out the door Thorkell had used earlier. He led her along a sandy path to a small building set a little apart from the others at the back of Thorkell's hall. It was built of logs and mud, a single room lacking the wood paneling of the great hall, with a firepit at one end and a raised platform along one wall. Piled on the platform, which served as both bed and sitting space, were woolen blankets, a straw-filled mattress, a few furs, and several pillows covered with the same lustrous cloth that had made Thorkell's robe. These were blue and green, bright spots of color in the drab room. On the tamped earth floor sat three ornately carved wooden chests. On top of one was a small oil lamp, its light, when Erik lit it, casting flickering shadows along the wall.

"This is my home. Here they leave me in peace," Erik told her.

He bolted the door and turned to her, his sea-green eyes gleaming in the light of the oil lamp.

"Do you live here alone?" Lenora asked, trying to order her swirling thoughts. She wished he would go away and let her sleep, but she feared he would not.

"You and I live here now. Where I am, there you live, until I sell you or give you away. But I do not think that will be very soon."

Seeing the look in his eyes, the same expression she had noticed earlier, she backed away from him. She felt again the sensation of successive waves of heat and cold passing over her body. She did not understand what was happening to her. She wanted to run away and hide from those green eyes that held her in a magical spell. And yet—and yet, she did not really want to leave him at all.

"Take this off," he said softly, touching the shoulder of her dress.

She hesitated a moment, then obeyed with shaking fingers. She felt his hands helping her, lifting the tattered woolen gown over her head and casting it aside. Her torn linen undergarment barely covered her.

Never taking his eyes from her, he removed his sword belt and then his tunic. His body was as tanned as his face. The heavy gold chain at his throat gleamed against his dusky skin. Silky,

dark hair grew on his arms and chest, and there
was a narrow scar running up and down his left
shoulder. He moved nearer, muscles rippling as
he put his arms around her.

Lenora stood rigid in his embrace. His mouth
hovered above hers, then lightly, briefly, touched
her trembling lips. His arms tightened, pulling
her hard against his tough, warm body. She shuddered at the feel of his bare skin on hers. They
stood locked together for a long moment before
his lips returned to hers, more firmly this time,
as he claimed his new possession.

His mouth was sweet, caressing her lips in a
way that sent little ripples of heat washing along
her body, throbbing into her limbs. Lenora, lost
in unexpected pleasure, was unaware that her
arms had encircled his waist.

Gently Erik's long hands caressed her throat
and shoulders, then moved lower to push aside
the remnants of her shift and cup her breasts. His
thumb flicked across one rosy tip. She caught her
breath and tried to move away, but he pulled her
back to him, bending his head to apply mouth
and tongue where his thumb had been.

She moaned, fighting against the strange melt-
ing she felt deep within herself as his tongue
played across her flesh. His hands slid along the
smooth curves of her hips in an intimate, sensuous gesture. Sweet fire laced through her. She
could feel her treacherous body molding itself to
his, urging him on. His hands traced quivering
sensations along her loins.

Suddenly she remembered this was a Viking,

and fear surged into her mind, erasing sensual delight. Vikings were wicked, brutish louts. Vikings had destroyed her family.

"No. No." She pushed frantically against his chest.

Ignoring her protests, Erik bore her down onto the rough bed, tearing off her shift. She lay completely naked before him, a sacrifice to Viking lust. She could not control the terror now consuming her. Her voice rose to an hysterical shriek.

"Don't touch me. Let me go. I'll kill you, I swear I will. Murderer! You are all murderers. Filthy Norse—"

On and on she raved, scarcely noticing when Erik moved away from her and sat on the edge of the bed, watching her. He waited patiently until her outburst ended in a flood of tears, finally tapering off into infrequent, weary sobs.

"Lenora," he said at last, "tell me exactly what Snorri did."

"I'm so tired. I only want to sleep. Please leave me alone."

"Tell me. I must know."

And so she recounted as much as she could remember of the raid on Wilfred's tun, and in addition all that Maud had told her.

"What did Snorri do to you?" he asked when she had finished.

"I just told you. He killed my family." Lenora gulped, trying not to cry again.

"I mean you. Did he rape you?"

The sharp question brought a flood of crimson

to her face and throat. She had been too shocked and confused to wonder what had happened after Hrolf had hit her.

"I—I don't know. I was unconscious most of the time."

"Of course he did. He is Snorri." The scornful curve of Erik's lips sent a cold chill to her heart.

She nodded in mute agreement, unable to speak, feeling totally, irreparably shamed by his words. She watched in silent anguish as he pulled on his tunic again, then threw her discarded gown over her.

"Stay here," he commanded. "Do not move until I come back. Do you understand?"

"Yes," she whispered miserably. She lay on the straw mattress, wondering if he would bring Snorri back with him, if he would turn her over to his brutal brother as unwanted, damaged goods.

Erik was gone only a short time. He returned alone, carrying a wooden bucket of water and a cloth.

"Get up and wash yourself," he said.

"What?" She thought she had misunderstood him.

"Snorri has touched you. You are dirty. I won't allow you to lie in my bed with his seed staining your flesh. Wash yourself."

The water was cold. His eyes never left her as she scrubbed at the dirt on face and arms and torso, on her legs and feet, and finally on her inner thighs. There was no blood to be seen there, but she knew enough to realize its absence did not

56

necessarily mean that Snorri had not violated her. She was too worn out to be embarrassed by Erik's steady gaze.

"Now get into bed," he ordered when she had finished.

She crawled back onto the straw mattress and he covered her with a woolen blanket, then lay down beside her, wrapped in a fur. She huddled against the wall, as far away from him as she could get.

"You need not fear me," he told her over his shoulder. "The thought of wallowing in Snorri's leavings like a hungry pig at a trough fills me with revulsion. I will not touch you in that way again."

It was not a flattering comparison, yet his distaste offered her a grain of comfort. This Viking, at least, would not rape her. But he had piqued her ever-ready curiosity.

"Why do you hate your brother so much?" she asked. The idea of disliking her own brother was so foreign to her that she could not comprehend it. Dear Wilfred, warm and funny and so protective of his two sisters, even of the competent Matilda. She dug her teeth hard into her lower lip to stop the tears that threatened at the mere thought of her lost family. In her concentration on controlling her feelings she almost missed Erik's next words, which issued forth in a low, hissed whisper of contempt.

"It must be a special delight to Snorri to know that out of deference to our father I have been forced to accept what he has used first. He must

Flora Speer

think it is a great joke. When you have to deal with him, Lenora, keep your wits about you, and never depend on his word. Now go to sleep.''

In spite of her weariness she could not do as he ordered, for she saw herself ensnared between contending brothers. She was terrified that when morning came Erik would give her back to Snorri as the next move in the dangerous game they were playing.

Her thoughts ran round and round, giving her no peace. Maud, who might have told her if Erik's accusation of rape against Snorri was true, had left Thorkellshavn with her new master. Lenora had seen them go. She knew Edwina could give her no information; Edwina barely remembered what had happened to herself. Lenora had ascertained that much before they had reached Thorkell's hall, and had been grateful for the forgetfulness that had eased Edwina's unbearable loss. She could not trust any answer Snorri might give on the matter, and certainly Erik would not believe his brother, either.

Erik stirred in his sleep and flung one arm over her. The warmth of his body was oddly comforting. He was clean, with a fresh, masculine body odor that was not repulsive at all. In that, as in other things, he was quite different from Snorri and his men.

She realized now how foolish she had been to fight him. She ought to have controlled her fear and encouraged him to take her, so he would keep her safe from Snorri. Much as she hated the idea of any Norseman touching her, she decided she ought to try to overcome Erik's distaste, to make him want her so he would not give her away or sell her. If he ever approached her again, she would force herself to accept his advances and try to please him.

Her taut muscles began to relax at last as she drifted into sleep. Her last conscious sensation was of Erik's arm across her shoulders, holding her close.

Chapter Six

Erik was gone when Lenora wakened. The room was dim, brightened only by the daylight showing at the bottom of the wooden door and through the hole in the roof over the firepit. Lenora swung her feet to the floor and groped about until she located her gown. She had just picked it up when the door flew open, letting in a blaze of sunlight. She blinked and clutched her bedraggled garment against her nakedness.

Erik entered, followed by the blond woman who had sat across from them at last night's banquet. As her eyes adjusted to the sudden bright light, Lenora looked again. Yes, it was the same woman who had gazed so often at Halfdan. Her dark blue eyes now regarded Lenora beneath raised brows. The woman carried a bundle of folded clothes in her arms.

"So, you are awake at last," Erik said. "It is past midday. I let you sleep. I knew you were tired."

"Thank you," Lenora whispered, embarrassed to have Erik and the blond woman watching her so closely when she was undressed.

"This is my sister Freydis," Erik went on. "She will explain your duties. You are to obey her in everything."

"Are you—" Lenora's voice squeaked in fright. She swallowed hard and tried again. "Are you giving me to her?"

"No," he replied. "I require a woman to attend me. One of Thorkell's women has been serving me. Now you will do that."

"Will I continue to sleep here?"

"You will. But I will not touch you, so have no fear of me." His expression clearly showed his disgust at the thought of taking what had once been Snorri's. "I warn you on pain of death not to tell anyone. I cannot insult my father by rejecting his gift to me, so no one must know we do not lie together. No one. Not even Thorkell's slave who was your friend. Let people think what they will."

"Very well, if you promise not to give me away. I do not want to be given back to Snorri."

He frowned at her. "You are my thrall," he reminded her. "I need not promise a slave anything. But I tell you that if I give you away or sell you, it will not be to Snorri. I will give him nothing."

Freydis had been listening to this conversation,

Flora Speer

which was conducted in a mixture of English and Latin, with a puzzled expression. Now she spoke sharply to Erik. He nodded.

"One thing more," he said to Lenora. "You must learn to speak our tongue. I will not always be with you to translate for you."

"I will try." She would have promised almost anything out of sheer gratitude at not being returned to Snorri.

"Now you must bathe."

"I washed last night."

Erik grinned at her. The smile lit up his face and made him look like a young boy. His sea-green eyes sparkled with humor, dazzling her.

"I do not like dirty women. Bathing often is a custom I learned in Miklagard, although it is not unknown here, especially in summer. We Danes are cleaner than you Saxons."

"That's not true."

"No?" His eyebrows went up, and she realized he was teasing her.

"I won't bathe," she declared. "It's unhealthy."

"Since I got you," he replied, "you have said little else to me but *no*. If you say *no* one more time, I will beat you. I will not live with a dirty woman."

Lenora's chin went up defiantly. She started to speak, but the look in his eye silenced her. He took the gown from her and gave her the rough woolen blanket under which she had slept.

"Wrap yourself in this and follow Freydis," he said. "And from this moment, you will speak only Norse."

62

There was nothing to do but follow his orders. Lenora covered her nakedness as best she could and left the cottage.

The mist and rain of the previous day were gone and the sun was warm on her head and shoulders. Lenora looked upon a landscape surprisingly like the one she had known all her life. Undulating green fields surrounded Thorkellshavn. Lenora, accustomed to living in a farming community, surveyed the fields with a practiced eye, recognizing a large strip of barley, another of rye, and noticing a herd of cattle grazing contentedly in the distance. The flat countryside beyond the farmlands was heavily forested. Looking in the opposite direction from the farm, she saw Snorri's longship drawn up onto a narrow ledge of sand at the river's edge. Beyond, along the far western horizon, she could glimpse between the sand dunes the blue shimmer of the North Sea. Over that sea lay her home, or what had been her home.

"Come," Freydis called over her shoulder. "You are too slow."

Lenora took a deep breath and straightened her back and shoulders in a gesture that was becoming habitual with her. Then she followed Freydis.

Some distance past the great hall and its surrounding buildings a clear, cold stream ran through a thick stand of trees before joining its waters to the river. Here, at a bend in the stream, a natural pool had formed. The trees, thick with their summer burden of leaves, provided complete privacy. Freydis indicated by a few words and gestures that Lenora should get into the pool.

With the tall, forbidding woman watching her, Lenora did as she was told. Freydis gave her a soapstone bowl filled with a fatty substance, which Lenora used to wash herself, even scrubbing her hair.

When she climbed out Freydis handed her a rough cloth with which to dry herself, and then helped her to dress. From the pile of garments she had carried to the stream, Freydis unfolded an undyed, pleated linen shift, long-sleeved and ankle-length, that could be tied at its round neck. Over this was draped a woolen, apronlike garment consisting of a straight panel in front and back. Wide shoulder straps connected these two panels, which were fastened over each collarbone with large oval brooches. Lenora handled the bronze jewelry with sensitive fingers, admiring the sinuous, interlaced curves of its design, which was composed of the stretched-out and contorted bodies of two animals.

"They're beautiful," she exclaimed.

Freydis looked pleased.

"Was mine," she said. "Erik bought for you."

"These were yours? Don't you want them?"

"Speak Norse tongue," Freydis told her sternly. She shrugged her wide shoulders. "I have many more."

In fact, Freydis was wearing twin brooches of spectacularly complicated design. Between them hung a necklace of glass beads patterned in brilliant colors and a second string of amber beads. From the right brooch hung several keys on silver chains, and a small iron knife with a carved bone handle.

"Erik bought? For me?" Lenora repeated carefully, still examining her own brooches.

"For you. You please him."

Lenora was not sure she had understood this last sentence.

The brooches were designed for Freydis' large frame, and so were too large for Lenora. It took her a while to arrange them properly. When at last she had them adjusted and had donned soft leather shoes that wrapped around her ankles, Freydis helped her to comb her hair with a carved horn comb. Then they tried to arrange it.

Freydis' straight, silver-blond hair was smoothly pulled back and twisted, the long, loose ends hanging almost to her waist like a well-cared-for horse's mane. Lenora's unruly curls would not go into a smooth knot. Her hair caught and snarled and had to be combed again. Finally she gave up. She took a strip of cloth and tied her hair back with that, fastening it at the nape of her neck. Curly tendrils escaped, framing her face in a damp chestnut cloud. Freydis nodded.

"Is good," she said. "Now come. You must work if you wish to eat."

Lenora had always hated the domestic chores that were so much a part of even a noblewoman's life, and had shirked them whenever possible. Now, under Freydis' strict but fair supervision, she controlled her dislike and dutifully applied herself to her work.

She learned that as Erik's personal slave she

did not have to do heavy manual labor. There were other slaves to do such chores and to help the free serving women who also worked in Thorkell's household. Lenora was required to help with the cooking, which was done in a separate room at one end of the great hall, and with the serving at each night's feast. She must also keep Erik's tiny cabin clean, and tend the fire in his firepit, for even in warm summer, the place was often damp and chilly, and Erik's injured leg ached when it was cold.

And always there was the spinning. Every woman of Thorkell's household had her own spindle and whorls, and whenever her hands were not occupied in some other task, she used them to spin wool or flax into thread.

Lenora had never disliked spinning as some women did. She was good at it, her nimble fingers pulling out the tufts of wool, sending the whorl toward the ground as she twisted the fibers into a smooth, even thread. She could spin and think of other things. She could spin and watch what was going on around her, learn new words of the Norse language, ask questions of the other women, and discover the relationships among various members of Thorkell's household.

It was weaving she disliked. She was too impatient, too eager to move about. She hated staying in one place at the upright loom that leaned against the wall. The stones weighing the warp threads were like weights on her own feet. She constantly got the threads tangled as she wove. Her cloth was uneven, too loosely woven in some places, too tight in others. She sat in the weaving room that opened off Thorkell's great hall and fought the loom.

Freydis was angry, her thin lips pressed into a sour expression.

"This is not good," she told Lenora.

"I know. I have never been able to weave."

"Then who will make Erik's clothes?"

"I'll try again." And she did, but with no more success than before. Freydis watched for a while, then shook her head and turned away. "Freydis, don't go. Please tell me, where is my friend, Edwina? It has been four days now since I have seen her."

Freydis frowned, concentrating on Lenora's strange mixture of English and Norse words. Lenora tried to speak the Danes' language, she worked hard, and she did not weep or complain as some of the other slaves did. But she constantly asked about the thin, pale girl who had been given to Freydis' father.

"She is with Thorkell," Freydis replied.

"For four days and nights?"

"I think she pleases him." Freydis went away and left Lenora to her weaving.

That night, as every night, there was a boisterous banquet in the great hall. Most of Snorri's crew had returned to their homes, but some of them were still there, reveling in Thorkell's generous hospitality. Bjarni and Hrolf were present, each with an arm about a serving girl, each with a huge horn of mead.

Also present were Thorkell's hird, his personal retainers, who were pledged to fight for him unto death, and to guard Thorkellshavn. These men lived with Thorkell, existing on his bounty, sleeping in the great hall, desporting themselves with the serving women. Altogether, there were close to fifty men at each night's meal, and nearly as many women.

There was hare for tonight's feast, dozens of them, cooked on spits and dripping juices. There was mutton boiled with leeks, boiled cabbages and turnips, wild mushrooms, wooden bowls of fresh porridge or thick buttermilk, and baskets of fresh berries, gathered from the nearby forest. Ale and mead flowed freely for men and women accustomed to heavy drinking.

Songs and tales performed by Thorkell's skald, wrestling contests, and an occasional drunken brawl provided the entertainment. Those who preferred quieter pursuits could play at chess or other board games, using pieces made of walrus ivory.

Lenora, having finished her serving chores, sat in her usual place next to Erik. Thorkell and Freydis sat opposite them. There was no sign of Edwina.

"Erik, do you know where my friend is? Please tell me." Lenora looked at him with anxious gray eyes.

"I have not seen your friend," he replied. "But do not worry. Thorkell will not hurt her."

He slid their shared silver cup along the table toward her so she could drink. The ring he wore on the little finger of his left hand glittered in the torchlight. When Lenora touched it, trying to see the design better, Erik snatched his hand away.

"Don't touch that," he hissed, glaring at her. "It was my mother's ring. It was all she had to leave me."

"I wasn't going to steal it," she said.

She knew it wasn't the ring. It was because of Snorri. Erik managed to avoid touching her at any time and did not want her to touch him. Never, when she was serving him in the little house they shared or sitting with him at each evening's feast, did he allow any physical contact between them.

He was gone most of each day, practicing with his sword and spear and battle-ax in the enclosed yard reserved for such activities. When he was not practicing battle skills he often rode out on horseback with Thorkell to inspect some part of his father's lands or spent time closeted with Thorkell in his private chambers, where, Freydis had told her, Erik kept Thorkell's business accounts.

Only at night, when at last he slept rolled snugly in his own blanket, did he occasionally move near her, and she would often wake in the dark to find his warm length pressed against her back as she lay near the wall. Once or twice his arm had slipped around her. Each morning he was gone before she woke.

Fearful that after a time he would give her to someone else, she had at first tried to find ways to bind him to her, but he remained indifferent.

Two halfhearted attempts to seduce him had failed miserably. She did not really know how to go about it and she was frightened. Finally, convinced Erik would never want her, she gave up.

As she pondered her situation, Lenora became aware that Halfdan had sat down beside her. He greeted her with a smile. Lenora's eyes widened at the red-splotched bandage on his right arm.

"What happened?" she asked. "You're bleeding."

"Only a little wound-dew. A small accident practicing with swords. It will be better soon."

Lenora thought she recognized the cloth of Halfdan's bandage.

"Did Freydis bind it up for you?"

The burly Viking's eyes met hers, and in their blue depths Lenora saw a world of anguish.

"Freydis has been good to me," Lenora said kindly. "She has been teaching me my duties here."

"She manages Thorkell's household very well," Halfdan said in a noncommital tone. His eyes strayed across the room toward Freydis.

Lenora saw her chance to learn more about Thorkell's family, but she knew she must be very careful or Halfdan would not talk to her. She had noticed he seldom spoke to women at all. She decided to approach the subject in a roundabout way. She hoped her scanty Norse would be adequate. Fortunately, Halfdan, like many Danes, had some command of English.

"You are Erik's good friend," she began, looking at him with what she hoped was an innocent expression.

"For many years," Halfdan told her solemnly.

"Do you live on Thorkell's lands?"

"No." Halfdan looked down at her with amusement. "My father is a king's jarl, like Erik's father. They are friends from their youth, when they went a-viking together to distant lands. Thorkell sent Erik to live at my father's hall when Erik was very small."

"Why did he do that?"

Halfdan glanced at Erik before answering, but Erik was apparently entranced by the song being sung by the skald. He seemed unaware of the existence of either his friend or his slave.

"Thorkell sent Erik to my father for safety after Ragnhilde killed Erik's mother. My father lives in the far north of Denmark, by the Limfjord. It is many days' travel from here, and Thorkell thought Erik would be safe there, with my father to guard him, and he was."

Lenora remembered the story Erik had told her on her first night at Thorkellshavn.

"Who is Ragnhilde?" she asked. "And why did she kill Erik's mother?"

"Ragnhilde was Thorkell's wife," Halfdan replied, confirming Lenora's suspicion. "Thorkell brought Erik's mother back from a voyage to the land of the Franks. Soon after Snorri was born to Ragnhilde, the Frankish slave gave birth to Erik. Thorkell was overjoyed to have two sons. Ragnhilde was jealous. One day Erik's mother was walking alone by the river, and she fell in and drowned."

"It could have been an accident."

"No one who knew Ragnhilde would ever believe that."

"Wasn't Ragnhilde punished?"

"Why should she be? The Frankish woman was only a slave. Ragnhilde may have paid Thorkell some compensation out of her own money, but the matter was between the two of them."

"Wasn't Thorkell angry?"

"I do not think so. He cared little for Erik's mother, and Ragnhilde was his wife. Two years later Freydis was born, so they must have been on good terms." Halfdan's eyes strayed across the room once more.

"But he was concerned enough about his younger son to send him to your father for safe-keeping?"

"Yes. My father has no other children. He was happy to have Erik as foster son, and I was happy to have a brother. We are blood brothers now. We have sworn the pact."

"I don't understand," Lenora persisted. "If Erik's mother was a slave, wasn't he born a slave too? How is it that everyone accepts him as Thorkell's legitimate son?"

"I can answer that."

Lenora swung around in surprise. Erik had been listening to her conversation with Halfdan. Lenora blushed at being caught discussing him and hoped he would not be angry. But Erik spoke in a quiet voice with no trace of irritation.

"When I was born Thorkell was so happy to have a second son that he set me free. He planned to free my mother also if I lived to be one year old. In the meantime, he hoped to have another son by her. At the yearly Assembly he sat me on his knee before the other men and legally adopted me. It was that which made Ragnhilde angry enough to kill my mother. She would have killed me, too, if my father had not sent me away from here."

"So you are legally as much Thorkell's son as Snorri?"

"Except that he is the older. By Odal law, when Thorkell dies Snorri will inherit everything."

"What will you do then?"

"I do not know." Erik's green eyes rested on Thorkell a moment. "My father is an honest man who has been fair toward me. I hope he will live for many more years."

"What finally happened to Ragnhilde?"

"She died of a wasting disease while I was away in Miklagard."

"Where is Miklagard?"

Erik scowled at her. "You ask too many questions, Lenora. I have told you enough for one night. Be quiet."

She obediently fell silent, and Erik began a conversation with Halfdan. Lenora did not mind Erik's brusque order. So much new information filled her mind that she needed time to think about it.

After what Halfdan had just told her she understood better the bad relations between Erik and

Snorri. She suspected Ragnhilde's evil deed had cast a blight over Freydis and Halfdan, too, for how could Erik's blood brother care for Ragnhilde's daughter, how hope for a future with her? Lenora remembered part of a verse Father Egbert had once read to her from the Holy Book: "The sins of the fathers . . . visited upon the children." The sins of the mothers, too, it would seem. Poor Freydis. Poor Halfdan.

Angrily, she dismissed the thought. Why should she care about the problems of these Norse? They were all heathen monsters. Let them settle their own feuds. The thing that mattered, the most important thing she had learned from her conversation with Erik and Halfdan, was that in this country slaves could be set free legally. Thorkell had freed Erik and would have freed his mother.

She would ask some of the other women about it. Surely someone would know how it could be done. She might even stir up her courage enough to ask Freydis, who, although not very friendly, was fair and honest with all of the slaves. Perhaps one day soon she and Edwina could both be free. Lenora hugged the thought close and smiled to herself, and thought of revenge against Snorri.

Chapter Seven

The next morning Lenora saw Edwina again. Freydis brought her into the weaving room where Lenora was struggling with the loom, and then quietly walked away, leaving them alone.

After a tearful embrace, Lenora looked at her friend more closely. Edwina was more thin and pale than ever. Her loose, unbelted Norse clothing, similar to Lenora's own, hung on her tiny frame like a shroud. Her honey-blond hair was pulled back and knotted, the ends hanging free down her back. The hairstyle emphasized her hollow cheeks and sunken eyes.

"Oh, my poor Edwina. Have you been ill?" Lenora tenderly stroked the girl's cheek.

"Not ill. Only unhappy."

"Is Thorkell cruel to you? Has he hurt you?"

"No, but I must share his bed each night. But

you know about that. Thorkell told me he gave you to his son. You know how it is for a slave."

Lenora had her mouth open to tell Edwina that she was more fortunate when she remembered Erik's threat to kill her if she told anyone he had not lain with her. She shut her mouth firmly.

Edwina wiped her eyes. "Thorkell is not unkind," she went on. "It's just that he is so old. He's almost fifty."

Lenora nodded sympathetically. In an age in which boys were considered adults at twelve and most men were dead before their thirtieth birthday, Thorkell was old indeed.

"Perhaps that is a good thing," Lenora said, hoping to provide some comfort.

"Yes. The first night was bad, but now he seems to want me just to lie beside him. He puts his hands on me. I do not like it, but it is all he does." She sighed deeply. "It really doesn't matter, with my beloved Wilfred gone. I don't care what happens to me now."

Appalled at the change in her friend, Lenora forgot discretion in a rush of anger.

"Edwina, I can't bear to see you like this. You were always so cheerful, always calming me when I was upset. I wish I could help you now. How I long to take revenge on them for what they have done to us. Especially Snorri."

"Hush, Lenora, don't say that. If anyone heard you, they would kill us both." Edwina looked frightened. "Think about your eternal soul. Vengeance is the Lord's. Father Egbert always said that. We must accept what has happened to us and trust in the Lord to give us strength to bear our misfortune."

"Trust in the Lord?" Lenora asked in exasperation. "These people are heathens. They don't know or care anything about the Lord. All they know is the law of the sword. Plunder and rape and burn and kill."

"They are not all violent and cruel. Thorkell is a learned man. So is Erik. I have seen them working together, how they love and trust each other. They both know how to read and write, and count, too." Edwina's eyes widened at the thought of these accomplishments.

"Are you defending them? How can you?"

"Because they are not as bad as you think."

"Snorri—"

"Snorri is a beast. Snorri is the worst of the Vikings. But they are not all like Snorri. Did you know Erik came to me and told me you were well and safe? Did you know he told Thorkell my betrothed had been killed, and to treat me kindly?"

"I did not know. He could have told me that you were well, but he never did. And what Erik told him did not keep Thorkell from taking you to his bed, did it?"

"No, that is true. He is an old man and settled in his ways. Owners bed with their female slaves. Thorkell would not change such things, but he is kind to me."

"I don't know how you can accept this misery so easily. I have tried so hard, but I will never be able to accept it. I hate them all. I wish I could find a way to make Snorri pay for killing our family." Lenora's eyes blazed with her desire for vengeance, her cheeks flamed.

"You will drive yourself mad thinking such thoughts." Edwina shook her head sadly. "There is nothing you or I can do to change what is. Accept it and make the best of it. And now let me help you at the loom. You never could weave properly, Lenora."

With this firm change in subject, Edwina went to work, quickly untangling the warp threads and setting their stone weights aright. She passed the skein of wool back and forth a few times, straightening the weft with the whalebone batten, producing a stretch of smooth, even fabric.

"You see? It's not so different from our loom at home. Now watch as I do this. You use the weaving-comb this way."

Lenora tried many times in the following days to change Edwina's passive attitude toward their slavery. She had never realized how stubborn her friend could be. Edwina would not budge. She would hear no word of any scheme for attaining revenge, and at last Lenora gave up, realizing there was nothing a lone woman could accomplish against the Norse. She would have to swallow her pride and be content with survival, as Maud had once advised her.

Freydis was pleased with Edwina's skill and speed at weaving and soon allowed her to take over Lenora's work at the loom while Lenora did the spinning. Lenora was relieved to be free of the weaving room, and guiltily relieved to be free of Edwina's mournful presence.

One sunny afternoon Lenora was returning to Erik's house with a pile of freshly done laundry. She had shortened an old linen shift that Freydis had given her and then washed it, along with two of Erik's short-sleeved linen undershirts. He wore them when at weapons practice, discarding his woolen jerkin in the summer heat, and one or two were always sweaty and dirty. After washing the garments and partially drying them in the sun, Lenora had had the unpleasantly warm job of pressing them on a whalebone board, using heavy, heated glass globules to smooth away the wrinkles. She had burned a finger, and now she was tired and irritable.

She stopped on her way home from the laundry house to watch the men of Thorkell's hird at weapons practice. It was important to keep their skills finely honed so they could fulfill their duty of protecting Thorkell, his home, and his family. The practice yard was busy all day long, no matter what the weather.

Today, Asmund, a tall, red-haired man, was working with a twisting spear, which was thrown with a cord looped about the shaft so it spun as it flew through the air and hit the target with fearful power and accuracy. Two other men practiced with swords, attacking each other with heavy, sweeping strokes, parrying each other's blows with their painted wooden shields. The Norse were proud of their ability to use their swords with either hand, and as Lenora watched, one of the pair switched shield and sword from hand to hand without missing a blow. Halfdan had once let her heft his sword, so Lenora knew how heavy such a weapon was. She watched the swordsmen appreciatively until her attention was drawn to a fourth man in the far corner of the yard, who repeatedly threw his battle-ax at a target, moving farther away from it each time.

When she had first come to Thorkellshavn Lenora had turned her head aside each time she passed this part of Thorkell's domain. The sight of those weapons had stirred unhappy memories of their deadly use on her dear ones. One day she had seen Erik and Halfdan at practice with their broadswords and had stayed to watch them as they dodged and ducked one another's blows, leaping sideways or backwards easily, laughing and joking as they worked. Erik's lameness seemed a minor inconvenience, so skillful was he at the acrobatic style of fighting the Norse loved. Only later did she begin to realize how much effort it took to overcome his handicap each time he took up his weapons. It was by dogged determination and constant practice that Erik had recovered and now maintained the agility, balance, and speed necessary to survive in battle.

Seeing Erik and Halfdan were not in the practice yard, Lenora walked on. As she approached the door of Erik's house, Snorri's closest companions, Hrolf and Bjarni, appeared before her.

"Lenora," Hrolf said, blocking her way. He had a high-pitched, nasal voice that contrasted unpleasantly with his heavy, bulky body. It was he who, on that day she could never forget, had as-

saulted Father Egbert and knocked Lenora unconscious. Lenora hated him only slightly less
than she hated Snorri himself.

"Let me pass," she said coldly.

"What a busy little slave you are," Hrolf
sneered, paying no attention to her demand.
"You wash his shirts during the day and warm
his bed at night. How fortunate Erik is that Thorkell gave you to him. Not many younger sons are
so favored."

Lenora tried to move around the two men, who
she now realized were drunk, but one of them
was always in her way.

"Would you like to warm our beds instead?"
Bjarni asked, leering at her. "Two full-bodied
men instead of a cripple. That should please
you."

"If either of you touches me," Lenora warned
them, "Erik will kill you both."

"That weak twig." Hrolf laughed. "I could kill
him by blowing on him."

"Your breath would destroy the strongest man.
You have had too much ale," she replied.

"Erik the Far-traveler is too weak to protect
you from us," Bjarni told her. "He was once a
fine warrior like Snorri, but those soft Greeks
ruined him so he no longer drinks or wenches
with us. He will not fight us over a slave woman."

"Come, pretty Lenora," Hrolf coaxed. "Let us
go into the summer fields and pleasure ourselves.
We will make joyous sacrifice to Frey."

"Get away from me."

As the two men advanced on her, Lenora felt

panic snuff out her indignation. She could not let them touch her; she would die if either of them laid a hand on her. She was terrified that she would faint and they would drag her away and do what they wanted to her.

She backed away, knowing they could catch her easily. She moved one step back, another, a third, and then she felt an obstruction behind her as a sturdy arm was wrapped about her waist.

"Oh," she screamed, and looked up into Halfdan's broad face. She nearly dropped her bundle of laundry, but Halfdan caught it in his free hand and gave it back to her. His left arm supported her as she sank limply against him, shaking with relief. She felt his strength and his firmness at her back.

"Well met, Hrolf, Bjarni," Halfdan said pleasantly.

"What do you want?" Hrolf growled.

"Snorri is working on his ship, down by the river," Halfdan told them in the same friendly tone.

"We know that. What of it?"

"Did you know he is talking of making another voyage soon?"

"He is?" Hrolf and Bjarni looked at each other in astonishment.

"You didn't know? I'm surprised he didn't tell you first, since you two made his last trip so successful. I would think you would want to volunteer to go a-viking again before winter comes."

"How do you know this?" Bjarni regarded Halfdan suspiciously.

"I heard him talking to Thorkell earlier. Don't you think you should ask him about it before anyone else takes your places? He will be choosing his crew very soon now."

"Yes. There is always plunder on Snorri's voyages. His luck is so good that many will want to go with him." Hrolf was thoughtful. His small eyes glanced from Halfdan to Lenora and back again. "You can have the woman if you want her. We won't tell Erik."

With sneering laughter, Hrolf and Bjarni went off to find Snorri. Halfdan released Lenora and stepped back.

"Thank you," she whispered.

"I would like to kill those two," Halfdan said in a conversational tone. "But that would only make things worse between Snorri and Erik."

"Is Snorri really going away?"

"I think so."

"Good. I hope none of them ever comes back."

"That would make Erik's life easier. But Snorri is cunning and lucky. He will be back." Halfdan's handsome face darkened. "And now he and Thorkell speak of his marriage to Gunhilde, who is the daughter of Thorkell's old friend, Sven the Dark."

Lenora digested this information.

"If that happens, will they live here?" When Halfdan nodded with a gloomy expression, Lenora added, "Then who will have charge of Thorkell's household? Will it be Freydis or this Gunhilde?"

"I do not know. I met Gunhilde once. She is a

cold, proud woman. She will not bow easily to
Thorkell's unmarried daughter."

"Freydis should marry," Lenora told him impulsively.

"Freydis should not marry."

Halfdan's face was etched in pain. Lenora
moved closer to this Norse giant who she had
begun to think of as her friend, and touched his
arm.

"Isn't there some way," she asked, "for Erik to
make peace with Snorri? Then you could marry
Freydis yourself. As a chieftain's son, surely you
would be acceptable to Thorkell."

"You do not understand our ways." Halfdan
took a deep breath before explaining. "Freydis'
mother killed Erik's mother. Erik is my blood
brother. His feuds are mine, but more than that,
because he is my brother, his sister is my sister
also. Brothers and sisters do not marry."

"But Halfdan—"

"Do not speak of it again. And do not speak of
this to Erik. I do not wish to cause him pain. I
will find Erik and tell him what has happened
with Hrolf and Bjarni. Stay in the house until
Erik comes." Halfdan set off toward Thorkell's
private chambers.

Lenora tried to fit Erik's shirts into one of the
carved chests that sat on the floor of his house, but
there was no room. A heavy fur cloak for winter
and a lighter but still bulky woolen cloak filled
all the space.

A second chest held bolts of the strange silk
fabric Erik had brought from Miklagard, and a

hoard of gold and silver jewelry. She had seen the contents once when he had opened the chest, but it was locked now. It was too full to hold anything more, anyway.

"Perhaps this one." Lenora moved the oil lamp off the third chest. It was unlocked, but Erik had never opened it in her presence. The other two were Danish chests, carved in the convoluted designs Lenora had learned to recognize as distinctively Norse. Like almost all Viking carvings, they were painted in brilliant colors. The third chest had human figures carved in neat panels and was unpainted. Because it was so different from the other two chests, Lenora decided it must have come from Miklagard, wherever that mysterious place was.

She lifted the lid and smiled. There was plenty of space here, on top of those flat blocks wrapped in linen. She laid the shirts carefully into the chest, then picked up one of the blocks and uncovered it. It was a book. Unfamiliar characters, hand-inscribed, covered the parchment pages. She laid it aside and picked up another block. It, too, was a book, this one in Latin.

It had been a long time since she had read anything. It took her a while to decipher the letters, but finally she began to read, her finger tracing the line.

"What are you doing?" Erik stood in the light from the open door. The white streak in his hair gleamed as he turned his head; his green eyes glittered in anger. "I said, what are you doing with my books?"

"I—I found them when I was putting your shirts away," Lenora stammered.

"If you have damaged them, I will beat you." He picked up the book from the ground and examined it critically.

"I meant no harm. I only read a page or two."

"Read? You?"

He clearly thought she was lying. She could tell from his expression she had better convince him quickly or there would be trouble for her. She showed him the book she was still holding.

"This one is in Latin. 'In the beginning was the word,'" she read, pointing to each word with her finger. "That's from the Holy Book, isn't it? Are you a Christian, Erik?"

"Only a provisional one. Do you really know how to read?"

"I can read and write."

"You can write too?" He stared at her, his anger forgotten in his interest in her accomplishments. He sank down on the bed platform, still holding the first book Lenora had unwrapped. A smile began to spread across his face. "You may be of some use to me after all."

"I couldn't read that one," she informed him, indicating the book in his hands. "What kind of writing is it?"

"Greek. I brought it from Miklagard."

Miklagard again. Lenora knelt on the earthen floor by the open chest and looked up into Erik's dark, handsome face.

"What is Miklagard?" she asked softly.

"The greatest city in the world."

"Is it like Rome?"

Lenora, raised in a small settlement in the midst of agricultural lands, was unable to picture a city, although she had heard of York, and Father Egbert had spoken of Rome.

"It is the second Rome," Erik told her, "and greater than the first, if you believe the people who live there."

"Greater than Rome?" she echoed. "How can that be? I don't understand."

"You don't need to understand." He picked up the piece of linen and began to rewrap the Greek book.

"But where is Miklagard? Is it near here? Can we go to see it?" Lenora's curiosity flared, intrigued at the frequent repetition of that name since she had met Erik. "I would so much like to see a great city."

Erik laughed, amused by her enthusiasm.

"It is many months' journey by sea and land and riverboat," he said. "To get there you must travel far east to Gardariki, where the Rus live, to the place the Slavs call Kiev. From Kiev you must sail down a dangerous river to the Euxine Sea, a great black sea far south of here. Across that sea lies Miklagard. In Grikkland. The Greeks call it Constantinople."

His eyes focused on something far away, remembering. He did not notice that Lenora had risen on her knees, and, leaning forward, had gripped his right forearm with both her hands. Her face was close to his as she listened to him. She forgot the damp, barren cabin in which they lived, forgot everything but Erik and his deep voice as he talked on, conjuring up wonders for her starved imagination.

"It is a city of gold and silver, and huge buildings of stone and brick and marble."

Lenora did not know what marble was, but it sounded wonderful.

"Buildings bigger than Thorkell's hall?" she asked.

Green eyes met gray ones with a smile. "Much bigger," Erik said. "The Emperor of the Romans lives in an enormous golden palace set in beautiful gardens. There are parades every day, and great ships lay tied up at the wharves, laden with gold and silks and spices and jewels, and merchants make huge fortunes buying and selling goods from all over the world. In Miklagard the sun shines every day and the air is warm, and life is sweet for a man with a purse full of silver."

"Oh," Lenora breathed, nearly overcome with wonder, "How I would like to see it. Will you go there again, Erik? Will you take me?"

They gazed into each other's eyes, so close Lenora seemed to see the same faraway vision filling Erik's mind. She could almost believe that she, too, had walked the distant streets of Miklagard and breathed its foreign air. Then the vision faded and she was once more aware of Erik's physical presence, of his tautly muscled body and his wide, smiling mouth so near her own. That mouth came nearer, almost touched hers, before he turned his head away.

"No." The light faded from his face. "I shall

not see Miklagard again. And even if I were to go, I could not take you. The journey is too dangerous. You would die before you reached the Great City. I was nearly killed getting there, and almost died again returning home."

"Is that when your leg was injured?"

The look in his eyes changed again. He stood up, shaking off her hands.

"I have told you before, you ask too many questions," he said harshly.

He had finished wrapping the Greek book. He replaced it in the wooden chest and held out his hand for the second book. She pressed it against her bosom.

"Let me keep it," she begged. "I want to read it."

"Give it to me. Now."

"Please." She was almost in tears. Why this one book meant so much to her she could not say, but she would not give it up easily.

He moved so quickly, she did not see the motion. Iron-strong hands reached out to grip her upper arms, pulling her to her feet. There was an angry expression on his face, but as Lenora bravely met his eyes, challenging him for possession of the book, she saw a softening of his habitual sternness toward her. Suddenly she was held tightly against him, only the book separating them. One of his hands left her arm and caught the hair at the back of her head, pushing her face against his. For one breathless moment they stared at each other, and then his mouth ground upon hers as his other arm slid around her shoulders, crushing her.

She was briefly aware of firm-sinewed thighs against her legs, and of one corner of the book she still held cutting painfully into her right breast, before she was swept into a sea of sudden desire. She had lost control of her own body. She felt herself pressing ever more closely against him, heard a low moan escaping from her own throat as her mouth opened and his tongue entered her, seeking, searching out the most sensitive places, lighting fires deep within her that excited and terrified her at the same time.

The kiss deepened, becoming almost violent before he tore his mouth from hers to rain scalding-hot kisses on her cheeks and her eyelids, finally returning to her lips, his tongue thrusting fiercely into her. She welcomed his assault, adding to the fire with her own response.

While one hand tangled into her hair, holding her head immobilized, his other hand and arm plastered her body to his in an unbreakable vise that grew ever tighter. Once more he left her lips, this time to set her throat aflame with his kisses. When his mouth met hers again, her surrender was complete. She leaned into him and gave freely of her own desire.

Held against him as she was, she could have no doubts about his arousal. She could feel his manhood pressing against her thigh, hot and strong. The touch added fuel to the fire raging in her brain and her bosom and further inflamed the strange, urgent ache deep within her. Not consciously aware of what she was doing, acting on instinct alone, she moved her hips, crying out softly as he pushed himself at her. Freeing one arm, she slipped it around his waist and up under his jerkin, feeling the smooth, warm skin of his back.

He recoiled from her touch. He let her go so suddenly she swayed and nearly fell. He caught her by the upper arms once more and flung her onto the bed platform. She lay there, skirts flaring up about her knees, her head against the wall, still clutching the book, waiting for his next move with mingled fear and anticipation.

"Give me that." His voice was drenched in barely controlled fury as he stretched out his hand for the book.

"No," she whispered. "Oh, Erik, please."

She was not certain whether she was begging him not to take the book from her or for him to take her. She lay watching him, her lips parted, her breasts still heaving with the unexpected emotions he had aroused in her.

One long hand reached out to her slowly, as though fighting some invisible force that held it back. Slender fingers traced her cheek and skimmed along the curve of her mouth. One finger slid between her parted lips and rested there before probing deeper, until it met her moist, warm tongue. It lingered a moment, testing, while his green eyes watched her and his tense body bent ever nearer.

Then his hand was snatched away as though it had been burned in a fire. He grabbed the book from her nerveless fingers and turned his back on her.

"Get up," he said, "and go about your work."

When she made no response, he turned on her. "You were Snorri's once," he said. "I do not want you. As a slave you are worthless. You lie about all day. If you do not work I will sell you."

His cold words stifled all the warm passion that had been building in her.

"I was not lying about until you threw me here," Lenora replied, stung by the injustice of his complaint. "I was working. I was putting your shirts away."

"You have done that. Go to the kitchen and help with the cooking."

"I am afraid to go out. Halfdan told me to stay here. Hrolf and Bjarni—"

"Yes," he interrupted. "Halfdan told me. It seems you are entirely too alluring to men."

"I did not encourage them," she declared, her anger matching his own. "I hate them. And Snorri. I hate them all."

"So you have repeatedly told me. What am I to do with you, Lenora? Shall I sell you to remove you from the vicinity of Snorri and his men? Would that please you?"

"It would not. I don't want to be sent away from—" She stopped, unable to complete the sentence.

"From?" He frowned at her, his dark brows drawing together in a fierce line. "There is someone. Who don't you want to be separated from, Lenora?"

"Edwina," she said quickly. "It is Edwina, of course."

"Ahhhh. Of course."

"I worry about her, Erik." Lenora dared not stop to wonder why she felt it necessary to explain at length a perfectly justified concern. "Edwina has not recovered from what Snorri did to us. Her thoughts are disordered, and she is unlike the Edwina I used to know. Her spirit is broken. I wish I could help her, but I don't know how."

"Lenora." His hand moved as if to stroke her hair, hesitated, and then, without touching her, withdrew. "There are some sicknesses only time will heal, and there are others that cannot be cured."

"Are you saying Edwina is mad?" She rose from the bed platform to face him. "How dare you suggest such a thing? If you had lived through the horrors she has known, lost what she has lost, you would be unhappy too."

"I have known my own horrors and you have lost the same things as Edwina, and neither of us is mad. The difference, my fierce, loyal little slave, is that you and I are strong, and Edwina is not. What a friend you are," Erik went on, smiling at her with an odd tenderness. "I won't sell you, Lenora. I could not send you away."

"You couldn't?"

"No. Never."

Green eyes lingered on her face, their strange, spellbinding light pulling her closer, ever closer to him. She sensed his arms reaching out to enfold her, felt her body bending toward him.

"We Danes value friendship and loyalty too," Erik told her, his matter-of-fact words breaking the spell that had held her. "I won't separate you from Edwina. I have an idea. I'll tell you about it soon."

He left her alone to wonder at his meaning. Several days passed, during which time Erik said nothing more to her than the few words necessary to give her an occasional order. Lenora decided he had forgotten his idea, whatever it had been. He avoided being alone with her, and since the afternoon he had caught her reading his book, he had slept elsewhere. She had seen him with a plump blond serving wench called Erna, who preened herself in front of Lenora and proudly displayed a bronze bracelet and neck ring. Wherever she looked in those days, Lenora's eyes fell on Snorri and his two friends, or on Erik with Erna only a step away, or on Edwina with Thorkell.

Edwina was becoming a complete stranger to Lenora. She moved through each day's duties like a sleepwalker, and slept in Thorkell's bed each night. She appeared to be totally reconciled to her status as slave.

Lenora was appalled to find Edwina had hope of becoming pregnant by Thorkell.

"Then he might free me and marry me," she told Lenora. "It is one way to regain my freedom."

"Only to exchange it for another kind of slavery," Lenora replied, her heart aching at the change in her friend. If only she could find a way to attain their freedom, Edwina might become herself again. Freydis had told her that slaves sometimes saved enough gold and silver to buy their freedom, but Lenora had no possessions except her clothing. Erik had never given her any jewelry, as some of the other men did for their slaves; Lenora had nothing to sell for the coins that might have freed her, nor could she do anything to help Edwina.

As she sat in the weaving room, spinning while Edwina and another woman worked at their looms, Freydis and Erik appeared.

"You are to go with Erik," Freydis told her. "But you must continue spinning in your free time. We need the thread, and no one is as fast as you at making it. Erna and Tola can take over your duties in the kitchen and laundry. Well, what are you waiting for, Lenora? Go."

"Where am I to go? What do you want?" she asked Erik.

"You told me once that you can write. How well can you count?"

"Only a little. But I can learn."

"I have discussed my idea with Thorkell and now we have new work for you to do. Come with me."

He led her out a door at the rear of the great hall, to a large room among the cluster of chambers reserved for Thorkell's use. Thorkell himself was seated at a trestle table reading from a square piece of parchment. He looked up as they entered, his sharp blue eyes appraising Lenora. His cheeks were pink above his white beard. In

Flora Speer

spite of his age, he looked strong and healthy.

"This is the woman," Erik told him.

"Good," Thorkell said. "If she works well, she can continue here while we are away."

"Where are you going?" Lenora asked.

She saw the glint that always appeared in Erik's eye when she began to ask questions, but he answered her patiently.

"My father and I will travel to the home of Sven the Dark. We go to arrange his daughter Gunhilde's marriage to Snorri, which we hope will take place this winter. Before we go, I am going to teach you what I have been doing for Thorkell. You will help me keep his records."

"Can't I go to Sven's home with you?"

"No. Do not argue with me, Lenora. You will do as you are told."

"Doesn't Freydis keep the household records?" Lenora had no wish to infringe upon the duties or rights of Thorkell's formidable daughter.

"Freydis does manage my household," Thorkell said. It was the first time he had ever addressed her directly. His voice was low-pitched and pleasant, but heavy with authority. "Erik is speaking of my business records, which I have always kept myself until recently. Now Erik helps me, and you will help Erik."

"Business? You mean—?" she stopped, embarrassed.

"Trade," Thorkell said. His blue eyes met hers, and a smile lifted the corners of his mouth. There was no physical resemblance between him and Erik, yet at that moment there was a remarkable

96

similarity of expression between Thorkell and his son. "The goods gotten on Snorri's voyages. I provide the supplies of food and drink, most of the weapons and ship's gear, and some of the men for those trips, and I reap the profits along with Snorri. The goods are traded in Hedeby and elsewhere."

"Plunder," Lenora whispered. The word slipped out thoughtlessly. She saw a distinct twinkle in Thorkell's eyes.

"Some of my wealth is accumulated by plunder, that is true," he told her frankly. "But an equal amount is gotten by trade. I have always preferred to trade. It is foolish to lose good men fighting in a raid where it is not necessary. After all, I may need those same men to fight for me another day."

He rose, and Lenora realized how very tall the man was. In spite of herself, she was impressed by his dignity.

"I am needed elsewhere," he told Erik. "You may use this room as long as you wish. Teach her well." To Lenora, he added, "You are friend to my slave, Edwina."

"Yes."

"You are the one who wishes vengeance on my son Snorri."

Lenora felt the blood drain from her face as Thorkell's cold eyes pierced her. She thought she would faint from terror of him.

"Well?"

Lenora knew she had to answer this man who stood watching her calmly as she struggled to

97

pull her confused thoughts together. She spoke through trembling lips, but her voice was steady.

"Snorri killed all of my family and destroyed my home. I would repay him for the deed if I could."

"If you could. But you are helpless to do so." There was no triumph or gloating in Thorkell's deep voice as he stated the obvious fact.

"I know that. Any attempt to kill Snorri would only result in my own death. I don't want to die. I want retribution."

To her surprise, Thorkell smiled at her.

"Thus do I hope my own daughter would react were she in your place. You have courage, Lenora, to speak to me so honestly." He drew nearer, towering over her. "I am at times a trader, so I will make a bargain with you, little slave. If you do your work in this room well, I will pay you. In time, a year or two, three years at most, you can earn your freedom. Would that please you?"

"Very much." It never occurred to her to doubt him. She simply knew Thorkell would not lie to her about so important a matter.

"In return, you will brew no plots against Snorri. That should not be too difficult for you. The day after tomorrow he is going a-viking once more, and when he returns he will be occupied with his marriage. You will not have to see him often. Are we agreed, Lenora?"

"Yes, Thorkell, I will agree to that."

"Good. Give me your hand." Lenora held out her right hand. She felt Thorkell's palm slap hard against her own.

98

"*Handsala,*" he said. "With this, our bargain is sealed. I know you will keep it well."

Then he was gone, and Lenora turned to Erik.

"Now you know why my father is called the Fair-speaker," Erik said.

"Did you know he would offer to pay me?"

"No."

"Are you angry that I can earn my freedom?"

"Why should I be? You are of no particular use to me. Now you had better get to work so you can earn your silver."

As she listened to Erik's instructions, one thought kept running through Lenora's mind: *Edwina told Thorkell I wanted revenge on Snorri. No one else knew. Because of that morning when I was angry for her sake and said things I ought to have kept to myself, my best friend betrayed me. Thorkell might have killed me; Edwina didn't know he would not. This is what it means to be a slave. I can't even trust my friend any more. I can never confide in her again.*

"Are you listening, Lenora? Pay attention."

"Yes, Erik, I understand. This list of numbers is to be copied."

Maud was right: I need only survive. Because Thorkell the Fair-speaker is a good man, I will earn my freedom one day.

Chapter Eight

On that night and the next great feasts were held to celebrate Snorri's leave-taking. Continual toasts to his good fortune and that of his men were drunk, and then it was necessary to toast Thorkell for providing supplies and weapons from his stores. Both ale and mead were imbibed even more lustily than usual.

Snorri, drunk and reeling, pulled himself to his feet and clapped a hand on Erik's shoulder.

"To my brother," he cried, lifting a silver-ornamented drinking horn. "May his luck improve."

There was a roar of laughter as cups and horns were raised to Erik's good fortune.

"You will certainly need better luck than on your last voyage," Snorri said, grinning down at Erik, "else you will suffer more broken masts.

May the next one break your neck."

Snorri raised his drinking horn and drained it a second time. He called out, and a serving wench ran to refill it.

"Here's to Erik," he cried loudly. "May he soon acquire a ship of his own and become a true Norseman once more."

"To Erik." The men cheered and drank again. "To Erik the Norseman."

Erik stood up quietly. Snorri, who had turned to face the revelers, did not see him. Lenora had by now grown used to the Vikings' custom of insulting each other when they were drunk. She knew such insults were usually taken as jests. Still, she felt a prickle of fear as Snorri persisted.

"We all know," Snorri informed the laughing men and women, "how Erik spent three years in Grikkland. And we have heard of the strange, unnatural customs of those clean-shaven, sweet-smelling Greeks, with their silken clothes and their pretty little boys and their eunuchs. To Erik," Snorri raised his brimming drinking horn yet again. "May he soon regain his lost manhood." Throwing his head back, Snorri began to drink.

Total silence fell in the hall. It lasted only a moment before the great drinking-horn flew out of Snorri's hand as Erik struck him. The horn crashed against the nearest carved pillar, spraying mead over anyone within range, then bounced on the floor, skittering along the bare, tramped earth until it stopped at the edge of the firepit. Snorri himself was thrown against the pillar, mead dripping off his blond beard in tiny golden droplets. Erik's left arm held him there, pinning Snorri across the chest. In his right hand Erik held his gold-hilted dagger. It pricked gently at one distended vein in Snorri's neck. Halfdan, his broadsword drawn, stood back-to-back with Erik, protecting him. Lenora held her breath, not knowing what to expect next.

"Take . . . that . . . back," Erik commanded.

Snorri's stained teeth showed in a vulpine smile. "Does the truth hurt, little Erik?" he asked contemptuously.

"Because I do not drink continuously and sprawl on the ground with every serving wench who passes me, you think I am not a true man? You are more stupid than I imagined, Snorri."

"You are not even a true Norseman, you half-Frankish weakling."

Erik's dagger blade pricked deeper. A thread of blood appeared on the side of Snorri's neck, but he did not flinch.

"At least my mother was not a murderer," Erik growled. "And I have never taken an unwilling woman."

Snorri's eyes flicked to Lenora, who stood horrified, watching them. He laughed again. Then he stopped, his blue eyes growing larger, as Erik's dagger slid a little farther into his neck, and Snorri at last realized Erik might be angry enough to kill him.

"In our father's hall, little brother?" he teased hoarsely, a twisted smile on his lips.

Green eyes and blue ones remained locked for

102

a long moment. Then Lenora saw Erik relax his hold and Snorri gather himself to spring at Erik.

"Hold!" Thorkell had risen. With his long white hair and beard and his red silk robe flowing about him, he looked like some mighty Norse god.

"This has gone far enough. Snorri, you bring bad luck upon your voyage by quarreling with your brother at your sailing feast. Erik, you must not draw your blade in my hall. I forbid it, although I know the insult is great. Here, wench, pick up Snorri's drinking horn and refill it. We will have one more toast to the success of Snorri's voyage, and then my two sons will sit side by side and eat and drink in peace."

Such was the force of Thorkell's personality, so complete his dominance over those in his hall, that everyone did as he commanded. The required toast was dutifully drunk, and Erik and Snorri seated themselves once more on the settle facing Thorkell and Freydis.

Halfdan helped Lenora to right their overturned bench, then seated himself beside her again. He grinned at her like a mischievous boy. "We almost had fun," he said. "Too bad Thorkell stopped it. There are a couple of Snorri's men I would like to skewer."

"Hrolf and Bjarni?"

"Among others." He grinned at her again.

On her other side, Erik drank steadily.

"Are you all right?" Lenora asked.

"Yes," he replied shortly, helping himself to a large portion of cooked, dried fish and smearing

103

it with sweet butter. He licked the thumb he had used to apply the butter and began to eat. Like his cup, his spoon was silver and of foreign design.

He was the strangest man Lenora had ever known. His anger at his half-brother had apparently vanished completely. Having had no experience with such things, she was not sure exactly what Snorri's taunt against Erik's manhood had meant, but she dismissed it. Recalling his prompt arousal when he had kissed her, Lenora felt certain there was nothing wrong with his manhood. Still, she understood that Snorri's jibes about Erik's luck and his half-Frankish parentage had somehow diminished him before the other men. She wished she knew how to comfort him.

"Erik?"

"What is it?"

"Snorri was only trying to make trouble. No one believed him."

She laid one hand softly on his arm, her anxious eyes meeting his. He gave her the smallest of smiles, and for once he did not pull away from her.

"I know," he said softly, so no one else could hear. "Everyone knows how Snorri lies. Thank you, my—Lenora."

That night Erik drank much more than usual, with the inevitable unhappy results when he stumbled into his house early the following morning. Lenora held his head over a large basin while he was sick, then wiped his face gently with a damp cloth. She stripped off his soiled shirt and helped him into a fresh one. When she would have unfastened his breeches, he protested.

"Leave me alone," he ordered, "I'm going to die now." He flopped facedown upon the mattress.

"You shouldn't drink so much," she told him, covering him with a fur.

"I don't drink as much as the others do."

"You did last night. You are all like children, trying to outdo each other."

"I've heard the Saxons are great drinkers too."

"I have never seen anyone drink like you Norse." She pushed him back as he tried to sit up.

"I should go to Thorkell. There is work to do," he insisted. "Oh, my head."

"Lie down," she ordered sternly, giving him a harder push that flattened him. She placed a cool, damp cloth across his forehead, then stood regarding him with a peculiar mix of feelings.

Try as she might, she could not hate him. She loved the times when, as they worked together on Thorkell's accounts, he talked to her of his travels and the strange places he had seen, when his memory and her insatiable curiosity merged in a close companionship such as she had never known with anyone else, not even her father. She felt compassion for him when the other men treated him as a weakling or outsider because of his lameness, and exasperation and anger when he treated her as the slave she was. There were times, like this morning, when she was overcome with a tender, almost maternal warmth toward him. And always, underlying all her mood changes and varying attitudes toward him, there was the undercurrent of his powerful physical attraction for her. But he would never touch her as a man touches a woman, of that she was now certain. She sighed deeply.

"Try to sleep," she said. "I will do your work for Thorkell."

She did not think he heard her, for he was already asleep.

She straightened the little house, then combed her hair and washed her face before heading toward Thorkell's chambers.

There was a crowd gathered at the river's edge. Good-byes and wishes of good luck were called across the water as Snorri's longship set out on its voyage. Fifteen pairs of oars dipped and rose in unison. Snorri stood in the stern of the *Sea Dragon*, next to the helmsman. Lenora wondered if he and his men were as sick this morning as Erik had been. She hoped so.

"Good-bye, Snorri," she whispered. "I hope you never return. May some good Saxon warrior hack you to pieces, very slowly."

I'm growing as bloodthirsty as the Norse, she thought as she made her way to Thorkell's room. No one was there, so she set to work, copying out a list of silver and gold items. Thorkell planned to send the pieces to Hedeby, where they would be traded for oil, for wine and glass from the Rhineland, for swordblades, for the silken cloth for which Thorkell had such a weakness, and most important of all, for dirhams, the silver Arabic coins that were the basis of Thorkell's private hoard. Arab silver was easily stored and could be traded for almost anything available in the northlands. Lenora had no idea where Thorkell's hoard was hidden, but it was rumored to be unusually large.

She looked up as Thorkell came into the room, followed by Edwina.

"Where is Erik?" Thorkell asked.

"Asleep. He was sick this morning."

Thorkell chuckled. "He never had a head for drink. I suppose it's because his mother was Frankish. Can you do this by yourself?" Thorkell indicated the parchment on which Lenora was writing.

"I can."

"Then I will leave you. There is something else I want to do right now. Come, Edwina."

Thorkell's smile made it quite clear what he wished to do. What shocked Lenora was the worshipful answering smile on Edwina's face.

She likes him, Lenora thought. She even wants him. She enjoys sharing his bed. Oh, Edwina, my dear, treacherous friend, how have we come to this? How can you care for a man whose son killed your betrothed?

When she finally returned to Erik's house, Lenora found him toweling himself briskly with a linen cloth. The room she had left so neat was an untidy mess, with Erik's clothes strewn about it. An empty wooden cup and a bowl half-full of porridge sat on one of the chests.

107

"I feel much better," Erik announced. "I went for a swim in the river."

"Thorkell said to tell you that you two will leave for Sven's home in eight days."

"So the decision has been made. Good. He feared Snorri would refuse to marry Gunhilde. Snorri likes to be free."

"If I know Snorri, he will be no less free once he is married. Poor Gunhilde."

Lenora began to fold the blanket Erik had tossed aside when he rose from the bed. He came up behind her and put one hand on her shoulder, turning her to face him.

"Thank you for caring for me this morning," he said softly.

"It is my duty to care for my master," she replied, not meeting his eyes. "You need not thank me."

He tilted her chin up until she was forced to look straight into his eyes. His fingers wove themselves through her chestnut curls, playing with the ends. His eyes were bottomless green pools, in which she would gladly drown.

"You are a beautiful young woman, Lenora. Do you know how difficult it has been to lie beside you all these nights and not touch you?"

"I am your slave," she answered with false meekness. "You may do what you want with me and I must obey."

"I do not want a woman who only obeys."

Still his eyes held her. She fought against feelings that threatened to burst out of control and overwhelm her. She wanted to put her arms around him, wanted his arms around her. Most of all, she wanted the touch of his wide, burning mouth on her lips. She put the idea firmly away, reminding herself that because of Snorri, she was repulsive to him.

"It has not been so difficult for you lately," she said, knowing she needed to recall herself to cold reality, and that this was the best way. "I have heard gossip about you and Erna."

"Erna?" He laughed, poking one finger at the wooden cup and half-filled bowl. "Erna brought me these. Take them back to the kitchen when you clean up." He saw Lenora's involuntary glance at the tumbled bed and smiled.

"No," he said. "I was too sick for such a thing. And besides—" He stopped, shrugging his shoulders.

She stood helplessly, watching him, wondering what it was he wanted of her, fearing the longing that would not leave her pounding heart, until he took her hand.

"Lenora, my sweet," he whispered, his voice a soft caress, "how I wish Snorri had never touched you."

"No more than I," she said ruefully, as Erik lifted her hand to his lips and held it there.

"Why do you torment me?" he asked. "Why can't I let you go and be done with it?"

"Erik, are you ready to go hunting?" Halfdan's tall form filled the doorway. "Oh. Shall I leave?"

"No, I'm coming." Erik quickly released Lenora's hand and picked up his swordbelt.

"Where are you going?" Lenora asked.

"Don't question my actions, woman." The tender moment was gone and Erik was his usual distant self once more, his cold words clearly intended to push her away from him. "Clean up this room. That shirt needs washing. And when you take those dishes back to the kitchen, tell Erna to wait for me tonight if I am late. She can serve my food as well as you."

He went out, slamming the door behind him, giving Lenora just a glimpse of Halfdan's startled face. She thought she heard a low laugh as the men left, and the sound infuriated her.

"Tell Erna yourself, you Norse animal!" She picked up the wooden cup and hurled it against the door. The sound it made was so satisfying that she picked up the bowl and threw that too. It hit the door jamb and split. Sodden gray porridge dribbled down the door frame and onto the floor. Lenora flung herself onto the bed, sobbing.

"Erik, Erik," she wept, pounding on the straw mattress, "I hate you so much. Don't leave me like that. Don't leave me. Please."

She did not see him again that day and she did not go to the great hall to eat that night. She cleaned the house a second time, took the dishes back to the kitchen, and managed to deliver Erik's message with some semblance of indifference.

She turned away from the triumph on Erna's face, picked up a piece of flatbread, some cheese, and a flagon of ale, and made her way back to the house. There, in a gesture of defiance, she took all of Erik's books out of the foreign chest and unwrapped and examined each one. She chose one to read and put the others back neatly, but deliberately not in the same order, so Erik would know what she had done. She lit a second and third oil lamp and read all night, slowly, tracing each word with her finger, trying to remember all the Latin her father had once taught her.

After that day, Erik did not seem to notice anything she did. He ignored her, except when they were at work together in Thorkell's rooms. He no longer slept in his own house at all. Lenora did not know where he was sleeping, but she thought she could guess who was sleeping with him. She had more than once interrupted the other women gossiping in whispers about Erna's undisguised desire for Erik, and had seen the sly glances aimed in her own direction.

Lenora could not look at Erna without wanting to slap the woman's smug face, and it took all of her self-control to be polite to Erik, to pretend not to notice what was happening. She feared if she made him angry, he would send her away from Thorkellshavn. Lenora did not think she could bear that. She told herself it was because of Edwina. She was surprised Erik had not put her out of his house and sent her to the women's quarters so he could bring Erna to live with him. So far he had not suggested it, and for that sop to her pride Lenora was grateful.

When Erik and Thorkell, after an enormous

farewell feast, left for the home of Sven the Dark, Lenora felt only relief. What did it matter whether Erik was at Thorkellshavn or elsewhere? He cared nothing for her. Nothing at all.

Chapter Nine

"Where is Edwina?"

Erna looked up from her weaving. With her overly plump face and figure she was not pretty, but she exuded an air of bored sensuality that Lenora knew many of the men found exciting. When she saw Lenora, Erna's hand went to the bronze bracelet on her left wrist, and she wore a mocking smile.

"Weren't you told?" she asked sweetly. "Thorkell took her with him this morning when he left for Sven's house. Thorkell cannot bear to be parted from Edwina, not even for one night. He says she is the best present Snorri ever gave him. That's very different from the feelings of some other men about their slaves, isn't it?"

Lenora did not answer. She would rather die

than let Erna know that Erik, like Edwina, had
not bothered to say good-bye to her. She sat down
on a low stool and leaned back against the cool
wall. It was an unusually warm day, with low-
hanging clouds threatening rain. The heavy,
moist air made her feel drugged. She pushed
damp curls off her brow, picked some wool out
of a basket, and began spinning. She would stay
in the weaving room just long enough to make it
clear Erna had not driven her away, and then she
would go elsewhere to work.

Erna continued to play with her bracelet.
When Lenora paid no attention, Erna thrust her
left wrist under Lenora's nose.

"Do you like it?" she asked.

"Very pretty." Lenora pretended indifference.

"Erik gave it to me." Erna's tone was almost
defiant.

"So you have said, many times."

"I please him." Erna smiled. "I am proud he
wants me."

"You must be, to talk about it so freely."

Erna smiled more broadly now, and ran her
hands along her lushly curved hips and thighs in
a sensuous motion. Then, her eyes fixed on Lenora, she slowly drew her hands across her abdomen, continuing upward to cup her heavy
breasts.

"And he pleases me too. Erik is a strong man."

Lenora stared at her coldly.

"I can hardly wait for him to return," Erna
went on, wriggling her hips. "He is so big and
strong," she repeated.

114

"If you are so eager for him, you will be in a sorry condition by the time he does return," Lenora told her sharply. "I understand he and Thorkell are to be away for a full moon's cycle and possibly more. Do you think you can wait?"

"He will come home to my bed, not yours."

"That is his misfortune."

Lenora suddenly rose. She threw down her spindle and the wool and started for the door.

"Where are you going, Lenora? Freydis told me you would be working here all day."

"I have more important things to do than listen to a she-cat in heat," Lenora snapped.

She ran across the end of the great hall and out the side door. The clouds had fulfilled their threat: it was pouring rain. She dashed into one of the buildings near Thorkell's chambers. It was a storeroom, recently swept and scrubbed. It stood empty now, awaiting the fruits of the harvest that would begin with the next full moon. She hurried across the room to a second door on the far side. All of the buildings on this side of the great hall were close together. Those that did not have connecting doors or hallways were only a few steps apart, for easy access during the cold, snowy winters. At the far side of these buildings, set a little apart from them, was Erik's house. Lenora knew she could scurry from one building to another and reach the house in a relatively dry condition. She moved quickly, wanting the privacy of her own place. She went through a second and a third room, then entered a fourth. She stopped suddenly, her skirts swirling about her ankles.

Halfdan and Freydis stood there, alone. They stood several feet apart, but the tension between them was so great it filled the room. They did not notice Lenora at first, then Freydis slowly turned her head and looked at Lenora out of dark blue eyes wet with tears.

"I'm sorry," Lenora said quickly. "I was trying to keep dry. I'll go now."

As she passed them, Lenora saw Halfdan reach out one huge hand and lay it against Freydis' cheek. Even with his back to the light, Lenora could see the sad look on his face.

Lenora burst out the door and ran straight to Erik's house, not minding the drenching rain. She slammed the door shut, barred it, and leaned against it, weeping and shuddering, though whether her sobs were for Freydis and Halfdan or for herself she did not know.

That night Halfdan sat beside Freydis during the evening meal, and in the morning he rode away.

"He says he is going to visit his father," Gutrid, one of the kitchen wenches, told Lenora. "Tola says he and Freydis sat up late in her room, talking. I wonder if talking is all they did."

"Tola is a gossip, and so are you," Lenora said. But she wondered, too, about Halfdan and Freydis, and about the reasons Halfdan had once given her to explain why he and Freydis could not marry. In spite of her determination not to like any of the Norse, she felt sorry for them both.

Freydis kept to her chamber the day Halfdan left. The following morning she appeared early, looking as if nothing had happened, and took charge of Thorkell's household as usual. She did not mention what Lenora had seen.

Soon the harvest began, and there was much to do to prepare food for winter storage. Although these processes went on all summer long, now the pace of activity quickened. Haying season had come, and everyone at Thorkellshavn, men and women alike, was required to work until this important harvest was done, for hay provided the only fodder for cattle, sheep, and goats during the winter.

At carefully determined intervals from now until the darkest days of winter, pigs and cattle would be butchered. The meat would hang in a coldhouse made of stone, through the center floor of which a diverted stream ran in a stone channel, its icy water helping to keep the meat cool. At the same time, fish and some of the meat would be dried, smoked, or preserved with whey or salt, for longer storage than the coldhouse afforded. Peas, beans, apples, and berries were dried and carefully stored. Nuts were gathered and piled in baskets or large wooden bowls in the storerooms. Freydis directed the making of cheeses. Thorkell's storerooms began to fill with wooden vats and tubs, with soapstone bowls and with baskets, overflowing with provisions.

After the haying was over, Lenora was spared much of the heavy labor that other servants were made to do. She spent part of each day working on Thorkell's lists and accounts and the rest of her time in the weaving room or assisting Freydis as she directed the household. Lenora was trying to weave a piece of cloth for a winter cloak for herself, but with her lack of skill at the loom she began to wonder if she would freeze to death before it was made.

The moon grew thin and then fat, and thin again, and now the nights were growing noticeably longer. Soon would come the time of equal day and night. A few bushes turned rusty-red and began to lose their leaves, and the green trees had developed a golden tinge. One quiet evening a rider appeared, his horse covered with foam, to announce that Thorkell and his son would arrive home the next day. Freydis ordered a welcoming feast prepared.

"I am eager to see my father and brother again," she told Lenora.

"I wonder if they were successful. Has Sven's daughter agreed to marry Snorri, do you think?"

"I am certain of it. My brother is too good a match for Gunhilde to reject him. Snorri himself will surely return soon too. He should have been here to help with the harvest. He will at least want to be here for the harvest feasts."

In spite of her cheerful words, Freydis did not look happy. Lenora thought she did not like the prospect of another woman at Thorkellshavn, trying to run Thorkell's household in a new way. Lenora herself did not like the idea of meeting Snorri again, but she was pleased and excited at the thought of seeing Erik. Her earlier hurt and anger at him had dissipated during his long absence.

The water in the little pool along the stream was by now uncomfortably cool. Most of the women had taken to using the bath house behind Thorkell's chambers, where the water could be heated, but Lenora went alone to the pool to bathe and wash her hair and then put on a clean shift. She did not want to hear whatever the other women might have to say about her careful toilet. She had no new outer garment, so she brushed and shook out the same blue woolen one she had worn all summer, fastening it at the shoulders with Freydis' brooches. Her uncontrollable hair she simply combed and left unbound.

Thorkell looked tired. He swung wearily off his horse and embraced Freydis.

"I am happy to be home," he said. "I am growing too old for travel. Lenora, it is good to see you again. Have you worked well in my absence?"

"I have tried to, Thorkell." Lenora was shocked at her own pleasure in greeting the Viking chieftain. Thorkellshavn seemed more complete, and safer, with his dignified presence in residence.

Edwina had not changed. She was as thin and pale as ever, and her huge blue eyes followed Thorkell worshipfully. She gave Lenora only the briefest greeting before hurrying after her master as he strode toward his chamber.

"Lenora." Erik stood before her. In a new scarlet tunic embroidered with gold and a red head-

119

band, he was far more handsome than she had remembered. His smooth, blue-black hair gleamed in the sun, the white streak catching the soft autumn light.

"Welcome home. Are you well, Erik?"

"Well enough." He picked up his bundle of belongings and headed for his cottage, nodding to her to join him. "And you?"

"I have completed all the work you left for me."

"I knew you would." His smile nearly stopped her heart with its warmth.

He entered his house as though he had never made a habit of staying away from it and began to unpack. He had brought her a heavy, oblong silver brooch.

"You will need it to hold your winter cloak," he told her.

Seeing a second brooch made of gold, Lenora asked, "Is that for Erna?"

"Who?" He looked at her blankly. "Erna? No, this is for Freydis. I always bring her a gift when I return from a journey."

He was changed, although she could not have said what the difference in him was. While he washed the dust of travel from his face and hands and carefully combed his hair before the small silver mirror Lenora held up for him, he asked for details of the work she had done for Thorkell and questioned her about the harvest.

"We must talk more," he said. "Later. I have much to tell you."

"Is anything wrong?"

"How serious you are." He laughed. To her surprise, he bent and kissed her cheek. "I promise you, nothing is wrong. It is only that, away from Thorkellshavn, I have had time to think. Since last you saw me, I have grown a little older and I hope a good deal wiser, and soon you will know everything I have decided. For now, come with me to the great hall. We can't insult Thorkell by being late."

He slipped an arm about her waist and pulled her out the door. He kept his arm around her until they reached the hall.

The feast that night was a happy one. In addition to the usual boiled mutton and roasted pig, a haunch of venison had been turning on the kitchen spit all day, watched over by a young male slave. With Snorri and his men absent, there were no violent incidents, but instead good-natured joking and laughter among the men of Thorkell's hird as they welcomed home their companions who had gone with Thorkell. Many casks of ale and mead were broached, and there was Frankish wine, a gift to Thorkell from Sven the Dark.

Erik had a new Rhinish beaker of pale green glass, which he filled with wine and handed to Lenora.

"I like this better than ale," Lenora told him.

"Don't grow too fond of it." He laughed. "It's very rare and expensive. We will only drink it on special occasions."

"Tell me about your trip," Lenora urged, encouraged by his obvious good humor.

"The marriage is agreed upon," Erik said, and

he began speaking about the details of Snorri's marriage contract. These were not private, but were being discussed openly by most of those in Thorkell's hall that evening.

As Erik talked, Lenora watched his dark face, smiling when his eyes met hers. It seemed to her his presence lit up the garishly painted, smoky hall, making everything around him more vibrant and alive.

He lavished attentions on her, cutting the best pieces of meat for her, covering her hand with his when she drank again from the new wineglass, and then turning the glass to drink from the spot where her lips had touched. Dazzled by his charm, her breath suddenly tight in her chest, Lenora responded with blushes and lowered lids and shy, happy smiles.

Her attention was so completely focused on Erik that in spite of all the noise and movement about her she was almost unaware there were other people in the hall. Then she lifted her eyes and saw, over his shoulder, Erna, standing in the shadows at one side of a pillar, clutching an ale pitcher with whitened knuckles and glaring at her in open hatred. Lenora was chilled by Erna's look until Erik spoke to her again, and she forgot the other woman in her delight at the funny story he was telling.

When at last they left the hall, Erik stood a while, looking at the dark gleam of the river.

"How strange," he said. "I long for distant lands, I ache for the feel of a good ship beneath my feet once more, I am excited by the thought of new sights and sounds and smells, and yet it is always so good to come back here. I spent most of my childhood away from Thorkellshavn, but this is still my home."

"We have all missed you," she replied dutifully.

"Have you? I know I have missed your gray eyes, Lenora, and your beautiful hair. I had no idea I would miss you so much." One hand played lightly with her curls. For a moment she thought he might kiss her, but he stretched and yawned instead. "It is hot tonight. Unusual, so late in the year."

They walked slowly toward his house, Erik calling out several times to men he knew, as those who had been present at the feast went off to their beds.

Their single room was stuffy and airless. Lenora expected Erik to leave and find Erna. When he made no move to go, she undressed quickly and wrapped herself in her woolen blanket. She lay down close to the wall, her back to the room, as she had always done when he was there. Erik stripped and lay down beside her on the straw mattress.

Lenora began to feel uncomfortable. The blanket was hot and scratchy against her skin, and she was almost unbearably aware of Erik's naked body next to her. She wriggled around, trying to get comfortable while still staying covered. It was impossible. She flipped over onto her other side and found him watching her.

"You forgot to put out the lamp," she said accusingly.

"I didn't forget. I wanted to look at you." Something in his voice caught at her senses, making her feel weak and lightheaded. It had been this way all evening, and now she realized the difference in him was his intense concentration on her.

"You have seen me before," she whispered, suddenly shy under his gaze.

He did not answer her at once. His hand tugged at the edge of the blanket, which she had tucked tightly under her chin. A teasing smile played along his wide mouth.

"It's not winter yet, Lenora. You don't need to bury yourself in blankets and furs to stay warm. Uncover yourself as I do."

Slowly, unable to tear her eyes away from his, she relaxed her tight hold on the blanket. He rose on one elbow and began unwrapping her as though he were uncovering a treasure.

"I thought of you constantly while I was gone," he told her, still pulling at the blanket. "I think I needed to be apart from you in order to see you clearly. I have made a decision about you."

"What is it?" Her voice quavered. She had begun to tremble with delicious, tantalizing expectation.

"I realized I have been wasting my most precious possession. You, Lenora. I decided to forget what is past, forget what was done to you against your will. You are beautiful, so beautiful, and I have wanted you since the first time I saw you.

I believe you want me too. Lenora, my sweet, tell me you want me."

Lenora closed her eyes against the green blaze in his. She sensed his mouth hovering just above her own.

"Yes," she whispered, and she felt his mouth take hers. Thought spun away and vanished until she was conscious only of feeling, her physical perceptions suddenly sharpened to exquisite sensitivity.

She was by now almost completely naked. She felt first the warm air on her skin, and then his hands, stroking along her shoulders. She swallowed hard as his fingers slid lower with maddening slowness, until they teased the sensitive tip of one breast. Then she felt his lips and tongue.

She had never forgotten his hands and mouth on her breasts on the night she had become his slave. Those caresses had haunted her dreams, but she had not known until this moment just how much she had longed to feel them again. A new, wonderfully warm sensation began to spread over her. She gave into it willingly.

He continued his exploration down the satiny length of her body, his mouth following his sensitive hands over abdomen and hip and thigh. Everywhere he touched her, her flesh sprang into eager life under his skillful manipulations, aching, yearning, hot with long-denied desire.

"Touch me," he whispered. "Touch me, Lenora. I want to feel your hands on me."

She could barely speak. It was nearly impossible to summon a coherent thought, to concentrate on anything but pleasure and warmth and Erik everywhere, touching her, holding her.

"I don't know what to do," she gasped.

"It doesn't matter. Just touch me and don't stop."

His mouth covered hers again, his tongue plunged into her, stars exploded in her brain. She grasped his head, her tense fingers pulling his hair as she forced his mouth harder against hers. Shyly at first, then with growing confidence, her hands caressed his shoulders and lightly touched the scar on his left shoulder and chest as she flirted with the feeling of his warm skin beneath her fingertips. She traced the corded muscles in his arms and neck and back, felt the straight column of his spine and the firm, hard mounds of his buttocks. She felt as though, with ever-increasing contact, he was more and more a part of her, as if they were absorbing each other, magically blending and fusing together.

He buried his face in her belly, and she was dimly aware of his hands stroking her outer thighs once more, then gliding around to separate them. She moaned when his long fingers laced through the tangle of red-brown hair between her legs, probing with delicate determination. As he pushed deeper she felt a sudden twinge of pain. She cried out, twisting away from him, striking his hand aside, just as he exclaimed in surprise and let her go.

"We were wrong," he said with an exultant laugh. "All these months I've kept away from you, and now I find that Snorri never touched you."

"What are you saying?" She still felt between her thighs an echo of the brief discomfort his fingers had inflicted.

"I'm saying," he told her, "that Snorri must have planned from the beginning to give you to my father, and thus he did not rape you. Your virginity was part of the gift. How angry he must have been when Thorkell gave you to me instead of keeping you for himself." He drew her nearer, his lips meeting hers.

"I can't." Shocked at what he had told her, Lenora began to fight him. "I'm afraid."

"I won't hurt you any more than is absolutely necessary," he promised. "It will be beautiful, my sweet Lenora. Let me show you."

He began kissing her again and whispering of his delight in her, until she relaxed once more. Through long, slow, magical moments his hands and mouth urged her to the edge of something wonderful.

In the dim light of the oil lamp she saw his tense face above her as he covered her body with his own. He took her gently, easing her fears with tender words. In spite of his care for her, there was an instant of sharp, tearing pain. Then she and Erik were one and the moment's cost to her no longer mattered.

He had been right; it was beautiful, incredibly, gloriously beautiful. He was cautious at first, moving slowly, as if to spare her further discomfort. His lips claimed hers again and again with infinite sweetness, but as she responded with growing eagerness his self-control disappeared.

127

He moved faster, plunging deeper, and she sensed his helplessness in the overwhelming tide of his own desire. She knew that she, too, was lost.

She looked into his eyes and thought she was drowning in the green, green sea. Waves lapped over her, softly, gently, in the beginning. Then larger, more tumultuous waves came, catching her up, tossing her back, ebbing and flowing over her, surging, crashing, thundering in storm-tossed swells. She gasped for air and gave herself to the sea. She felt it coming, felt its inevitability, as the final, huge, unstoppable wave enveloped her and spun her toward the sky in a dizzying spiral, flinging her upward and out of herself into a thousand pieces of spindrift.

It seemed only an instant, and at the same time long, long years, before she drifted slowly into the sea once more and was borne safely to shore by gently rolling swells.

"Lenora." Erik's voice was soft as the summer breeze swirling along the sand dunes at the sea's edge. "Now you are mine, my sweet, and only mine."

"Yes." Happy tears glittered on her long lashes as he kissed her once more. "I am yours."

Erik's head rested on her breast, his breathing quiet. She smoothed back his hair and he burrowed deeper into her softness.

What of vengeance now? she asked herself. How could she dream of harming Erik, or anyone he loved, after he had brought her such joy, such beauty? How could she want to hurt Thorkell or

Freydis, who had both been fair and just to her? None of them was responsible for what Snorri had done, and now Erik had blurred the memory of that horror and replaced it with peace and contentment.

Erik. In the light of the oil lamp she wrapped her arms around the sleeping man and smiled at the shadows on the wall.

Chapter Ten

"Lenora, you have done well. I am pleased with you."

"Thank you, Thorkell." Lenora waited expectantly, and at last Thorkell smiled at her.

"I will begin paying you now," he said. "Freydis tells me you have caused no trouble while I was away, and you have done more than your share of work for her."

"Will you pay me in Arab silver?"

Lenora knew such coins were acceptable almost anywhere, although not for their face value. It was the purity of their metal that was important, for payment in silver was by weight. Every trader had his own scales, and purchasers short of coin had been known to hack off a piece of a silver necklace or an arm ring and throw it into the pan to balance the scales.

"Where will you hide your hoard, Lenora? Is there any place that is safe for a slave?"

"In Erik's house. I'll hide it there."

"That's not wise. Anyone may take it while you are elsewhere, and should Erik die, everything in his house will be assumed to be his, nothing yours. No, I have a better idea."

"What is it?"

"I will write down your earnings and keep the record with my accounts. Your silver will be safely hidden with my own hoard. When you have earned enough to buy your freedom, I will give you all of your coins. Should I die, your earnings will be paid as one of my debts. Will you agree to that?"

"I will. Will Erik? Doesn't my master have to approve of this also?"

"I will speak to him."

Erik began to teach her to read and write Greek. He made her work on her Latin again, and continually tested her on her counting.

"The more you know, the more useful to me you are," he told her.

Now Lenora seldom had time to spend with the women, for Erik and Thorkell kept her busy. She learned to make ink for them by mixing soot with vinegar or blood she had brought from the kitchen, and she watched as Erik carefully trimmed parchment leaves to the correct size. Parchment, which Thorkell bought in Hedeby, was expensive. Every piece, no matter how small, was used and then reused if possible. Lenora took the tiniest scraps and slivers to practice writing her Greek and Latin letters.

Each night they barred the wooden door of Erik's house and lay in each other's arms. Lenora, who one midsummer day had wondered about the attraction between men and women, now found all her questions answered. Erik was a skillful and demanding lover, taking as much delight in her pleasure as in his own. The memory of Snorri's brutal crimes against her family was, if not entirely forgotten, at least set aside, and Lenora's desire for revenge against the Norse ebbed to nothing as her attachment to Erik grew.

She was devastated when he left to visit Halfdan.

"Take me with you," she begged.

"I want you to remain here. Thorkell needs your help."

"I'll die without you."

"Never. You will merely wait for my return," he said, one long hand stroking her in the places she liked best. She moved against him with a sensuous purr.

"Don't leave me behind," she whispered. "You know you'll need a woman."

"Then I'll find one where I am."

"If you do, I'll find another man," she threatened.

"You dare not do that. Never forget, sweet Lenora, that I am your master." And then, to her mingled fury and delight, he proved the truth of his statement.

* * *

The harvest was over and the winter storms had begun before Snorri and his men returned. Once more the plunder from his raids was piled before Thorkell in the great hall and carefully divided. Lenora watched, pitying the wretched captives who huddled to one side. She remembered too well her own introduction to Thorkell's home.

Snorri had sailed to the west of England and to Ireland, from where he had brought Thorkell a new slave. He led her forward, a tall, gray-eyed woman with flaming red hair. She stood quietly before Thorkell, showing no emotion when Snorri tore off her saffron-dyed mantle to reveal a near-perfect body, barely covered by a torn linen undershift.

"This is Maura," Snorri said. "She is fiery enough to warm your bed for many a winter."

From her position behind Thorkell's chair, Edwina stared coldly at the newcomer.

"I was angry that you and your men were not here to help with the harvest, but now I am pleased," Thorkell said. "There is more profit here than from any of your previous voyages. In the spring we will take a great baggage-train to Hedeby and trade our goods for Arab silver. You are a good son, Snorri. I am proud of you."

Snorri flushed with pleasure.

Early the next morning, Lenora found Edwina in the kitchen, weeping.

"I spent the night in the women's quarters," she said in response to Lenora's question. "Thorkell took his new woman to bed last night."

133

"What else did you expect?" Lenora asked.

"I thought he cared for me," Edwina whined. "He said he did. He gave me clothes and jewelry. But he's angry that I did not conceive. Now everyone will know what has happened. I'm so ashamed."

"He is the master and you are the slave," Lenora said, thinking of Erik.

"Don't you think I know that? Oh, I'm so unhappy. How will I ever get with child if he sleeps with her? He'll never marry me now." She ran from the kitchen, sobbing loudly.

Lenora recalled this conversation when Erik returned a few days later. She watched him carefully for signs of indifference as he sat beside her at the evening's feast. He raised his eyebrows in amusement at Thorkell's red-haired slave, adorned with heavy gold jewelry and a green silk caftan brought from the Arab lands. Edwina, placed several seats away from Thorkell, looked very unhappy and ate little.

Any concern Lenora had felt about Erik's interest in her was banished once they were alone in his house.

"How glad I am to be home with you," he said. He pulled her into his arms with urgent tenderness, holding her close, her face buried in his throat. After a while, he stirred.

"Take this off," he murmured, unfastening the brooches at her shoulders. "I want to touch you. I want nothing between us." He let her go only to remove his own garments.

As she dropped her woolen overdress and

134

pulled off her long-sleeved linen shift, letting it fall to the floor, he moved against her again, his hands sliding down her arms until his long fingers twined between her own and held her hands against his naked thighs. She put her head on his shoulder, and his lips set fire to the pulse in her throat.

Then they were pressed tightly together and she could feel the whole hard, masculine length of him, shoulders and breast and hip and thigh, bonded against her own joyfully yielding body.

Her arms were about his neck as their lips met at last. She felt like one who, dying of thirst, has been given cool, perfect water in an exquisite silver goblet. She drank him in greedily. She could not get enough of his mouth, which had suddenly become essential to her continued existence. She moaned in grief when he raised his head, barely aware that he had lifted her into his arms and was carrying her to their bed. She clutched at him as he laid her down, not wanting to let him go for a moment, pulling him back to her, aching for the touch of his mouth again.

"I have missed you," he whispered, as his lips rained kisses of sultry fire from fingertip to elbow to shoulder to breasts, until she cried out in delight.

"Lenora, my sweet," he breathed, his mouth setting toes and calves and knees and thighs aglow with heat and flowery explosions of joy.

"You are so beautiful," he told her, his face buried in her throat, her breasts, her abdomen.

And then finally, when she thought she could

bear no more pleasure, when her senses were spinning and her eyes were unfocused and half-closed, when she was totally bewitched by his tender explorations, she heard him out of the shimmering space above her.

"You are mine, Lenora," he said at last, his voice trembling with emotion, his body fierce yet gentle with her as he led her to the ultimate joy.

"Yes," she cried out while she could still speak, "I am yours, Erik. Always, always."

Again and again before morning he awakened her with deep, passionate kisses and the most intimate of touches. She was not always certain whether she was dreaming about him, as she had so many nights during his absence, or awake and holding him in her arms while he carried them both to the heights of delirious rapture, until she lifted her lids and found his green eyes looking deeply into hers as he made her his yet again.

"Erik," she sighed, "I have been so lost, so empty without you."

"You are not empty now."

"No, I am full of you. Never leave me again. I want to sleep beside you every night. There, do that again, and that. Ah, Erik, Erik . . ."

Snorri's marriage to Gunhilde was to take place at the turning of the year, during the great Yule feasts that celebrated the time when the days began to lengthen. He and Thorkell and a large retinue of men left for the home of Sven the Dark. Erik and Freydis were responsible for the preparations to welcome the bridal party on its return ten days later; then Sven and a group of his friends would accompany his daughter to her new home.

The guest chamber where Sven would stay and the great hall where his men would sleep along with Thorkell's hird were cleaned and decorated with evergreen boughs. Snorri's own room received special attention. Lenora, unwilling to enter the room, stood at the door, watching, as Freydis put the finishing touches on the decorations. Lenora regarded the little statue of the god Frey that had been placed near the bed and nervously crossed herself.

"Stop that," Freydis ordered. "You will bring them bad luck. This is for fertility, so they will have many children."

"If anything will work, that will," muttered Edwina, considering the statue's enormous, erect phallus. "Maybe I should have placed my faith in Frey."

"Don't say that, Edwina. You are just upset because Thorkell took Maura with him." Lenora was genuinely shocked. Edwina had once been deeply religious, had often scolding Lenora for her laxity.

"I don't know what I'm going to do. Thorkell hasn't slept with me since Maura came. I thought he would marry me."

"Edwina, come and help me in the kitchen," Freydis advised. "You will be much happier if you do some work. You think too much about your problems."

When the bridal party returned Lenora was

fascinated to find the bride's father tall and thin, with thick, silver-blond hair and pale blue eyes.

"Why do they call him Sven the Dark?" she asked Erik, who had just greeted the returning Halfdan, arrived for the feasting.

The two men laughed uproariously.

"Because," Erik said, when he had calmed himself, "when Sven was born he was a deep red color, no one knows why. It was believed he would not live, but he did. In fact, he has never been sick a day in his life. His father thought it was a great joke to call him Dark." With this, he and Halfdan burst into laughter again.

Lenora shook her head, understanding that this was another of those strange jests the Norsemen found so amusing, like the friendly insults they often hurled at one another.

Sven's daughter Gunhilde was extremely tall, almost as tall as Snorri. She was coldly beautiful, with red-gold hair and pale, creamy skin. In spite of many friendly overtures made to her, she maintained an unbending aloofness toward the women of Thorkell's household, preferring the companionship of the people she had brought with her to Thorkellshavn from her old home. Lenora did not like Gunhilde, and she believed Freydis did not either.

The wedding feasts continued for days. On the third night, in the midst of noise and revelry, Lenora was talking with Halfdan when she became aware of a growing quiet in the hall. She turned in her seat to see by the firepit a tiny old woman, gowned in white and holding in her right hand a staff taller than she was. There was a majesty about the woman, a serene and profound stillness. And something more, a quality of unknowable mystery, of darkness, that Lenora felt even before the woman's eyes briefly met hers. Lenora had been about to cross herself for protection against the power she felt emanating from the woman, but her hand was arrested in mid-motion by those deep, impenetrable eyes. In an instant the woman's gaze had moved on to rest on others in their turn, but still Lenora could not move.

As those in the hall fell into an unnatural state of complete silence, Thorkell rose from his seat beside Snorri and Gunhilde. At the same time, Lenora found her tongue again.

"Who is she, what's happening?" she asked Halfdan.

"It's the volva," Halfdan whispered back in an awed tone.

"The what?"

"Hush." Halfdan's voice sank even lower. "Thorkell is the officiating chieftain here; he will speak. You must be quiet. She is the volva, the seer, the Angel of Death. I do not know the word in your language."

"You are welcome," Thorkell told the old woman. "Do you come to prophesy?"

"I do." In spite of her apparent frailty, the woman's voice was strong and commanding. She looked around the hall, as though assuring herself of everyone's complete attention, then drew herself to her full height. In a gesture almost too rapid for the eye to follow she threw something into the firepit. There was a flash of light and a billow of gray smoke, followed by an appreciative murmur from the audience, as though most men and women in the hall had seen exactly what they expected to see. Borne on a whisp of smoke, the smell of bitter herbs pricked at Lenora's nose, making her want to sneeze.

Again the volva waited until silence was restored. When all was quiet once more, she lifted her staff off the ground to point its base toward Thorkell.

"You, my old friend Thorkell the Fair-speaker, will not see another Yule. I will come for you."

A gasp was heard around the hall, followed by frightened whispers. Thorkell nodded at the volva's words, unafraid. Lenora was more than ever impressed by his great dignity.

"I am ready," he said. "But what of my sons?"

The volva's long staff pointed now at Snorri. Lenora thought she saw a tremor of fear pass over his face before he recovered himself and sat impassively, staring back at the volva.

"Snorri," the woman intoned, "your end lies far from here. I see treachery and double treachery."

Snorri laughed. "What of my reputation?" he asked. "Will it live after me?"

"You will be long remembered."

Snorri nodded in satisfaction, for such was the wish of every Norseman.

"Will I have sons to follow me?"

"You will have twin sons, but you will never

see them. Before they are born, you will die the most shameful death of all. You will die at the hands of a woman."

"I don't believe you." Snorri's face had turned bright red. He began to rise, but Thorkell stopped him.

"Sit," he commanded, and Snorri sank back into his seat.

"My other son," Thorkell asked. "What of Erik?"

The volva turned to face Erik and pointed her staff at him.

"Ah," she said, "such a long path. So far away. Other lands, other gods. And treachery. Danger. Trust no one, son of Thorkell. Your way is long and difficult. I cannot see, I cannot see . . ."

The old woman fell onto the earthen floor in a crumpled heap. Freydis hurried forward with a cup of mead to revive her. No one else moved. Lenora felt a cold chill along her spine.

Suddenly, Snorri leapt across the firepit, his sword drawn.

"You," he shouted at Erik. "It is you who have done this."

Sven, on this occasion seated next to Erik, put out a restraining hand.

"Would you bring shame to my daughter's marriage feast by spilling your own brother's blood?" he asked.

"This is no brother of mine," Snorri rasped, showing his yellowed teeth. "You did it, Erik. You brought the old crone here to curse me."

"You know perfectly well the volva goes where

141

she wishes," Erik replied cooly, "and she spoke not curse but prophecy."

"Snorri, sit down." Thorkell's voice rang across the hall. "I will have order in my home. Sit down, I say."

With a scowl, Snorri recrossed the room and sat down. Lenora noticed the icy expression on his bride's face and her rigid shoulders. *I would not be Snorri's wife for all the gold in Grikkland,* she thought.

The disturbance had spoiled the once-boisterous mood, and the night's feasting ended early.

"I'm glad Snorri didn't hurt you," Lenora said when she and Erik were alone in his house. She ran her hands along his finely muscled arms and locked them behind his head. She kissed his lips, but to her surprise found no response. "Erik?"

Reaching up, he took her wrists in his strong grip and held her away from him.

"I should kill you," he said.

"What?" She stared at him in shock.

"I believe yours is the hand that will strike down my brother. You are the woman the volva spoke of, who will destroy him in shame. You will bring disgrace to my family. Why can't I kill you?"

Since the first night he had owned her, Lenora had never feared Erik, but now she was terrified at the look on his face.

"What are you saying?"

"I think you have bewitched me, Lenora. You are more seductive than all the dark-eyed beauties of Grikkland. I swore I would never touch what had once been Snorri's, and yet every night I lie with you and I cannot help myself. I told myself I would find another woman when I visited Halfdan, but there was no one I wanted. Erna wants me again, and I look at her with disgust. What have you done to me that I want no other woman?"

"You need no other. You have me. And you know full well I was never Snorri's woman."

"Do you deny you want revenge against him?"

"I had thought of it, but I gave up the idea as impossible for a slave. Besides, I promised Thorkell—"

"I know what you promised. And I know what the volva said."

"I remember a night when you almost killed Snorri yourself, after he insulted your manhood," Lenora responded. "Why do you worry about his safety now? He would kill you if he had the chance and not think twice about it."

"On the night you mean, I did think a second time, even in the heat of anger," Erik told her. "I remembered that we have the same father, that I was born a slave yet Thorkell freed me and adopted me, that he has always treated me fairly. In that thinking lies the greatest difference between Snorri and myself. I am so grateful to Thorkell, I love him so well, that however angry I may be, however much I might wish I could, still I will not harm any son of his."

"Not even to save yourself?"

"It will not come to that."

143

His confidence dismayed her.

"It almost came to that tonight," she responded quietly. "Snorri would have killed you and laughed to see you die. He is dangerous, Erik. Please, be on your guard against him."

He would not listen to her. His hold on her wrists tightened.

"If I ever catch you in treachery, Lenora, I will kill you slowly. I know how you Christian Saxons fear death."

"That's not true. I'm not afraid to die, but I haven't done anything wrong. How can you treat me like this because of what a half-mad old woman says?"

"She is the volva."

"You don't believe that heathen nonsense?" Lenora would not admit that she herself had felt a thrill of fear at the volva's prophecies. She knew what Father Egbert would have said about such witchcraft.

"The volva has powers you do not understand." Erik dropped her hands and she rubbed her wrists where his fingers had bitten into her. "Go to sleep, *slave*. I am going to talk with Halfdan, and then I will go to Erna."

But he was back later that night, after Lenora had cried herself into exhaustion. He lay down beside her on the straw mattress and put his arms around her.

"I need you," he moaned as his mouth found hers. "Only you. Lenora, you beautiful witch, I can't do without you. What in the name of all the gods have you done to me?"

At his touch, a heavy, throbbing desire stirred in Lenora, stronger than the fear and anger she had known earlier. She could feel her own hot blood coursing through her veins.

"Erik," she whispered, "whatever I have done to you, you have also done to me. I can't stop wanting you, and when I am with you, nothing else matters."

There was no gentleness in their coming together. They tore at each other's garments, gasping and sobbing in their urgent, primitive need, until they were both naked. Her fingernails raked his back as he pulled her roughly to him. She cried out like some wild animal, totally lost in the sensation of his skin against hers, his body demanding equal passion from her, until suddenly she lost all control and was swept away beyond thought, beyond time and place, to some strange realm where all the stars in the sky exploded at once and fell in shimmering pieces into the quiet sea.

And then, only then, there was peace between them at last. Erik slept in her arms, and she marveled at the passion that had flared between them. She thought of Snorri, holding Erik more closely, as if to protect him, and wondered where Snorri's hatred of his brother would end.

Three days later Lenora found Edwina singing happily at her loom.

"Have you heard the news, Lenora?"

"I have heard nothing. I've been working in Thorkell's chambers."

"Maura is gone," Edwina announced.

"Gone?" Lenora looked for confirmation at Freydis, who had just come into the weaving room.

"It's true," Freydis said.

"Sven wanted her," Edwina reported. "So Thorkell gave Maura to him for a gift. She departed with him early this morning."

"Did no one ask Maura what she wanted?" Lenora knew such things happened, and she had not especially cared for Maura, but the casual exchange of a human gift was cruel.

"She's only a slave."

"So are you, Edwina."

"Not for long. Thorkell took me to his bed last night. Soon he will ask me to marry him." Edwina went back to her weaving, a sly smile on her face.

Freydis followed Lenora out of the weaving room.

"She's mad," Lenora said. "Thorkell will never marry her, will he?"

"Edwina has always been mad," Freydis replied, "Since the first day she came here. Mad and weak. She is not strong like you. No, Thorkell will never marry her. Why should he? She is only dreaming."

The gray, wet, cold winter continued, with only the slightest lengthening of the days to give hope that spring would ever come. Storms blew in off the North Sea, bringing snow and stinging rain and sleet. Hands and feet were constantly cold, faces chapped red from the ever-present wind.

In the cold weather Erik's injured leg ached badly and his limp worsened. At night Lenora wrapped hot stones in cloths and laid them against his old wounds.

It was an unhappy time, for Freydis was often at odds with her new sister-in-law over who would manage the household. Snorri, quickly bored with his cold and distant wife, was anxious to be off on another voyage. Because of the volva's prophecy, there was general agreement among his former crew members that Snorri's good luck was gone. Few wanted to sail with him again, most fearing they would be involved in his predicted shameful end. Snorri's temper grew ever shorter.

"Forget the freemen. I'll buy slaves to sail with me," he snarled one day, striding about Thorkell's chamber. His angry presence upset Lenora as she struggled with a long list of Thorkell's goods and a bad pen. She wished Erik were there, but he had gone riding with Halfdan.

"You will never make good sailors of slaves," Thorkell observed mildly.

"I will if I promise them their freedom at voyage's end," Snorri replied.

"They'll throw you overboard before you are out of sight of land," Thorkell said. "No, you need free men."

"Give me part of your hird. You support them; they owe you their allegiance. You can order them to go with me. They are well-trained fighters, and any true Norseman is a sailor."

"If I do, who will protect my lands while you are gone?"

"Then give me half of your men, and I'll make up the rest of my crew from your farmers and my few loyal friends who will still volunteer."

"Take my farmers? Who will sow my fields when spring comes? Besides, they are free men. I cannot order them to go."

"They will go if you ask them to."

"No, Snorri."

Snorri's huge hands doubled into fists. Lenora sat watching this scene, terrified of Snorri's vicious temper. But Thorkell stared him down, unafraid.

"Will you strike your own father?" he asked with a smile.

"I need to go a-viking," Snorri ground out between clenched teeth.

"Have you gone berserk in the dark winter, as the men of Sverige in the far north do? Or is it your cold wife you long to leave?"

"I will return in time for the spring planting. I give you my word."

Thorkell's knotted fingers stroked his long beard.

"Perhaps it would be best for you to go. I grow weary of stopping your constant arguments with Erik, and if you continue to quarrel with Gunhilde, you will soon get all my serving women with child. Very well, go find yourself some other diversion."

Snorri grinned happily. "You will provide the supplies I need?"

"Don't I always do that? But I warn you, I want a large profit on my investment. And see to it that as many of my men as possible return in good health."

"I will. I must find Hrolf and Bjarni. They will want to go with me." Snorri, his good humor restored, slapped his palm against Thorkell's to seal their bargain, then hurried from the room. He sailed six days later, and most of Thorkell's household was glad to see him go.

"I hope he brings no more slaves home," Edwina said. "Thorkell is happy with me now."

Privately, Lenora thought Thorkell looked more tired than happy, but she was too involved in her own life just then to give much thought to others. On a cold night, as they lay snug under layers of furs, warm and content after their lovemaking, she told Erik her secret.

"I am carrying your child," she said.

She felt his body tense beside her, and then his strong arms drew her closer.

"Are you sure?"

"Completely." She laughed softly. "I think it was that night you returned from visiting Halfdan. Do you remember? We scarcely slept all night."

"I remember." His lips brushed her cheek. "A son. It must be a son."

"It will be whatever you wish, Erik. Are you happy?"

"I am."

His mouth covered hers, and she snuggled against him in blissful peace. He had not men-

149

tioned marrying her, or even that he would set the child free. Surely he would do for his own son what Thorkell had done for him. They still had months in which to discuss it. So much time. She fell asleep with Erik's fingers splayed across her fecund belly.

Chapter Eleven

"It's not fair," Edwina wept. "I can't conceive and you are carrying a child."

"I thought you would be happy for me."

"Do you really want it? You always said you hated all the Norse. I thought you wanted revenge."

"I did, but I've changed. I want Erik's child. I want to give him a son."

"Perhaps he'll free you and marry you. Has he said he will?"

"We haven't talked about that, Edwina."

"If I were with child, I'd make Thorkell marry me. He would, you know. He really cares about me. It's just that I can't conceive. I try so hard. But he can't—he won't—" She broke off as Freydis entered the weaving room with a cup of mead.

"Drink this," Freydis told Lenora. "You must

eat and drink well, to give strength to the child."

"You will grow fat." Edwina giggled, "And Erik won't want you any more."

Lenora and Freydis exchanged glances, Freydis shaking her head sadly. Lenora drained the cup.

"I must go to Thorkell," she said. "He has work for me to do."

"Keep warm," Freydis advised. "Some of the farmers and their families are ill. Don't get chilled or you will be sick too."

"I won't." Lenora hurried off, glad to get away from Edwina. Her friend's unhappy condition was a constant weight on Lenora's heart. There was nothing Lenora could do to help, but being with Edwina always made her feel guilty.

Ten days later the illness that had first infected the farmers and their families invaded Thorkell's immediate household. Several of the servants died of it. Women and children were the most severely afflicted. Freydis was soon short-handed in the kitchen and laundry, as slaves and serving women took to their beds. Lenora temporarily gave up her work for Thorkell to help Freydis care for the sick.

"I don't know why you are doing this," Gunhilde said to Freydis. "You are working like a slave yourself. These people will recover or not, depending on each one's own luck and strength. It is in the hands of the gods. You can add nothing to anyone's recovery with your broths and hot ale."

"I know there are many who believe as you

do," Freydis replied, "but the labor of these men and women adds daily to my father's wealth. I will not desert them when they are too ill to fetch water or food for themselves." She filled a bowl with steaming gruel and gave it to Lenora to carry to the women's quarters. "See that Tola eats all of this. She ate nothing yesterday. I'll carry a full bucket down to the farmers' houses. Gunhilde, will you help me?"

"I refuse to make myself into a servant for slaves," Gunhilde said coldly. "I am going to my chamber to spin in peace."

"Go then," Freydis muttered under her breath. "You are no help anyway." She wiped her damp brow with her sleeve.

"You're not well," Lenora said. "Go to bed. I'll do this."

"No. No, I can do it."

But the next day Freydis could not leave her bed, and the following day Thorkell was ill. Edwina was frantic.

"He won't eat, Lenora. What shall I do?"

"Give him just a little at a time. Insist that he swallow it. Now go, Edwina. I'm busy."

With Gunhilde refusing to help, Lenora now supervised the household. The young woman who had once hated domestic chores managed with an efficiency and skill that surprised even herself. Erik, agreeing with Lenora's methods, silenced Gunhilde's arguments against providing care for the sick and stopped her attempt to take over the running of Thorkellshavn in Freydis' absence. Erik and Halfdan together assisted Lenora and the few other women who were still on their feet.

Evening meals were no longer merry and boisterous feasts. A few men and women sat somberly in the great hall, trying to keep warm and wondering who would fall ill next.

"Lenora, you are worn out," Freydis told her one day. "I'll get up tomorrow to help you."

Lenora took the empty gruel bowl from Freydis and handed her a cup of ale. She wrapped her shawl more closely around her shoulders. Freydis' chamber, a small room attached to Thorkell's quarters, with its own separate entrance, was cold in spite of the blaze of logs in the firepit.

"You are not well enough yet. You are still too weak." Lenora stood up from the bed platform, stretching, her hands on her hips.

"My back aches." She laughed. "I spend my days bending over the cooking fires, stirring soups and gruels. Tola is helping me. She is out of bed but still weak. And Gutrid and Erna are sick now. Will spring never come?"

"It will come soon enough. Some years are like this. Everyone is sick and many die. Other years it's not so bad. No one knows why."

"I'll come back later." Lenora moved toward the door.

"How is my father?"

"Very weak, but Edwina says he is getting better. He says he wants to die in battle. Sven the Dark told him the Franks will attack in the spring, and Thorkell is planning to take his men on a march to the south to meet them."

154

Freydis chuckled, nodding. "That is his duty. When he was given these lands, he was charged by King Horik, whose jarl he was, to protect the east and the south of Denmark. Thorkell never fails in his duty, though Horik is dead for many years and there is no true king in Denmark now."

As she left Freydis' room, Lenora wondered if Erik would have to ride with his father to fight the Franks. Surely his leg would be improved by then so that he could ride for long periods of time. She did not want to think of Erik in battle.

The wind off the sea was cold and damp. There had been much flooding this stormy winter. Thorkellshavn, wisely built high on the slope above the river, had so far escaped the waters, but freezing rain had filmed tree limbs and buildings with a thin crust of ice. Lenora cried out as one foot broke through the brittle surface and sank into a deep puddle.

"Oh, it's so cold." As she tried to get out of the puddle, her other foot slipped on an ice-glazed stone. She lost her balance and flew through the air, landing hard on her bottom and skidding across the frozen ground almost back to Freydis' door. The bowl and cup she had been carrying went clattering away with a noise that rang loudly in Lenora's head as blue and white stars exploded before her eyes.

She wakened to bitter cold. Her clothes were soaked from the rain and caked with ice. Her head ached and her buttocks were sore where she had fallen. It took great effort to push herself to a sitting position. Wet, ice-stringed hair flapped into her face.

She began to shiver. She took a few moments to gather her strength, then tried to stand.

"Ahhh—" she screamed in pain and sank to her knees.

"Help," she cried. "Freydis, can you hear me? Someone, please help me. Freydis!"

She heard a sound from within Freydis' chamber, and then the door opened. Freydis, weak and pale, clung to the frame, her woolen winter shift billowing in the cold wind, a shawl clutched about her upper body.

"Lenora?"

"I hurt my ankle. I can't stand up."

Lenora crouched on the icy ground, rocking back and forth from the pain surging up her leg and weeping because of a strange, aching malaise that was steadily creeping over her. Freydis stumbled to her and tried to help her rise.

"It's no use. I'm too weak. I'll try to find one of the men." Freydis, now nearly as drenched as Lenora, staggered barefoot across the courtyard toward the great hall.

Lenora collapsed into a sodden, miserable heap. Endless cold time passed before Halfdan scooped her up in his brawny arms and carried her to Erik's house. Freydis was already there, busily feeding the fire into a high, warming blaze.

Halfdan lay her on the bed, and he and Freydis quickly stripped off her wet clothes, rubbed her down with linen cloths, and wrapped her in blankets and furs. Tola appeared with a hot drink.

Lenora took it gratefully, as much for the warmth of the cup against her numb fingers as for the heat that curled into her stomach as she swallowed it.

"Let me see your ankle." When Freydis' fingers probed the swollen flesh Lenora cried out in pain. "I don't think it's broken. We'll bind it up. Tola, fold that linen into strips."

"Freydis, you are wet. You should be in bed."

"I don't mind the cold. You have tended me for days, Lenora. Now it's my turn."

Lenora's ankle was soon bound. The pain in it subsided, but she lay shivering and aching.

"My back hurts," she told Freydis. "I fell so hard. I feel so strange."

Freydis and Tola exchanged knowing glances.

"Oh—Oh!" Suddenly Lenora doubled up as pain lanced through her. "Freydis, help me."

Freydis' hands caught hers. Another pain came, worse than before, and now Lenora understood.

"My baby," she moaned. "No, not my baby."

Through a thick mist she heard Freydis speaking. "I am certain she will miscarry. Tola, bring me more cloths and a basin. Halfdan, you had better tell Erik. He will be in Thorkell's chambers."

The mist around Lenora's head got thicker. She felt far away, separated from everyone. Halfdan's low voice rumbled through the small room, echoing in Lenora's fevered brain as another pain tore at her.

"Freydis, you are cold...cold...cold...dry

clothes . . . clothes . . . clothes."

Only Freydis' steady voice made any sense to Lenora. "Hold on to me, Lenora. Very well, Halfdan, send a woman to my room for a dry shift and my blue shawl. I'm here, Lenora. I'm here."

Time was divided into the short spaces between waves of pain that were ever more severe. Erik and Halfdan came and went, looking worried. Edwina appeared briefly, weeping, to throw herself on Lenora's writhing form until Freydis ordered her out. Gunhilde's cold voice spoke from a great distance.

"I do not understand why you are all so upset. She is only a slave, after all."

"Get out." Erik's voice was dark with pain and fury. "Never set your foot in my house again. Go!"

"When Snorri comes home I will tell him of this insult."

"Do. And then make him tell you what he once did to this woman's family."

The pain came again, blanking out all else.

Only Freydis was always there, holding her hands, encouraging her through hours of wrenching agony, finally sponging her body with cool water and covering her with a fresh blanket.

"Drink this."

"I can't."

"You must, to regain your strength. Tola put an egg in it, and some herbs to help stop the bleeding."

Too weak to protest further, Lenora swallowed the hot ale.

"It's over," she whispered, the tears streaming down her face.

"Many women miscarry, Lenora. It is sad, but you will recover and bear other children."

"I wanted this one. For Erik."

"Erik will give you more babies."

"I want to see him."

"He is with our father. Thorkell is very ill."

"He's getting better. Edwina said so."

"Go to sleep, Lenora. Go to sleep."

The fever attacked her the next day. She lay at the edge of death for many days and nights, delirious and wracked with cruel nightmares about the child she had lost. When finally she came to her senses again, she was so weak she could scarcely move. It exhausted her to turn her head to watch Tola enter with a cup and bowl.

Freydis' serving woman fed her in a silence far different from her usual gossipy chatter.

"How long have I been sick?" Lenora whispered weakly.

"Eight days."

"So long? What has happened while I've been in bed?"

"Nothing."

"No gossip, Tola?" Lenora managed a chuckle. "I can't believe that."

Tears appeared in Tola's eyes. Seeing them, Lenora was filled with alarm. She struggled to sit up but could not. She lay back, panting.

"Erik," she gasped. "Where is Erik?"

"He is well."

"Freydis?"

"She is well too. And Halfdan. And that bitch Gunhilde." The tears were now rolling down Tola's plump cheeks. "It's Thorkell."

"Is he still sick?"

"He is dead."

"Thorkell? No, it can't be. He was getting better."

"He was, but something happened to him. He could not breathe. Erik made him sit up and fed him hot soups and ale, but his breath came harder and harder, and then five days ago he died. I do not weep for his death," Tola explained, wiping away her tears, "but for the manner of it. He should have died in battle. He was a good chieftain and he deserved an honorable death. Now he must journey to the underworld of Niflheim to live with Hel. It is sad. A brave man like Thorkell should have been welcomed into Valhalla by Odin himself."

"I don't understand what you are saying. Where is Thorkell now? Isn't he buried?"

"Of course not. He will not be buried until he is burned. But that is not for five days yet."

Lenora gave up, unable to comprehend Tola's rambling explanations.

"I want to see Erik. Please send him to me."

"I don't know if he will come. He's busy with the funeral arrangements."

"That's the first thing you've said that I can understand. Tell him I want to see him, Tola."

Erik did not come until evening. Lenora had drifted in and out of sleep all day, and she had eaten again. She felt stronger by the time he arrived.

"I cannot stay long," he said. "I must return to the feast."

"I am sorry to hear of Thorkell's death."

"He was a good and just chieftain. He was well named the Fair-speaker."

"Aren't you sad that your father is dead?"

"It is not good to weep for the dead."

Lenora did not answer. She knew Erik had loved his father, and she was certain that beneath the apparent indifference to Thorkell's death, Erik was deeply grieved. Perhaps he was afraid if he began to speak of his sorrow it would overcome him. She decided to change the subject.

"How is Edwina? May I see her? She must be heartbroken."

"Edwina is cheerful enough. She is at the feast."

"I want to see her. I must speak with her." Lenora could not believe Edwina was cheerful. Surely she was distraught and would need her best friend. Their recent differences were forgotten in Lenora's concern for Edwina. "I wish I could get up to go to her, but I'm so weak."

"You must remain in bed until—for a few days more. I will ask Edwina's companions to bring her to you tomorrow."

"What companions?"

But Erik had gone.

Edwina entered the house the next afternoon, accompanied by two serving women.

161

"I want to speak to my friend alone," Lenora told them.

"We dare not leave her," they responded. They sat impassively on the earthen floor by the door.

"I am sorry you miscarried your babe," Edwina said. She walked unsteadily to the bed platform and sat down hard. She giggled, and a whiff of mead fumes reached Lenora's nose.

"My poor Edwina. I know you cared for Thorkell. You must miss him terribly."

Exerting all her strength, Lenora sat up and tried to put her arms around Edwina, but the girl pushed her away.

"This is not a sad time." Edwina giggled. "It is a happy time. I do miss Thorkell, but I will be with him again soon."

"Edwina, Thorkell is dead."

"I know." A crafty smile spread across Edwina's thin features. "But they said I could join him."

Lenora was now convinced that Edwina was totally mad with grief and further confused by strong drink.

"They asked us all," Edwina told her with mock sobriety. "They said, 'Who will journey to Niflheim with Thorkell and live with him there?' And I said, 'I will,' and then they were all so happy. I will go with Thorkell and he will set me free and marry me and I will bear his child."

Cold terror gripped Lenora's heart at these words. "Edwina, what have you done?"

"It's true," one of the serving women said. "She is the sacrifice. When Thorkell is burnt Edwina will go with him."

"NO!" Lenora clutched at Edwina's thin shoulders. "You can't do this!"

"She volunteered," the serving woman said. "She is doing it freely."

"Volunteered? Can't you see she's mad? She has never been herself since the day my brother Wilfred was killed. Where is Erik? I must speak to him. He will stop this idiocy."

"Erik was pleased with Edwina's decision. In any case, once a woman agrees to die with her lord, she cannot change her mind."

"Freydis. Freydis will help me."

"Freydis is busy planning the funeral feasts. You should be working, too, Lenora. You should be helping to sew Thorkell's funeral clothes."

Lenora stared at the serving woman, unable to believe her ears.

"Helping? Do you imagine for one moment that I'm going to participate in this heathen ritual? Edwina, for God's sake, you are a Christian! Don't do this."

"Now, Lenora," Edwina said in a soothing tone, "You are much too upset, and you have been ill. You must know that this is the wisest thing for me to do."

"Wise? Never!"

"Don't you see? Snorri is the oldest child. He will inherit all of Thorkell's goods, including his slaves. I do not want to belong to Snorri. I am Thorkell's woman. I want to be with him. This is my only hope."

"Erik could buy you. We could be together."

"Do you really think Snorri would sell me to

Erik? He's too vicious to do such a kind thing. You know what he will do to me, out of spite."

"No, no." Lenora leaned her head on Edwina's shoulder and wept.

"It's all right," Edwina said. "I'm perfectly happy. I don't mind at all."

She stood up. Lenora noticed how pathetically thin she was.

"Edwina—"

"I must return to the feast. We must eat and drink every night from now until the funeral." Edwina went out without a backward glance, her two companions trailing after her protectively.

"She's mad. I know she's mad. They can't hold her to a promise she made out of grief. Freydis. Freydis will help me." Shaking with weakness, caught in the grip of a terrible nightmare, Lenora dragged herself out of bed. "Freydis will be in the kitchen, or perhaps the great hall if the feast has begun. I have to find her."

With desperate determination, Lenora made her way through the cold dusk toward the kitchen. She could barely stand and had to stop frequently to rest against the buildings along the way. At last, her meager strength nearly dissipated by her efforts, she clutched at the kitchen door and, pulled by its weight as it swung inward, lurched into the warm room.

Freydis, in her best gown, with all her jewelry on display, was giving orders to the slave who turned a spit on which hung the carcass of a sheep. She whirled at the draft of cold air.

"Lenora, what are you doing here?"

"Freydis, you have to stop it. She's mad; you know she is. You said so yourself. Don't let them burn her. Please, please."

"If you mean Edwina, she has given her word to go with Thorkell and that is the end of it. If it is a comfort to you, know that she will be dead before she is burnt."

"She has lost her wits. She didn't mean it. You can't let them do it." Lenora swayed, holding herself upright by clinging to the edge of the door. "Please, Freydis," she begged again.

"I can do nothing. Go back to your bed."

"Erik will help me. Where is he?"

"Erik is at the feast, and I will not let you disturb him. Here, Erna, help Lenora to bed, and then come right back here. I'll need you to carry in the mutton."

Crying uncontrollably, Lenora retraced her steps on Erna's arm.

"Poor Lenora," Erna hissed in her ear. "It was foolish of you to miscarry just when Erik needs a woman to sit with him every night for the funeral feasts. But Erik and I celebrate life without you."

"Leave me alone," Lenora screamed. With her last bit of strength she slammed the cabin door in Erna's face and bolted it shut.

Chapter Twelve

The next morning Lenora forced herself out of bed again and went along the path to Thorkell's chambers. She found Erik in the room where they had so often worked with his father. It seemed strange not to see Thorkell's tall, white-bearded figure seated at the trestle table. She wondered briefly where Thorkell's body was. She was afraid to ask.

"What do you want here?" Erik showed no sign of affection toward her. "There is no work for you here any more."

Lenora sank onto a bench, feeling lightheaded.

"Please don't let Edwina die," she begged. "She is my friend. She is all that is left of my home and my family. Help her, please."

"The choice was Edwina's and it was freely made. There is nothing I can do."

"She didn't know what she was doing when she decided."

"I cannot change anything. 'Odin made it a law that all dead men should be burnt,'" Erik recited, "And one of the dead man's people must go with him. It is an honor for Edwina."

"How can you allow this? You told me you were a Christian."

"I am only a provisional Christian so I can trade with the Greeks."

"I don't understand that."

"It doesn't matter what you understand. Nor does it matter what I believe. Thorkell was a Danish chieftain, a king's jarl, and he will have a worthy funeral. It will be done as he would have wished it."

Lenora looked into Erik's pain-filled eyes and knew he would not help her.

Although still weak, she made herself help with the preparations for the feast that evening, and she assisted with the serving. She still believed there might be a way she could save Edwina. She would not chance missing any opportunity by hiding in her bed.

The men drank steadily, as though they were deliberately trying to get drunk. There was much overloud laughter. Coarse jokes were told, and men threw bones and pieces of food at each other like naughty boys. Thorkell's seat was empty, but Gunhilde sat next to it, looking smug.

"She is saving Snorri's place," Tola said. "When he comes home he will surely be elected chieftain, and in any case, he will inherit everything. I'm glad I'm Freydis' slave and not Thorkell's."

"What do you think Erik will do now?" Lenora roused herself from her concern over Edwina to ask the question of this woman, who had been friendly toward her.

"Who knows?" Tola shrugged. "Erik never reveals his plans. But I don't think this hall will be large enough for both of them without Thorkell to keep the peace. You had better be careful." Tola nudged Lenora's ribs. "Erna has been taking advantage of your absence."

At that very moment, Erna was sitting on Erik's lap, trying to feed him a morsel of meat while he shouted to a man across the room.

Even Halfdan, who never looked at any woman but Freydis, was fumbling at the skirts of a serving wench. He sat with Erik on the carved and painted settle across the firepit from Thorkell's old seat, and as he reached after the woman, he nearly fell out of the chair. This brought raucous laughter from all the men.

Lenora turned away in disgust. Freydis, coming out of the kitchen, sent her a knowing look.

"It means nothing," Freydis said. "They are always like this after a death. It is their way."

"It is not my way," Lenora answered.

Erik appeared in the house they shared only to change his clothes. He scarcely spoke to Lenora and would not listen to her continued entreaties for him to save Edwina.

In addition to her deep concern for her friend, Lenora desperately needed Erik to comfort her in her grief over the loss of their unborn child. She longed for him to put his arms around her and tell her that he cared too. He seemed indifferent to her pain. Lenora tried to excuse him, telling herself he had his own grief over Thorkell to deal with, but she could find no excuse for Erna's frequent appearances at Erik's side. Lenora had trusted Erik, and now his apparent infidelity was one more pain for her to bear.

In the three days remaining before Thorkell's funeral, Lenora felt she was walking through a deepening nightmare. No one would listen to her. No one seemed even to understand what she was saying. There seemed to be no way to save Edwina, and yet Lenora would not give up hope.

Edwina herself was unusually cheerful. She ate and drank heartily. Whenever Lenora tried to talk to her she appeared to be drunk. Lenora suspected Edwina was being given special herbs to make her so happy, but she could not discover what they were.

Two days before the funeral, the volva who had prophesied at Snorri's wedding feast reappeared, now dressed in dusty black robes.

"What is she doing here?" Lenora wondered aloud.

"She is the Angel of Death, come for Thorkell and Edwina," Erna answered. "She will supervise the final arrangements for the funeral. It is she who will dress Thorkell in his new clothes. And," Erna added maliciously, "it is she who will kill Edwina."

Lenora shivered and left the great hall. She

could not bear to look at the old woman, and could hardly endure Erna's presence.

The day of Thorkell's funeral dawned with a silver-bright sun glaring down on the ice and snow left by the most recent storm. High clouds began gathering early in the day, presaging yet more sleet and freezing rain.

Lenora, consumed by thoughts of the horror the next day would bring, had not slept until it was nearly light. She was pulled into groggy wakefulness by a loud knocking on her door. It was Erik, with Halfdan by his side.

"Get up," Erik told her. "You have to leave."

"Leave?" she repeated stupidly, rubbing her swollen eyes. "Where am I to go?"

"Freydis said for you to go to her chamber. Hurry."

Lenora did not understand what Erik was talking about, but perhaps, she thought, still half-asleep, just perhaps, he had found a way to save Edwina after all. She would do as he asked without making a fuss.

"I won't be long."

Erik and Halfdan waited outside until Lenora stepped through the door, fully dressed. Half-blinded by the brilliant, low-slanting winter sun in her face, she did not see Edwina and her two companions until her friend stood next to her on the path.

"Edwina!" Lenora threw her arms around the slender girl, hope changing to near-certainty. "Is it all right? Are you safe now? Can we go away

together? Can we escape? Is Erik going to help
us after all?''

Edwina's cool little smile stopped the rush of
questions. On this day Edwina was perfectly
sober and quite calm. She spoke and moved with
great dignity.

"All is well, Lenora. I am going away, but you
must stay behind. Go with Halfdan."

"Why with Halfdan?" Lenora asked, still not
willing to understand. "What about Erik?"

"Do as I bid you. Farewell, Lenora. Always remember that I love you." After a quick embrace,
Edwina turned to Erik. She said quietly, "I am
ready. I will follow all your instructions."

Erik nodded. "Take Lenora away, Halfdan."

There was no resisting the gentle but determined pressure of Halfdan's large hand on her
arm. Lenora was propelled down the path toward
Freydis' chamber.

"No," Lenora said, trying to twist her arm free.
"I'm going with Edwina."

"That's impossible," Halfdan told her. "You
were not one of Thorkell's slaves."

"But—" She stared at his stern face, the morning's brief hope draining away. "Isn't Erik going
to save Edwina? Isn't that why he told me to
hurry, so I could go with her?"

Halfdan shook his head, and Lenora knew the
terrible thing was really going to happen. She
was wide awake now, and she wished with all
her heart that she were not. Even knowing Edwina's fate was certain, Lenora made one last
attempt, for the sake of the close friendship she

and Edwina had once known, and for the love she still had for Edwina.

"I'll prevent it somehow. We'll run away." She started back toward the little group still standing in front of Erik's house. She had moved only a single step when Halfdan stopped her.

"You can walk to Freydis' chamber," he said, "or I will carry you. But you are going right now."

Halfdan's hand on her upper arm tightened, and he pulled her in the direction he wanted her to go. He was too strong for her to fight him with any hope of winning. Defeated and unable to find words to protest any more, Lenora let Halfdan lead her to Freydis' room. As they went along the path, she saw, drawn up onto the sandy beach at the river's edge, a longship, with logs and brush piled around it. A shimmering silken tent had been erected on its deck. Halfdan saw her looking.

"That is the place," he said gently, and Lenora's knees buckled.

"I can't, I can't bear it," she moaned. "Oh, Halfdan, help her. Please, why won't someone help?" She knew her plea would make no difference, but she uttered it all the same.

"Lenora, you don't understand. We *are* helping her. This is what she wants." Halfdan put his arm around her waist and half-carried her into Freydis' room.

"There is food and mead for you," he said. "Freydis told me to bolt the door on the outside to prevent you from attempting anything foolish. We will open it again after the pyre is lit."

"No! No!" Lenora made for the door, but Half-dan's bulk stopped her.

"Let me go," she demanded hysterically, beating at his chest with clenched fists. "I have to stop this madness. Let me go, Halfdan."

"I'm sorry, Lenora, I cannot. It would be better for you if you could simply accept our ways in this, as Edwina has." Halfdan went out, and Lenora heard him fasten the door and walk away.

"Let me out!" she shrieked, tearing at the door, pounding, scratching until her nails broke and her hands were bloody. She beat and kicked until she was worn out, but the strong wooden door held.

"Edwina, Edwina," she sobbed as she slid along the door frame and lay weeping on the floor. "Edwina!"

The long day passed. She heard movement along the path, voices and occasional laughter. Once she heard Edwina's voice. There was no fear in it. Then all was quiet for a while, until she heard singing coming from the direction of the river.

Half-mad with fear for her friend, Lenora picked up the food bowl and flung it across the room. A pitcher followed. She gave one of Freydis' clothes chests a wild push. As it grated across the hard earth floor her eyes fell on a knife lying half-hidden beneath it. Lenora pounced on it and ran to the door.

By wedging the knife blade between the frame and the door she could just make contact with the wooden outer bolt that held the door shut. She worked frantically, carefully, trying to be quiet lest someone hear her, until finally she lifted the bolt and the door swung open.

It was dark with the heavy blackness of night and an impending storm. The only light was by the river, where torches cast a lurid glow into the night. Lenora hurried toward the light. There was a crowd around the longship on the beach. All the folk of Thorkellshavn were arrayed around an open space immediately in front of the ship.

Erik stood at the edge of the open space, completely naked and holding a torch in his hand. As Lenora watched, he ran backward toward the ship and flung the torch over his head into the brush piled against it. The flames exploded upward, enveloping the ship and its contents, as family and friends came forward and added their torches to the pyre.

With a shriek wrung from her very soul, Lenora ran for the ship.

"Edwina! Edwina!"

The first person she met was the old volva. She was wearing the gold neck-ring Thorkell had given Edwina.

"Witch!" screamed Lenora. "You hideous old witch!"

Then she saw Freydis, her mouth open in astonishment, and Erik, still naked.

"Murderers," she screeched. "You are all murderers. Filthy, murdering Norse—"

Erik's hand swung out and struck her. She crashed to the ground and lay there, weeping inconsolably, as the flames leaped higher and higher into the winter sky and then slowly died.

Chapter Thirteen

The great, final funeral feast took place that night and lasted until the following morning. Lenora heard the noise and the laughter coming from Thorkell's hall as she crept past it. There was no reason for her to remain weeping by the longship. It was only smoldering embers now, and ship, Thorkell, and Edwina were one.

It was raining again, a heavy, ice-laden downpour that quickly soaked everything, but Lenora felt as though she were on fire. She staggered to the trees that surrounded the little bathing pool, broke the film of ice on the surface, and sluiced her burning face and arms with the frigid water. She was no longer hot. Now she was cold and numb. The temptation to slide into the pool and remain there forever was almost overwhelming. Lenora fought the part of herself that wanted to give up and join Edwina and the rest of her family in death.

"No," she said through chattering teeth. "I won't do it. I'm the only one left. I won't let my family end here."

She returned to Erik's house, threw off her wet clothing, and covered herself with a shawl. She added logs to the fire with reckless abandon.

"Tonight I must be warm," she muttered, "or I'll die too."

She collected all the furs and winter cloaks and blankets she could find and piled them onto the bed on the shelf along the wall, then got into it and pulled the coverings over herself. She lay there a long time, staring into the fire and thinking of Edwina, before she fell asleep.

Erik stumbled in sometime during the icy-gray morning that followed. He was very drunk and looked as though he had not slept for days. Dark circles underlined his eyes, and his mouth was set in a bitter line.

"Get me water to wash with," he ordered.

Lenora sat up among the furs, pulling the woolen shawl around her shoulders. When she tried to get out of bed, her legs trembled and gave way. She sank back, sitting on the edge of the bed platform.

"I can't stand," she whispered, stating the obvious.

"Are you still sick?" He reached out a hand toward her, moving nearer.

"Don't touch me," she cried, evading his hand.

177

"Stay away from me, you disgusting murderer."

"I am no murderer."

"You killed Edwina."

"The volva killed Edwina. Edwina wanted to die," he said wearily. He staggered, landing next to her on the bed. His arms wound around her. He did not seem to notice her shrinking away from his unwelcome embrace. "I need you, Lenora. My father is dead and I need you. Let me hold you."

As his mouth sought hers, Lenora smelled mead and wine. She pushed at his shoulders.

"Leave me alone, you pig."

"If I am a pig, then let us wallow together and make little piglets," he chuckled drunkenly. He reached for her again, pushing her down on the bed and falling on top of her. His hands groped clumsily along her body in a grotesque imitation of his usual lovemaking.

Lenora fought him, struggling with sudden, panic-stricken strength. She was appalled to find that in spite of his drunken condition and her deep anger she still wanted him. His familiar touch set her body tingling with desire. Valiantly, she fought against her own awakening need.

"You will never have me again," she declared, panting as she tried to push him away. "You are no better than Snorri. I hate your whole family for what you've done."

They wrestled together, rolling back and forth on the bed. Erik was perilously close to achieving his objective when Lenora, with a desperate effort, pushed him onto the floor. He sat up, shaking his head with a stunned expression.

"Get out, you drunken brute," she cried. "You are truly Snorri's brother to take an unwilling woman. Go back to Erna."

He pulled himself to his feet and stood blinking down at her, swaying slightly.

"You are not unwilling," he announced with mead-induced gravity. "And I do not want Erna. I want you."

"Well, I do not want you. I never want to lie with you again." Lenora's voice cracked with anger as she slapped at him.

He caught her hands and pulled her roughly against his chest.

"You have nothing to say about it. When your master desires you," he reminded her, "you must submit."

"Leave me alone," she screamed, all self-control gone. "I can't stand the sight of you."

Relentlessly he bore her back onto the bed. Lenora fought and clawed and bit and scratched, but he would not be stopped. In her weakened state her strength soon ebbed.

"Put your arms around me, hold me," he pleaded.

"No, no." She was nearly sobbing now. The harder she tried to get away from him, the closer his body pressed against hers. She tossed her head from side to side, trying to avoid his mouth. It was hopeless. As she twisted helplessly beneath him, his lips met hers.

She would not give in to him, she would not.

She despised him. But, ah, his mouth was sweet, and even in his drunken and angry condition he was not brutal. There was no fighting him; he was too strong for her. Her body, that weak vessel for her bruised yet unconquered spirit, was even now surrendering, rising to meet him, accepting him, enfolding him.

She wanted no pleasure from their union; she wanted only a quick martyrdom under his imperative masculinity. He would not allow it. He caught her up with him and carried her along on his passion until at last her unwilling arms did encircle him, and in the instant before his final cry of joy and despair her mouth softened and opened and drew him in and held him, and he tasted her tears and her sweetness together.

"I hate you," she whispered into the thick hair of his muscular chest. "I will always hate you. I'll never stop."

"Lenora." His arms held her in unbreakable bondage. "My sweet, comforting Lenora." He sighed deeply and pulled her closer.

"Erik?" She lifted her head to meet his eyes, but he was asleep. She tried to slip out of his grasp, but his arms tightened. Finally she gave up and snuggled into his warmth, drifting off to sleep beside him.

Snorri came home two days later to find a divided family.

Gunhilde, always jealous of her position, had taken over management of Thorkellshavn as soon as the ashes from Thorkell's funeral pyre had been gathered up and buried. Although there were a few who would have preferred to see Erik elected to fill Thorkell's position as chieftain, there was general agreement that Snorri would be chosen once he arrived home safely from his latest voyage. Thus there was no opposition to Gunhilde's actions.

"Snorri has inherited his father's possessions," Gunhilde announced unnecessarily, "even though he does not know it yet. As his wife, I will manage his affairs in his absence. Give me the keys, Freydis."

Gunhilde's stubborn chin tilted upward and she looked at Freydis with a mocking expression, not troubling to hide her pleasure at Freydis' enforced submission.

Freydis, her face white with fury at such treatment before all those assembled for the evening's feast, unfastened the keys that hung suspended on silver chains from her right shoulder brooch. Silently she handed them to Gunhilde.

"Tola," Gunhilde said, "from this day you will follow my orders only."

"Tola is my personal servant." Freydis' voice dripped scorn. "Since you are so well informed about household matters, I thought you knew that. Tola belongs to me."

"Then my woman Signe will take over Tola's duties in the kitchen and hall," Gunhilde replied. "Let Tola help you with your clothes and your hair, dear Freydis. You will need such assistance for you are to wed soon, and you must look your

181

best for your bridegroom."

Freydis went even whiter at these words. "I have no plans to marry."

"But I have plans for you, sister. My cousin Kare is coming to visit in the spring. You will like him, I know."

"Ha," Tola whispered to Lenora. "I've seen that Kare. He's fat, and his eyes look in opposite directions. My mistress won't want him."

"Gunhilde doesn't want a rival in her home," Lenora observed. "That's why she wants Freydis to marry and leave Thorkellshavn."

"You had better be careful too," Tola said. "Gunhilde remembers how Erik kept her from ruling Thorkellshavn while Freydis was sick. For that insult, she dislikes Erik almost as much as Snorri does, and she doesn't like you much more. She will make trouble for the two of you if she can."

Later that night Lenora returned from the kitchen to find Halfdan and Erik in deep conversation in Erik's house.

"Come in and shut the door," Erik said. "Are you alone?"

"Yes. Tola has gone to Freydis."

"Good. Tola means well, but she talks too much. You are not to repeat anything you hear, Lenora." Turning to Halfdan, Erik continued. "We will dig it up a little later, after everyone is asleep. If you leave early enough, just before dawn, no one will notice how much you are carrying. Are your men all trustworthy?"

"Completely. Shall I return here afterward?"

"I think you should stay with your father. I may need someone in a place of safety."

"I wish I could take Freydis with me," Halfdan said. "I am worried about her. Gunhilde hates her."

"She will not leave until Snorri returns. After she talks with him, if Snorri agrees with Gunhilde about this proposed marriage, then Freydis may decide to go. I am certain she will refuse to marry Kare, and that is her right. Gunhilde cannot force Freydis to marry."

"Gunhilde can make life very unpleasant for Freydis if she does not agree to marry," Lenora put in. "Gunhilde is a determined woman."

"So am I determined." Erik stood up. "Let's go, Halfdan. Lenora, remain here while we are gone. Open the door only to Halfdan or me. We won't be long."

Muffling their faces in their cloaks, the two men went out. Lenora fastened the door and sat down to wait.

She needed this time alone to sort out her confused thoughts. Her old hatred of the Norse, and her desire for revenge against them, had returned in a great surge of fury as she watched Thorkell's funeral pyre burning. She could not bear to think of what had been done to Edwina.

She blamed Erik, believing he could have stopped Edwina's death if he had wanted to do so. She would never forgive him for letting her friend die. And yet she knew he had done what he had out of love for his father, and in her deepest, most secret heart, she acknowledged Edwina's eagerness for her fate. Lenora could not deny she had wanted Erik when he had come to her, wanted him to hold and comfort her for her loss while she did the same for him. How could she hate him and need him so desperately at the same time? No matter how long or how hard she thought, Lenora could find no answer to that question. The only thing she was sure of was that, with Snorri and Gunhilde ruling Thorkellshavn, her safest course was to be as agreeable as possible to Erik, and to stay as close to him as he would allow.

When Erik and Halfdan finally returned each man carried a heavy leather sack, encrusted with dirt and leaves. These they dumped out onto the bed. Lenora cried out in wonder.

"Be quiet," Erik ordered, his voice low and urgent. "We don't want anyone to hear us. Snorri's friends must not know what we are doing this night."

"I'm sorry," Lenora said in hasty apology. "I was just so surprised. I have never seen so much silver in one place before." She could not take her eyes off the lustrous metal. Cups and plates, twisted wires made into neck-rings and armbands, but most of all, coins, lay scattered before them on the bedshelf. "Where did you get this? And if it has been buried, as it must have been from all this earth on the bags, why isn't it black?"

"It hasn't been buried very long," Erik said. "This is my portion of Thorkell's hoard. He gave it to me when he became sick. He remembered

184

the volva's prophecy and thought he might die. He decided to provide for me in advance."

"We are lucky Snorri is away," Halfdan added. "There will surely be trouble when he returns. You see, Lenora, although the oldest son inherits, he will usually pay the younger ones some compensation, so they can travel abroad to make their fortunes, or so they can set up their own homes. Snorri will never do that for Erik, and Thorkell knew it. Now, Snorri's absence gives us time to make other arrangements."

"What will you do with all of this?" Lenora picked up a coin. There was strange writing on it. "What does it say?"

"I don't know. I can't read Arabic." Erik's worried eyes searched her face. "Can I trust you? Well, it's too late if I can't. Halfdan is going to take this hoard to his father for safekeeping. You are going to help us pack it. Unload that chest. We will also need the chest from Miklagard. Take everything out of it but the books."

"You are sending the books away too?"

"Snorri will only burn them if there is trouble. Go on, Lenora."

They worked as quickly as possible. When the chests were packed and locked, Halfdan left, returning with two strong male servants. The four men carried the chests out to load them on a cart, leaving Lenora to bundle the last few pieces into the leather sacks.

"Here." She thrust the package at Halfdan when he returned. "It is almost daylight. You must go."

185

"Be careful, Lenora. This is a dangerous place now that Thorkell is dead." Halfdan's blue eyes were shadowed. "If Freydis asks for me, tell her only that I have gone to my father. For her own safety, she cannot know of this hoard of Erik's."

"Freydis and I do not speak much these days," Lenora said, "but I will tell no one about the silver."

Halfdan's big hand patted her shoulder.

"Till we meet again, Lenora. Keep well, brother." The two men embraced, clapping each other on the back, and then Halfdan was gone.

It was later the same morning that Snorri's ship appeared, oars moving rhythmically as it progressed upriver to its anchorage at Thorkellshavn.

Snorri did not seem at all distressed at the news of his father's death. He strode into the great hall and seated himself on the arm of Thorkell's chair. He did not take the seat itself, for that was reserved for the master of Thorkellshavn.

"We will elect a new chieftain tonight," he announced, to uproarious acclaim. Turning to Gunhilde, standing at his side, he added, "And then we will celebrate my homecoming seated together upon Thorkell's chair."

Gunhilde's expression as she looked back at her husband was warmer and more respectful than Lenora had ever seen it.

Next, Snorri made his way to Thorkell's chambers, followed by Erik and Lenora.

"I have completed Thorkell's work," Erik told him. "Here is a list of all our father's lands and possessions."

Snorri, who could not read, squinted at the sheets of parchment.

"What do I care for lists?" he said. "I own Thorkell's hoard now. And even you, clever Erik, do not know where it is buried. Thorkell told only me."

Erik shrugged. "I know the law," he replied. "All of Thorkell's debts have been paid. It was done with Gunhilde's agreement. Now everything that was Thorkell's is yours."

"Except for one debt," Lenora spoke up. "Erik, you forgot to pay me. Thorkell promised me silver coins for the work I did for him in this room, so I could eventually buy my freedom. He was holding the money for me. There is a record of it."

"I did not forget," Erik said, looking annoyed that she had raised the subject. "I did not want to discuss it with Gunhilde. I will take care of that debt myself."

"Indeed you will." Snorri laughed. "I will not pay my silver to any slave, certainly not to another man's wench. Now leave me, both of you."

Lenora would have said more, would have protested the unfairness of Erik having to pay a debt his father had incurred, but the look he gave her stopped the angry words before they left her tongue. It seemed to her that Erik was pleading with her to remain silent. Looking from his face to Snorri's, she understood how foolish it would be to antagonize the man who was now the most powerful one in Thorkellshavn.

"I told you to get out," Snorri said rudely. "This is my room now. Don't enter it again."

In silence Erik opened the door, holding it so Lenora could pass.

"Treat your slave like that," Snorri said, noting the courtesy, "and before long she will rule you. But you are easily ruled, aren't you, Erik?"

Without responding to the taunt, Erik closed the door behind himself and Lenora. Then, with his arm across her shoulders, he took her up the path and into his own house.

"Now we can speak more freely," he said. "Don't talk to Snorri or Gunhilde unless it's absolutely necessary, and then be extremely polite."

"He has cheated me of the silver I earned," Lenora began.

"The money is unimportant." He made an impatient gesture with one hand. His apparent indifference angered her.

"It is important to me. I want to buy my freedom. It's the only hope I have left," she ended in a broken whisper.

"I understand." With a deep sigh he put his arms around her. "But for the moment it is safer for you to have no coins of your own, and to remain my slave. Trust me, Lenora, please."

"How can I, after the things you've done?" She tried to pull away from him, but he held her so that she was forced to look into his shadowed eyes.

"You will trust me," he said just before his mouth touched hers, "because in Thorkellshavn there is no one else to trust, and because you desire me as much as I want you."

Chapter Fourteen

That night, as almost everyone had expected, Snorri was elected chieftain to replace Thorkell. He took his seat on Thorkell's wide chair to cheers and applause. Gunhilde, her head held high and her eyes sparkling, proudly took her place beside him. She glittered with gold and silver necklaces and many bracelets, as befitted a chieftain's wife. Her shoulder brooches were huge and ornate in design, holding up a gown of fine, gold-colored wool.

"She likes him better now," Tola said. "Gunhilde likes a man with power. Signe says they spent a long time alone in their chamber. Snorri will want a legitimate son as soon as possible. Although, if Gunhilde proves barren, he has illegitimate sons he could adopt. Half the children in Thorkellshavn are his. Snorri will never lack for an heir."

"You gossip too much, Tola." Lenora's antipathy toward Snorri was stronger than it had ever been. She could not see him without remembering what he had done to her family and how he had cheated her.

Lenora picked up a pitcher of ale and carried it to the double seat across the firepit from Snorri, where Freydis and Erik were sitting. After filling their cups, Lenora took her place on a stool by Erik's side.

Now came the time for the members of Thorkell's hird to pledge themselves to the new chieftain. One by one the tall young men of the bodyguard came forward, knelt on the hard earthen floor, set their hands on Snorri's sword hilt, and swore loyalty unto death. Lenora noticed a few who hung back, coming forward only reluctantly after being cajoled by their fellows. There were several who stayed in the dark corners of the vast hall and did not come forward at all.

Toasts were drunk to Snorri's good health, and then to Gunhilde's. More toasts followed, to the large number of sons the couple was expected to produce, to the success of Snorri's latest voyage, the spoils of which had been divided that afternoon, and, finally, toasts to the well-being of the folk of Snorri's household.

"Erik," Snorri called across the room, "where

is your friend Halfdan? Why is he not here to wish me well?"

"He left early this morning to visit his father," Erik replied. "Had he known you would return so soon, he would have waited."

"I'll send a man after him," Snorri said. "Hrolf, Bjarni, which of you will ride after Halfdan and bring him back?"

Lenora glanced anxiously at Erik. The pleasant expression on his face revealed nothing of what he must be feeling at Snorri's suggestion.

"Do not take your men away from the celebrations, Snorri," Erik said easily. "Halfdan is too far along the road to Limfjord for them to catch him quickly. Once he has seen his father he will return, and we can have another feast then."

"*I* can have another feast," Snorri replied, emphasizing the pronoun, "but only if *I* chose. I make the decisions here now, Erik."

"I know that." Erik refused to rise to Snorri's challenge. "I only meant the family could welcome Halfdan's return."

"You are not part of my family."

"Thorkell adopted me. I am your brother and you are mine."

"I don't care what Thorkell did. I want nothing to do with you. It would please me to see you dead. It would please me even more to kill you myself."

The great hall had grown steadily more quiet during this exchange. Now Snorri's harsh, grating tones were the only sound in the room, seeming all the harsher when followed by Erik's almost gentle voice.

"You may try whatever you like, Snorri."

"Stop this." Freydis sounded strained. "Whatever you might wish, Snorri, you and Erik are brothers."

Gunhilde's cold tone cut her off. "For once I agree with Freydis. If you do not wish to recognize Erik as your brother, Snorri, then he remains your guest. I know you could kill him easily"— here Snorri smirked with pleasure, as Gunhilde continued—"but it would be bad luck for you to kill a guest while we celebrate your elevation to chieftain. Kill him later if you wish, but not tonight. Besides, you have something more important to do right now. It is time to announce your sister's marriage."

"So soon? So soon?" The murmur rippled around the room. Freydis sat like a statue, her face marble-pale.

"Yes, yes," Snorri said, raising his drinking horn. "I nearly forgot. We are arranging my sister Freydis' marriage to Gunhilde's cousin Kare. It is an excellent match. Kare is related to the king. That will be good for us, will it not, men?"

There was a cheer at this suggestion of royal favors to come, but it was not so hearty as Snorri might have wished, perhaps because the present king was not accepted by all the jarls, and his position was so insecure that he could not be depended upon to distribute largess to his relatives. Nevertheless Snorri continued boldly, setting out his plans for Freydis.

"Kare is coming to visit in the late spring, once the planting is completed. The wedding will take place then, although it might have been more appropriate just before the planting. Then Kare could plow his field and sow his seed with the rest of us."

Now there was boisterous laughter, followed by more ribald jokes. In the midst of the noise, Freydis rose and walked slowly across the room to face Snorri and Gunhilde.

"I do not wish to marry," Freydis said, loud and clear, so all could hear her. The revelers quieted again at this unexpected diversion.

"Why?" Snorri laughed, caught up in the bawdy mood of his men. "Has Kare's row already been planted? By Halfdan, perhaps?"

Lenora caught at Erik's arm as he began to rise. It took all her strength to pull him back into his seat. She was helped by a tall man standing behind Erik, who put both hands on Erik's shoulders and pushed down hard. Erik looked around in surprise, then relaxed when he saw the man's face.

Snorri was addressing Freydis again. "I have chosen Kare for you. You are fortunate that he wants you."

"You mean Gunhilde has chosen Kare." Freydis' dark blue eyes regarded the pair on the settle with contempt. "I was never consulted about this match. I have repeatedly said that I do not wish to marry."

"What you wish," Gunhilde sneered, "is to

194

marry Halfdan. But Halfdan will never marry his blood-brother's sister."

Freydis winced, then recovered her composure.

"I do not wish to marry," she repeated a third time, making it official. "I am a free woman. I am not obligated to marry anyone. You cannot force me to do so."

"You will marry Kare or you will go out into the world alone," Snorri declared. "I will banish you from my home."

"Then do so, but I will not marry Kare."

Lenora felt pure admiration for Freydis. Tall and big-boned and strong Freydis might be, but she looked frail and very lonely as she stood before Snorri and his wife. Lenora knew how much Freydis loved Thorkellshavn, and from her own experience she had some idea how hard it would be for Freydis to leave her home. When Erik, shaking off the restraining hand of the man who still stood behind him, rose from his seat and went to stand beside his sister, Lenora followed him.

"Freydis is right," Erik said. "There is no law that says she must marry your choice for her. And until she marries, this is her home. You cannot put her out."

"Have you become a lawspeaker in my absence? How dare you tell me what I cannot do, you Frankish bastard? I tell you that unless Freydis agrees to marry Kare, she must leave my home by midday tomorrow. As for you, you sniveling, Greek-soft cripple, you have no place here.

195

The sooner you go, the better."

"Then I will leave with Freydis tomorrow."

"I'll be well rid of you," Snorri declared. "Get out and take your whore-sister with you!"

In his determination to avoid physical conflict with Snorri, Erik might have tolerated endless insults directed at himself, but the crude term applied to Freydis goaded him beyond self-control. Suddenly his sword was in his hand. He took a purposeful step toward Snorri. Lenora saw other blades flash as men readied themselves for the bloodshed all must have believed would come within moments.

There was a sound behind her. Lenora spun around, her nerves on edge. She found three tall Vikings standing close to her. The tallest of them was the man who had helped her to hold Erik in his seat. These three were among the men who had not sworn loyalty to Snorri.

"Snorri," called out this man, stepping casually between Erik and his half-brother.

"Ingvar the Bold," Snorri exclaimed. "Well, what is it?"

"Asmund and Olrik and I were members of Thorkell's hird. We served him and protected him faithfully. For many years we slept in his hall."

"I know that. What of it? Do you want some reward for your service to my father before you join me?"

"We ask as our reward only a promise, Snorri. We want your word as a chieftain."

"Tell me what promise you expect me to make."

"Give us your word that you will send no one to harm Erik or Freydis or any other member of their party for five days. In turn we will escort them away from Thorkellshavn."

"And in six days," Snorri jeered at Ingvar, "Erik will return with an army to destroy us. No, I will not do it."

Ingvar held up his hand to stop the angry flow of Snorri's words.

"We ask a promise of Erik also, and for the same reason we ask one of you. We loved and respected Thorkell. We do not want to see his sons kill each other. We want children and grandchildren of Thorkell's to live and remember his name and his reputation. Erik," Ingvar turned to the dark man who stood beside Freydis, "will you swear to leave Denmark at the earliest opportunity, and not to take up arms against Snorri until you do?" Then Ingvar added in a low voice, "For I think now Thorkell is dead you mean to return to Miklagard if you can. That long distance will keep you safe from Snorri, and him safe from you."

Erik and the tall Viking locked eyes for a long, tense moment. Finally, Erik sheathed his sword and turned back to face Snorri.

"I swear," Erik declared, his firm voice carrying clearly throughout the hall, "that until I leave Denmark I will not use my weapons against Snorri or his men, unless I or my companions are attacked first. I have the right to defend myself and my friends."

Ingvar nodded approvingly at this speech. "That is fair. Snorri, will you agree?"

Snorri laughed his nasal, unpleasant laugh. "I was right about you," he said to Erik. "The Greeks have addled your wits. Any true Norseman would stand and fight." He surveyed the group standing before him.

"You are all traitors to me," Snorri added. "I should kill every one of you for your disloyalty. But, as Gunhilde has said, this is a joyous occasion. For Thorkell's memory, let there be no bloodshed this night. Be gone, all of you, by midday, when Freydis must leave. And you three, Ingvar, Asmund, and Olrik, do not return here. If ever I see you again, I will kill you."

They walked from a silent hall into the cold night.

"I must pack my belongings," Freydis said. "Lenora, find Tola and send her to me. She will go with us."

"Pack as little as possible," Erik said when Lenora had joined him in his house. "We will leave as soon as we can, and travel quickly. I don't trust Snorri. I'm sure you noticed, he seemed to agree with Ingvar, but he never swore to give us those five days."

"Where are we going?" Lenora asked as she folded Erik's clothes into his saddlebags. "Will we go to Halfdan's home?"

"You are going nowhere," Erik replied. "You would only slow us down."

"You told me this afternoon that I am safest as your slave, with you." With a furious gesture, Lenora threw onto the bed the shirt she had been holding. "I will not remain here without you. I know too well what Snorri will do to me once your protection is removed. I will go with you, or I will follow Edwina." Her voice cracked on the last word. She had not mentioned Edwina by name since the night of Thorkell's funeral and it was hard to do so now, but she was close to panic from fear of Snorri.

"You have been ill recently, and you are still weak," Erik said, looking at her with a critical gaze. "It would be a difficult journey for you."

"Not as difficult as staying here." Lenora's chin lifted with just a touch of defiance. "I am growing stronger every day. If Tola can go with you, so can I."

Still he hesitated.

"You told Freydis you wanted to depart as soon as possible," she reminded him. "Yet you are delaying."

His hand reached out to catch a chestnut curl that lay against her cheek. As though it had a life of its own, it curved about his fingers. He gave it a playful tug.

"Wench," he said softly, "what am I to do with you? Nothing has been the same since Thorkell gave you to me. Sometimes I wonder which of us is the slave."

"Take me with you," she begged, pressing her advantage. "Don't leave me to Snorri."

He spoke almost under his breath, as though he were thinking aloud.

"If you did not want to come, I think I would drag you along with me. I only hope you are strong enough, my sweet." Then, louder, he said, "Very well."

Having made up his mind, he at once became efficient, rapping out orders.

"Finish what you are doing, then pack a few things for yourself. Not too much, and do it quickly. Use the other saddlebag."

"Where are we going?" Lenora asked again, trying not to let her feelings show, although she was limp with relief.

"We go first to Hedeby. It is the safest place for us. I will send Olrik north to intercept Halfdan and tell him to join us there. He will bring with him some of my silver. Halfdan, Ingvar, and Asmund will take you and Freydis and Tola back to his father at Limfjord. There you will be safe from Snorri."

"What will you do?"

"As Ingvar guessed, I will return to Miklagard."

"Take me with you." He frowned at this suggestion.

"I have already agreed to take you away from Thorkellshavn. I cannot take you to Miklagard. It is too far, and the way is too dangerous."

"Are there no women in the lands you will travel through?"

"Of course there are."

"Then I can go too."

With an annoyed expression, he handed her her cloak.

"I will hear no more argument," he said in a stern voice. "You are not going to Miklagard."

Part Three

*The Varangian Way,
Denmark to Constantinople
March to September, A.D. 868*

Chapter Fifteen

Long before the sun had risen they left Thorkel-lshavn. Olrik rode north to find Halfdan. The others crowded themselves and their few possessions into a small boat Ingvar had stolen.

"Quiet," Erik warned as a cloth-wrapped bundle thudded into the boat's hold. "We don't want anyone following us."

"There is nothing to fear from them," Tola said. "Erna told me they all drank themselves to sleep last night. They won't wake up until the day is half over."

"I hope you are right," Erik replied. "And I hope you spent more time packing food than gossiping with Erna."

With Erik at the tiller and Ingvar and Asmund rowing, they made their stealthy way downriver to the sea. Then, as the sky brightened with the dawn, they raised the sail and headed southward.

It was a rough passage. The fierce west wind whipped at them, blowing water into the boat and threatening to drive them aground on sandbars or on one of the many islands that fringed the western coast of Denmark. Occasional blasts of snow or sleet stung their faces.

Lenora thought they would all freeze to death. In spite of their discomfort, she had the distinct impression that the men were enjoying themselves. They handled the little boat with skill born of years of practice. They laughed in sheer physical exhilaration as they sailed past rocks and shoals with a breathtakingly narrow margin of safety.

Even Freydis looked happier than she had for some time. She handed Lenora a wooden bucket and they bailed water out of the hold until their hands were red and numb.

"We should have gone by land," Tola grumbled. "And we should have gone directly north to Limfjord instead of stopping at Hedeby first."

"Be quiet, woman," Freydis ordered. "Erik knows what he is doing. Keep bailing."

They were all soaked and half-frozen before they finally sailed into the estuary of a broad river. Now they traveled eastward, after a time moving into a smaller tributary river where they dropped the sail. Ingvar and Asmund picked up the oars again and began rowing.

It seemed an eternity to Lenora before they landed at the edge of a village that sat on a low slope above the marshy river valley. Small wattle-and-daub houses clustered together, overshadowed by ships of all sizes moored at the river's edge.

"They come here from the lands to the west." Freydis had seen her gaping. "They are unloaded here and their cargo is carried overland to Hedeby. It is safer than making the long trip north around the tip of Denmark, then south to Hedeby. There are pirates and treacherous tides and shoals in the waters north of here."

"How far is it to Hedeby?"

"Only half a day's ride. Erik will find horses for us in the morning."

They pulled their boat out of the water a short distance from the village and laid it on its side, propping it up with the oars. They built a fire and huddled together in the shelter provided by the boat's hull. Their evening meal was flatbread and dried meats and fruits, washed down with ale. Lenora slept in the curve of Erik's arm, covered with his damp fur cloak.

The next day they traded the little boat and some silver coins from Erik's purse for three horses. They paused to eat their morning meal before setting out for Hedeby.

"No sign of Snorri yet," Erik remarked. "Let's hope our luck continues."

"He will follow us," Ingvar said. "I know Snorri too well. You will keep your word, Erik, but Snorri will not keep his. He will claim he never gave you those five days' start, though his words made it appear he had agreed to my suggestion. He is not to be trusted. He will make a poor chieftain. His people will not fare well."

Lenora did not want to think about Snorri and what would happen if he caught them. She tried to change the subject.

"What will you do after we reach Hedeby?" she asked Ingvar.

"We will remain with Erik so long as he needs us. Afterward we will find another chieftain to serve."

"You could take service with Halfdan's father," Erik suggested. "Another good sword arm is always welcome to guard Limfjord."

"Perhaps we'll do that."

They headed east, riding double, a woman behind each man. They rode with a wide earthen rampart on their right side. It was topped by a wooden palisade that towered a good three handspans above Lenora's head. The fortification stretched behind them to the river's edge, while before them it reached to Hedeby itself.

"That is the Danevirke. It was built to keep out the Slavs and the Franks," Erik told her.

They entered Hedeby by the western gate, crossing a wooden bridge over a wide ditch and then passing through a plank-lined opening in the town's protective earth wall. They continued along a street paved with heavy wooden planks, past wood houses with thatched roofs, barns, stables, warehouses, and workshops, all jumbled closely together and seething with busy commercial life.

Erik had told Lenora about Hedeby and the goods that were brought there to be traded. The town faced Hadeby Noor, a lake at the end of a long, winding fjord, which provided protection from invasion or the pirates who lurked in the Baltic Sea. On the landward side of the town an old Roman road ran north to Limfjord and south across the border into Frankland.

Hedeby sat at the crossroads of two great trade routes. Leather, skins for making parchment or vellum for bookbindings, soapstone bowls and cups from Norway, beeswax for candles and bronze casting, honey, cattle, smoked and salted meats, dairy products, furs of fox and seal and bear, antlers or walrus tusks for combs and pins and chesspieces, whalebone, sea salt and grain, soft down and feathers for pillows and quilts, and amber, called sea-gold and prized by the Greeks and Romans, came to Hedeby from the northern countries.

From the south and west came olive oil and slaves, marten furs and gold jewelry from Ireland, and soft, deep blue wool from Frisia. Millstones for grinding grain into flour, fine glassware and swordblades, and wine came from the Rhineland. The black slaves whom the Norsemen called "blue men" were brought by ship from the faraway lands across the Middle Sea. From the east came sable furs and Slavic slaves.

From the greatest distance of all, along the trade route that went east across the Baltic Sea then south through the land of the Rus to Constantinople and Bagdhad and beyond Bagdhad to the very ends of the earth, along this Varangian Way came gold and spices, silks and other rare textiles, Arab silver, finely wrought jewelry and enamels, pottery, and the occasional small statue of some foreign god. Also along this way came a few adventurous Arab traders. From time to time they were to be seen in the streets of Hedeby—small, dark men with carefully trimmed black beards, wearing long, flowing robes and wrapped headdresses called turbans.

To Lenora, Hedeby was a magical place, over-crowded and noisy and exciting, but Erik was concerned at the lack of activity and the small number of merchants he saw.

"It is too early in the season," he said. "Another two cycles of the moon will bring more merchants. Then there are twice as many people here and more ships than you can count drawn up at the edge of Hadeby Noor. All summer long the trading contines, until the merchants sail home again in the autumn. Then it is easy to find passage on a knarr traveling east. At this time of year it will be difficult."

Erik led his little party to the house of a man he knew.

"Holgar is an old friend of Thorkell's," Erik said, introducing them. "I have traded with him in the past. We will stay with him."

"If he is a friend of Thorkell, will he not also be a friend of Snorri?" Asmund objected. "Can we trust you, old man?"

The plump, pink-faced merchant spat on the ground. "That for Snorri," he said contemptuously. "That misbegotten thief has cheated me too many times. He gives all Norsemen a bad name. Oh, I could tell you stories, young man, tales that would bring tears to your eyes. I'll have nothing to do with Snorri Thorkellsson, and I will gladly help anyone trying to escape him. My house and all I have are yours."

"Good enough." Asmund laughed, laying a hand on Holgar's shoulder. "Any man who hates Snorri must be an honest man and a friend."

Holgar's house was not small, but it was soon crowded as the six members of Erik's party tried to make themselves comfortable. The wattle-and-daub walls seemed to close in upon them.

Lenora escaped from the main room through a door at one end and found herself in a smaller room that served as a kitchen. She found Holgar's serving woman removing bread from a domed clay oven.

"Let me help you," Lenora offered.

The woman looked up, startled, and replied in a strange tongue. Her wide, pale face was intense with the effort of communication.

"She won't understand you," Holgar said, coming into the room. "She's a Slav. I bought her from a Frankish merchant who got her from the grasslands east of his country. She only speaks a few words of Norse."

"How do you tell her what you want?" Lenora wondered.

"I point to something, or yell at her. If she doesn't do what I want, I beat her." Holgar patted the woman on her ample buttocks. "She's nice and warm to sleep with in the winter," he said contentedly.

"What is her name?" Lenora asked.

"I don't know. I never bothered to find out. I call her Alara. That's good enough."

A few gestures made it clear Holgar wanted the woman to serve food to his guests. This she did, with Lenora's help. A shy touch to Lenora's arm and a quick smile indicated the woman's gratitude.

Holgar's property was surrounded by a wooden fence, the gable end of the house facing the street. Behind the house, the land sloped down to the stream that ran through the center of Hedeby, supplying its inhabitants with fresh water. A barn stood to one side, a storehouse for merchandise on the other. Holgar proudly told them he had a larger warehouse down on the waterfront. Erik and Ingvar inspected the premises and pronounced them defensible should the need arise.

"There is little room in the house. Asmund and I can sleep in the barn," Ingvar offered.

"We had better stay together," Erik said. "It will be safer that way if Snorri should come during the night. We need someone on guard at all times too."

"We can take turns. I'll begin the watch, then Asmund can take over," Ingvar agreed.

Furs and rugs were spread upon the wide platform running along each side of the main room, and the party settled down for the night. Lenora lay wrapped in Erik's arms, drifting between sleep and wakefulness, the fear and tension she had felt during the journey from Thorkellshavn beginning to dissipate at last.

Erik stirred, pulling her closer.

"You are so warm and sweet. I'll miss you when I go away," he murmured into her ear.

"Then take me with you," she breathed softly. "I want to see Miklagard."

She felt him stiffen and move apart from her, the tender moment gone.

"You cannot go with me, Lenora. I have made up my mind and nothing will change it."

Erik spent the next day trying to find a merchant ship that would soon sail eastward. He took Holgar with him, for the merchant had many contacts among those who came each year to trade at Hedeby. Asmund and Ingvar remained at Holgar's house to protect the women should Snorri appear.

Lenora used her time well, helping Alara with the cooking and washing, but she quickly tired of her confinement within the house and the enclosed courtyard behind it.

"Tomorrow I am going with you," she told Erik that night. "If I'm to be exiled to Limfjord, then I want to see a real city first."

"I'll let you go if you promise not to delay me," Erik replied. "We have been lucky so far, but I want to find a ship before Halfdan comes. Then I can send you and Freydis north with him at once, and we will all be gone before Snorri finds us."

Erik's luck held. At midmorning of the following day they found a merchant loading goods into a large cargo vessel. The merchant's name was Rodfos. He was a big man, with a red face to match his bushy beard and the beginnings of a belly from too much food and drink. He wore enormously full, baggy breeches of bright blue wool, and high boots of soft leather, criss-crossed and fastened with thongs. This sartorial splendor was further embellished by a wide green cape that fastened with a large gold pin on his right shoulder, leaving his sword arm free. Under his cloak, a small silver hammer, symbol of Thor, dangled against his chest on an ornate silver chain.

"I am sailing to Bornholm, in the middle of the Baltic Sea," Rodfos announced grandly, "and then on to Aldeigjuborg on Lake Ladoga. I leave the day after tomorrow at dawn. Be here tomorrow night and sleep aboard. When I am ready to sail, I go whether you are here or not. I wait for no latecomers."

"I won't be late," Erik promised. "I will travel with you to Aldeigjuborg."

"Bring your own food. There will be casks of ale and water on board."

"If you don't need my help any more, I will leave you," Holgar said as they parted from Rodfos. "I should be about my business."

Erik drew Lenora to the water's edge. They sat down on the upturned hull of a small fishing boat. Lenora looked around her with interest at the ships drawn up on shore or moored to the strong wooden posts set in the water. Sturdy wooden warehouses lined the harbor. The inhabitants of

Hedeby, secure in the strength of the Danevirke that guarded them, and in the additional safety of their own town walls, went about the business of trade that was the town's only reason for existance. Ships were loaded and unloaded, goods bartered for other goods, silver weighed and exchanged for merchandise.

The waters of Hadeby Noor sparkled deep blue and silver. Gulls wheeled and dipped above, their cries a raucous punctuation to the human voices below. The sun shone brightly, but it was chilly, with a sharp breeze from the water. Soon the days would be longer than the nights, and here and there a bit of green had appeared, but winter had still not entirely loosened its grip on the land.

Lenora glanced at Erik. His eyes were fixed on the eastern horizon, his profile sharply chiseled against the blue sky.

"You are gone from me before you have left," she said softly.

"Not really gone, just planning."

"I hate Snorri," she burst out. "This is all his fault. If it weren't for him, we would all be comfortable at Thorkellshavn."

Erik did not answer her.

"I know you have reason to dislike Snorri," Lenora said, "but why does he hate you so much?"

Reluctantly, Erik withdrew his attention from the distant sky and looked at her.

"I think he believed I was his rival for Thorkell's affection. Our father was kind to me when I came home injured, and Snorri was jealous. He thinks I am weak because my leg is lame. He has hated me since then. He is unable to understand that Thorkell could love us both."

"I thought he had always hated you."

"We were never friends, that is true, but we did not fight so much before I went to Grikkland. We were both away a good part of each year and seldom saw each other. Snorri went a-viking to England or Frankland, and I traveled here to Hedeby to trade, or on to Gardariki, where the Rus live. I always preferred to trade peacefully, but Snorri likes to take his goods by pillage and fighting. He enjoys bloodshed."

"And you do not?"

"I like a good fight." Erik grinned. "There is a feeling that comes over me when I stand sword in hand before an enemy and know I will defeat him. I cease to be Erik and become someone else, a berserker, until the battle is over. Then I look around me and scarcely remember what I have done."

"Yet you let Snorri call you a coward and did not fight him."

"Sometimes it is wiser not to spill blood. There are other ways of getting what I want. I learned that from the Greeks. That night it was more important to get Freydis safely away from Thorkellshavn than to defend my name. And you." His hand stroked her hair, feeling the crisp, shiny curls, blown by the sea wind. "I wanted you away from Snorri too. I did not want him to have you. I can pay him back later for his insults to me. You know better than anyone, Lenora, that I do not want to kill Snorri, but I think, if we meet again, he will force me to it. He is an evil man, a true son of Ragnhilde." Erik sighed.

Lenora moved closer, feeling his warmth, smelling the good masculine scent of him.

"But you wanted to leave me in Thorkellshavn," she said.

"I could never have left you behind for Snorri to harm. I was worried that you were not well enough to travel, and I did enjoy arguing with you about it," he teased, his mood lightening. "Arguing is something else I learned from the Greeks."

She smiled, too content at that moment to be angry with him. As he had said, there were other ways than fighting to get what she wanted. Just now she wanted all the information she could learn about Miklagard. There was not much time left before he would be gone for good.

"Tell me about your last voyage to Grikkland."

"We gathered a huge fleet of ships," Erik said, his voice heavy with memories. "Askold and Dir were our leaders. They are the rulers of Kiev. We were going to attack Miklagard."

"Attack the greatest city in the world? Why?"

"Gold. You cannot imagine all the gold there is in Miklagard. And jewels and silks, spices and slave girls. We were going to take them for our own. We were all going to be rich forever." He laughed softly, remembering. "I was so young then. Only seventeen and full of dreams. I thought I would bring chests of gold back to Denmark to repay Thorkell for his goodness to me."

"What happened?"

"We sailed across the Euxine Sea to Miklagard and laid siege to it. There was a terrible storm. Most of our ships were sunk. Many men died."

"Is that when you were injured?"

"The ship's mast split and fell on me. The man next to me was killed. My shoulder and leg were broken and I got this." He touched the scar that ran from his left eyebrow to his hairline.

"I was lucky not to lose my eye, but that was the end of my luck. The ship began to list badly and I fell overboard. I remember trying to swim, but my left arm and leg wouldn't work. I don't know how I got to shore. There is a long time, many days, that I cannot remember. One day I woke up in a house outside Miklagard. The people caring for me were Greeks, and I spoke no Greek.

"Do you know, Lenora, the rulers of Miklagard will not allow the Rus traders to live within the city walls? They fear our swords. They only let small groups of Northmen enter, no more than twenty-five at a time, and the men are forced to leave their weapons outside the gates. And every autumn all the Rus must go home again, back to Kiev." He laughed. "The emperor of the greatest and most powerful city in the world lives in fear of a few Northmen."

"Who can blame him, if you send fleets and armies against his city?"

"Eirena told me there were special religious ceremonies to thank their god for sending the storm to wipe out our fleet."

"Who is Eirena?"

"Eirena Panopoulos. She is the woman who cared for me when I was injured. Her brother Basil is a merchant. Because I was so badly injured I was unable to travel. Basil got special permission for me to remain in Grikkland. I lived with Basil for three years. It was from him I learned both Greek and Latin.

"I will go back to Miklagard," Erik told her. "I will take silver coins and goods to trade with Basil. Perhaps I can go into business with him. I could travel far to the east to trade. I have always wanted to see what lies beyond Miklagard."

Erik's eyes were focused on sights half a world away, but Lenora did not notice. She cared nothing for the intricacies of international trade. Her interests lay elsewhere.

"Is this Eirena very beautiful?" she asked.

Erik considered her question for a while. "I'm not sure," he said at last. "She was different from any woman I had ever met before, but later I realized she was not so different from other Greek women. She is small and dark, with big brown eyes, and she is learned. But beautiful? I don't know."

"Did you lay with her?"

"Certainly not. The Greeks are Christians. Their women remain virgins until they marry. Their male relatives can become extremely violent on that subject."

"Did she want you?" Lenora asked.

"How should I know that?"

"I think you would know if a woman wanted you. Perhaps you don't want to tell me?"

219

"Stop asking so many questions."

But Lenora would not be discouraged from pouring out the unexpected jealousy suddenly welling up in her. First there had been Erna, now some Greek woman. She felt as though she had been stabbed through the heart.

"I hate this Eirena," she cried. "I know she wanted you. You'll go back to Miklagard and be with her. I hate her."

"You hate too many people, Lenora. Snorri, Gunhilde, Bjarni, Hrolf...how many others? Hatred is a bitter thing. It will destroy you, not those you hate. You should forget the past and take what pleasure you can from life now."

I would, Lenora thought, *if you were not leaving me and taking with you all the pleasure my life might hold. Oh, Erik, what will I do without you? Why do I feel as though my heart is breaking in two?*

Chapter Sixteen

When Erik and Lenora returned to Holgar's house they found Halfdan waiting for them. He handed Erik a sack of coins.

"Olrik caught up with me on the road," Halfdan said. "I sent him on to Limfjord with the rest of your hoard. He will tell my father what has happened and that we will be in Limfjord soon."

"Good."

"Why didn't you all simply ride north with Olrik?"

"Because I am going to Miklagard."

"Then I am going with you."

"No, you are to take the women to your father for safety. Did Olrik tell you Snorri plans to marry Freydis to Kare?"

"Snorri has no right to force her."

"Snorri does what he pleases. He cares nothing

for the law. But once Freydis is with your father and protected by his guards Snorri cannot harm her."

"Erik, if Snorri finds you, he will try to kill you."

"My fight with Snorri is long overdue, postponed for the sake of our father. Now it must be, and I can no longer avoid it. But," Erik added, "when we do fight, I plan to take Snorri and at least a few of his men to Valhalla with me."

Hearing the two men laugh cheerfully at this, Lenora shuddered. She helped Alara to cook and serve the evening meal, but she could eat little.

On this, her last night with Erik, Lenora was possessed by conflicting emotions so strong they nearly paralyzed her. She still hated the Norse for all Snorri and his men had done to her family, and she resented Erik, Halfdan, and Freydis because they had done nothing to save Edwina. And yet all three of them had been kind to her. Halfdan had become almost like a brother to her. Freydis had cared for her when she had been sick. And Erik, whose touch could send her spirit soaring into the sky, whose kiss was a sweet drug, whose body had been so intimately a part of her own, Erik who had been unfaithful to her with Erna, and who was planning to rejoin his Greek Eirena with not a thought for the pain it would cause Lenora—what did she really feel for him? Her confusion intensified at the end of the meal when Erik rose and took her hand.

"Lenora," he said, "before he died, Thorkell charged me with payment of his debt to you. He wanted me to tell you that you had done your work well and that although you are a slave, he counted you among his friends."

Into her hand Erik pressed a small leather purse. It was filled with silver coins.

"I never earned this much," Lenora whispered, her throat tight.

"It is what Thorkell told me to give you."

"I am honored, not only by the extra silver, but even more because Thorkell called me friend."

"Now," Erik went on, "I call all of you here to witness what I say. Lenora has been my slave. I hereby set her free."

Lenora gaped at him, not believing what she had just heard.

"Tomorrow," Erik said to her, "you and the others will leave Hedeby and travel to Limfjord. From there Halfdan will arrange your passage home to East Anglia."

"What are you saying?" She still did not fully comprehend what Erik had just done.

"You are a free woman, Lenora. You can go home now."

"I have no home. Snorri destroyed my home."

"You must have relatives somewhere. You have told me your father was an important man. You will find your rightful place again."

Before Lenora could say anything more, Halfdan swept her into his bear-hug of an embrace. Holgar scurried about the room, filling his guests' cups with mead. Ingvar and Asmund raised theirs and toasted Lenora's freedom. Tola kissed her, weeping. Alara hovered in the background,

Flora Speer

not understanding what was happening but her expression clearly showing how glad she was to see her new-found friend the center of rejoicing. Even cool Freydis took Lenora's hand and said she was pleased.

Only Lenora stood unsmiling, trembling, watching Erik, wondering what she would do now that her last bond with him was severed. After tomorrow she would never see him again.

Halfdan pressed a cup of mead into her hand. She forced herself to smile as the party drank a toast to Erik's good luck on his dangerous voyage to Miklagard.

"You should look happier, Lenora. You have what you wanted." Tola was helping to clear away the remains of their meal.

"I am happy," Lenora lied. "It's just so unexpected. I don't know what to do next."

"That Erik. He's full of surprises."

"Yes." Lenora glanced at the men, sitting about on the bed platforms, making plans for the morning. Erik was in deep conversation with Freydis. Lenora followed Alara and Tola into the kitchen.

"Better hide that," Tola advised, indicating the bag of coins Lenora still held. "Someone might steal it."

Lenora pulled the strings tight and tied them about her neck. She tucked the bag under the neckline of her dress and patted at it until it was nearly flat.

"That will do for now," she said.

She wondered if she and Erik could slip out to

the barn later. She wanted to be able to speak to him without the others hearing, to thank him for her freedom, to hold his naked body in her arms and abandon herself to his caresses. Just once more. Just one last time.

"Lenora," Freydis interrupted her thoughts as she joined the other women in the kitchen, "I wanted to ask you—"

There was a loud crash in the main room, and an unmistakable sneering laugh, followed by Asmund's shout.

"Snorri!"

Tola dropped the wooden plates she was holding. Freydis turned white. Lenora moved to the doorway to see what was happening.

Snorri, sword ready in his hand, had thrown back the wooden door to the street, smashing it against the wall as he entered. He was followed into the house by Hrolf and Bjarni. More armed men could be seen crowding behind them at the doorway.

"Come in, brother." Erik was apparently unruffled by Snorri's sudden appearance. "How did you find me so quickly?"

"Erna," Snorri replied. "Let me give you a lesson in women, cripple. When you leave a wench like Erna for another woman you must do one of two things. Either you kill her or you pay her well. Otherwise, she will seek to do you harm. Erna was your woman once, but you neglected her completely after Lenora arrived at Thorkellshavn, and the other women teased her about it. Her pride was badly hurt. You poured salt into that wound by going away without even saying good-bye to her. Tola, gossiping as usual, had told her friend Erna where you were going. Erna told me. An entertaining woman, that Erna. A bit quick to lift her skirts, but then, unlike you, I paid her well."

"I will remember your advice," Erik said dryly.

"You won't live long enough to use it, thief."

"I am no thief."

"I have learned you stole part of Thorkell's hoard. I want it back."

"Thorkell gave me that silver for my own use."

"You lie. You stole it," Snorri insisted. "I think you have loaded it on some ship, disguised as cargo. I think you plan to take it to Miklagard with you."

"Do you?" Erik's smile was guileless.

"I know what a coward you are, how you hate to fight. Give back the silver and I'll let you go without hurting you."

"If you want to bargain with someone, you should not begin by insulting him. What about Freydis?"

"Freydis will return to Thorkellshavn with me, and marry Kare."

"That is something over which we will never haggle, Snorri. Freydis is not for Kare."

Lenora saw Snorri's sword flash as he raised his arm to strike. She saw Erik duck and leap aside, unsheathing his own blade. The room erupted into battle as Snorri's men forced their way inside.

Halfdan cut down one man before he came

226

through the door. Holgar attacked a second, Half-dan a third man. Asmund and Ingvar struggled with Hrolf and Bjarni. Snorri and Erik, locked in combat, lurched through a side door into the courtyard.

The room was too small for so many people. There wasn't enough room to maneuver. Swords and shields and battle-axes got in the way of movement.

Halfdan dispatched another of Snorri's men, swung around, and leapt toward the kitchen.

"Freydis," he shouted, "go to the barn. Get the horses ready." Snorri's men attacked him again, and Halfdan moved back into the main room.

As Freydis turned toward the door leading to the courtyard, Hrolf entered the kitchen, the fire of battle in his eyes.

"There you are, Freydis," he called. "You are the cause of this dispute. It is time for you to die."

He raised his glittering battle-ax. Freydis stood unmoving, seemingly fascinated by the weapon poised above her head. Tola, seeing Hrolf's in-tent, screamed. As Hrolf swung his ax downward, Tola ran in front of him, pushing her mistress out of the way and taking the blow Hrolf had meant for Freydis.

Suddenly Asmund was there, shouting. Hrolf spun around, forgetting Freydis. Yelling a wild battlecry, he pursued Asmund into the main room.

Freydis stooped to be certain there was nothing she could do to help Tola, then raced out the kitchen door, heading for the barn.

"Lenora, follow me," she cried.

Lenora caught the terrified Alara by the hand and pulled her into the courtyard. Light from the open kitchen door made a dim pathway across the darkness. A shadow blotted out part of the light as another of Snorri's men appeared with Ingvar in pursuit. Seeing Lenora, Snorri's man reached for her. Alara pushed at him and he ran her through. Now Ingvar engaged the man, and they moved off into the darkness, leaving Lenora alone.

Alara lay on the ground, bleeding heavily. Lenora bent over her. Alara looked up, smiled, and closed her eyes. Lenora knew without touching her that Alara was dead. Too many people were dead or dying in this small space, and all for Norse greed and cruelty. All for Snorri. Lenora drew a deep, shuddering breath and stood up, covering her ears to shut out the sounds of battle reverberating off the buildings edging the courtyard.

"Stop it!" she screamed, "Stop it! Oh, Erik, where are you?"

A cluster of men, all arms and legs and swords and shields, surged out of the door from the main room into the courtyard. Freydis had disappeared. Lenora ran back into the kitchen, through it, and then entered the main room by the serving door. She was in time to see Hrolf turning from Holgar's inert body to face Erik.

Grimly the two men fought, swords whacking against wooden shields, as Erik slowly backed

Hrolf into a corner until he could go no farther. Erik lifted his sword for the last blow, took a step forward, and slipped in a puddle of blood. His lame leg gave way as he lost his balance and went down. His sword, knocked out of his hand by the impact, slid lazily across the floor to stop at Lenora's feet. Hrolf laughed and raised his own sword, taking his time, relishing the moment.

Lenora snatched up Erik's heavy blade in both hands and ran forward. The sword felt light as a feather to her. She knew what to do: three steps more and a slashing blow from right to left, just as she had seen the men do at weapons pactice back at Thorkellshavn. But first she had to distract Hrolf from Erik.

"Hrolf, kill me first!"

He saw her coming and leapt over Erik, who caught at his ankle, unbalancing him. Hrolf spread his arms to steady himself, moving his shield away from his body. It was the opening Lenora needed.

So fierce was her anger at Hrolf that she felt nothing as the sharp sword met his body. Hrolf crashed to the floor.

"That's Saxon revenge, you murdering Norseman," she screamed.

As the red mist before her eyes cleared a little, the astonished face of Bjarni swam into view. He moved into the room, sparing only a glance for Erik, who was now slowly pulling himself to his feet.

"I see you need a woman to protect you, cripple."

229

"Are you afraid of a woman, Norseman?" Lenora taunted, brandishing the sword at him.

Bjarni grimaced at the insult.

"Of no woman on earth, slave."

"Well, you should be, murderer." Holding the sword in both hands, totally unconscious of its great weight in her renewed fury, Lenora slashed at him with all her strength. The blade barely nicked his side before Bjarni deflected it with his shield. He jumped to the right and laughed at her.

Lenora turned a bit to face him, her back toward the open door into the courtyard. She had forgotten about Erik. Her attention was completely focused on Bjarni, whose sword was now poised above her. Lenora felt no fear at all, only excitement and rage.

An iron-strong arm circled Lenora's waist from behind, lifting her off her feet and carrying her through the door and away from her opponent. Another arm slammed the door of the house shut and bolted it, sealing Bjarni inside. Erik roared with laughter as he half-carried, half-dragged her to his horse, which was saddled and waiting thanks to Freydis' quick work.

"Put me down," Lenora yelled. "I'll kill Bjarni. Let me kill him. Erik, let me go."

"Stop it, Lenora. Calm yourself." She still held his sword. He pried it out of her stiff fingers, then flung her across the horse, stomach-down. "What a berserker you are. Are you sure there's no Norse blood in your veins? You fight almost as well as a Danish woman."

"What do you mean, almost? Let me up. *Erik!*"

He paid no attention to her outraged cries. Mounting quickly, he rode at a canter along the straight road running through the center of Hedeby to the shore.

"Erik...where...is...Halfdan?...Where is Freydis?" Lenora gasped. The jolting she got as the horse ran was making her feel very ill, and all she could see was the road beneath the horse's hooves.

"They will meet us. Be quiet, Lenora. We don't want to be followed, and you are too noisy."

Those who had survived Snorri's attack reassembled inside Holgar's warehouse by the edge of Hadeby Noor. Erik rode right through the big open door, and Halfdan shut it behind him.

When Erik lifted her off his horse, Lenora found to her astonishment that she was trembling so violently she could hardly stand, and tears were running down her cheeks.

"It happens sometimes after a battle," Erik said gently. He kept his arm about her until she was seated on a bale of Holgar's goods.

"Snorri and his men have withdrawn," Halfdan told them. "He ran away."

"Make no mistake about him." Freydis was busily binding up a gash on Asmund's left arm. "Snorri will come looking for us again, Erik, and soon."

"I know. Tomorrow you are all to leave Hedeby as we had planned. I will stay out of sight in this building. After dark I'll sneak out to Rodfos' ship

231

and hide there. With any luck, Snorri won't find us."

"I won't let you remain here alone." Halfdan was adamant. "I am staying with you."

"And I," Freydis said. "This trouble is partly over me. I can fight, too."

"And I," Lenora added.

"You are going to Limfjord, Freydis. I cannot rest easy until you are safe from Snorri and Gunhilde. As for you, my former slave," Erik's green eyes twinkled as he looked at Lenora, "I know you can fight like a man when you want. I thank you for your help earlier. You saved my life, and I am grateful. I can no longer order you, but I ask you to go with Freydis. I want to know you are safe."

"Send the women with Asmund and Ingvar," Halfdan suggested. "I will stay with you tomorrow in case there is any trouble, and when you are safely at sea, I will ride after them."

They finally settled on Halfdan's plan. With their nerves stretched tightly, sleep was impossible, but they tried to rest in anticipation of a long ride the next day.

Lenora had finally gained some control over the tremors that had shaken her limbs, but every time she thought of Tola or Alara, her stomach heaved. She resolutely put out of her mind the gruesome sights of that evening, and the memory of Snorri's taunting voice, but she could not forget the fear that had stabbed at her heart when she had thought Hrolf would kill Erik. The idea of a world in which Erik did not exist was unbearable, and so, instinctively, she had acted to save him. But equally intolerable to her was the thought of caring for the man who had let Edwina die.

Love a Norseman? Not Lenora, daughter of Cedric! Cold pride came to her rescue, telling her the sooner she was parted from Erik, the better for her. No, she would not even weep when he left her. Let him go to Miklagard and his Greek Eirena. She, Lenora, would go to Limfjord as he wanted her to do, and then back to East Anglia, and once she was there, she would think no more of Erik the Far-Traveler. If she were fortunate, she would never have to think of, or see, a blood-thirsty Norseman again as long as she lived.

Among the goods in the warehouse they found woolen fabrics that Holgar had planned to sell. These they tore or cut into warm cloaks to replace the outer garments they had left at Holgar's house and scarves to cover their heads and faces until they were safely gone from Hedeby.

They delayed their departure so Asmund, wrapped in brown wool, could hurry out to buy food for their journey. There was no sign of Snorri.

"He's waiting for something," Erik said. "I'm sure he has a plan. I wonder what it is?"

They left the warehouse late in the day. Through Freydis' quick thinking, they had been able to bring all three of their horses from Holgar's barn.

"Ride double and leave one horse for me,"

Halfdan said. "Go safely, all of you."

Freydis' fingers lingered an extra moment in his big hand. Lenora turned away from them, saddened by the expression in Halfdan's eyes.

Erik kissed Lenora lightly on the cheek before helping her to mount behind Ingvar.

"Be happy, Lenora. I wish you well." That was all he said. Lenora, her feelings locked behind stiff pride, was glad he had not tried to embrace her. He opened the warehouse door and they rode out.

It took only a short time to pick their way through the streets of Hedeby. Soon they were out of the town, following the Danevirke westward until it met the Haervej, the old military road that would take them north to Limfjord. As far as they could tell, they were not followed.

The dusk deepened, throwing long shadows.

"We will travel until it is too dark to see anything," Ingvar said. "We want to get as far away from Hedeby as we can before we stop."

They moved off the path and into the shadow of the Danevirke to let a troop of armed men ride past them toward Hedeby. Asmund and Ingvar were busy with the restive horses and Freydis had her head down, but Lenora, curious as always, stole a glance at the men going by. She pushed back her face-concealing headscarf to see better, then caught her breath and clutched Ingvar's waist more tightly.

There was no mistaking the red-gold hair and proud carriage of the woman who rode at the head of that troop, nor would Lenora ever forget

234

the tall, thin man with unusually pale blond hair riding beside her. There was another, closely muffled female form, but Lenora, more concerned with those she had recognized and relieved that she and her companions had not been noticed, only cast a quick look at this second woman and then dismissed her. She had more important things to think about than other people's slaves.

"Ingvar," Lenora whispered urgently.

"What is it?" Ingvar spoke over his shoulder. "Don't hold me so tightly. I can't breathe."

"Didn't you see them? That was Gunhilde and her father."

"What is Sven the Dark doing here?" Ingvar exclaimed.

"Sven? Going to Hedeby?" Asmund pulled his horse around so they all sat close together.

"With a small army," Ingvar said. "That's why Snorri didn't come after us again. He was waiting for reinforcements."

"I would wager my best brooches that Snorri knows which warehouse we were hiding in," Freydis said bitterly. "With Sven's men to help him, he will attack, hoping to take me captive and kill Erik. And Halfdan."

"I'll ride back to Hedeby and warn Erik." Asmund gathered up the reins. "Get down, Freydis."

"No. Wait." Lenora caught at the reins, pulling Asmund's horse closer. "I have a better idea. Let me go."

"Don't be silly. A woman against those warriors?"

"If he could still speak, Hrolf would tell you I can fight as well as a man." Lenora glared at Asmund, and in the dimming light she saw him grin. "Erik has charged you two with Freydis' safety until she reaches Limfjord. You must stay with her to guard her."

"We are to keep you safe, too, Lenora," Ingvar said.

She ignored him. "Asmund, if you go riding off, you leave three of us with only one horse," Lenora said. "What are we to do then?"

"I hadn't thought of that."

"I know. Now listen to me. I will go back on foot. No one will pay any attention to a woman hurrying home at day's end. You three ride on as fast as you can. I will find Erik and Halfdan and warn them about Sven's warriors. We will see Erik safely aboard ship, and then Halfdan and I will ride after you. We'll catch up with you somewhere along the Haervej."

"What do you think?" Asmund asked his friend.

"It's a better idea than yours," Ingvar told him.

"I think we should all go back," Freydis said. "Then we will be four to help Erik against Snorri."

"Freydis, he wants you out of Snorri's reach." Lenora's voice was hoarse with tension and impatience. "There will be no trouble if I get there in time to warn Erik before Snorri attacks. The longer we sit here and talk, the better chance Snorri has to take Erik. And you know he won't spare Halfdan either."

236

Freydis bowed her head in silent assent. Lenora slid to the ground from her perch behind Ingvar.

"Good luck to you, Lenora."

"And to you, Freydis."

Lenora watched as the horses moved off into the gloom. Then, wrapping the woolen scarf more closely about her face, she set out for Hedeby.

Chapter Seventeen

Lenora passed through Hedeby's north gate by mingling with a group of people with carts who were arriving to trade. They were hurrying to reach the town before nightfall and thus paid no attention to her. Once inside the town she moved cautiously, not wanting to meet Snorri or any of his friends. She made her way to the waterfront and then found Holgar's warehouse.

The door was unbolted. She tiptoed inside. It was so silent in the building that for one terrible moment she thought Erik and Halfdan had already left, or worse, that Snorri had come and gone, leaving them dead.

She took a step, then another, and hesitated. A familiar arm caught her about the waist and a long, supple hand stifled her scream.

"Erik," she whispered against his fingers. "Oh, Erik."

He dragged her into a storeroom at one end of the building, where an oil lamp was burning and he could see her.

"By Thor's hammer," Halfdan exclaimed, "what are you doing here? Where is Freydis?"

"Well away. I came back to warn you." Her news was quickly told.

"What now?" Halfdan asked Erik. "You said you think Snorri will come after us at dawn and we should leave before then. With Sven to help him, he may come sooner. Shall we stay and fight them?"

"We dare not. There will be too many of them. They will kill us and then discover Freydis is gone. Snorri will search until he finds her, and our deaths will be for nothing." Erik thought a moment before continuing. "We have to draw Snorri's attention to us so he doesn't notice that Freydis has slipped away. Then we must make him follow us and keep him occupied long enough for Freydis to get to Limfjord."

"How can we do that?" Halfdan asked.

"By taking my sister and my friend with me as far as Bornholm. Lenora, come here." Erik took a silken cloth from a bundle in a corner of the room. It was a pale, creamy color, almost the shade of Freydis' hair. "Wrap this around your head. Be sure you cover all your own hair. Then put the woolen scarf on top of it. There. Your name is now Freydis."

"Erik, you can't make her do this," Halfdan objected. "She's not your slave any more. She has the right to refuse."

"I forgot." Erik's bright smile flashed, dazzling Lenora. "Will you help us?"

He's enjoying this, Lenora thought. He thinks it's fun to outwit Snorri and the others. She had to admit her own heart was beating faster with excitement.

"I'll help you," she said, "but I'm not as tall as Freydis."

"It doesn't matter. Just keep your hair covered. If anyone catches a glimpse underneath the scarf, he'll see the silk and think it's your hair."

"You hope," Halfdan said doubtfully.

"It will be dark. I'll call her Freydis once or twice in front of others, just before we go aboard ship."

"You will bring Snorri's men down on Rodfos' ship. We will never get away." Halfdan was still uncertain.

"I don't think so. My sister Freydis here and I will slip out and go to the ship. A little while later you will come along, after creating a diversion that will draw most of Hedeby, including Snorri and Sven, to this warehouse. It won't be until much later, when he starts asking questions along the waterfront, that Snorri will learn we have sailed away."

A slow smile spread across Halfdan's face.

"What do you want me to do?" he asked.

"Something simple and spectacular. Holgar has no further need for this warehouse now that he's dead, and he left no heirs."

"A funeral pyre would be suitable. Too bad we haven't got the body."

Lenora shook her head.

"Halfdan, that's not funny," she said.

"Snorri would agree with you. Perhaps he will think our bodies are here." Halfdan's broad shoulders were shaking with laughter. "We should rearrange the merchandise first, don't you think?"

"A good idea," Erik agreed. "Come on, Lenora-Freydis. You have to work too."

They shifted barrels and bales of goods to strategic locations within the warehouse, making certain to spill the contents out against the walls. They sprinkled as much lamp oil as they could find onto these untidy piles.

"It will burn better that way," Erik said.

"We could use some of these things," Lenora remarked.

She had pulled out a long, loose garment made of silk. It was a rich blue-green color that glowed in the light of the single oil lamp they were using to illuminate their work.

Erik glanced at her in annoyance, then smiled as she held the robe against herself, measuring its length.

"That color becomes you," he said. "You are right, we should make other use of some of Holgar's goods. It would look very strange for us to go aboard ship with no belongings at all. We may as well take a few things to trade along the way."

They quickly made up three bundles, using

241

large pieces of woolen cloth to wrap their choices. They took fabrics and jewelry, a few marten skins, a walrus tusk, a couple of knife blades, and a packet of amber.

"You carry this," Erik said, giving Lenora the amber. "If we are separated, or if Halfdan and I are killed, it will buy your passage home."

Lenora added the packet to her bundle. She folded the silk robe and tucked that in too. Erik divided their food into three piles and they each took one. Halfdan found a tent and put it on his pile, folding it as small as possible. He included an iron cooking pot, along with the tripod and chain necessary to support it over a fire.

"That will be too heavy to carry," Erik objected. "You are only going as far as Bornholm, you know."

"We can't go anywhere without a cauldron. It will be useful, and if I don't want to cook in it, I can always sell it."

The night was nearly over before they were ready. Erik and Lenora crept out of the warehouse and made their way to Rodfos' ship by a roundabout route. Rodfos met them at the gangplank, blocking their way.

"No women on my ship," he declared. "Women are bad luck."

"This is my sister Freydis," Erik announced. "We must both go to Aldeigjuborg."

"No women, I said. If you had told me earlier that you wanted to bring her, I would have refused you passage."

"I'll pay you well, Rodfos. It is a family matter.

Freydis must come with me."

"Must? What are you running away from, Freydis?" Rodfos turned his attention to the woman with Erik, inspecting her with an eye fully appreciative of feminine charms.

There was a moment's tense silence before Lenora-Freydis found her voice.

"A man I do not wish to marry."

"Ha. And is this handsome fellow with you truly your brother?"

"Of course." Lenora managed to sound offended.

"He had better be. Where is your father?"

"Our father is dead," Erik answered. "I am taking Freydis to our uncle, a trader who lives in Aldeigjuborg."

"To avoid this man she does not wish to marry?"

"Yes."

"A likely story." Rodfos regarded them suspiciously.

"Please," Lenora begged. "Please let me go too."

"Well," Rodfos hesitated. "For a family matter I might make an exception. But it will cost you double the amount we agreed on. For each of you."

"That's robbery," Erik protested.

"Then save your silver and stay in Hedeby."

"All right. I'll pay you."

"Before you come on board." Rodfos' bulky form still blocked the gangplank.

Erik opened the leather purse at his belt and

243

counted out the silver coins. Rodfos inspected
them carefully before pulling out his portable
scales and weighing the coins. The scales balanced, with two pieces of silver left over. Rodfos
gave a low laugh and tossed the extra coins into
the pan, sending the scales tilting as the coins
overbalanced his weights.

"Fair enough. Come on, then." Rodfos moved
aside to let them onto the ship.

Erik looked annoyed but did not protest the
overpayment.

"Stay in the bow," Rodfos instructed, "and
keep out of my sailors' way. They don't like
women on board either. Now, I have things to
do. We are leaving earlier than we planned."

They made their way to the half-deck at the
bow of the ship, climbing over the cargo piled
amidships.

"Where is Halfdan?" Lenora wondered anxiously.

"Don't worry. He'll be here."

In fact, Rodfos' men had the cargo lashed down
and were ready to sail before Halfdan arrived.
He ran lightly up the gangplank, his huge bundle
and the wooden tent frame slung over one shoulder, a mischievous smile on his face.

"By Odin's beard," Rodfos roared, "what is
this? What kind of tricks are you playing?"

"This is my friend Halfdan," Erik replied
calmly. "He is coming to Aldeigjuborg with us."

"Is he, too, running away from someone he
does not wish to marry?"

"He will help me to protect Freydis."

"He will not. I have no more room on my ship."

"I will pay you," Halfdan said. "And I will work too. I am a good sailor."

"So is every man in Denmark. There is something strange going on here, and I wish I knew what it is. You are all too free with your silver. Well, I suppose I have to take you too. Come aboard, come aboard. It's time to sail. Put out the torches and cast off there."

A few men were loitering about the dock, listening to this discussion with much amusement, calling out advice and joking with Rodfos and his sailors.

Erik winked at Lenora.

"Well, sister Freydis," he said out of the side of his mouth, "if Snorri comes looking for news of us along the waterfront, he will hear that you and Halfdan have sailed with me."

"I wish I knew where Snorri is now," Lenora muttered.

"He's probably wondering if we are being roasted alive," Erik said, pointing over her shoulder. "That should leave him confused for a while. Let's hope he thinks we died in there. If not, he'll come after us, but at least Freydis will be safe. Snorri will be in Aldeigjuborg, or even Kiev, before he realizes she isn't really with me. Look." He pointed again.

Lenora turned to see Holgar's warehouse in flames. Dark figures, silhouetted against the light of the fire, ran toward it, gesturing wildly. A few figures with buckets were dipping water out of the harbor in a vain attempt to quench the fire.

245

Red and orange flames reflected in the rippling water of Hadeby Noor and leapt in tall fingers against the gray dawn sky. The same wind that sent the fire billowing ever higher caught the sail of Rodfos' ship as they glided past the burning building.

"I was beginning to think you hadn't started it well." Erik clapped Halfdan on the shoulder. "I should have known you wouldn't fail."

"I used strips of linen dipped in lamp oil and laid on the earth floor," Halfdan explained. "It took a little while for them to burn back to the fabrics and wood we had piled up, but then everything burst into flames at once. It looks nice, doesn't it?"

He watched the burning building with a satisfied smile as they sailed beyond it and out the fjord toward the sea.

"Did you do that?" Rodfos, coming up behind them, jerked a thumb toward the flaming warehouse.

"How could we? We were all on your ship when it started." Halfdan's handsome face was the picture of innocence.

Rodfos balanced himself lightly on the forward deck of his ship, his giant fists planted firmly on his hips. He looked his three passengers over with an irritated expression.

"I want no trouble from you," he said. "If there is any, all three of you go over the side."

"There will be no trouble," Erik assured him.

"There is a change in plans," Rodfos now informed them. "We are not going to Bornholm after all. I've no cargo to unload there and there are too many pirates in that area. We are going directly to Aldeigjuborg."

"What?" Erik was plainly angry. "You told me you'd put in at Bornholm."

"Well, I've changed my mind. It shouldn't matter to you anyway. You wanted to go to Aldeigjuborg, didn't you? If we don't stop at Bornholm, you will be there that much sooner. With your dear uncle, who lives there."

"You—" Erik began.

"That's wonderful," Lenora interrupted. "I can't wait to see my uncle again. I'll feel so much safer with him."

Rodfos smiled at her, his gruff exterior softening a little.

"What is your uncle's name?" he asked. "I do a lot of trading in Aldeigjuborg. I may know him."

"I don't think so," Erik put in.

"Gorm," Lenora said, using the first name that popped into her mind. "Uncle Gorm. He's a wonderful man."

"Never met him." Rodfos went off to attend to ship's business.

"Afraid of pirates," Erik said scornfully. "He's a pirate himself. The silver he took for our passage would buy a ship of our own. I wanted to send both of you back here from Bornholm and now you will have to go all the way to Aldeigjuborg."

"Hush," Lenora soothed. "He might hear you."

"You can hardly blame him for not trusting

247

us," Halfdan said reasonably. "We did come aboard in a very strange way."

"I suppose so, but I don't trust him, either. Halfdan, you and I will take turns sleeping. One of us will always be awake to watch Rodfos and his men and to guard Lenora—er—Freydis."

Erik squinted at the sky, then glanced back toward Hedeby. The sun had just risen on a clear, beautiful day. The flat landscape of Denmark slid by as the ship made its way down the fjord toward the Baltic Sea. The plume of smoke and fire from Holgar's warehouse dipped lower. Erik drew a deep breath and let it out in a whistle.

"Farewell, Denmark," he said.

"I wonder if we will ever see it again," mused Halfdan.

"You will. I won't."

Nor I, Lenora thought. Edwina's bones lie buried there with Thorkell's, and my babe's remains too. I never want to see that place again. She turned her back on the land and resolutely faced the eastern horizon.

Chapter Eighteen

Rodfos' knarr, the wider, deeper, cargo-carrying version of a Viking longship, was heavily built to withstand the rough northern seas. There were short decks at the bow and stern only, leaving the midship area open for cargo, which was securely lashed down and covered with oiled canvas. There was a square sail of brilliant red and yellow stripes. The ropes holding the sail were made of strips of twisted and waxed walrus hide.

In spite of its heavy load, the ship skimmed easily over the waves with no pitching or rolling, only a gentle rocking motion that Lenora found very relaxing. She slept well at night, knowing either Erik or Halfdan was standing guard.

Her last trip at sea, aboard Snorri's longship, had been a journey of sorrow and dread. This time it was different. Lenora accepted the rigors of shipboard life without complaint. Cold, dried food, a shortage of fresh water with which to wash, the confinement of the knarr's forward deck, bothered her not at all. She was filled with a sense of adventure and of curiosity about what lay ahead.

Early in the trip she had taken the little packet of amber out of her bundle of clothes and goods to be traded, and had hung it on a thong around her neck. It lay against her skin under her gown, along with the purse of silver Thorkell had paid her. When she wrapped her makeshift woolen cloak around her shoulders and pulled it close to her throat against the sea wind, the thongs were hidden.

It's my own private hoard, Lenora thought. I'm a free woman now, not a slave. I can do what I want. Erik can't send me back to Denmark or Anglia if I don't want to go.

What she wanted, she now knew beyond any doubt, was to go to Miklagard with Erik. She had had time during this sea voyage to think about and make her peace with the events at Holgar's house. She realized that the deaths of Tola and Alara had been quick and relatively painless. She said a few silent prayers for those unfortunate women, but she had no regrets for Snorri's men who had perished. They all, but especially Hrolf, had deserved their deaths, and Lenora had no regrets for what she had done. Having thought this far, Lenora let herself remember Snorri's taunting words to Erik, before the fight had begun.

"Erik?"

"Yes?" He was lying beside her, rolled in his woolen cloak. A pace or two away Halfdan sat on the deck, keeping watch. The starry night sky arched above them. Lenora could hear the rustle and slap of water along the ship's hull, the creaking of timbers, the straining of the sail under a stiff breeze, and, out of the dark, the occasional gruff comment of one of Rodfos' sailors.

"Snorri said," Lenora needed all her courage for this, but she had to know, "Snorri said you neglected Erna completely after I arrived at Thorkellshavn. Is that true?"

Erik stirred, turning toward her. His hushed voice sounded close to her ear.

"If you mean," he said, "was Snorri telling the truth that it was Erna who told him where we were going, yes, I believe for once in his life Snorri was being honest. Erna would have betrayed us without hesitation if she thought it would be to her own advantage."

"Was it because she was jealous of me?" Lenora took a deep breath and asked the all-important question again. "Is it true you had nothing to do with Erna, you never lay with her again, once you met me?" She waited tensely until he answered her.

"Yes, it's true."

"But all those months before we—And Erna showed me a bracelet and said you had given it to her."

"I gave her a bracelet half a year before you came to Thorkellshavn." Erik moved restlessly. "Don't talk any more. Let me sleep, Lenora. I must keep watch soon."

He rolled over, turning his back to her, but Lenora did not mind. She could not have spoken again if she had tried. She was near to open tears of joy and relief. Erna had lied, had deliberately and spitefully tried to make Lenora unhappy. Lenora forgot all the decisions she had made out of pride just a few days earlier. Denmark and East Anglia had no claim on her. She would stay with Erik. They would make the journey to Miklagard together. They would be lovers again, and all would be well between them.

She was still thinking about her private plans the next afternoon when Erik approached her.

"Freydis, do you want some?" That, she knew, was for the benefit of the two sailors who were working nearby. Erik handed her the wooden cup of ale from which he had been drinking. Lenora accepted it and sipped at the brew. It tasted sour. She wrinkled her nose. There would be nothing better until they reached Aldeigjuborg.

Erik's eyes scanned her sunburned face and her tangled curls. She had removed the pale silken scarf as soon as they were out of sight of Hedeby, and since then had let her hair blow free. The sun had soon burnished its natural chestnut shade with streaks of gold. Her brows and lashes were by now touched with gold too. He bent toward her.

"How I would like to lie with you," he mur-

252

mured. "I want to feel you against me. I want your arms around me."

Lenora's gray eyes were brimming with laughter and happiness as she looked up at him. He and Halfdan were letting their beards grow, and Erik looked strange and vaguely sinister behind the black hair newly sprouted on his chin and upper lip. Only his green eyes were the same. Seeing the intensity in them and recalling their present circumstances, she giggled, choking on the sour ale, and then sobered.

"You can't do that," she said demurely. "I'm your sister."

"I haven't forgotten," he replied through clenched teeth, but with a spark of humor to answer her own. "It's driving me mad."

"Poor Erik," she teased. "Remember, it was your idea."

He scowled ferociously.

"Just wait until we get to Aldeigjuborg," he said. There was a world of erotic promise in the simple statement.

"You should also remember that I am no longer your slave," she replied sweetly.

"You want me as much as I want you."

He was right, she did want him, more than ever now that she knew the truth about Erna. She missed their nightly lovemaking. The tension between them, unreleased during the journey from Thorkellshavn, was building up and would before long urgently demand relief. She hoped they would reach Aldeigjuborg soon.

* * *

Rodfos was a bold sailor. Where other Norse merchantmen hugged the shoreline of the Baltic Sea, fearing pirates and landing each night to make camp and to sleep, Rodfos sailed directly northeast toward the land of the Finns. He had faith in Thor, who had so far protected him and helped him to prosper, and he reasoned that pirates would lurk close to land, seeking out and pouncing upon those more timid souls who took the safer way. The open reaches of the Baltic were the place for fearless men who knew their gods were with them.

The winds were favorable, and on the tenth day they reached the flat marshland, half hidden in mist and fog, that the Finns called *neva*, or swamp. With a skill resulting from years of travel through this wild and empty land, Rodfos navigated his knarr up the broad, swift-flowing Neva River to Lake Ladoga. There, not on the lake itself but on a river that emptied into it at the southern shore, secure behind an earth rampart and a deep ravine, lay the trading center the Norse had named Aldeigjuborg.

Goods from the northlands and from the west of Europe were unloaded at Aldeigjuborg and exchanged for merchandise brought north along the river system from Holmgard and Kiev. Some of this merchandise had originally come from Constantinople, which the Norse called Miklagard, or from the Caspian Sea and Bagdhad, far to the east.

Almost always, merchandise traveling along these routes went through the hands of a series

of traders, each plying his own territory overland
or his own section of a river. As the goods passed
from merchant to merchant at trading posts
along the way, always with a profit for the han-
dlers, the costs rose and rose again. It was possible to make a fortune working along the trade
routes or, if one's luck were bad, to lose everything including life, for these routes attracted
thieves and roaming nomadic tribesmen in addition to the natural perils of flood and storm that
were stoically accepted as routine hazards.

Rodfos traded regularly in Aldeigjuborg. He
liked the place. It was exciting. Beyond the open
market at the river's edge and the square log
houses in which the more settled traders lived
were the gaily colored tents and camp fires of the
men and their women who were passing through
the town on their way to almost anywhere in the
known world. In Aldeigjuborg there was always
something new to see, someone interesting to
meet.

Rodfos stood on the deck of his knarr and
watched the bustle on the waterfront. He was a
happy man. It had been a good voyage. Once
more he had evaded the pirates who haunted the
northern sea, and he had made a nice pile of
unexpected silver from his unwelcome passengers, who had proven to be much less trouble
than he had feared. He turned as the passengers
approached him. He thought the men were nothing remarkable, but the woman was a real
beauty. She reminded him of a girl he had known
once, long ago, who had been forced to marry

someone else and then had died in childbirth.
Rodfos sighed, remembering.

"Good-bye," Lenora-Freydis said, holding out
her hand. "Thank you for helping us, Rodfos."

"I hope you find your uncle in good health."
Rodfos held her hand, gazing into dark gray eyes
and recalling his lost youth.

"Yes. Uncle Gorm. I'm sure we will." She
smiled and gently withdrew her hand from his.

Rodfos' eyes followed the woman's slender figure until she and her companions disappeared
behind a crowd of men bidding for Saxon slaves.

They pitched the tent Halfdan had brought
with him and set up the tripod and chain to hold
the cauldron over their cooking fire.

"We fit right in," Halfdan observed. "No one
would know us from any other traders."

"Snorri can't have followed us so quickly, can
he?" Lenora looked about nervously, as though
she expected to see Snorri's bearded face mater-
ialize at any moment.

"I hope it is a long time before he gets this far,"
Erik said. "It will take us a while to find a ship
going back to Denmark and buy your passage on
it. Then I can head for Holmgard and Kiev."

"I am not going back to Denmark," Lenora said
flatly.

"Neither am I," Halfdan added.

"I've told you before, Lenora, you can't go to
Miklagard with me. You have no idea how hard
the trip is, or how dangerous." Erik was plainly
irritated at this rebellion against his carefully

laid plans. "I never intended that you should come this far with me. Were it not for Rodfos, you would be on your way westward this very day, sailing from Bornholm. You will do as I say, Lenora, and return to Denmark. Halfdan, you must guard Lenora and see that she gets safely to Limfjord."

"I don't want to be safe, I want to go to Miklagard," Lenora declared. "I'm not your slave any more. You can't tell me what to do." Lenora was hurt, and her pain sounded in her voice. She had thought all was well between herself and Erik, and now here he was, trying to get rid of her. She began to be angry. Even Halfdan's support did nothing to calm her rising temper.

"We won't leave you, Erik," Halfdan said. "You are going to have company on your trip, and that is that."

Erik ignored his friend to glare at Lenora. She looked back at him in open defiance.

"I don't want you," Erik said slowly and clearly. "It is too dangerous for you. Go home. That is what we planned."

"It is what *you* planned, so you will be free of me when you meet your precious Eirena again, isn't that it?" In her relief about Erna, Lenora had forgotten that cursed Greek woman Erik had told her about, but now she remembered. If Erik didn't want her with him, it must be because of Eirena.

"I don't want to worry about you any more. I want to know you are safe in Denmark." Erik stalked off toward the waterfront.

"We're almost out of food," Halfdan said. "We had better see if we can trade some of this woolen cloth for a piece of meat and a few vegetables."

"I hate him," Lenora ground out, her frustration and rage spilling over.

"I know. So do I. That's why we both want to follow him to the ends of the earth." Halfdan's boyish smile calmed her more effectively than anything he could have said. Halfdan understood.

When Erik returned later, Lenora had a tasty stew simmering in Halfdan's cauldron. He ate silently and then wrapped himself in the piece of wool from Holgar's warehouse that served him as both cloak and blanket and fell asleep.

Wrapped in her own tattered cloak, Lenora lay between Erik and the gently snoring Halfdan. So this was their first night ashore, for which, during the sea voyage, she had so yearned. She had hoped to spend it in Erik's arms. She ached for his touch. His proximity, within the close confines of their tent, only increased her discomfort. The sky was light and the busy town was stirring into life before she finally slept.

Their argument went on for days, with only slight variations. Erik continued to search for a ship sailing to Denmark. Both Halfdan and Lenora repeatedly insisted they would not leave him. Stubbornly determined that they must go, he paid no attention to their protests.

Erik also tried to find a party of traders traveling to Holmgard and on to Kiev, but in this quest, too, he was unsuccessful. The traders who had come to Aldeigjuborg were there to stay until their goods were sold and new cargo bought. Most were waiting for the ice to break up on the rivers that were the roads to the interior of Gardariki. This year the spring thaw was late. Until the ice was gone and the floods had subsided enough to make travel safe, the traders were forced to remain where they were.

Erik grew more and more irritable and restless, and Lenora responded in kind. With Halfdan sharing their tiny tent, the intimacy that might have resolved their quarrel was impossible. Their tempers grew ever shorter with each other.

"It's your Greek woman, your precious Eirena," Lenora stormed at him for the hundredth time, humiliated by the realization that although she cared for him deeply and wanted him badly, Erik apparently no longer wanted her.

"I am weary of you, Lenora. I grow more tired every day of your sharp tongue and your stubbornness. I want to be free."

"Then go, and I will stay here," she retorted.

"You wouldn't last long. These traders are rough men, and they know a nice piece of merchandise when they see one. You have been safe so far only because Halfdan and I are here to protect you."

"How I despise you," she cried, stung by an argument she knew was true.

He laughed at her insults and refused to argue further.

One midday, when their supply of food was nearly used up and Erik and Halfdan had gone

259

off to talk to a trader from Kiev, Lenora set out by herself for the market. She was fascinated by the variety of goods to be had there, and stopped several times to look at silks and furs and gold jewelry, but she avoided the area where slaves were sold. She did not want to be reminded of her recent past.

She had just begun to bargain for some turnips and a particularly fine cabbage when she looked toward the edge of the market area and a man caught her eye. Her heart skipped several beats.

It was Sven the Dark. No one else could be so very tall and thin, or have such thick, pale blond hair. He turned his head and she was certain. Where Sven was, his son-in-law Snorri could not be far behind.

She had to hide before he saw her. Lenora looked around the crowded waterfront in frantic haste, searching for a safe place. There was none.

She left the baffled vegetable seller and hurried in the opposite direction from Sven. She dared not glance over her shoulder for fear he would see her face and recognize her. She noticed with surprise that Rodfos' knarr was only a short distance away. She had thought he had sailed back to Hedeby, but there sat the knarr, looking to Lenora like a place of refuge. Rodfos himself stood on the dock next to his ship, talking to another man. As Lenora watched, the man walked away, leaving Rodfos alone. She hurried forward.

"Freydis, what are you doing here?" Rodfos' deep voice boomed out. Lenora was certain Sven must have heard him on the opposite side of the market.

"I need your help," Lenora said, putting one hand on his muscular arm. "I'm in danger."

"Are you? Someone here?" Rodfos looked about the waterfront. "Where is he?"

"It's the man who wants to marry me," Lenora lied. "He has followed my brother Erik and me from Denmark. I just saw him. Will you hide me? It's only for a little while, just until he goes away."

"I'm glad you came to me." Rodfos hurried her up the gangplank onto his ship. "You will be safe here. I'm the only one on board. All my men have gone ashore. Come under the rear deck."

Rodfos led her to a part of the ship where she had never set foot. She had spent most of the trip from Denmark confined to the ship's forward deck.

"These are my quarters," Rodfos said, pulling aside a red woolen curtain that hid a cozy alcove. "No one will look for you here."

The space held only a carved wooden chest and a bed made of piled-up furs on a wooden shelf. Rodfos went out and Lenora sank down on the bed. She was still trembling with the shock of seeing Sven. As soon as it was safe, as soon as Sven had left the marketplace, she must find Erik and Halfdan and warn them. She hoped Sven would not find them first.

Rodfos returned with a large pitcher and a beautiful silver cup filled with mead. He handed it to her and she drank. He sat beside her on the fur-piled bed.

"Now tell me the truth," he said.

"I have told you the truth," Lenora lied between sips of mead. "Sven wants to marry me, but I do not want him. Our father died, and now my brother Erik must protect me from Sven."

"What about your Uncle Gorm, the merchant who lives here in Aldeigjuborg? Can't he make this Sven stay away from you?"

Lenora met his eyes unwillingly. She tried to look honest, but she wasn't sure she was succeeding. The mead, taken on an empty stomach, was confusing her.

"We have no Uncle Gorm," she said, tossing him a small bone of truth. "That was a story we made up. We were afraid you would refuse to take us aboard your ship, and Sven was after us."

"I thought as much. And this Halfdan fellow, is he your lover?"

"Oh, no." This time Lenora could meet Rodfos' gaze with perfect sincerity. "Halfdan wants someone else. A woman back in Denmark."

"I see. Drink some more mead, Freydis. You are still trembling. Are you really so afraid of this Sven?"

"He is a terrible man," Lenora said with great seriousness. "He beats women."

"You think he would beat you?" Rodfos was sympathetic.

"Probably." Lenora knew Sven would do worse than beat her if he ever caught her. She trembled again at the thought.

"I won't let him hurt you." Rodfos' big hand rested on her shoulder. He was staring at her in an odd way, as though he saw someone other than Lenora-Freydis sitting in her place. "You don't look very much like her, but you are alike. It's the way you hold your head, and your voice."

"Who?"

"Someone I knew once, long ago, when I was too young and foolish to fight for what I wanted. She had to marry someone she feared. She's dead now. I won't let that happen to you, not if I can help you."

Lenora was suddenly ashamed of the lies she had told him. Inside this big, gruff half-pirate there was tenderness and a kind heart. Impulsively, she threw her arms around his neck, nearly spilling the cup of mead she was still holding.

"You are a good man, Rodfos."

"It's been years since anyone called me that. Here, now, take your arms away or I'll forget you are young enough to be my daughter. Not that that has ever stopped me before. Still, you are so much like *her*, I'd not harm you. You should save yourself for some lucky fellow your own age. Youth with youth." Rodfos disengaged himself and stepped to the other side of the tiny cabin, keeping his back to Lenora. "I know I'll regret this tomorrow, when I remember how sweet you felt, cuddled against me like that. Now. Let us talk seriously about this Sven."

"I hope he has gone from the market. I have to find Erik and warn him."

"If Sven has come such a long distance search-ing for you," Rodfos said, "you may be certain he's not alone. He may be hoping to kill your brother and his friend and take you away with him and marry you by force. Freydis, I will try to help you, but you must be honest with me. What are your brother's plans?"

"Erik wants to go to Kiev," Lenora said, care-fully not adding that Erik did not want her to go with him, "but he can't find anyone who is trav-eling there in the next few days, and he says it is too dangerous to travel alone."

"He's right about that. Yes, if you get out of Aldeigjuborg and away to the south, Sven might lose your trail. I'll see what I can arrange for you. I know a few people here in Aldeigjuborg. This is what you must do. Find your brother and his friend and stay at your tent until I come to you. Just be sure Sven doesn't see you."

"I will. But, Rodfos, you don't know where we've camped."

"Yes, I do. I've been keeping my eye on you, Freydis. I'll find you. Now, run along. I have to locate an old acquaintance of mine."

That evening Rodfos brought a man to their tent. Lenora had told Erik and Halfdan about seeing Sven.

"Now that Sven is here," Halfdan had told Erik, "and surely Snorri with him, we can't waste any more time looking for a ship to Denmark for Lenora and me. We must all leave for Kiev as soon as possible."

Erik had said nothing to this, but he looked worried. Lenora, hopeful in spite of her terror of both Sven and Snorri, had had sense enough not to press Erik, but instead silently occupied herself with preparing and then cleaning up their dinner.

"This is Torgard," Rodfos told them, striding boldly into their camp. "He is taking two boatloads of goods to Holmgard and then to Kiev. I think you can arrange something agreeable to everyone."

Torgard was a nondescript man, of medium height and medium build with lackluster brown hair, but his pale blue eyes were bright with intelligence, and as they all learned later, with cupidity. He made his living transporting goods from Kiev to Holmgard to Aldeigjuborg and back again.

"The ice has melted at last. The river is still flooding, but I am leaving tomorrow," Torgard said. "I'll get my goods to Kiev before anyone else. Three of my men were killed in a brawl yesterday. I will hire you to take their places if you are willing to do hard work, but I don't want to take the woman with me."

"She's strong and healthy," Rodfos said helpfully. "She could cook for you."

"I do my own cooking. A woman will only make trouble."

"No, I won't. I'll keep to myself and I won't slow you down. I promise."

"She is a good traveler, Torgard," Rodfos put in. "I had no problem when she was on my ship."

265

"Well," Torgard looked annoyed at this insistence, "I do need more men, and there are few for hire in Aldeigjuborg. All right, but I want you to know I'm not happy about this." Then, dismissing Lenora with a shrug, Torgard promptly began discussing the trip to Kiev with Erik and Halfdan.

"Thank you," Lenora said to Rodfos, one hand on his arm.

"Good luck, Freydis. We won't meet again." Rodfos' huge hand covered hers for just a moment.

When their business was finally concluded, the men separated, Torgard and Rodfos going off together. Lenora watched them until they were out of sight.

"You will have your way after all, Lenora. You and Halfdan will have to go with me." Erik was frowning at her. "What did you tell Rodfos that made him bring that man to us?"

"I told him Sven had followed us from Denmark, that if he married me, he would beat me all the time. I made no changes in the story we first told him, except to let him believe Sven is the one who wants me."

Lenora was still angry with Erik. She decided not to tell him what she had learned about Rodfos that day, or why he had helped them. Instead, she wiped out the cooking cauldron and began to pack their supply of food for the journey south.

Chapter Nineteen

The journey from Aldeigjuborg to Kiev forever
after lay in Lenora's memory as a confused jum-
ble of painful impressions.

The trip had not begun too badly, as they sailed
and rowed south on one river to the lake where
Holmgard lay, then, a day later, moved southward again on another river. Lenora felt op-
pressed by the thick, dark forests surrounding
them, and lonely in the vast, unpeopled land, but
she could bear that so long as they were heading
toward Miklagard. Neither she nor her two companions made any protest about the pace Torgard set. The faster they moved, the farther away
from Snorri and Sven they would be.

Once on their way they had quickly dropped
the fiction that Lenora was Erik's sister. She was
relieved to have her own name back again.

The trouble began with their first portage. They paused while the men felled trees, using the trimmed trunks as rollers upon which they dragged Torgard's two boats for miles across land to the next river. The path through the forest had been cleared by others who had traveled that way before them, and they even found a few tree trunks left ready for their use, but it was slow, hard work, made worse by swarms of mosquitoes and the sudden advent of humid heat. Erik and Halfdan willingly joined the other men in their labors, while Lenora did menial jobs, cooked for the men, and nursed their inevitable injuries.

The problem was Torgard. He wanted to travel even faster than they had been doing. He explained to them that because of dangerous rapids in the river south of Kiev, the trip to the Euxine Sea and Miklagard could be made only in early summer.

"After the ice has broken the spring floods begin," Torgard said. "At that time the river is too dangerous for travel, but as the waters recede, the traders of Kiev assemble their loaded boats at Vitaholm, just downriver from Kiev, and then, when the water level has dropped to a certain point, they sail south together. They always travel in large groups for safety from the Khazars, who live on the steppe south of Kiev, and who will attack anyone on the river. The rapid flow of the water makes travel faster and carries the boats over many of the rocks and shallow spots. It is still a difficult journey, with portages around cataracts and rapids, but it is easier at midsummer than at any other time of year. For the man who successfully takes his merchandise to the sea, the rewards are great."

Torgard was determined to reach Kiev in time to sail with the merchant fleet that summer.

"Otherwise I must wait until next year," he said. "I have never been to Miklagard before. I have always sold my goods in Kiev, to others who carried them south and reaped the profit. This year I will go myself. I expect to return a rich man. For that to happen, we must reach Kiev before the fleet sails. Unfortunately, we are already late because the ice on the northern rivers did not melt soon enough and I was delayed in Aldeigjuborg."

He drove them mercilessly. He scarcely gave them time to sleep or eat. The tired men grew surly and accidents multiplied.

Only Lenora never grumbled. She knew none of the men was happy at her presence, and she was afraid if she did complain they would simply leave her behind.

The first portage successfully accomplished, they enjoyed the brief respite provided by river travel before transferring to land once more. The second portage took ten days and was much more difficult than the first. One man lost a leg in an accident and soon died of infection.

Erik, as tired as everyone else and convinced they were far enough away from Snorri to feel safe at last, quarreled with Torgard, insisting they stop for a few days.

"The men will work better if they are rested,"

Erik argued. "Let them sleep a bit and then hunt for a day. Fresh meat will make us all stronger. You won't make any profit if we are too weak to take your boats to Kiev."

Torgard gave them one day.

The damp wilderness on either side of the river teamed with animal life. The hunting party returned with ducks, squirrels, and a small deer. They ate well that night, and Torgard grudgingly provided a barrel of mead from his stores.

After the meal, Erik took Lenora's hand and pulled her into the trees. They lay on a bed of pine needles that was only slightly damp, and he took her into his arms.

"Aren't you glad I came with you, instead of going back to Denmark?" she teased, holding him close, enjoying the feeling of his strong masculine frame against her own softer body. At his touch, the yearning had begun somewhere deep inside her. She forgot their recent quarrels in anticipation of the pleasure they would give each other. It had been so long since they had lain like this, back at Thorkellshavn. Her lips parted in expectation as she moved against him eagerly, wanting him.

"No," he whispered into her hair, one hand reaching down to raise her skirt, "no, I am not glad you are here. You should be safe at Limfjord by now. Then I wouldn't have to worry about you."

Lenora struck at him so suddenly that he let her go in surprise. She rolled out of his arms and away from him and knelt on the ground. She felt as though he had thrown her into the cold river.

"If you don't want me here," her throat was tight as she forced the words out, "then don't try to make love to me. I am no longer yours to use as you once did, without my consent. In case you have forgotten, you freed me, before witnesses."

"I haven't forgotten. But I want you, and I know you want me. Come here."

"No." She got to her feet, nimbly sidestepping his reach when he would have pulled her down beside him again. In a state of angry confusion, she started back toward the campfire. She did not understand her own feelings. She wanted Erik, had wanted him badly for weeks, but she could not lie with him that night. He wanted a woman, but any woman would do. Lenora wanted Erik to want her, and her alone.

She wrapped her frayed woolen cloak around herself and lay down by the fire. She saw Erik return, fill a cup with ale, and drain it at a gulp. His expression was stormy behind his thickly grown beard.

I don't care how angry he is, she thought. I'm not his slave any more.

Torgard roused them at first light. The heavy, seemingly endless labor began again. Slowly, painfully, the boats were dragged on the tree trunk rollers, a few feet at a time, over the swampy ground between the two rivers.

"There," Torgard cried late one afternoon, pointing to a wide band of silver just visible between the trees. "The Dneiper River at last."

The next morning they launched the boats and headed downriver to Kiev. Torgard urged them on, resenting each night's darkness when they were forced to draw the boats to the side of the river to wait for daylight, waking them again before dawn so they could set off as soon as it was light enough to see.

They were all reeling with exhaustion by the time they arrived at Kiev. When Torgard learned the yearly flotilla of boats bound for Miklagard had already left, there was no controlling him.

"You delayed us," he raged at Erik. "If you hadn't made us stop and rest, we would have been here in time. I did you a kindness, letting you travel under my protection, and now you have ruined me. You'll pay for this."

Erik laughed and walked away from the angry man.

"What shall we do now?" Halfdan asked. "We can't stay in Kiev for an entire year, waiting for Snorri and Sven to find us."

"We won't have to." Erik was undaunted. "Despite what Torgard says, there are traders who leave later in the season. We will just have to find one and offer him our services. The trip is more difficult because the river is lower, and more dangerous because the Khazars are more likely to attack small parties of travelers, but it can be done."

Once more they pitched Halfdan's little tent on the outskirts of a trading town. Erik set out to find someone, anyone, who was going to Miklagard and could use two strong fighting men as guards.

Lenora was amazed by the change in Erik. The farther they traveled from Thorkellshavn, the more confident and self-assured he became. He stood taller and straighter, and even his limp became less noticeable. He moved easily among the mixed population of Kiev, speaking the Danish tongue, or Greek, or even Latin when necessary. His brilliant smile flashed often as he talked with strangers.

He had made no further attempt to possess her. He treated her with casual indifference. She told herself she did not care.

The Rus, most of whom came from Sweden, had built Kiev on the western bank of the river, on a bluff safely above the high waters of the spring floods, and well-fortified against attack. Below the town, sandy beaches fringed the islands that lay in mid-river, and the dark green forest grew almost down to the water's edge. Sturdy log houses with oak fences around them attested to the prosperity of the Northmen who had settled this wild land.

When Erik had sailed to Miklagard seven years earlier, it had been in the force assembled by Askold and Dir, the joint rulers of Kiev. His bravery and shrewd intelligence had brought the young Dane to Askold's attention during the expedition. Erik had visited Askold on his way back to Denmark three years after the disastrous storm that had shattered his leg and ruined Askold's hopes of conquering the Great City. Erik's friendship with Basil Panopoulos had helped Askold in his secondary goal of establishing regular trade with the Greeks. Now, leaving Lenora to attend to their campsite, Erik and Halfdan went to call upon Askold, hoping he could direct them to a merchant traveling south.

With the tent set up and some of the goods from their rapidly shrinking bundles bartered for food, Lenora tried to repair the ravages of the difficult journey from Aldeigjuborg. She washed her face and hands and combed her hair. She really wanted a bath, having grown used to that luxury while at Thorkellshavn, but Erik had warned her not to go away from the tent unless he or Halfdan accompanied her. Kiev was a dangerous place for a young woman alone.

The linen shift and woolen overgarment she had worn since leaving Denmark were filthy and tattered. Lenora pulled from her scanty pile of belongings the blue-green silk caftan she had found in Holgar's warehouse just before leaving Hedeby. It was badly wrinkled and had a water spot on one sleeve, but she put it on. In the damp, early-summer heat, the light fabric was like a caress against her skin.

"That's very pretty, Lenora."

She whirled to see Torgard watching her. She wondered how long he had been standing there, just outside the tent.

"Are you all alone?" he asked.

"Erik will be back soon. Did you want to speak with him?"

"Yes, but it can wait. You should have a gold

necklace to go with your new dress." Torgard's eyes held hers, making her uncomfortable. "I have one among my wares. Would you like to come and see it?"

"I can't go with you. Erik told me to stay by the tent."

"Do you always do what he says? He treats you like a slave."

This was so close to Lenora's own sentiment about Erik's present attitude toward her that she forgot her dislike of Torgard for a moment and smiled at her visitor.

"I am no man's slave," she said.

"Then you are free to come with me. You could at least look at the necklace."

"I really shouldn't."

"It isn't far from here. You will be back before Erik returns from Askold's hall. He will never know you disobeyed him. I can show you the marketplace as we go. Would you like to see the silks that come from far to the east? Some of them are even more beautiful than the robe you are wearing."

"Well . . ." Lenora hesitated.

"Are you frightened? I will protect you. After you have seen the necklace, I will bring you safely back here, and then I'll talk to Erik. I may have found some traders who will let you travel with them to Miklagard."

"That's wonderful." Torgard seemed to have forgotten his anger against Erik, and after what he had just said, Lenora did not want to remind him of it. Perhaps he wasn't as unpleasant a person as she had thought. "I can only be away for a little while. I'm supposed to watch over our belongings."

"I understand, Lenora." Torgard took her arm and guided her toward the bustle of the marketplace. Lenora soon forgot her initial reluctance to go with him and became absorbed by the sights and sounds around her. Kiev was larger than Aldeigjuborg or Hedeby, its market filled with goods more exotic and bountiful than Lenora had ever seen before. She paid little attention to the direction in which Torgard was leading her until he paused to open the door of a square log house.

"Where are we?"

"This is my home. Come inside, Lenora. I'll show you the necklace, then I'll take you back to your tent."

Lenora stepped through the door. Torgard followed, bolting the door securely behind himself. Lenora began to feel uneasy.

"I think I should leave," she said.

"You will remain here."

Lenora suddenly recalled something Torgard had said earlier. "How did you know Erik had gone to see Askold?"

"My servant has been watching you. I know everything you three have done since we all arrived here in Kiev."

"Why? What do you want?" Her uneasiness was increasing rapidly.

"Erik has nearly ruined me, delaying us on the

trip downriver until the flotilla had left. I lost huge profits because of him."

"That is ridiculous. The traders' boats had left for Miklagard days before we got to Kiev. You could never have been here in time."

Torgard laughed. It was not a pleasant sound. "What Erik cost me, I will begin to make up on you."

Lenora had gone beyond uneasiness. She was now very afraid of the harmless-looking man before her.

"What are you going to do with me?"

"Sell you. I will gain some silver from the transaction. Erik and Halfdan will delay their departure from Kiev to search for you. The delay will allow your pursuers to catch up with them." Seeing the look on Lenora's face, Torgard laughed again. "Rodfos told me you were running away from someone who had followed you across the Baltic Sea. He paid me to take you to safety. He did not know who your pursuers were, but I reason that anyone who wants you and your friends badly enough to travel such a long distance will be willing to pay for information on your whereabouts. I will know where Erik and Halfdan are, so I will make a lot of silver from that. Then, if your pursuers want you, too, I'll sell them that information also, and let them fight your owner for you. In fact, I might even warn him your pursuers are after him, and make a little more money as a reward for my kindness to him."

"Who are you going to sell me to?" Lenora

could only hope that whoever Torgard was dealing with would be a decent person who would accept her explanation that she had been abducted and let her go.

"He will be here shortly," Torgard said. "In the meantime, we may as well enjoy ourselves."

Torgard grabbed Lenora by the wrist and dragged her toward a bed platform that was covered with dirty, matted furs. She fought him every step of the way. She was overcome with disgust and loathing of Torgard, and with anger at herself for leaving the safety of Halfdan's tent with the man. It did not occur to her until much later that Torgard would have gotten her away from the tent by any means, however violent, so he could carry out his plan.

Torgard threw her roughly onto the furs and then flung himself on top of her. Lenora continued to fight him. If she could just get away from him, get out of his house, find her way back to the tent and find Erik, then all would be well.

Torgard's hands were all over her, pinching and bruising and probing. He ripped the silk robe off one shoulder. At last she lay still, watching him through slitted eyes. He ignored her reactions, intent on satisfying his own lust before Lenora's purchaser arrived. When he loosened his hold on her to pull down his breeches, Lenora wriggled aside, and then, just as he uncovered himself, she jabbed him in the groin with her knee. He screamed in pain.

Lenora scrambled off the bed and ran to the door. She fumbled with the bolt, then slid it open.

She plunged through the doorway, falling into the arms of a blond giant who had lifted one fist to knock on the door. He caught her around the waist, lifting her off her feet and slinging her carelessly over his shoulder, then carried her back into Torgard's house. There, still holding the kicking, fighting Lenora, the newcomer burst into laughter.

"What's this, Torgard? Are you sampling my merchandise before I have a chance to try her?"

Torgard, his breeches down around his knees, was sitting on the edge of the bed platform, still doubled over, clutching himself and moaning.

"She's a fighter, is she?" The blond stranger laughed even harder. "Too strong for you, I see, but I'll soon tame her."

With his free hand he pulled a leather purse from his belt and tossed it at Torgard, who snatched it up and began to count the silver coins it contained.

"You're not as badly hurt as you thought you were," the blond man observed. "Or is it that silver cures all ills? It's all there, Torgard. Weigh it and see. Now I'll be on my way."

"You can't buy me," Lenora cried. She was still dangling across his shoulder, and she kept on pounding at his back with both fists. "I'm not a slave, I'm a free woman. Torgard abducted me."

The blond man put her down at last.

"Is this true, Torgard?"

"Of course not. She lies all the time. That's why her master wanted to sell her." Torgard limped to Lenora's side, holding his breeches up with

279

one hand. He regarded her with an expression of pure hatred. "Just don't believe anything the wench says."

The blond man looked Lenora over from head to toe, considering her.

"Well," he said softly, "whatever you were before, you are a slave now."

He put out one hand to take her arm. The hand was covered with fine golden hairs and it looked strong enough to crush her with no effort at all. Lenora stepped back, out of his reach.

"I won't go with you," she declared. "I'm going back to Erik."

She headed for the open door. Torgard caught her shoulder and spun her around. His fist connected with her jaw. The last thing she heard was his exultant laugh.

"Where is she?" Erik's sharp eyes scanned the area around their tent. "I told her to stay here."

"Lenora wouldn't wander off," Halfdan said. "She understood your warning, and she has too much good sense to defy you about something so important."

"Has she? I hope so. She has been remarkably difficult since we left Denmark."

"She wants to be with you," Halfdan said. "She loves you."

Erik stared at him in amazement, and Halfdan saw a flicker of something in his friend's eyes. Ordinarily, he would have teased Erik about his feelings for Lenora, so clearly revealed by that look, but the situation was too serious for joking.

Halfdan could think of several explanations for Lenora's absence and none of them was pleasant.

"At least," Halfdan said, "we can be sure Snorri or Sven had nothing to do with this. Neither of them could possibly be in Kiev so soon. Why don't you search the tent, and I'll look around out here."

Erik ducked into the tent and came out holding Lenora's cast-off woolen dress and dirty linen shift.

"Here, see this. Where could she go without clothes on? Halfdan, *what has happened to her*?"

"Your concern has clouded your reason," Halfdan reproved gently. He knew if it were Freydis who was missing, he would be as upset as Erik was. Halfdan was fond of Lenora, but he could see things more clearly than his friend. He took the garments from Erik's hands and held them up for inspection. "They're not torn or bloody, Erik. That means she took them off herself. Didn't she have another dress, a blue silk thing? She'll be wearing that. We will look for a girl in a blue silk dress. We had better start asking questions right at the next tent."

"When I think," Erik said, "of what might happen to a young and beautiful woman in Kiev— Halfdan, *we have to find her*."

Chapter Twenty

She was being smothered. She was wrapped in a shroud and she could not get out. She struggled, moaning at the pain in her jaw and clawing at the choking fabric. She heard a laugh coming from a great distance.

"Awake, are you?" said a vaguely familiar voice. "Hold still."

She was released from the shroud and saw it was only a blue wool cape. She gasped for air. She looked up to see the blond giant watching her. They were standing in a courtyard enclosed by a tall wooden fence. At one end of the court-yard was a large log house, with several wooden buildings to one side. She took another deep breath as the blond man steadied her.

"That's better. I thought you were dead. I was

going to get my silver back from Torgard. Who needs a dead slave?"

"I'm no slave. Let me go, please. I must find my friends."

"No more lies." He touched her jaw. His hand was surprisingly gentle; but still she winced. "That will soon heal. Tell me your name."

"Lenora. I am *not* a slave," she insisted.

"I'm Attair. If you behave, I'll treat you kindly. If you try to escape, I'll kill you, slowly and painfully. Do you understand?"

"I'm not a slave."

Attair caught the hair at the back of her head and pulled her face close to his. He had smooth, lightly tanned skin with a golden tinge to it. His eyes were golden-brown, like two pieces of sea amber. They slanted up at the sides above his high cheekbones. He had a full, sensuous mouth.

"You are a slave. Mine. I bought you." The amber eyes softened. "I may have gotten a better bargain than I originally thought. You will be beautiful once you are clean and dressed. This will be an interesting night."

When Lenora opened her mouth to protest, Attair stopped her.

"One more word and I will order your tongue cut out. That is what I did to these women, and I will do it to you." He beckoned to two women who stood by the door of the log house. "Bathe and prepare her, then bring her to me," he ordered.

The women bowed their heads silently, and

Attair strode off toward the gate, where a group of armed men was admiring a horse.

The women indicated by gestures that Lenora should follow them. They conducted her to one of the outbuildings, a bathhouse. They stripped her of her clothes. She began to object, but then realized Attair had spoken the truth. The women could not speak. It seemed to Lenora they were trying to convey to her that she should be silent and do as Attair had commanded or she would suffer the same fate.

When they took her clothes away, she did insist, albeit silently, by gestures, on keeping the two bags that had hung around her neck, one with the silver coins Erik had given her, the other containing the amber they had found in Holgar's warehouse in Hedeby.

The women scrubbed her and made her sit in a room with hot stones onto which they threw cold water. The room filled with steam, choking her. Then they washed her again, scrubbing her hair, too, this time, and rinsed her with cold water.

They massaged scented oils into her skin with firm, rhythmic motions. Next they rubbed her body with linen cloths until her skin flushed rosy-pink. They trimmed and cleaned her nails and polished them with a piece of silk to make them shine. One of the women opened a vial of silver-black powder. Into this she dipped a pointed stick and used the stick to outline Lenora's eyes. The other woman rubbed a reddish-brown powder onto Lenora's cheeks and lips.

If she had not been so frightened, she would have enjoyed these ministrations, but fear lay like a cold stone at her heart. Where was Erik? Would he, as Torgard believed, search for her, delaying his departure from Kiev until Sven and Snorri found him? Or would he shrug his shoulders in that gesture so characteristic of him, and go on to Miklagard and forget her? She thought that was possible, considering their recent quarrels. She did not believe he cared about her at all.

Finally, when her naked body had been cleansed and oiled and scented and painted to the satisfaction of the two serving women, they dressed her. They brought her a gown of heavy, pale green silk. There were patterns woven into the fabric, branches of flowers and little birds and strange round symbols that seemed to be some kind of writing. The wide sleeves were lined with sheer, peach-colored silk. The gown wrapped across the front, and was held with a jeweled gold sash.

The women combed her hair, letting it ripple down her back in thick chestnut curls that glowed against the pale green of the gown. They put soft, silk-lined slippers on her feet.

Lastly, they gave her a cup of hot liquid brewed with herbs. It tasted bitter. She would have refused, but they made it clear she must drink it. She obeyed.

They led her to Attair's house, into his private chamber, and left her there alone. Lenora had never seen such richness. Thick carpets covered the floor and the extra-wide bed platform along one side of the room. More carpets were hung on the walls. Where there were no carpets, there were panels of silk draped in brilliant, shimmering colors.

Everywhere Lenora looked there was pattern and color. The rugs were red and blue and gold and turquoise, woven in designs of flowers, leaves, vines, and geometric patterns.

On top of the rugs covering the bed platform were thrown thick furs and silk-covered pillows in violet, gold, or azure blue, with silk tassels on the corners. Before the bed stood a low, ornately carved wooden table, topped with a huge gold tray that was piled with dishes of food. The oil lamps hanging on long chains from the high rafters were of pierced brass or colored glass.

The air smelled of incense and of another, oddly sweet scent Lenora did not recognize. It made her dizzy.

She heard a sound behind her and turned. Attair had entered the room. He closed the door and drew across it a panel of green and gold silk, hiding the door and enclosing them in the ornate, fragrant opulence of his private quarters.

He, too, had bathed. His dark gold hair was still damp, but it was carefully combed, as was his beard. He was robed in a long, gold, velvet caftan, trimmed at neck and sleeves with gold embroidery. When he moved toward her the fabric swished softly against the carpets. His yellow-amber eyes glowed as he looked at her.

"I was right. You are beautiful," he said.

Lenora backed away from him.

"Will you eat?" He gestured toward the gold tray.

"I'm not hungry."

"Some wine, then."

He picked up a long-necked gold pitcher encrusted with jewels and poured purple-red wine into a delicate glass goblet. He handed it to her.

"You are afraid of me," he said. "You needn't be. You will enjoy this night. I will give you as much pleasure as you will give me." He sat down on the bed platform, lounging against the glowing silken pillows.

"Sit here," he invited.

"I'll stand."

"As you wish. You will lie down soon enough." Looking amused, he leaned forward and lifted the cover from one of the dishes on the gold tray. A mouthwatering odor of chicken mixed with cinnamon and herbs assailed Lenora's senses. Attair selected a piece and chewed it thoughtfully. "This is very good. Are you sure you don't want to try some?"

"I want to go back to my friends."

"Impossible. What is that you are holding?"

Lenora held out the two leather bags.

"This is all I own," she said. "I'll give it to you if you will let me go."

Attair took the bags and opened one. He shook it over the bed, and silver coins scattered across the soft pile of the carpets.

"There is not enough here to buy your freedom."

287

Lenora watched his fingers tugging at the thong that fastened the second purse. Amber flowed out of it, filling Attair's open hand, glowing in the gentle light of the oil lamps; soft, rounded lumps of yellow-gold and brown-gold, blending with his tanned skin and golden hair and eyes.

"Ah." He expelled his breath in delight. "Lovely sea gold."

He selected a piece and held it up, contemplating a tiny insect trapped forever within the translucent globule.

"The Greeks believe sunlight shining on the waves of the northern ocean solidifies, making amber," he said. "They treasure it. They believe it has magical properties."

"Then you can sell this purseful to them. Surely it is enough to buy my freedom."

"I don't want to free you." Attair scooped the pieces of amber back into the bag and tossed it aside. He rose and approached her. "This amber, and the silver coins, are mine. I bought them when I bought you, though Torgard did not know you had them."

"They are mine," she declared, nearly in tears.

"Not any more." His large hands rested on her shoulders. "You are not going to drink?"

"No." Pulling away from him, she set the goblet of wine down on the little table. She knew she could not escape this man. It was useless to think of Erik. He could not help her now.

Attair followed her. He wrapped his arms about her, pulling her back against his chest, her head on his broad shoulder.

288

"Don't you like me?" he whispered. His moist, full lips nibbled at her earlobe, then inched slowly down to the hollow of her throat. She felt his strong, masculine body pressed firmly against her back.

"How can I like you? I don't know you," she said.

His left hand holding her at the waist, Attair's right hand began wandering over her, sliding under the loose folds of her green robe to enclose one breast in his huge grasp.

"You will know me well enough before tonight is over," he murmured. His hand moved lower, creeping slowly down her body.

"Are you a Dane?" she chattered nervously. "Did you come down the river from the northern sea?"

"I have no country. My father was a Norseman from Birka, my mother a Petcheneg woman he captured on a journey home from Bagdhad. The Greeks call us Rus, so that is what I am, a Rus trader." He lowered his voice, modulating it seductively. "I am a rich man, Lenora. If you please me, I will cover you with jewels and silks, and furs in the winter."

Both of his hands now worked at the golden sash that held her gown closed. She put her small hands on top of his and tried to stop him.

"I want to know more about you," she said, hoping to delay the inevitable.

"You know all you need to know for now. Be silent, Lenora. I do not like women who talk. Do not speak again until we are finished."

He brushed her restraining hands aside and went on with his explorations. He finally succeeded in pulling off her sash. It slithered to the floor as the edges of her robe slipped apart. Reaching beneath the soft silk he ran his golden-haired hands across her abdomen and down between her thighs, rubbing gently against her. She stiffened. Only Erik had ever touched her in that way. Erik. She forced back a sob and closed her eyes. She could not stop thinking about Erik, and how much she wanted him. But Erik did not want her. She kept her eyes tightly closed and bit her lower lip to stifle a cry as Attair's determined touch moved upward on her thighs. He held her immobilized, his hands never stopping their motions.

Lenora did not want Attair, she wanted to leave this luxurious prison, she wanted Erik. *Erik!* And yet, as Attair continued to stroke and rub and press, and his breathing in her ear quickened with his rising passion, Lenora was flooded with an insistent, pulsing need that throbbed in rhythm with the slow, sensuous pressure of his hands. She began to moan softly and move herself against him. She felt a shock when she opened her eyes and saw not Erik, but Attair. She whimpered in disappointment, then choked back the sound.

Attair was being remarkably gentle for a man who claimed to own her, which gave him the right to take her with violence if he so desired. But behind every caress of his expert hands, every sensation of purely physical pleasure those hands imparted to her body, lay the threat of violence. She could not forget the women who had bathed her, whose tongues had been removed at Attair's command. She believed that if she wanted to survive this night, she would have to submit to her new owner.

Her *owner*. Attair was right; however much she might protest, she was a slave once again, subject to the desires of the man who had bought her. She hated him and hated herself even more for the desire he was creating between them. No man but Erik should ever make her feel this way. She should not be responding to Attair.

He did not notice her distress. He was concerned only with her body, with preparing her to receive him for his own pleasure. He pushed the silk robe off her shoulders and then, in a smooth, purposeful motion, divested himself of his only garment. His body gleamed gold in the lamp-light, covered with soft golden hair, hard-muscled; totally, powerfully male. When he looked at her his amber-gold eyes flamed with a fire that threatened to burst out of control as he drew her to him and his arms surrounded her and his mouth fixed itself upon hers and would not let her go. She was imprisoned in his golden embrace, like an insect caught in molten amber, trembling with fear and unable to free herself.

She was not aware of walking or of being carried, but by some mysterious means he brought her to his bed and lay her there. The oil lamps above her swung on their golden chains and the scented air filled her lungs. She knew in another moment Attair would possess her completely, and then she would belong to Erik no more. Two large tears welled out of her eyes and ran across her cheeks to moisten the pillows on either side of her head.

Attair separated her legs and knelt between her thighs, poised. She saw his tongue come out and moisten his full lips. She closed her eyes, unable to look at him any longer.

He heard the hammering on the door before she did. She felt him moving away from her, heard him swearing a hideous oath. Lenora's eyes flew open. Attair was off the bed platform, wrapping the gold velvet caftan about his waist. She watched him tear back the silk panels over the entrance with a violent gesture. He wrenched open the door and shouted into the darkness. There was an answering cry, a question, and another oath from Attair. He came back into the room, pulling the caftan over his shoulders as he walked. Lenora, seeing his angry face, quaked with fear. This did not look like the same man who just a little while ago had been caressing her tenderly and murmuring words of desire.

"Our pleasure will have to wait," Attair said. "The Khazars have attacked one of my baggage trains coming overland from the Volga River. I am needed there. I may be gone for a day or two. The women will attend to you until I return. When I do, we will finish what we started tonight." A large hand reached out and clasped one of Lenora's breasts in a firm grip. "Do not try to escape, my beauty. Do not even dream of it. I leave my compound well guarded, and I have an unbreakable agreement with my men. They never touch my female slaves, except the foolish few who try to escape. Those women, my men are free to use as they wish. So be wise, Lenora. Remain here, and wait for me." Attair removed his hand from her breast and walked out of the room.

Lenora fell onto the cushions, weeping in shame and relief. She had not wanted Attair, but her body, starved for so long for Erik's lovemaking, had responded to him against her will, had demanded release from weeks of anger and frustration. She cried harder. She had a reprieve, but Attair would return, and when he did he would make her his. Once Attair had lain with her, she was certain Erik, even if by some wild chance he found and rescued her, would never take her to his bed again. Lenora cried herself to sleep in hopeless anguish.

She wakened, still alone, uncertain what part of the day it was. There were no windows in this chamber; the only light came from the ornate oil lamps. The two silent, nameless serving women arrived with fresh food. Lenora was famished. She downed chunks of lamb cooked with rice, nibbled pastries filled with honey and almonds, and drank the heavy red wine the women poured for her. Then they took her to the bathhouse, where the routine of the day before was repeated. She was bathed and scented and painted and dressed, this time in a deep blue caftan trimmed

in silver. The women escorted her back to Attair's
room, which had been tidied in her absence.

Lenora waited. And waited. She was bored,
and she feared Attair's return. The serving
women brought more food. Lenora ate again of
unknown dishes redolent with spices and drank
cooling fruit juices, then fell into a deep slumber.
She woke up to a day that was a repetition of the
one before. A third day followed, equally boring,
until, returning from the bathhouse in late afternoon, she found Attair waiting for her at the door
of his private room.

He looked down at her, taking in her flowing
rose-colored silk gown and her freshly washed
hair. He fingered a long, slender knife stuck into
his belt, caressing it with voluptuous pleasure.
Lenora sensed a barely restrained anger in him.

"I don't like that color," Attair said, glancing
at her dress again.

"I'll change it," she offered.

"Never mind. You won't be wearing it long."

Fear stabbed through Lenora. She knew he was
going to take her in a very few minutes. Something in the way he looked at her told her that
this time he would not be stopped by anything
and, further, he would not be as gentle as he had
been before. She wished he would leave his knife
alone.

"Did you catch the Khazars and get your goods
back?" she asked, hoping to distract him from
the blade.

"No, I did not. An entire caravan loaded with
silks and silver, lost to me. If I had found just one

Khazar, I would feel better." His fingers stroked the knife again.

"I'm sorry." Perhaps sympathy would soothe his temper. She did not want to be the outlet for his rage over his failure. "Did you really lose so very much? Surely, if you are a rich man, as you said—"

"Torgard is bringing me another woman tomorrow," he interrupted her. "After tonight, you will work in the kitchen."

"Have I displeased you in some way?" She did not know whether to be relieved or more frightened. Then Attair smiled at her, and fear won. When he spoke, she remembered the silent serving women.

"You talk too much, Lenora. You ask too many questions. I have something special planned for you tonight, to silence your clattering tongue, and then in the morning, you leave my chamber."

As his hand continued to fondle his knife, Attair's eyes shifted toward the door to the courtyard, where there seemed to be some kind of excited exchange taking place. He stepped to the door.

"What's going on out there?" he called.

"I wish to speak to Attair the trader."

At the sound of that familiar masculine voice, Lenora's heart nearly stopped.

"Who are you?" Attair called.

"I am Erik, called the Far-traveler. I need to discuss with you a matter concerning your reputation."

"There is nothing wrong with my reputation." Attair laughed.

"But there is. You have been tricked by that weasel, Torgard. Now he is telling the story to everyone he meets, and laughing at you."

"You had better come in."

Attair stepped aside and Erik entered the house, looking calm and faintly amused.

"You, go away." Attair jerked his head at Lenora.

"Let her stay," Erik said. "It's about her that I've come. Shall we go in here? You don't want your servants to hear this."

He walked lightly into Attair's private chamber. He looked around at the luxurious decor, raised his eyebrows, and grinned at Lenora.

"What is it you have to say to me, Erik the Fartraveler?" Attair was abrupt, not troubling to disguise his irritation at this intrusion.

"Four days ago you bought this slave woman from Torgard. He cheated you."

"How?"

"She was my slave when Torgard stole her from my tent. I come to you openly because I believe you purchased her honestly, not knowing she was another man's property. I want her back."

"I am not your slave," Lenora declared angrily. When she had first seen Erik, she had had to resist with all her strength the desire to run into his arms, but now she was furious with him. How dare he call her his slave when he had freed her in Denmark? Why did she not simply tell Attair that she was a free woman? All her bitterness and resentment at Erik's cold treatment of her flared anew.

Erik behaved as though he had not heard her angry exclamation. He smiled at Attair in a friendly way.

"If she were not my slave," Erik asked, "why would I bring her on such a dangerous journey? I care nothing for her, but I paid good silver for her, as you paid Torgard. He cheated you by paying me nothing and then charging you too much for her. It was all profit for Torgard."

"How do you know this?" Attair asked.

"I overheard Torgard boasting to someone about it. He thinks it's a marvelous joke, and says he is going to do the same thing again tomorrow."

"Is he?"

"Isn't he?"

The two men stared at each other. Attair turned his eyes away first. He gave an uncomfortable laugh.

"That Torgard is a clever thief. Someday, one of his victims will finish him. He is bringing me another woman tomorrow," Attair admitted.

"I can help you. I will buy this woman from you for more than you paid Torgard. Then you can boast of your profit on her and everyone will know what a shrewd trader you are."

"And what of your reputation? You would look foolish indeed after such a bargain, losing silver to both Torgard and me."

"I'm on my way to Miklagard. I won't return

to Kiev. I care nothing what men here say of me."

"I doubt that. Still, I am growing tired of this woman's constant chatter. And I could use the silver. I have suffered a business loss. Yes, perhaps I will consider selling her." Attair named a price. Lenora knew it was inflated.

"Of course," Attair added, "I have fed and clothed and housed her for four days. I should be paid for that."

As the two men haggled, Lenora watched Erik. By no glance or word did he reveal any personal interest in her. She was merchandise to him, nothing more. And yet she was not really his slave, and well he knew it, whatever he told Attair. Erik had not wanted her to travel with him to Miklagard. Why, when he had been conveniently relieved of her unwelcome presence, had he come to rescue her?

At last Erik held up his hands.

"According to Torgard, you bought Lenora for one hundred twenty dirhams. I will pay you two hundred dirhams. It is all the silver I have left. Since you know how Torgard tricked you, you can probably convince him to give you the new slave woman at a lower price."

"I like your boldness, Erik. Few men would dare to walk into my compound alone and unarmed as you have done." Attair looked from Erik to Lenora. His full lips curved in a peculiar smile. He ran his tongue over his lips, moistening them. "How much did you say?" he asked.

"Two hundred dirhams. It's good Arab silver."

"I'm sure it is. Very well, take her."

Lenora could not repress the sound of relief and joy that escaped her lips. However angry she might be with Erik, it would be wonderful to be free of the fear and the stifling confinement of Attair's house.

"Find the serving women," Attair told her. "Get from them the clothing you wore when I bought you. That gown is mine."

"Yes. I won't be long." Lenora hurried to the door, then stopped. "My silver and my amber. I want them back. They belong to me."

She saw Attair's expression harden.

"Lenora," Erik said, his voice harsh with tension, "do as Attair has told you."

"But—"

"*Now!*"

She ran out the door. When she returned to the log house a short time later, clad in her torn blue-green dress, Erik was waiting for her just outside the door. There was no sign of Attair. Erik took her by the wrist and headed for the courtyard gate.

"What about my silver?" she asked, hanging back.

"You're lucky to get away with your life. Stop worrying about a bag of coins," he replied angrily.

"But it's mine. I earned it."

He stopped so suddenly that she bumped into him.

"Would you like me to give you back to him? Would you like to learn first-hand what he does to his discarded women?"

"He said he would send me to work in the kitchen." Lenora resolutely rejected the vision in her mind of Attair stroking his knife with loving fingers, and the memory of his words about silencing her tongue. Erik was just trying to frighten her.

"Is that what he told you? The kitchen? I won't terrify you by telling you the truth. I heard a lot about Attair while I was searching for you, and none of it was good. Torgard deliberately sold you to Attair, knowing full well what he would do once he was bored with you. Now keep quiet until we're safely away from here."

"That's what all men tell me," Lenora muttered. "'Just keep quiet, Lenora,' 'Be silent, Lenora,' 'Don't talk so much, Lenora.'"

"You should take the advice." Erik jerked her wrist, pulling her after him once more. "We aren't free of this compound yet."

They were approaching the heavy wooden gate of the stockade surrounding Attair's property. Three guardsmen stood before the gate. Erik, still holding tightly to Lenora's wrist, stopped and fixed his gaze on the men. After a period of time that seemed to Lenora to last forever, the leader grinned sheepishly and gave an order. The gate began to swing open. Lenora could see Halfdan waiting outside, mounted and holding the reins of a second horse that stamped and snorted its impatience to be away.

Erik hurried her through the gate, but when she would have broken into a run, he held her back.

"Easy," he said quietly. "Try to look natural and unconcerned."

"What's natural in a situation like this?" she responded. Only now, outside those wooden walls, could Lenora begin to admit to herself the overwhelming terror she had hidden for four long days. "I just want to be gone from this place."

"Hello." Halfdan greeted her as though she had returned from a walk to the marketplace. "It's good to see you."

Erik boosted her onto the spare horse, then mounted behind her. He turned his horse and they rode away. She leaned her head against his chest for a moment, feeling suddenly weak.

"You slept with him." Erik's face was grim.

"I did not," Lenora snapped, strength and anger both returning. "He was called away before—before that could happen. But I might have, if you had not come when you did. Erik, I was his slave and I was afraid. He has two serving women whose tongues he had ordered removed."

Erik's arms tightened about her.

"He probably tore them out himself. From what I've heard of Attair, he likes to torture women. I have occasionally wanted to silence you permanently myself, but—" His green eyes were serious in spite of his light tone. "Did he hurt you?"

"No, but I believe what you've said. I'm sure he is a cruel man." She shivered and drew closer to Erik once more. "Thank you for rescuing me. I hoped you would come to set me free."

"You are not free," he told her. "I paid the last

301

of my silver to buy you."

She could not believe what she had just heard.

"You set me free in Denmark," she said.

"Only because I thought I would never see you again. If I had known you would be dragging after me all this distance, I would never have freed you." He laughed down at her, seeing her stricken expression, and once more his arms tightened, nearly taking her breath away. "Now you are mine again. And this time I may never set you free."

Lenora was silent a while, absorbing this. She noticed they had circled around to the south of the settlement that was Kiev, and were approaching the river.

"Where are we going?" she asked dully, her mind still primarily focused on her newly enslaved status.

"We are going to Miklagard," Erik told her. "Today. Torgard is taking us."

Chapter Twenty-One

"Torgard? Are you mad?"

Lenora slid to the ground and watched Erik dismount. They were in a grove of closely clustered trees. Through the dense underbrush she could just see the gleam of the river.

Halfdan had also dismounted. He and Erik lifted heavily packed saddlebags off their horses. Halfdan looped each horse's reins securely about its saddle and smacked each on the rump. The horses wandered off through the trees.

"They'll find their way home," Halfdan said.

"Too bad we couldn't sell them," Erik remarked. "There's no silver left."

"How much did you pay for them?" Lenora wondered.

Halfdan laughed, the cheerful boyish sound she remembered so well.

"We stole them," he said. "Here, Lenora, you carry this." He tossed a bundle at her, then crashed through the bushes after Erik. Lenora followed.

Torgard was tied securely to a tree near the river. He had a black eye and a large bruise on his jaw.

"Are you glad to see us alive?" Erik teased. "I didn't have to tell Attair where to find you after all."

Torgard whimpered.

"What is he doing here?" Lenora demanded. She circled Torgard, wishing she had a weapon handy.

Halfdan chuckled. "Well, after he told us where you were, we invited him to join us on our journey. It seemed the hospitable thing to do. He wouldn't have a chance if Attair found him after learning what a cheat he is. You can slice him up any way you like later, but for now he has provided our supplies."

Lenora saw a boat pulled up among the trees. It was a small copy of a Viking longship, similar to the fishing craft in which they had escaped from Thorkellshavn. Erik was adding their saddlebags and the bundle Lenora had carried to a pile of fresh provisions already lashed into the bottom of the craft. Lenora recognized in the pile the cauldron in which she had cooked so many meals.

"We're going to Miklagard in that?" she asked doubtfully.

"To the Euxine Sea at least," Erik said. "That's

304

why we are letting Torgard live. It will be easier with four of us to move it over the portages."

"Four of us?"

"You aren't in Attair's harem any more, Lenora. You will have to work with the rest of us." She had the strangest feeling that Erik was laughing at her.

"We had better get started," Halfdan said. "It will be dark soon, and I have no doubt Attair and his men will be close behind us."

"Why should he come after us?" Lenora asked.

"For the pleasure of killing all of us slowly now that he has our silver and has teased us by letting us believe for a while that we are free of him," Erik said. "That is Attair's way. Let's get the boat into the water, then I'll untie our friend Torgard."

"Not so fast!" The tall, lean figure of Sven the Dark stepped through the trees, his pale blond hair catching the late-day sunlight. Several bulky shadows with drawn swords loomed behind him.

"Sven, help me," screamed Torgard.

"Why should I help you, you sniveling coward?"

"I told you where they were," Torgard's eyes rolled in fright. "Untie me, Sven, so I can escape this battle. Please, please."

"You were no help to me. After you told me where they used to be camped, I had to track them for half a day before I found them." Sven the Dark turned to Erik. "Where is Freydis? Where is Snorri's silver?"

"Freydis is where you can't find her," Halfdan

said. "She is safe with my father, and so is Erik's silver."

"That's Freydis," Torgard exclaimed. "That woman there. They called her Freydis at first."

"I see," Sven said slowly. "They tricked you, Torgard. They tricked all of us. Lenora pretended to be Freydis to draw us away from Denmark until the real Freydis was safe."

"That's it," Erik said. He moved about casually, as though he had nothing serious on his mind, but Lenora, watching him, was certain he was trying to maneuver Sven into a position where the sun would be in his eyes. Surely Sven, veteran of combat that he was, would realize this too. But Sven was more interested in baiting Erik than in securing his position in preparation for battle.

"You even tricked your brave friend Rodfos," Sven continued. "That was unkind of you, Erik. Rodfos paid dearly for your falsehoods."

"What have you done to Rodfos?" Lenora's mouth went dry as she recalled the red-haired sailor.

"He was a hard man to kill," Sven said. "He wouldn't tell us where you had gone, but we found another man who remembered seeing Rodfos and Torgard together, so we followed Torgard to Kiev, hoping to find you. Our guess proved correct."

Lenora staggered with the shock of Sven's news. She leaned against a tree for support and tried vainly to blink back the tears. "Rodfos," she whispered. She could only hope that Rodfos had met in the afterlife that woman he had loved long ago, the one she had reminded him of.

"Rodfos will be avenged," Erik promised her.

"By whom?" Sven sneered. "You are all going to die just as soon as Snorri arrives. I would like to do the job myself, but I promised I would wait for him."

"Erik," Lenora said, "I want a sword."

"To do what?" Sven laughed.

"To use it. I killed Hrolf. I may kill you, for Rodfos' sake."

Sven looked surprised at her angry words.

"You won't have the chance, wench," he told her.

Halfdan put his sword into Lenora's hands. She grasped it tightly, feeling its great weight tugging at her muscles.

"I have Bone-biter," Halfdan said, pulling his battle-ax from his belt.

"You would let a woman use your sword?" Sven scoffed.

"Only this woman. I won't be without a sword for long. I'll take yours, once I've killed you."

"You are welcome to try, Halfdan."

"Please let me go," Torgard begged, still straining at his bonds. "Please. I'll leave here, I won't bother anyone, I promise."

The stream of pleading words was cut off as Sven casually stabbed Torgard. Sven straightened, stepped back, and met Halfdan's battle-ax. He fell without a word. Halfdan picked up Sven's sword.

"I told him I'd have another one soon," he said

cheerfully. "Be careful now, Lenora. Watch your back."

"I will."

Sven's men surged forward as they spoke, determined to avenge their fallen leader. There were only four of them, but they were large and strong, and blood-lust flamed in their eyes.

Lenora stood with her back against a tree. Erik and Halfdan stood before her, protecting her. Each quickly brought down a man. They had fought without shields, having packed their own into the boat, but they now picked up the shields of Sven's dead comrades.

Lenora watched, holding her breath, as the men fought, dodging around trees, ducking blows, retreating only to return to the attack, shields raised to ward off blows as they slashed and parried.

Halfdan was wounded. Lenora saw the blood running down his arm, but he laughed and, dropping his shield, tossed his sword to his other hand and kept on fighting. In a short time Sven's men lay dead.

Lenora began to bandage Halfdan's arm.

"No time for that now," Erik panted. "Do it later. Into the boat, Lenora. Halfdan, help me push it off."

A familiar harsh laugh floated through the trees; a bulky body forced its way through the underbrush.

"What's this? Sven dead? Am I next? If I had known you were going to be so brave, cripple, I'd have brought more men with me."

"I have been waiting for you, Snorri." Erik left the boat, which he had been pushing toward the river, and turned to face his brother. Bjarni stood beside Snorri.

"Where is Freydis?" Snorri demanded.

Erik told him. Lenora noted that Erik did not mention the disputed hoard of silver. Snorri's face grew red with rage as he listened.

"Now, Erik, I am going to feed you to the eagles at last. As for you, you miserable slut," he roared at Lenora, "How dare you pose as my sister? I should have killed you the first day I saw you."

Snorri's battle-ax whirled in his fist as he took a step toward Lenora. Before he could let it fly, Erik's sword sliced across his arm. Snorri dropped the ax and pulled his sword out of its scabbard with his good hand. Erik lunged at him again. They fought, snarling and panting, dodging among the trees, until Lenora lost sight of them in the thick growth.

Meanwhile, Bjarni attacked Halfdan. He hefted his short-handled spear, a confident smile on his face. Bjarni was proud of his prowess with this weapon. Lenora had often seen him in the practice yard at Thorkellshavn, working on the twisting throw for which he was justly famous.

Halfdan moved forward, sword in hand. Bjarni let go of the spear with an effortless thrust that spun it through the air and imbedded it deep in Halfdan's chest. Halfdan dropped the sword and crashed backward like a great tree being felled.

Before the spear had left Bjarni's fingers, Lenora had begun to run toward him, holding the sword Halfdan had given her. Bjarni reached for his own sword, but Lenora was too quick for him. Before Bjarni's blade was free of its scabbard, Lenora had struck at him, and he went down.

Lenora turned to Halfdan, tears streaming down her face. She was shaking with grief and rage combined. Kneeling, she lifted his head onto her lap.

"You are a true friend, to avenge me so soon. And with my own sword." Incredible as it seemed, Halfdan was smiling at her, although his voice was weak. "Where is Erik?"

Lenora looked around to see Erik moving toward them through the underbrush.

"He's coming now. Halfdan, we have to get that spear out of you."

"Not yet. Let me talk to Erik first."

Erik came to them quickly. He knelt and clasped Halfdan's hand.

"Brother," Halfdan said.

"Brother. I wounded Snorri, but he ran away."

"He would. He'll be back." Halfdan took a deep, obviously painful breath. "Don't cry, Lenora. This is a good death. My own Valkyrie will come for me soon."

"Oh, Halfdan." She could not stop the tears.

"When you see Freydis, tell her my last thoughts were of her. Get you safely to Miklagard, Erik. Don't worry about a funeral. I don't need one."

"I'll raise a runestone for you."

"Carve on it that I died in Gardariki in a good cause." Halfdan took another difficult breath.

"Give me my own sword. I want it in my hands."

Erik picked it up and laid it in Halfdan's cold hand, wrapping his fingers around the hilt.

"Lenora used it well," Halfdan murmured, his voice weaker. "She has avenged me. She killed Bjarni."

"Lenora did? Yes, she would."

"Now, Brother, pull out the spear and let me go."

Erik rose. He placed his hands on the spear handle and tugged. Halfdan grunted in pain. Erik tugged again.

"Stop it, stop it," Lenora cried. "You're killing him."

"It has to be done. He's dying anyway. Better quickly with us here than leave him to the wolves, or to Snorri and his men."

"Try again, Brother." Halfdan's voice was calm. "I would help you, but I'm indisposed."

Erik looked at Lenora. "Help me," he said.

"No, I can't, I won't."

"Lenora," Halfdan whispered, "do it for me." His blue eyes met hers in a painful plea.

Reluctantly, Lenora set her hands over Erik's on the spear shaft and together they pulled. And pulled again. As the spear came out they stumbled backward.

"Freyd—" Halfdan's last breath whispered away on the wind. Lenora fell beside him, weeping uncontrollably.

"Enough of that, Lenora. Come away."

"We can't leave him like this."

"There is nothing we can do for him now. He

311

wanted us to save ourselves. Come on." Erik pulled her toward the boat.

"Why aren't you crying?" Lenora demanded, still unable to stop her own tears. "He was your blood-brother."

"Norsemen never weep for their dead. You should know that by now." Nevertheless, there was a hard, tight look to Erik's mouth, as though he were holding back a cry of pain. He pushed at the boat, and it began to slide into the river.

"Get in," Erik ordered.

"Wait! Please wait for me."

At the sound of a woman's voice, Erik spun around to face this latest intrusion, sword in his hand once more. A tall, slender figure in a tattered dress ran between the trees, her long hair streaming behind her.

"Help me," she cried. "Don't let Snorri capture me again."

The woman stopped abruptly, looking at the bodies that lay scattered among the trees. She stepped to one and nudged it lightly with her foot.

"Sven is dead. I'm glad." She looked more closely at Erik. "You are Thorkell's other son."

"I am, but I don't know you." Erik did not relax his guarded stance. His eyes flicked behind the woman, looking for possible attackers, then moved back to her face.

"I am Maura," she said.

Erik looked perplexed until Lenora explained. "I recognize her. She's an Irish woman Snorri brought home as slave for Thorkell. Your father later gave her to Sven."

"I remember now."

So did Lenora. Bitter memories came back to her. This was the woman whose gloriously beautiful, red-haired presence in Thorkell's bed had made Edwina so unhappy. She was no longer lovely. She was pale and looked half-starved. She lifted one hand to push back her lank, dirty hair and her sleeve fell away, revealing bruises on the pasty-white flesh of her bony forearm. She saw Lenora looking.

"Snorri did that, and Sven did worse," she said. She looked straight at Erik. "I escaped while they were fighting you. Wherever you are going, it will be better than remaining with Snorri. Take me with you."

"Am I to drag two women with me all the way to Miklagard?"

"I won't be any trouble to you," Maura said hopefully.

"That's what Lenora said before we left Thorkellshavn, and she has been nothing but trouble ever since."

"Trouble!" Lenora glared at him, forgetting for a moment her grief over Halfdan. "I have been more help than trouble and you know it."

"Were you help when you had to be rescued from Attair?"

"That wasn't my fault."

"Oh, don't waste time quarreling," Maura begged. "Snorri will return soon. He has more men at his camp. We must leave here."

"That is exactly what we are going to do, once my lazy slave gets herself into my boat."

Lenora, too angry to respond, climbed over the side, moving Halfdan's cauldron to make room to sit down, barely resisting the urge to heave it at Erik. She would settle this foolishness about her being his slave again once they were safely away from Snorri.

Maura tried to get into the boat after her, but she was too weak. With an annoyed exclamation, Erik picked her up and dumped her in. He gave the craft one last shove, then leapt aboard as it spun out into the current. He moved to the stern and took the tiller, steered into the middle of the river where the current was strongest, and headed south.

Chapter
Twenty-Two

"Open the sail," Erik ordered brusquely. "If you want to travel with me, you will both have to work."

The two women strained at the twisted hide ropes. Maura was too weak and exhausted to be much help, but Lenora hauled with all her might until the small square sail lifted and caught the wind. They sailed until after sunset, until the clear sky was a deep lavender-blue and a nearly full moon rose, lighting the empty river with silver.

Lenora had expected they would stop when darkness came, but Erik continued at the tiller. The river's current was strong, pulling them southward, past the dark forest and the pale, ghostly beaches of the islands dotting the river. There were no sounds but the ripple of the water, punctuated now and then by a soft command from Erik. He spoke seldom, and Lenora suspected he was thinking of Halfdan.

It was not until the moon had nearly set that Erik directed the boat toward a beach on one of the islands and told them to lower the sail. The women climbed out, stiff and weary, to help him pull the boat up onto the sand.

"We will be off again at dawn," Erik said. "We'll take turns standing guard, and I don't want either of you to fall asleep when it's your turn. Snorri is sure to come downriver after us, and we had better watch out for Attair too."

The mention of Attair reminded Lenora of her argument with Erik. Somehow she had to convince him she was a free woman, but for now she was too tired. She collapsed onto the sandy beach and fell asleep at once, not caring that she had no covering. It seemed she had only blinked her eyes when Erik was shaking her shoulder and telling her it was her turn to keep watch.

"Wake me as soon as it is light enough to see the river," he instructed.

She sat on the sand in the darkness, leaning against the side of the boat, listening to the water moving past the little island.

Erik had told her once that the journey from Kiev to the sea was the most dangerous part of the voyage to Miklagard. It took at least forty-two days and sometimes much longer, with dangerous rapids and violent nomadic tribesmen along the way. They had no choice—they had to go on, for behind them were Snorri and Attair, either of whom would soon be at their heels.

Lenora stretched, moving her stiff shoulders. She could see the faint glow in the eastern sky that foretold the dawn. Soon it would be time to wake the others. If only Halfdan were with them. She wiped away a tear. She must not think of Halfdan. She would think instead of a subject that ought to bring her satisfaction.

The retribution for which she had once yearned with such a violent passion was nearly complete. Hrolf and Bjarni were slain; of the leaders of the raid that had destroyed her family only Snorri remained, and she would do anything in her power to make him pay for the blood he had shed. But there was no comfort or even relief to be found in that knowledge, and for the first time she considered the possibility that the cost of vengeance might be too high.

She had not expected to find friendship among the Vikings, yet friendship had been given to her. She thought of honest Thorkell, of Freydis, of Ingvar and Asmund and Tola. She thought again of Halfdan. Then, finally, inevitably, her thoughts dwelt upon Erik, upon the child they had conceived together in tender pleasure, and of the way he had rescued her from Attair.

Laying her head back against the boat she looked up toward the stars, but she did not see them for the many tears blinding her. So many dead to claim her tears, so little joy to be had from revenge, so much pain caused by hatred. She had in the past year wept too often from rage or bitterness or grief or frustration. These tears were different. They cleansed her heart, so that when the soft breeze had dried the last moisture upon her cheeks she felt renewed and at peace. She looked around, a little surprised to find herself still sitting in the same place. She felt as though she had ended a long and difficult journey.

It was lighter now. The sky and river were both a pale, rose-tinged gray. She saw Erik's sleeping form stretched on the sand near her, his naked sword by his hand. She reached toward him to touch the warm skin of his face, to brush back a lock of hair that had fallen over his forehead.

He caught her wrist, pulling her down onto his chest until their mouths nearly touched. She could feel his warm breath and the firm, steady beat of his heart.

"It's almost dawn," she whispered.

They reached Vitaholm at midday. This was the place where the merchant fleet assembled each year after leaving Kiev. With summer waning and the flotilla gone on its way to Miklagard, the fortified outpost was nearly deserted, the lookout tower on the hill standing as a last, lonely sentry before the wild southern steppelands.

"We will stop," Erik told them. "If there is anyone going south on the river, it will be from here. It would be safer to join a party, rather than trying to make the trip alone."

They soon learned there was no such group.

"We go on quickly then," Erik said. "If we can

have no protection from numbers, speed must be our safety."

The women pleaded for a night of rest within Vitaholm's ramparts. Maura was plainly exhausted. She had told Lenora of being repeatedly beaten and nearly starved by the coldly sadistic Sven. Lenora feared she would not survive the trip to Miklagard, and said so.

In spite of his eagerness to be gone, Erik admitted his sympathy for the bone-thin woman. He allowed them to stop long enough to trade some woolen cloth for bowls of a hot, meaty stew, coarse brown bread, and flagons of ale from an old woman in the marketplace, who stirred a huge cauldron over a fire.

Maura ate her food with the concentrated intensity of one who has gone without for too long.

"Eat it slowly," Erik cautioned. "You don't want to be sick."

"I haven't eaten this much at one time since I left Thorkellshavn," Maura said. She wiped her bowl with a last crust of bread, swallowed it, and licked her fingers. "That was so good."

Well fortified by their meal, they set out again. Once more they traveled until the moon had nearly set and then slept briefly.

Attair found them at dawn, as they pushed the boat back into the river. He came with a dozen mounted companions. He signaled for his men to wait and rode alone onto the beach to confront Erik and the women.

"Get into the boat," Erik said softly.

"I won't leave you." Lenora had needed only

one look at Attair's cruel, handsome face to know she would rather die at Erik's side than ever belong to Attair again.

"Obey me, Lenora," Erik said. "I want to be able to sail quickly."

"Please, Lenora," Maura begged, nervously eyeing Attair. "I'm afraid of that man."

The two women gave the boat another shove, waded into the river with it, and clambered aboard. Lenora picked up the oars. Using them as poles, she and Maura held the craft steady, waiting for Erik.

"Erik Far-traveler, give me the woman and I'll let you live," Attair called.

"I bought Lenora from you in an honest sale," Erik replied. "She is mine."

"I followed you and found Torgard dead. Is this the second woman he was to bring me? Did you steal her from him? She's not very pretty, and much too scrawny for my taste. You may keep her. I'd rather have Lenora back. There are a few things I would like to do with her. You understand."

"Only too well. You have my silver. Lenora stays with me."

"Shall we fight for her?"

Attair's horse picked its way daintily to the water's edge. Erik slowly backed away until he was knee-deep in water.

"Come out and fight on land," Attair coaxed, urging his unwilling horse into the river.

He raised a huge battle-ax and brought it down with a slashing motion, bending far out of the saddle to do so. Erik leapt toward the horse, moving inside the deadly circle of the ax's swing. Catching Attair off-balance, Erik pulled him from the saddle. Water splashed around them, obscuring Lenora's view of the fight. The horse reared, neighing loudly. Attair lay stunned, half under water, his ax lost as he fell. Erik's sword flashed once.

Attair's men had begun moving forward with menacing expressions.

"Raise the sail," Erik shouted, splashing through the water toward the boat.

A volley of arrows flew through the air, several thwacking into the side of the boat. Maura gave a loud shriek. Lenora was too busy with the sail to pay attention to her. Erik caught the stern of the boat and pulled himself over, his sword still in his hand.

Lenora pulled wildly at the ropes, her nervous hands slipping and burning. She felt Erik next to her, helping. More arrows whizzed through the air. One tore right through the unfurling sail. Then the sail was completely open and they were moving out of range of the arrows. Attair's men rode restlessly back and forth at the river's edge, shouting after them.

"Is he dead?" Lenora asked.

"He is. I'm sorry it was so quick and easy. He deserved something much more painful. I doubt his men will follow us to take vengeance for his death. I think they are more likely to ride back to Kiev to divide Attair's belongings among themselves."

"Are you hurt, Erik?"

"No, but Maura is. Tend to her, will you? We'll run aground if we're not more careful."

Erik scrambled to the stern to grasp the tiller. Lenora turned to Maura. She lay on a pile of supplies, her face ashen, her eyes closed, an arrow protruding from her left shoulder.

"Pull it out," Erik advised. "Wash it with river water and bind it up."

Biting her lower lip, Lenora did as he said. She was afraid Maura would die as Halfdan had done, but she only moaned. Lenora moved her to a more comfortable position and covered her with a rug she found in one of Torgard's bundles. She found a cask of ale, unplugged it, and filled a wooden cup. This she held to Maura's lips.

"Thank you." A bit of color had come back into Maura's pale face. "Where is Erik?"

"He's safe. We are far away from those men now."

"At first I thought it was Snorri coming after me." Maura began to weep. "Don't let him capture me, Lenora. Promise me you'll help me."

Lenora felt sympathy flood through her, washing away all her previous resentment against this once-beautiful Irish slave.

"I can imagine what Snorri did to you," she said. "We won't let that happen again. We'll get away from him, you'll see."

Lenora was not at all sure she and Erik could keep that promise, but she knew Maura needed the reassurance. After Maura had drifted into sleep, Lenora crept to the rear of the boat to kneel near Erik. He put one arm around her waist and pulled her against his side. She rested there, watching the riverbank slip by.

The landscape had changed. The dark green northern forests had disappeared. Now in all directions stretched the flat, golden steppes, endless and monotonous.

The weather had changed too. Gone was the heavy, humid air of northern swamp and forest, exchanged for a dry, frequently windy heat that steadily increased as they traveled southeastward.

No one bothered them. They moved through the wide, empty land in isolation. There was no sign of pursuit, no hint that Snorri was following, but still Erik insisted they take turns keeping watch each night. As day followed identical day, Lenora longed for a night of uninterrupted sleep.

The sun was relentless. Erik and Lenora were soon tanned to a deep brown, but Maura burned. They pulled cloths from the bundles Torgard had packed into the boat and covered her head and arms and shoulders.

"I will always be grateful to you," Maura said one day as Lenora put a clean cloth on her now-healing wound. "You saved my life twice, once by making Erik bring me with you and a second time when I was wounded. I won't forget it."

"No one makes Erik do anything," Lenora said. She added a question about Maura's home in Ireland.

"I don't want to talk about it. It's too painful. Snorri killed my husband and my child and did terrible things to me. He is an evil, heathen man. Sven was no better. Erik seems to be different, and I must admit his father was kind to me, but I have finished with men. Erik says this Miklagard to which we are traveling is a Christian city. Perhaps I will enter a convent there."

If you live until we get to Miklagard, Lenora thought, considering Maura's too-thin body. Then she asked about a matter that had been preying on her mind ever since they had left Kiev.

"Maura, while you were in Aldeigjuborg, did you ever see a man called Rodfos? Or hear Snorri or Sven talking about him?"

"A big, heavy man with a red beard? Was he a sailor?"

"That's the one. Do you know what became of him?" Lenora had to know what Rodfos had suffered for her sake. She felt she owed that much to him, to know his final fate.

"Was he a friend of yours?" Maura's haunted silver eyes were huge in her thin face. "That poor man. I tried to help him, but Snorri wouldn't even let me give him a little water. And then Sven beat me again for thinking of helping a prisoner."

"What did they do to Rodfos?"

"You don't want to know, Lenora, and I don't want to tell you. Please don't make me say the words."

"They really did kill him then. I thought Sven might have been lying."

"Sven didn't know what really happened."

"What do you mean, Maura?"

"After Sven beat me I lost my senses for a

while. When I woke again it was night, and I was still lying on the ground, not far from Rodfos. I could just see him in the firelight, and I saw he was breathing, but it must have been painful for him. I'm sure Snorri had broken his ribs. Then two men came out of the dark and carried Rodfos away."

"Snorri's men, carrying him off for more torture." Lenora could hardly speak. Pity for Rodfos and rage at Snorri and Sven constricted her throat.

"Oh, no." Maura's bony hand reached out to take Lenora's, offering what comfort she could. "I think they were Rodfos' own men. I knew those who were traveling with us, and I had never seen those men before. I wanted to ask them to take me, too, but I was in such pain I knew if I tried to move or speak I would have to cry out. I wouldn't be able to help myself, and then Snorri's guards would hear and come to investigate, and see what was happening. So I just lay there watching them until they vanished into the darkness. When Snorri discovered what had happened, he was furious. I pretended I was still unconscious so I wouldn't have to answer any questions. He beat me again, anyway, but I never told what I had seen, until now."

"Thank you for telling me, Maura." Lenora pressed the hand holding hers. "At least now I know Rodfos had a chance of living. He tried to help us. I wouldn't want him to come to harm because of me. Curse Snorri! How can one man be so wicked?"

"He thinks Erik has done him an injustice. He wants vengeance, but he was a bad man even before that."

"When will it end?"

"Not until Snorri is dead, Lenora." Maura's face was sad. "Snorri will never stop so long as there is life in him." Lenora knew she was right.

Maura recovered her health slowly. Lenora thought this was because she was so exhausted and hungry when she was wounded. She slept deeply each night, and Erik and Lenora often extended their time on guard to allow Maura to sleep longer.

One evening, when Maura had settled herself to sleep beside the fire and Lenora was about to lie down herself, she brought up the matter of her status as Erik's slave.

"You freed me in Hedeby," she reminded him. "Why must I be your slave again?"

"Don't you understand? Attair had so many armed men that Halfdan and I could not rescue you by fighting our way in and out of his compound. The only way to get you out of there was by tricking Attair. I had learned enough about him to know he would agree to sell you if he thought he had the better of the bargain, and if it would make him look clever. That is why I offered to buy you."

"Did you really use all of your silver?"

"Every last dirham, and all Halfdan had too."

Lenora digested this for a moment, blinking back the tears that still rose to her eyes every time she thought of Halfdan.

"I'm grateful to you," she said at last, "but I don't want to be a slave any more."

"No one does, Lenora. In your case, it is the safest thing for you to be. Let everyone we meet know that you belong to me and that my sword will defend my property."

"And after we reach Miklagard? Will you free me then?"

"We'll see. I make no promises. Perhaps I'll decide to keep you permanently."

She turned from him in anger at his words. He stepped in front of her, his eyes glowing like emeralds in the firelight.

"Lenora, I ask you to trust me. I don't want you to come to any harm."

"I want to be free."

"What of me? I'm as much a slave as you are." His hands rested lightly on her shoulders. "Sometimes I think I'll never be free."

"Erik?" She stared at him, puzzled by the tone of his voice.

He drew her closer.

"Trust me," he repeated, his voice tender.

"I am beginning to." She raised one hand to touch his heavily bearded face.

Beside the fire, Maura stirred sleepily. "Is it time for my watch?" she asked.

Erik walked away from Lenora into the darkness.

"Not yet, Maura," he said over his shoulder. "Go back to sleep. You, too, Lenora."

They did not discuss Lenora's situation again.

* * *

At last they came to the place where the river turned due south and, rushing downward between walls of granite rock, dissolved into the rapids and cataracts that had taken the lives of countless voyagers.

"This is the most dangerous part of the journey," Erik told them. "Even more so now because the water is low. We will rest for a day and eat well. This passage will require all the strength we have."

They took advantage of the pause to bathe. Maura washed modestly at the river's edge, keeping her back turned and dressing again quickly when she was finished. Lenora pulled off her soiled garments and plunged into the water. After the endless heat and the windblown dust of the steppe winds, the coolness was wonderfully refreshing.

She moved farther out from shore, sinking down into the water until she was covered to her chin. She tilted her head back to wet her hair. She did not notice Erik telling Maura to keep watch, or see him strip off his clothes and follow her into the water.

As Lenora floated toward the middle of the river, she felt the power of the current and realized how strong was the force against which they would be contending the next day. It nearly pulled her off her feet when she tried to get back to shore. She floundered about in the water until a pair of muscular arms caught her and she was pressed against Erik's warm, naked chest.

"Be careful," he teased, his mouth near hers.

"I don't want to lose you to the river."

"Oh, Erik," she cried in surprise. She put her arms around his waist to steady herself. "I didn't know you were here."

"But here I am."

He held her body so firmly to his that they were almost one. She closed her eyes, half-fainting with sudden desire that came unbidden, flooding over her. He knew it. He knew everything about her.

With a strong kick he lifted himself off the riverbed, floating backward toward the shore, pulling Lenora on top of him.

"We're going to drown," he whispered, and kissed her.

Both their heads went under water. They came up spluttering and laughing. Lenora clung to him, her whole being suffused with joy at his nearness, radiant with happiness as their laughter and their entangled bodies in the swift-flowing river combined to dissipate whatever residual anger and bitterness had lain between them. She knew at last that she had been wrong about Erik. He did want her. She could feel how much.

She wound her arms about his neck and kissed him, feeling his happy response in his hard mouth as he left her breathless. He let her go reluctantly.

"We're shocking Maura." Erik stood up in the shallower water where they had floated and hauled Lenora out with one hand. The late-afternoon sun shone on droplets of water running over his chest and arms and down his torso. "Go dress or I'll forget Maura is here. I wouldn't mind, but I don't think you would want her watching us."

"Erik." She caught at him, not willing to let him go. His green eyes met hers, reading the depth of passion he had stirred in her.

"Soon," he promised. "One day soon, my beautiful Lenora."

He dove into the water again, swimming into the cold depths with strong, sure strokes. It was a long time before he waded out and dressed.

The next day they traversed the first of the series of rapids. Erik fastened three twisted hide ropes to the boat. They unstepped the mast and lashed it and the sail into the hold, along with their other gear. They took off their outer clothes, piling them into the boat. Then, each grasping a rope, they stepped into the icy water. Carefully they felt their way around submerged stones and unexpected holes as they inched along, wading close to the looming cliffs, pulling the boat with them.

The sound of water roaring and thundering among the rocks and boulders—some the size of small islands—that littered the middle of the river had lulled Lenora to sleep for two nights. Now that she was in the midst of that sound it was terrifying. The swift-moving river crashed against the rocks, breaking into white foam and swirling in dangerous whirlpools and eddies. The current tugged at their feet.

They could hear nothing but the water. Erik

gave them directions by gestures or by nodding his head. Several times the current caught the boat, nearly pulling them with it into midstream, where they would be dashed against the rocks and killed. It took all of their combined strength to haul the boat back toward shore, where the current was less strong and they could manage the craft more easily.

Lenora wanted to run, to get to the other side of this noisy torture as quickly as possible. She could see the white-faced Maura was as frightened as she was. But Erik was slow and patient, edging his way along, step by careful step, until they reached the other side of the rapids and the river began to run more calmly.

They pulled the boat up onto a narrow, rocky beach. Lenora sat on the ground, her knees shaking with relief. Her ears still rang with the tumult of the water against the rocks.

"That one wasn't too difficult." Erik dropped down beside her, laughing. "Wait until you see the next one."

"You have no fear at all," she said in wonder.

"A clear head is more useful than fear for a journey like this."

The rapids were protection as well as danger. That night, for the first time since leaving Kiev, they did not keep guard.

They made their way downriver more slowly in the following days, occasionally pulling the boat through rough water, more often making a portage. They unloaded their cargo, carrying it overland past the rapids or waterfalls, sometimes needing an entire day for this. Then they trekked back to the boat and half-dragged, half-carried it overland. It was a small boat, scarcely big enough for the three of them and their bundles. Lenora had thought it was too small for such a long trip, but with each day that passed it seemed to her larger and heavier.

They had to stop frequently to rest when moving it overland, for Maura, though willing, was still weak from her wound, and Lenora, try as she might to keep up with Erik, was not as strong as a man. As they progressed farther south on the river, a constant guard was necessary in case the Khazars attacked them.

"It's luck," Erik said one evening. "They must have raided the merchant fleet that went before us and got plenty of loot from it. Perhaps they think no one else is coming downriver so late in the season. We have been very fortunate so far."

"Or perhaps," Lenora said, thinking of Attair's ill-fated caravan, "they are raiding inland this season."

It was just before the last cataract that Snorri finally caught up with them. They had slept late, worn out from their labors of the day before.

"We will rest for one day," Erik had said, "and then make the portage."

The women were repacking their belongings to better distribute the weight they would each have to carry when they heard Erik unsheath his sword.

"Put all the bundles into the boat and lash them down," he ordered. "Take the extra sword,

Lenora. Maura, you use that short-handled spear."

They watched as Snorri's men beached their boats a short distance upriver from them. There were eight men and Snorri himself. He wore a scarlet cloth around his upper left arm, where Erik had wounded him at their last meeting. His expression was murderous. Seeing him, Maura began to cry.

"There are too many of them. They will capture us. Erik, kill me now. I don't want Snorri to touch me again."

"Be quiet, woman," Erik replied impatiently. "I'll do my best to keep Snorri away from both of you. Now, Lenora, when I call to you, I want you to push the boat into the water. Get in it and head for the rapids. Don't worry about me. I'll catch up with you."

"All right," Lenora answered. "We'll do as you want."

Snorri led his men toward them. Erik stepped forward. "Well met, brother. Have you come all this way just to see me again?"

"You are not my brother," Snorri growled. "I repudiate you."

"Whatever you say. You are still my guest, however, since I was on this beach first. I regret I have no feast to set before you. What entertainment would you like? That I can provide, and with pleasure." With a cheerful smile, Erik lifted his broadsword and held it poised.

"Oh, you'll entertain me," Snorri snarled at him, "but the pleasure will be mine. I'm going to kill you, cripple, and those two witches with you, after my men and I have used them a while. Then I'll take the silver you stole from me and go home and rule Thorkellshavn."

"Shall it be man-to-man combat?" Erik suggested politely. "Just the two of us? No point in spilling anyone else's blood, is there?"

"Just what I had in mind," Snorri responded. "It won't take me long to finish you off."

"Then ask your men to stand back and give us plenty of room. Tell them not to touch the women until we have fought."

"Do you imagine you are going to win? Even if you should, my men will hack you to pieces and then take the women."

"Make them move away. I need space."

"Move back," Snorri ordered his men. "You don't want this weakling's blood to spurt all over you. It would soil your pretty clothes and bring you bad luck."

With much laughter the men stepped aside, leaving a wide area between themselves and the river's edge, where the two women stood by the boat. In the center of this space Erik and Snorri faced each other with drawn swords. Snorri also carried a battle-ax instead of a shield.

Lenora glanced around, appreciating how clever Erik was. He had arranged the field of combat so she and Maura could easily get the boat into the water before Snorri's men could reach them. Before the men got to their own boats up the beach and began to pursue them, the women would be well into the rapids that began a short distance on the other side of a rock promontory that jutted out into the river. She and Erik had climbed up onto the promontory the evening before, and Lenora had seen the white water downstream. What would happen to them once they reached those rapids, Lenora did not know. During their trip downriver she had learned a good deal from Erik about handling the boat, although she was still only a novice. But she had come to trust him completely; she would do whatever he told her to do.

Snorri slashed at Erik with his sword. Erik ducked, raising his shield to ward off the blow, and struck at Snorri's legs. Snorri jumped aside. His heavy battle-ax thudded into Erik's shield and stuck there. Erik threw away the now-unbalanced shield. Their swords clashed together, flat blade against flat blade. They strained against each other, hand to hand, eye to eye, wavering back and forth until Snorri broke away. When he fell back Erik pursued him.

Lenora knew what Erik was doing. The eyes of all Snorri's followers were fixed upon the two men fighting before them. They had temporarily forgotten the women by the boat. Erik was maneuvering Snorri so his back was turned to the river and he could not see what the women did. This left Erik's back open to Snorri's men. Lenora bit her lip hard to keep from crying out, but not one of Snorri's men made a move toward Erik. They were all engrossed by the intense fury of the battle between the two brothers.

Erik beat at Snorri with relentless determi-

335

nation, forcing him toward the high, rocky promontory. Step by step they moved closer, as Snorri's men turned to watch the action.

"Now," Erik called out, "now."

Lenora turned to the boat, throwing into it the sword she had been holding in both hands.

"Come on," she said quietly to Maura, glancing around to be sure no one noticed them.

"What for?"

"Do you want to wait for Snorri? We are doing what Erik told us to do. We're getting away from this beach. Push, Maura."

With all her strength Lenora leaned against the boat. Maura added her weight, and then it was in the water. They scrambled aboard and Lenora picked up the oars and put one into Maura's hands. They began to row toward the middle of the river.

Lenora spared one quick look at the battle on shore. Erik and Snorri had progressed farther along the slant of the promontory. Snorri's left arm hung uselessly at his side.

Erik must have opened Snorri's old wound, Lenora thought. Then all of her attention was given to the boat as the current caught it and spun it around, pushing it farther out into the river.

"You take both oars," she told Maura.

She caught at the tiller and struggled to make the boat turn its bow downriver. As she did, she heard a shout from the beach and knew Snorri's men had noticed them at last.

"Are they following us?" she asked anxiously,

336

still trying to make the boat obey her, too busy to look back at the beach.

"Not yet. I think they are waiting for Snorri. These oars are useless. The current is too strong." Maura drew the dripping oars into the boat.

It made no difference how Lenora steered or how hard she tried to direct the boat; the river seemed to have a mind of its own. The boat spun around twice more and then drifted toward the end of the promontory.

"Look!" Maura pointed to the topmost rock, where Erik and Snorri now fought at the very edge. As they watched, Erik took a wild swing at Snorri, wounding his right arm. Snorri stumbled back. Erik flung down his sword, turned, and dove into the river on the far side of the rocks.

The current carried the boat around the end of the promontory and into a pool of calm water. Lenora could hear shouts, but she could no longer see what Snorri and his men were doing.

A dark, laughing face appeared at the side of the boat.

"Move to the other side, Maura, and balance my weight while I get in," Erik said.

He swung a leg over and then lay dripping in the bottom of the boat, convulsed with laughter. Blood streamed from a cut on his leg. Lenora dabbed at it with the hem of her skirt.

"I lost a good sword blade, but it was worth it. You should have seen Snorri's face. He had no idea what was happening."

"They'll be after us, Erik," Lenora said.

He sobered at once, moving to her side. "Give

337

me the tiller, Lenora. Row until we're in mid-stream."

It took only a few strokes before the current caught them once more, moving them ever more quickly toward the foaming white water Lenora could see ahead.

"Erik, you said we had to make a portage around this stretch of river."

"Not with Snorri so close. Tie down everything you can and sit in the middle of the boat. Hold on tightly."

Lenora hurried to do his bidding. Maura's face was so white with fear, it was almost green. She tried to help Lenora, but her hands were shaking too much.

"We can't do this," she cried.

"If you want to go back to Snorri, I'll put you ashore," Erik offered.

Pressing her lips firmly together, Maura shook her head and set to work. Once their gear was arranged as safely as possible, she sat down in front of Lenora and clutched the side of the boat.

There was no time to do or say anything more. They had reached the rapids and the noise of the river filled their ears. They were hurtled through a granite gorge, water roaring around them as it foamed and dashed against the rocks scattered about the river.

Erik navigated with great skill, but he could do little more than aim the boat. They brushed against a rock, tilted, swung away, and continued their wild ride downriver. Lenora was certain the boat would be broken into pieces against the

338

rocks; the only question was when.

The noise grew louder. It echoed and re-echoed against the granite walls around them. Surely the water was moving even faster now. Lenora felt as if she was sliding downhill, unable to stop herself. She heard Erik shout something, but she could not understand the words.

Suddenly, there was an abrupt downward drop, a rush of sound and white water, and the boat seemed to sail through the air.

She was falling and she heard someone scream. She hit the water so hard it knocked the breath out of her. As she sank through endless fathoms of cold, black water, Lenora knew she would sink forever.

Chapter
Twenty-Three

Something touched Lenora, wrapped around her ankle, and pulled her. She fought, but it would not let her go. She emerged into sunlight, spluttering and coughing, beating with her fists against the thing that pulled her back.

Erik let go of her ankle. He caught her hair and swam to shore, dragging her after him. Then he heaved her onto rocky land and left her.

As she struggled to rise, coughing up the water she had swallowed, Lenora saw Erik swimming toward her with Maura's motionless form. Their boat bobbed, hull up, a short distance away.

Erik thrust Maura at her and set out again for the boat. Lenora dragged Maura out of the water, laying her on the rough beach.

Maura opened her eyes, then closed them

again. There was a large blue bruise on one side of her forehead.

"You have to sit up," Lenora urged. She tried to pull Maura upright, but found she was suddenly too weak. She slumped beside the unconscious woman.

Erik had the boat nearly beached and was standing in the water, trying to turn it rightside up. Lenora gathered all of her strength and went to help him. They were both shivering from the cold water and the shock. Somehow, after many attempts, they righted the craft. Miraculously, two of their bundles of belongings, the one remaining sword, and the oars and sail remained, securely lashed into the hold.

"Everything is soaked," Lenora said.

"We'll attend to that later. We can't stay here. Snorri's men will come around the rapids by land. I'm too tired to fight again today."

Lenora looked up at the cataract pouring foamy white water into the pool where they had fallen. Viewed from this angle, its height made her dizzy.

"It's hard to believe we went over that and lived," she said.

"Luck," Erik replied, managing a smile for her. "So far ours has held. Let's bail out the boat and be on our way before Snorri arrives."

By the time they had finished and Lenora had at last bandaged Erik's wounded leg, satisfying herself it was nothing serious, Maura was sitting up on the beach, looking bewildered. When Erik picked her up she clung to him, weeping.

"No more rapids," she cried. "I can't bear any more."

"Only a little farther," Erik assured her. "Just a short distance from here the river is calm again." He lowered her gently into the boat, then helped Lenora to get in.

As Erik had promised, it was not very long before the river became calmer, widening into a lakelike body of sparkling blue. They stopped briefly to restep the mast and unfurl the wet and heavy sail. It soon dried in the hot wind. They sailed until evening.

When they finally stopped Erik had to lift Maura out of the boat. She was weak and unable to stand. The bruise on her forehead showed dark blue against her pale skin.

"I'm sorry," she said. "You are both so brave, and I'm no use to you. You should leave me behind."

"You are just tired," Erik told her. "You'll feel better tomorrow."

They did not make a fire, not wanting to attract attention. Maura ate a bit of soggy bread and drank some ale, then drifted into a feverish sleep. Lenora had coaxed her into removing her wet clothes and wrapping herself in a large piece of wool. Lenora took off her own soaked clothing and spread the garments on the ground, hoping they would dry overnight.

She lay wrapped in a damp woolen cloak, staring up at the brilliant stars. Erik sat down beside her. She could just see his shape outlined against the sky.

"What do you think Snorri will do now?" she asked.

"He probably sent men overland right away to see if we survived the cataract. When they don't find our bodies he will surely search farther. It will take his men at least two days to move their boats and supplies around the rapids. Snorri's wound may be severe enough to stop them for a day, not more. So we have gained a little time."

"He will follow us all the way to Miklagard." It was not a question, for Lenora already knew the answer.

"For that silver, which he thinks is rightly his, Snorri would follow us to the ends of the earth."

"We will never be safe so long as he lives."

"I know." Erik sighed. "Were he anyone else, I would kill him with pleasure. And yet, he is still my brother, my father's son. I wish there were some other way."

She felt his hand on her shoulder.

"Come with me," he urged softly. "Just a little distance away. It is safe here, and Maura is asleep."

She rose and followed his shadowy form. When he stopped he took the cloak from her shoulders and spread it on the ground. The rug he had wrapped about himself followed, making a bed on the grass.

They stood naked and silver-pale in the dim starshine. The dry steppe breeze blew softly upon them, brushing their skin with its tender summer-night warmth.

Erik's hands slipped lightly along her shoulders and down her arms, barely touching her. He caught her hands and raised them to his lips. As he kissed each finger and then the palm of each hand, she felt a warmth radiating from his mouth, spreading up her arms and suffusing her body with tingling delight. He pulled her hands around his waist, drawing her against him. Slowly his arms encircled her. His embrace tightened as his mouth met hers.

Nothing had changed. They had been separate from each other for more than four cycles of the moon, but it was as though that time and all that had happened during it was nonexistant. She remembered every detail of his body, as he remembered hers. She touched the scar on his left shoulder and the shorter scar over his eyebrow, then ran her fingers through his thick dark hair. She knew just where to touch him, what to do to please him.

His mouth was hard, as it had always been, and sweet, and when his tongue slid into her she moaned with joy.

They sank down upon her cloak, still locked in that endless kiss. His hands caressed her breasts, teasing and enticing. Pulling his mouth away from hers at last, he scattered kisses of sweet fire over her face and eyes and throat. He encouraged her eager response until she cried out, then stopped her cries with his lips.

"Don't wake Maura," he teased between hungry kisses. "We'd have to stop."

"I couldn't stop and neither could you," she whispered. The glorious, demanding need was rising in her. It could not be denied; it would be assuaged or she would die of it.

His eyes glinted with starlight when he raised his head to take her mouth again. Then his hands and lips began to move ever lower, while he caressed her breasts until they ached, then inscribed wide circles across her abdomen, stroking her smooth, eagerly responsive skin with such inflammatory effect she had to choke back a scream. At last he found the sensitive, secret spot for which he had been so lovingly searching. There he lingered, knowing well what to do, until she was nearly mad with longing, writhing and twisting and gasping in unrestrained ecstasy, not caring now who might hear her cries.

"I want you," she moaned. "No one but you. Tell me you feel the same."

His shadow rose above her, blotting out the stars. And then they were no longer separate. He was hers, all, entirely hers, and she was his. She would never belong to anyone else. Only Erik; only Erik. Her heart was his, and it nearly burst with joy as he cried out his need for her and his unending desire.

"I'll never stop wanting you, Lenora. Never."

The stars spun through the night sky, then blurred and faded. The bearded shadow above her was all that existed in the world, their blended bodies the source of all delight.

The painful past disappeared, vanished like gossamer smoke. Let Snorri pursue them; he did not matter. The dangers of the voyage yet to come did not matter, nothing else, no one else mattered. Only Erik.

As their lips met in a climactic kiss, and earth and sky paused for a brief, tense moment before the joyous explosion of their mutual rapture, Lenora knew Erik was all she had ever wanted or ever would want until the very end of her life.

Lenora opened her eyes. Over her head, against the background of a clear blue sky, a tiny yellow butterfly fluttered and danced. She smiled at it, stretching in delicious satisfaction. After a moment she sat up, looking around her. The calm river glittered in the early morning sunlight, like a child who has worn itself out with tantrums and will now be good for a while. Maura was washing her face by the water's edge. Lenora's glance skimmed past the woman to settle on the man a little distance away. Erik was examining the hull of their boat, checking for damage inflicted by rocks and cataracts. Seeing his intense concentration on his task, Lenora smiled again.

She stood, not caring that she was naked, enjoying the sensation of the warm breeze against her skin. With the proud carriage of a woman who knows she is desired, she walked toward Erik. She had nearly reached him when he looked up and saw her. His eyes wandered over her, appreciating every curve and line of her body, his expression acknowledging that this display was for him alone.

"One day," he said, "I will see you gowned in silks and wearing jewels, but you will never be more beautiful than you are now."

"If I am beautiful, it is your doing."

It did not matter that her clothes were still damp and uncomfortable from their dowsing in the river. It made no difference that their morning meal was stale bread and flat, sour ale, that searing heat quickly followed the early morning coolness, that swarms of insects rose, stinging them or flying into ears and eyes and mouths, that the ceaseless steppe wind began to blow, bringing sand and dust to add to their physical discomfort. To Lenora the world was beautiful; the day was perfect.

Maura declared herself nearly recovered from the previous day's injuries.

"My head aches, that's all," she told Lenora. "I don't remember much of what happened except that I was afraid."

"We went over a waterfall. Erik thinks you hit your head on a rock. He saved both our lives."

"You are so brave. I wish I weren't such a coward. I used to have courage, but ever since Snorri killed my family I'm frightened all the time."

Later in the day they came to a large island, where several heavily laden boats had been pulled out of the water near a cluster of tents. As they beached their own boat, a bare-chested, blond man strode forward to greet them.

"Welcome to St. Gregory's Island," he said to

Erik. "I hope you are an honest merchant."

"I am traveling to Miklagard and mean no harm to anyone."

"Perhaps you would like to join us? We are sailing soon. We were with the main fleet from Kiev, but some of our men were badly injured when the Khazars attacked us, and we decided to rest here to recover. The last section of the river is safer than the part that has gone before, but there are still dangers. It is always wiser to travel in a large group. I am surprised to see you with only one boat."

"We lost the rest of our party along the way," Erik lied glibly. "I was concerned about going on alone. I will consider your offer."

"Do you always travel with two women?" The blond man laughed.

"They are my slaves. I'm not old yet," Erik declared, a twinkle in his eye.

The other man laughed again. "If you can afford to feed them," he said, "it's your affair."

The man, who said his name was Harald, showed them a good spot to pitch their tent and even brought them some fresh meat from his own supplies.

"The fleet from Kiev always stops here to rest and to give thanks after surviving the rapids," Harald told Erik. "You see that huge oak tree over there? The men make offerings to Thor around it, bread or meat, or whatever they have to give."

When Erik did not seem too interested in this, Harald added, "Of course, I don't do that. I'm a

Christian myself. I have to be to trade with the Greeks. They're very particular about not dealing directly with heathens. You could have yourself signed, you know. For a little silver, a priest will make the sign of the cross over you, and then they say you are a provisional Christian so you can trade with them. It doesn't hurt a bit, and afterward you can do whatever you want about worshipping and they won't care. They just like to keep up appearances. They're sly folk, those Greeks. They have a thousand rules and it looks as though everyone is obeying them, but for the right bribe you can get away with almost anything."

"I know," Erik said. "I've been to Miklagard before."

"Then you understand what I'm talking about."

While listening to this conversation Lenora had been unpacking their still-wet belongings and, with Maura's help, spreading them out to dry. There wasn't much left. She was glad Halfdan's cauldron and tripod had been saved when their boat capsized. She ran her hands around the pot, remembering Halfdan's carefree laughter and boyish jokes, and then began filling it with meat and vegetables for their meal.

When Harald finally left them for his own tent Lenora joined Erik as he sat near the cooking fire cleaning his extra sword, which had suffered somewhat from immersion in the river.

"Didn't you tell me once you were a provisional Christian?" she asked.

"That's right. You heard Harald. The Greeks won't trade with heathens."

"I recall you saying Norsemen aren't allowed into the city."

"Only in small groups and unarmed. They camp outside the walls at a place called St. Mamas."

"When we reach Miklagard where will we live?"

"We could stay at St. Mamas, but it's the first place Snorri will look for us. I'm hoping we can stay with my friend, Basil Panopoulos."

"And Eirena, your precious nurse."

Erik grinned and said nothing.

"Are you certain we will be welcomed by this Basil?" Maura had joined them, and now she looked anxiously at Erik.

"Of course we will. There's not a thing to worry about." Erik's confidence silenced them both.

They left St. Gregory's Island a day later, traveling with Harald's boats. This last portion of their journey downriver was uneventful. As day followed beautiful day, Erik joked cheerfully about his luck. Lenora began to hope Snorri might have given up his pursuit. Perhaps Erik had wounded him more seriously than they had realized.

At last they reached the delta of the Dneiper River and the island called Berezanji, beyond which Lenora could see the open surface of the Euxine Sea. Erik sold their boat at the trading post on Berejanzi, and whatever belongings they could spare. It was with a tear that Lenora watched a tall, fur-clad trader walk off with Half-dan's cauldron.

Harald owned a large knarr, which he kept at Berezanji. He would sail it to Miklagard once it was loaded with the goods he had brought from Kiev. He had agreed to take Erik and the women with him for a high price.

"I know it's not enough," Erik said, putting an assortment of silver coins into Harald's hands. "I'll work on the ship to make up the difference, and the women will cook."

"Why don't you sell one of them? The skinny one wouldn't bring you much, but you could get a good price for Lenora."

"I won't sell either."

"I'm just trying to be practical. Women are more trouble than they are worth, and you can always find another one. What else have you got? I know you would never sell your sword, but what about your ring? It's gold, isn't it? I'll take it in partial payment."

"Never." Erik looked at the ring on the little finger of his left hand. "It was my mother's. I won't sell it."

"Well, then, I guess you will have to work. You could also introduce me to this merchant friend of yours, this Basil Panopoulos, who will surely know how to get around the restrictions the Greeks have put on our trade with them. For a favor like that, I might reduce the price of your passage."

* * *

One bright morning they finally sailed into the dark, choppy waters of the Euxine Sea, and on an equally sunny day they entered the Bosporus, where they dropped anchor and waited for the Byzantine customs men to come aboard and inspect Harald's cargo.

The leader of this group, the first Greek Lenora had ever seen, was a short, wiry man in a long-sleeved tunic and a long cloak, fastened at one shoulder with a buckle. His costume was simple, but the silks from which it was made were heavy and luxurious, and his manner was that of an important man accustomed to submission from those under his command. Under his supervision all of Harald's merchandise was inspected, and metal rods run through some of the bales, to detect contraband. Then the usual duty of one-tenth the value of the cargo was paid in gold. In spite of Harald's open manner and obvious honesty about the goods he had brought to Constantinople, the inspector seemed annoyed, an attitude modified only a little by the sereptitious crossing of his palm with an extra pouch of gold for his own use.

"You are late in the season," the inspector said, speaking slowly and clearly so this rude barbarian might understand him better. "Your fellow traders have already arrived, and many of them have finished their business and gone home."

"I was delayed. The Khazars attacked us," Harald explained.

The inspector was not interested.

"You do know you are permitted to stay at the

Holy City for three months only? And you know where the Rus encampment is? Good. The Prefect will be informed of your arrival. One of his representatives will decide on the exact prices of your goods and inform you where and when you may sell them. Until then, stay out of trouble, and do not attempt to enter the city without permission."

"I am not a trader," Erik spoke up. "I have come from Denmark to see my old friend, Basil Panopoulos, and I would like to enter the city as soon as possible."

"I know Basil; he trades with you Rus." The inspector's dark eyes rested on Erik. "The Bureau of Barbarians will want to know about you. You may have information they can use. Meanwhile, stay with your friend Harald."

"When I go into the city," Erik said, "these two women go with me."

"That is a matter for others to decide." The little man turned his back on Erik.

It was dawn before Harald received official permission to proceed, a slender youth in a short tunic bringing him a note on parchment that he was to display when required.

The anchor was lifted and the knarr moved slowly through the Bosporus toward St. Mamas, where traders from Kiev and Holmgard were allowed to stay. This settlement lay on the European shore of the Bosporus, across the Golden Horn and some distance away from the rich temptations of Contantinople. It was a ramshackle suburb of tents and a few badly built houses, fringed with heavy-laden boats pulled up on the shore or anchored nearby while their owners awaited permission to sell the cargoes.

"The Greeks don't trust us," Harald joked. "They keep us even farther away from their beloved city than they keep the Venetians, who have their own little village between St. Mamas and the Golden Horn, and who would like to buy Constantinople for themselves if they could. I'm told the Greeks think we northerners smell bad, but at least we smell like men and not like a flower garden." Harald waved his hands in front of his face as if to brush away the last traces of the heavy perfumes worn by the Greeks who had boarded his ship.

Lenora stood in the prow of the knarr, straining for a sight of the great city, although she knew on this day they were forced to stop short of it.

"I'm almost sorry our voyage is over," she said. "If only Halfdan were still here to see the wonders of Miklagard with us."

"Yes, I wish that too." Erik's arm tightened across her shoulders. "You must have Norse blood, Lenora. You have the Viking passion for adventure, and the desire to see new sights, just as I have."

Before she could answer, there was a cry from Maura.

"Look," Maura called excitedly, pointing across the water. "Erik, is that it?"

A great domed building topped with a golden cross rose out of the early morning mist like something in a dream. It shimmered a soft, creamy gold as the sun broke through the clouds and a brilliant ray shone directly on it.

"Hagia Sophia," Erik said softly. "The Church of the Holy Wisdom."

As they watched, the mist began to dissolve and other buildings drifted into view through the clear, liquid light: a smaller domed building in front of the great church of St. Sophia, then a long cluster of red-roofed buildings, and the high, many-turreted wall that on two sides of the city plunged straight down into the water.

The straits were swarming with gaily painted boats, ferrying goods and passengers from one side to the other. A flock of birds suddenly swooped by them, flying close to the water, the beating of their wings the only sound they made.

"There is Miklagard," Erik said, as though he were giving them a gift.

"It's so big," Maura whispered, awe-struck.

"It's beautiful," Lenora breathed. "Erik, will they allow us inside? We have come so far, they can't keep us out."

"I think they will let us in eventually. We just have to be patient. The Greeks are peculiar people. Those who want to deal with them have to do things their way."

"They must feel very safe behind those walls," Maura said softly.

And now, as if he had been teasing them with just a glimpse of the city they had traveled so far to reach, Harald turned his knarr toward land and dropped anchor on the northern side of the Golden Horn.

They camped ashore that night with Harald and his men. Harald had set sturdy guards around his ship.

"The Greeks don't trust us, but if we are wise, we don't trust them, either," he observed.

From the beach they could see the end of the triangular peninsula on which stood Constantinople. Protected on two sides by water—the Bosporus and the famous waterway known as the Golden Horn, where treasure-laden ships from all over the world were safely moored behind a protective chain—and further guarded on all three sides by high, strong walls, the city sat, rich and secure. As the sun set, Lenora watched the lovely shapes of its buildings darken and become silhouettes against the evening sky.

"I hope they let us enter soon," she said with a sigh.

Erik laughed, put his arms around her, and held her close.

It was near the middle of the following day when a messenger, a dark-eyed, curly-haired young man named Georgios, came to escort them to the home of Basil Panopoulos.

"Good luck," Harald said. "Don't forget me."

"I won't," Erik promised. "I will speak to Basil about you. In the meantime, I leave you my sword. I can't take it into the city, so you keep it for me."

As she stepped into the messenger's boat, Lenora could hardly contain her excitement. The bright yellow sail of the small craft opened with

356

a smart cracking sound as the stiff breeze caught it, and then they were skimming across the water to a wall-enclosed landing area that made a tiny harbor just beneath the high wall of the great city. Lenora looked with stunned wonder at the huge, high-decked galleys of the Imperial Navy laying at rest just inside the Golden Horn.

They were met at the landing by an official, who recorded their names and demanded their weapons. He seemed surprised when Erik said he had no sword, but finally let them pass.

Georgios led them on foot to Basil's house. They passed through a bazaar where tradesmen had set up booths and benches to display their goods. Sellers called out their wares and argued with customers, their combined voices rising to a roar of excitement that found an echo in Lenora's pounding heart.

Nearest to the Golden Horn were the fish markets. Then came rice, flour, lentils, salt, and other foodstuffs, in sacks or wooden barrels. Next, sumptuously beautiful cloths of silk and linen and wool, some embroidered with gold and jewels, were displayed, followed by booths showing sculptured ivory, jewelry, perfumes and spices, sheep and horses and pigs for sale, candles and honey and cheeses and cloissoné work and furs. All were organized in their respective sectors of the marketplace according to some plan that Lenora vaguely recognized but was too overwhelmed by the myriad sights and sounds and smells to sort out and make into any kind of sense. It all ran together in her mind like some brilliant tapestry. She had never seen anything like this, not in Hedeby or Aldeigjuborg or even Kiev.

And the people; there were so many different kinds of people, mostly male. There were hook-nosed men with pointed beards and long black hair, men in turbans and flowing robes, Venetian merchants in brocaded silks and furs and jewels, Northmen with mustaches and the firm stride of those accustomed to ships' decks and open spaces, and Greeks in tunics and long, swirling capes. Each spoke his own language, voices mingling together until the babble rose higher and higher and words became incomprehensible in the general tumult.

There was music, made by a group of exotic-looking men and women with brightly-printed scarves on their heads and golden earrings made of coins. The women danced and deftly scooped up the money thrown by the onlookers, tucking it into their bosoms without missing a step, while the men prodded a trained bear to do tricks.

Maura clung to Erik's arm, wide-eyed and pale, nearly overcome by the pressure of the throng through which they slowly made their way.

On Erik's other side, Lenora moved in a near-dream, looking eagerly from side to side, afraid she might miss something, breathing in and absorbing all the smells, even the unpleasant ones, wanting to stop to look at and touch the merchandise and listen to the strange voices in this great city in which she had imagined herself since first Erik told her of it.

Georgios was openly pleased by this provincial woman's delight in his native city, but he would not allow her to stop. He hurried the three foreigners on through the busy market to a narrow side street only a little quieter than the main thorofare, then to another, narrower street where it was quieter still, though by Lenora's standards noisy and crowded with men rushing past them on the way to conduct unknown business.

They came to a neighborhood of houses two or three stories tall, faced with brick and stone in geometric designs, with arched windows overlooking the street. The tall buildings blocked out much of the light, making the street dark and damp.

Georgios stopped before the ornate portico of one house and rapped on the iron door. It opened slowly. An elderly man looked out at them.

They had washed themselves and tried to brush and tidy their clothes, but they were a distinctly bedraggled trio, especially in contrast to Georgios, with his oiled, carefully combed curls and scarlet cloak.

Lenora's silk gown, once blue-green, was now faded closer to gray, dirty, torn, and waterspotted. Maura had long ago lost the belt from her undyed woolen dress, and it hung from her thin shoulders in ill-fitting folds. She was barefoot. Erik's untrimmed hair, heavy black beard, and the scar over his left eye all made him look like a pirate. When he stepped boldly forward the old man closed the door a little, glancing anxiously at Georgios as if for help.

"Tell your master Erik the Far-traveler is here. He will remember me."

"My master is not at home."

The servant tried to close the door, but Erik caught it and pushed it wide open. He strode inside, beckoning his companions to follow.

Georgios spoke in quick Greek, and the old man seemed to lose some of his anxiety.

"I will leave you here," Georgios said. "Perhaps we will meet again. Spyros will deal with you now." With a polite bow, their guide disappeared out the door.

"Is your mistress still the lady Eirena?" Erik demanded of the elderly Spyros.

"She will not see you," sputtered the servant. "She would not expose herself to the indignity of an interview with barbarians. We have armed guards here. I will call them if you do not leave at once."

"I am no barbarian. I am a friend of Basil Panopoulos and of his sister, who was once my nurse. You will be punished if you do not tell them I am here."

The servant's expressive face showed his fearful reaction to Erik's threat. "Wait in this room."

Spyros left, and a moment later a tall, muscular man entered. He stood impassively by the inner door, a gleaming sword in his hand. He never took his eyes off Erik.

"Is this a palace?" Maura whispered. "I thought your Basil was a merchant. I have never seen a house like this before."

Lenora looked about her. The entrance hall had

a high, vaulted ceiling and a marble floor. On the walls were painted murals of hunting scenes. The only furniture was a long stone bench at one side of the front door. Lenora imagined would-be visitors sitting in a row on the bench, waiting to gain admission to the presence of Basil or his sister.

They were made to wait a very long time. Maura eventually sank down on the hard stone bench and leaned her head against the wall. Lenora wandered about the room, looking at the murals. Only Erik stood quietly in the center of the room, waiting patiently.

At last there was a sound from behind the tall guard. The servant Spyros had returned.

"I have told my mistress of your presence," he said, his tone revealing just how offensive that presence was to him, "and also of your disgraceful appearance. She will see you, but you must wait here. You will not be admitted to the house until she is certain you are who you claim to be." As he finished speaking a woman entered the hall.

Eirena Panopoulos was twenty-six, one year older than Erik. She was elegant rather than beautiful, a tiny, small-boned woman, with large brown eyes, a high-bridged nose, and full red lips. Her black hair was braided with silk ribbons and coiled around her head in an ornate style, leaving frizzy curls on her forehead. She wore a long, wide-sleeved gown of deep green silk, into the fabric of which was woven a red-and-gold flower pattern. Around her shoulders was draped a shawl of brilliant orange, patterned in blue and yellow, with a border of gold threads. She wore heavy gold and carnelian earrings.

Her posture was stiffly erect, her movements carefully controlled. She advanced a few steps into the room and stood still, studying the three travelers before her.

Lenora felt Eirena's eyes on her with a cold, dark gaze, speaking nothing of warmth or welcome. Looking back at that exotic, glittering apparition, Lenora felt like the crudest of country wenches. If all the inhabitants of Grikkland were like this one, it was no wonder they thought the Norsemen, with their rough woolen clothes and easy, open manners, were barbarians.

Lenora could see Eirena had impressed Maura in the same way. Maura had risen from the stone bench and moved to a position where she was partly hidden behind Erik, yet could still have an uninterrupted view of this vision of Byzantine splendor.

Eirena had been regarding Erik carefully, from a safe distance, as though she feared he would smell bad if she got too close. A faint smile barely touched her beautifully painted features.

"It is you," she finally said. "Erik. After so long a time. I could not believe it when the Prefect sent word you had come."

She spoke slowly. Lenora could not understand everything Eirena said, but the Greek Erik had taught her at Thorkellshavn and had insisted on speaking with her and Maura during the last days of their journey, now stood her in good stead.

She could at least make out the general meaning of Eirena's words.

"I apologize for coming before you clothed like this," Erik said formally, "but my journey has been long and arduous, and I have no other garments. When we were permitted to enter the city we came directly here."

The smile on Eirena's face became just a little more pronounced and now spread to her eyes. She took one step forward.

"You were so eager to see me again that you forgot your manners? How like you, my impetuous love," she said. "I knew I was right to wait for you. I always knew you would return to me. Erik, *agape mou*, my beloved, enter my home and be welcome."

Part Four

*Constantinople
Early September
to late October,
A.D. 868*

Chapter
Twenty-Four

A manservant appeared to lead Erik away. The women were conducted by another servant through the interior of Basil's house to a large, second-floor chamber decorated with mosaic floors and walls and containing a huge metal tub. Eirena, who had accompanied them, gave abrupt orders to two female servants, then disappeared without explanation. One of the servants approached Lenora.

"*Te banio,*" she said carefully, as though speaking to a child. "*Nea foremata.*"

"What are they going to do to us?" Maura asked fearfully.

"We are to take baths and put on new clothes. They won't hurt us," Lenora assured her. "These people are Erik's friends."

Lenora did not mention her shock at Eirena's

manner of greeting Erik. She hoped she had misunderstood Eirena's words, which had seemed to confirm her own fears about the Greek woman's relationship with Erik.

They bathed and washed their hair with the assistance of the servants. Afterward they were led to meet Eirena in a luxurious bedchamber. The windows of this room looked out over the water to hazy purple land in the distance. Lenora hurried to the window to see the view.

"That is Asia," Eirena informed her. "Over there lies Anatolia. It is part of the Empire too."

"Where is Erik?" Lenora turned away from the window in time to surprise a flash of suspicion in Eirena's eyes at the mention of Erik's name.

"He is being cared for as you are. He has asked that we all eat together this evening. You will see him then."

"Will Basil be there too?" Maura asked timidly. "Erik has told us so much about him. I would like to meet him."

"My brother is in Thessalonica on business," Eirena said. "He will return in another week or so."

They were given silk gowns to wear, cut straight and full in the Greek style, but caught at the waist with corded belts, and with long, wide sleeves. From their size, Lenora suspected these clothes were Eirena's castoffs.

Maura was so tall her pale green gown did not reach her ankles, and the sleeves were far too short. She pulled the belt tightly around her narrow waist.

"It will have to do," Eirena said impatiently, and turned to Lenora.

Lenora's dress was a light brown, brocaded in deep blue and red, with a red belt. It was almost long enough, but she had bigger bones than Eirena, and her figure was fuller. The gown was too tight, especially across the bosom. Each time she moved, Lenora was certain the seams would split.

"Your skin is too brown. It's disgusting," Eirena said, looking at Lenora critically.

"I have been in the sun every day," Lenora said mildly, not wanting to antagonize the woman. She noticed Eirena's olive complexion was smooth and untanned, and she was carefully made up. "Could I wear paint too?"

"Lenora," Maura gasped. "Why would you want to do such a thing? Only wicked women wear paint."

"This is a civilized city, and we use cosmetics," Eirena said sharply. "If you are going to stay in Constantinople, you must do the same."

She commanded her servants to bring cosmetics, and with their assistance Lenora applied color to eyes and cheeks and lips. Maura watched in fascination, and when Eirena stepped out of the room, she dipped her own finger into a pot, and, giggling, tried a little red on her pale cheeks.

They were conducted to yet another room, where they were to dine. The walls of this chamber were painted with flowers and trees and the figures of men and women in ancient Greek costumes who were consuming an assortment of ex-

otic foods, all depicted in bright colors. The floor
of the room was pale marble; the table and chairs
were carved and gilded wood with blue silk cushions. The dining room opened onto an inner
courtyard, where bright flowers bloomed in
carved marble pots and a marble fountain
played.

When Erik appeared Lenora hardly recognized
him. His ragged beard was gone and his hair was
trimmed just below his ears in the Greek style,
with a fringe across his brow.

"I see your old clothes still fit. I saved them for
you," Eirena told him.

He did look handsome, in a knee-length tunic
of deep blue silk, edged in gold and green embroidery, and a gold belt. His hose were a lighter
blue and his shoes were of fine, soft leather.

He was gravely polite to Eirena, but when he
looked at Lenora over the Greek woman's head,
she saw laughter in his emerald eyes.

"You two look much improved," he teased.
"Thank you for helping them, Eirena. You are
very kind."

"I am happy to do whatever you wish," Eirena
replied.

Lenora had the odd feeling Eirena was not
happy at all, but was in fact angry that Erik had
appeared on her doorstep with two female companions. She thought Eirena would have much
preferred to have Erik all to herself.

They ate a meat soup, followed by roast kid
with onions, leeks, and garlic, and a dish of rice
and lentils, all washed down with a resinous

wine. Then they were served fruits and honey tarts. The food was heavy and oily, but after the meager rations available on the trip from Kiev, they all ate heartily.

After the meal was finished, Eirena spoke to one of her ever-present maidservants, and then to Lenora. As she had done before, she spoke slowly and carefully, leaving Lenora with the impression that Eirena wanted to make certain her ignorant northern guests could understand the elegant Greek speech of their hostess.

"You will be shown to your sleeping chamber now. I know you must be tired after your long journey. Feel free to sleep as late as you wish tomorrow. I will give orders you are not to be disturbed."

"Erik?" Lenora looked at him in perplexity. He must know she wanted to speak with him, to learn what his plans were for her. Would he free her a second time, now they were safely in Miklagard? She was suddenly uncertain about wanting her freedom from him.

It was apparent Eirena did not know her true situation. Sure her haughty hostess would swiftly banish her to the servant's quarters or worse if she ever found out, Lenora did not dare to mention it until she and Erik were alone. But when would that be? There he was, standing relaxed and smiling at Eirena's side, and bidding her and Maura good night.

"Sleep well," he added.

"You are weary too," Lenora said, too stubborn to give up and go away quietly. She was rewarded by an exasperated look from Eirena, who started to say something before Erik interrupted her.

"It doesn't matter. I have much to say to Eirena. I'll see you both tomorrow."

Annoyed, Lenora followed the servant to the chamber appointed for herself and Maura. There she lay in a soft bed and fumed as the night crept slowly by.

She had known all along, ever since she had first heard of the woman's existance, that Eirena wanted Erik. Now she had seen them together, she was certain of it. She imagined Eirena pressed into Erik's arms, her dark head barely reaching his chest.

No, Erik would never do such a thing. He had said he wanted her, Lenora. Still, Eirena was obviously clever, and, Lenora suspected, also devious.

She had to see Erik, to feel his reassuring arms around her. She slipped out of bed, being careful not to disturb Maura, and went to the door. The corridor outside was empty, lit by a few oil lamps in ornate dishes. She did not know where Erik's room was, but she would find it. She took a few tentative steps along the corridor.

A hand caught at her arm. With a stifled scream, Lenora stopped. A man in a simple servant's tunic stood before her. Lenora recognized the elderly Spyros.

"Where are you going?" he asked.

"To find my friend Erik."

"You must stay in your room. I am to guard

your door. I will be punished if you leave."

"I don't need a guard." Lenora drew herself up and faced Spyros proudly. "I order you to take me to Erik," she commanded.

"Lady, I dare not."

"What is this noise?" Eirena appeared from a door a short distance down the hall, looking angry. She was wrapped in a cream wool shawl, and her curly black hair tumbled over her shoulders in disarray. "How dare you disturb my household at this late hour?"

"I want to see Erik," Lenora told her.

"In the middle of the night? You should be ashamed of yourself. No respectable woman would go to a man's room after dark."

"In Denmark, Erik and I lived together," Lenora told her boldly, "and I saw him whenever I wanted."

Eirena went pale.

"I am shocked you would admit such a thing publicly," she said, "but I knew from your manners you were a loose woman. You are too familiar with Erik, and you are too outspoken. I would never allow you to stay here, except that Erik wishes it."

"I want to see him."

Eirena smiled, a maddening, distinctly superior smile.

"He is sleeping," she said, but did not say where.

After a few moments' silence, during which Lenora choked back both anger and tears, Eirena, apparently pleased with the effect her words had

373

had, spoke to the manservant.

"Take this woman to her room and see she stays there until morning."

There was nothing Lenora could do, for in spite of his age, Spyros was clearly stronger than she.

She got back into bed beside Maura and lay there, so furious with Eirena that she was unaware of the tears streaming across her cheeks and onto the silken embroidered pillow.

Chapter Twenty-Five

It was noon of the following day before the women were allowed to leave their room. When she asked for Erik Lenora was told he had gone out. She believed Eirena was trying to keep them apart.

Lenora was totally baffled by Eirena's behavior. The woman acted as though their confrontation of the night before had never happened. She was, in her stiff, distant way, pleasant to both her guests, finding more of her old clothes for them to wear, speaking easily of her life as mistress of her brother's house, even advising Lenora how to paint her face.

"Is it true you saved Erik's life?" Maura asked.

"Yes," Eirena answered. "Basil has a villa outside the city, on the Bosporus, where we go to escape the summer heat. He was away from home when the Rus made their unexpected attack. After they had been driven off and a great storm sent by heaven to protect us had wrecked many of their ships, they sailed back to their own country. The next morning I found Erik washed ashore at the edge of our garden. I was certain he would die, but he lived in spite of his grave injuries."

"I'm surprised you didn't turn him over to the government as a prisoner. That would be the proper thing to do, wouldn't it?" Lenora said with acid in her voice.

Eirena ignored the scarcasm.

"It is our Christian duty to care for the sick and injured" was Eirena's bland reply. "Basil was angry with me when he returned home and found Erik in the villa, but he soon grew to like Erik. My brother has a great many important friends in our government bureaucracy, so he was able to make arrangements with the authorities for Erik to return to the city with us at summer's end. Erik stayed here with us for three years. Together, he and Basil were instrumental in devising the new trade agreements with the Rus."

"From which your brother has profited a great deal," Lenora added.

"Of course; that was their purpose." Eirena smiled.

Lenora was quickly bored in the rich seclusion of the Panopoulos house. She missed the easy freedom of her former existance. Only her brief stay in Attair's house had been as restrictive as the cloistered luxury from which she now suffered.

Adding to her feelings of confinement were the armed guards who watched over the house. There were always one or two in the entrance hall, usually one outside the front door, and others placed throughout the house. She later learned two of these men always accompanied Basil when he went out.

"They are necessary for our safety. My brother is a wealthy man and many are envious of him," Eirena told her. "Basil also needs protection when he has business to transact with the barbarian merchants from the north and east."

Lenora thought with some amusement that fabled Miklagard, even with its strong walls, was no safer than the northlands Eirena so scathingly called barbaric.

She saw little of Erik, and never alone. He seemed to be out a great deal on what Eirena vaguely described as "business," and when he was present Eirena monopolized the conversation.

Lenora did learn from the servants that Erik had been ordered to present himself to the Bureau of Barbarians. When she expressed concern about this, Eirena only smiled and shook her head.

"You don't understand at all," she said, as though Lenora were a foolish child. "Our government needs to know everything it can learn about the barbarians who surround us. How else can we deal with them? They come in great numbers to our city, and the police must know what to expect of them, how to control them. Some day we may even convert them to Christianity. How marvelous that would be."

Regardless of Eirena's complacency, Lenora remained concerned until Erik had safely returned from his interview.

"There was nothing to worry about," he told her. "They only wanted to know about trade in Kiev. Once I had mentioned Basil's name, they treated me very well."

"You see," Eirena said with a smile that plainly indicated just how silly she thought Lenora was, "I told you so earlier. You don't understand us, Lenora. We are different from you northerners."

"I want to see the city," Lenora declared one afternoon when she and Maura sat in the courtyard with Eirena. "I have come so far and heard so much about Miklagard, and I have scarcely seen anything at all."

Eirena was scandalized. "No virtuous woman would show her face to a stranger," she said piously.

"Don't you ever go out?" Lenora asked, incredulous. "Don't you want to see what is happening beyond the walls of this house? Wouldn't you like to travel and learn something of the world?"

"The best of everything in the world is here in Constantinople," Eirena responded. "I cannot imagine why anyone would want to leave it. We have our villa on the Bosporus, and I go there each summer. That is far enough from the Holy City."

"But your menfolk must travel, to trade. Erik has told me of all the merchandise that comes here from all over the world, and I have seen a little of the bazaar."

"The merchandise is brought to us. There is no reason for any of us to leave Greece, and those who do—soldiers on campaign, for instance, or the governors of foreign provinces—always long to return home. This city is the center of the world." Eirena folded her hands complacently.

"You must feel very secure here," Maura observed. "This house looks safe, and the city walls are so strong."

"No one could ever imagine conquering us." Eirena laughed. "We are invulnerable to any attack."

"The Rus besieged you once," Lenora reminded her.

"Their attempt failed." Eirena's placid confidence remained unshaken.

Lenora secretly resolved to speak to Erik. She was sure she could cajole him into taking her about the city, if only she could see him alone.

She had no chance to do this before Basil returned home. There was a flurry of activity one afternoon, and one of the servants came to tell her and Maura to wear their best clothes to meet the master of the house at dinner.

They dressed in the best they had, Maura in a cream silk gown embroidered with red and gold roses. It was ridiculously short at ankle and wrists, but it set off her flaming red hair, which she had tied back with a ribbon, disdaining the ornate Byzantine hairstyles. Adequate sleep and plenty of food had done wonders for Maura. She was still timid, fearful that Snorri would somehow find her, but she looked better than Lenora had ever seen her.

Lenora had a gown of irridescent silk that shimmered now green, now gold as the light caught it. There were two wide embroidered bands of gold running down the front of the dress on either side, and a gold belt. Her chestnut hair was still streaked with gold from her long days in the sun, her skin glowing rosy-tan. She painted her face with new-found skill, then bound her hair into a loose knot, letting the errant curls straggle free about her face. Lenora saw her image in the silver hand mirror Eirena had given her guests and knew she looked beautiful. Eirena's unkind comments about her tanned complexion meant nothing.

It was not usual for a merchant in Byzantine Constantinople to become wealthy. The government placed too many restrictions on trade and levied too many harsh taxes to pay for the luxurious Imperial Court and the military aspirations—and occasional military follies—of the Byzantine Emperors. Basil Panopoulos was an exception to the usual.

Basil had been clever enough to see the possibilities of doing business with the Rus, those wild, fur-clad men from the far north who, eight years earlier, had attacked Constantinople and then had begun trading with her. Basil did not hold the northerners in the same haughty disdain as did some of his fellow merchants. With the rescued Erik as willing interpreter, Basil had been among the first to deal with the Rus. Soon he was very rich.

It was not wise to flaunt one's wealth. The spies of the government bureaucracy were everywhere, and not only exorbitant fines but public flogging and unpleasant forms of capital punishment were meted out to those who disobeyed regulations. Basil was careful. His two houses, though beautifully decorated, were not extravagant. His way of life was circumspect, his attendance at church services regular, his payment of taxes prompt but not too prompt, his donations to Orthodox monastaries and churches exactly what would be expected, almost to the last gold solidus.

His sister Eirena guessed at Basil's fortune, but her guess fell far short of the reality. Eirena well knew her brother was rich and that she would never want for any material thing. If she wished, she could make a good marriage, with a handsome dowry, but Basil would not press her to do so. He liked having Eirena in his house, running it efficiently and providing just the degree of sisterly companionship that was all he needed at the end of a busy day. Basil had never married and was not interested in the various recreations and vices that his native city offered. His nature cautious to a fault, Basil was content with the quiet, private way of life the Orthodox Church recommended to its adherents. His work was his principal interest.

It was, until the day he returned home from a trip to Thessalonica to learn his old friend Erik had returned from the northlands, bringing with him two strange women.

Basil was in his middle thirties. He was short, with brown eyes and curly brown hair carefully combed to cover a growing bald spot. He looked remarkably like his sister, but there was in him a restless energy that Eirena lacked.

Lenora noticed this at once. Basil prowled about the room, never lighting anywhere for long. When he did sit he crossed his legs and constantly swung his upper leg back and forth. His hands moved expressively when he talked.

He wore a brilliant orange-red tunic and a wide jeweled belt. He had several gold rings. He wore the heavy perfume favored by Greek men, but just enough of it to leave a pleasant fragrance behind him when he moved.

He was a congenial host, talking constantly on many subjects, asking questions of his guests, helping them to the various dishes of a splendid feast, of fish stew, two kinds of roast fowl with eggplant and artichokes, and fine white bread and the best wine from Chios, followed by sweetmeats and raisins. But there was something wrong, some underlying tension that grew during the evening between Basil and Erik, which Lenora could not ignore.

The women left the dining room shortly after the meal was finished, Eirena announcing in a tone permitting no opposition that they would now retire for the night.

Once in the bedchamber she shared with Maura, Lenora waited, standing by the window and listening to the distant sounds of the city.

"Aren't you going to bed?" Maura asked.

"No, I'm going to see Erik."

"We aren't allowed out of this room at night. You know that. There is always a guard at the door."

"Perhaps not tonight. With so much excitement over Basil's homecoming, they may forget about us. It's worth a try. I know where Erik's room is now. I've learned my way around this house."

Lenora waited a little longer, then slipped out the door. Her guess had been correct. There was no one in the corridor. She hurried to Erik's room, only to find it empty. She dared not linger, for there would be a servant coming soon to prepare his bed for sleep. She would have to come back later. She was about to leave when the door opened and Maura appeared.

"You frightened me," Lenora whispered. "What are you doing here?"

"I came to warn you. Eirena is still awake. I heard her talking to someone in the corridor. I think the guard will be at our door soon. Oh, and the men are still in the dining room. Eirena said so."

"Let's join them."

"Do we dare? Eirena will be furious."

"She doesn't need to know. I have to see Erik without that woman around to interfere."

"All right. I can keep watch, and if someone should find you with Erik, it won't look so bad if I'm there too."

"That's a good idea, Maura, though I'm tired of always following Eirena's rules for us. Come on."

Silently they made their way along the corridor and down the wooden stairs, which creaked at every step. Lenora was sure they would be discovered, but they reached the dining room without meeting anyone, either the servants or the imperious mistress of the house.

They paused outside the half-closed wooden door, stopped by Basil's angry voice, and now Lenora understood the tension she had recognized in him earlier.

"You came naked the first time and I took you in because my sister requested it. I fed and clothed you and gave you gold when you went home. Now you return, with two extra mouths to feed, and again you bring nothing. I do not call this friendship."

Erik's answering voice was full of humor, refusing to accept the offered insult.

"Basil, you forget, I brought to you my connections with the Rus traders. Because of my friendship with the rulers of Kiev, you have made one fortune and will soon make another. That is payment enough for your former kindness to me. This time I come as a friend, as an equal. I want to stay in your city, as your partner."

"That is impossible. There have been changes with the new Emperor, stricter regulations on foreign trade. Life is difficult these days for a poor merchant."

"You are not poor, Basil."

"In any case, you would not be permitted to stay in the city permanently. The last time you were injured and sick, and I had to pay entirely too much gold in bribes to keep you here. This time, three months is the limit. The Emperor himself would not change the new laws for you."

"I see. Well, then, the women and I must go when our three months are over."

Maura suddenly brushed past Lenora, pushed open the door, and ran into the dining room. She stopped before Basil, her creamy silk skirts swirling about her, her red hair gleaming in the candlelight like a fiery beacon. She looked like some angry northern goddess.

"No," she cried. "We can't leave. It's safe here behind the walls. If we leave Miklagard, Snorri will find us again. I can't bear that." Maura burst into tears.

Lenora had never seen anyone cry so beautifully. Maura did not wrinkle up her face as she cried, nor did her nose turn red. Her skin retained its normal creamy tone. Maura's soft gray eyes simply filled with glistening tears that ran down her cheeks in great round drops. Her long, dark lashes fluttered as she blinked. She sniffed delicately.

Basil rose from his chair with an angry exclamation. "Were you eavesdropping?" he accused.

"No, no, we came to find Erik." Maura gestured toward Lenora, who had followed her into the room. "I only heard a little, but it was more than enough. Basil, you can't be cruel and send us away, just when we have found safety. I know you are a kind man. Please help us." Once more Maura was overcome with tears as she looked at Basil with a piteous expression.

Lenora saw Basil's face change as he regarded the slender, flame-haired creature before him. Basil's stern anger disappeared when he tried to comfort Maura.

"Something will be done," he assured her. He put one arm around Maura's slim waist, and she bent toward him like a willow tree in a spring breeze. "Don't worry, Maura, I'll think of something. Please don't cry."

Maura's head was now on Basil's shoulder and he was patting her back as she wept. Since Maura was a full head taller than Basil it was an awkward position. Lenora noticed that Basil, unaware of any awkwardness, had taken on a protective attitude. Struggling to subdue a giggle, Lenora glanced at Erik and saw answering laughter in his eyes.

"Sit down, *poulaki mou*, my dear little bird. Sit here." Basil led the still-weeping Maura to his own chair and settled her in it, tucking an extra cushion behind her back. He rapped out an order. "Erik, pour her a glass of wine."

Erik, his face a study in careful self-control, obeyed. Basil held the glass to Maura's lips, watching attentively as she drank.

"Everything will be all right," Basil soothed. "Who is this Snorri? Why do you fear him? Tell me all about it." He drew a second chair close to Maura and prepared to listen.

As Maura talked, Basil's eyes remained fixed on her face, oblivious to everything else. Erik grinned at Lenora.

"Walk with me in the courtyard," he suggested. "We aren't needed here."

Arm in arm, they circled the marble fountain. Its gentle splashing muffled the voices from the dining room, but Lenora could see Basil still sitting close to Maura and listening to her as though spellbound.

Then she forgot Basil and Maura as she felt Erik's arms around her, and she lifted her face for a long, satisfying kiss.

"I've scarcely seen you since we got here," she accused.

"I have been busy."

"With Eirena?"

He laughed and kissed her again. "Not with Eirena. With Harald. Making plans. It is always good to have an extra plan for an emergency." Sensing the query that rose to her lips, he stopped it with a third kiss. "Ask me no questions inside these walls, my sweet Lenora. Trust me."

"I do. Oh, Erik, if we must leave as Basil said, I don't want to go away without seeing this city. I want to see the hippodrome and Santa Sophia and the golden statues, and all the other wonderful things you told me about, but Eirena won't let us go out. She says virtuous women remain indoors unless they are going to church."

"Does she? Yes, Eirena would say that." He seemed amused.

"It's like being in prison," Lenora went on. "And worst of all, I never see you unless Eirena is there. I think she's afraid of what we'll do if we are ever alone together."

"No doubt. Aren't you afraid?" he teased.

"Not of you."

"Then come to my room. Now."

"Yes. But what about Maura?" Lenora glanced through the arch into the dining room, where Maura still sat talking to her host.

"She's safe enough with Basil. She'll keep him talking half the night. Come on. This way."

Catching her hand, he led her through darkened halls, up a staircase at the back of the house, and thence to his room. The servant Lenora had feared meeting earlier had come and gone, leaving a single candle burning beside the luxurious, silk-covered bed. She heard Erik bolt the door behind them, and then she turned to see his outstretched arms. She went into them without hesitation.

His hard mouth covered her trembling, eager lips, leaving her aware of nothing but his presence. She clung to him, aching with swiftly stirred desire. She opened her mouth to lure him, and when she felt the moist surge of his tongue she answered with her own urgent thrusting. She would devour him if she could, and make his body completely one with hers. Her fingers trailed through his hair, kneaded his strong shoulders, dug into his back. His mouth slid along her throat as his hands tugged at the neckline of her gown. He was defeated by the silk fabric, which lay close at the base of her neck.

He let her go just long enough to lift the gleaming green-gold robe over her head and drop it on the floor. Her sheer linen undertunic followed the same route. She pulled at his tunic, helping him, until he, too, was completely naked. Then she was crushed against him, lost in the sweet sensation of flesh on flesh. His hands stroked slowly along her spine, leaving traces of fire in the wake of his fingertips. Before she could recover her breath his lips met hers in another passionate onslaught that sent her senses spinning.

He lifted her off her feet and carried her to his bed. There he tenderly laid her and, taking the candle, held it above her to gaze upon her body. His eyes traveled from her strong, slightly squared shoulders to the wonder of her full, rounded breasts with their rose-brown tips to her slender waist and gently curving belly. He scrutinized the rich promise of hips and thighs, missing no detail, and then moved on to her long, beautifully formed legs and delicate, high-arched feet. And then he lifted his eyes slowly, lingering once more on each curve and hollow, until his attention rested on her lovely face.

She felt not the slightest shame as he looked at her, but moved about so he could see her better, preening for him while he smiled his pleasure. When at last he replaced the candle on the table by the bed, he bent his head and kissed the sensitive tip of each breast in turn, teasing them gently until they both stood erect and firm, and her breath came in soft gasps. He searched on, moving lower with calculated slowness, while his skillful hands turned her flesh to rosy fire.

They were very quiet. Lenora knew that in this house there was always someone listening, some servant nearby. They dared not speak above the faintest whisper, but this stricture only intensified their passion, forcing them to communicate by touch and taste and the ardent movements of their bodies. The words they dared not utter aloud were spoken with eyes and fingertips, and silent lips and tongues, and finally by the deep, urgent union of both body and spirit that went on and on for a glorious eternity of sweet sensation until it ended in a long, soft sigh.

With infinite tenderness she brushed back his dark hair, smoothing down the white streak, stroking the Greek-style fringe over his forehead. He kissed her, his mouth a promise of yet more passion to come.

"Tomorrow," he whispered into her ear, so softly she could hardly hear him, "I'll take you to see a church near here. Eirena can't object to such an excursion. We will talk then. Now I must take you back to your room."

"Not yet," she breathed. "Just a little longer."

Her hands teased at him until he gave a smothered chuckle at his body's response. He put his mouth against her ear. "You are a dangerous woman," he murmured. "How could I let you go now?"

It was nearly dawn when they crept out of Erik's chamber in their bare feet and tiptoed along the corridor to Lenora's room at the other side of the house. The servant posted to guard the door sat on the floor, his head resting against the wall, snoring softly. With great care, Lenora opened the door and slipped silently inside. Erik waved and headed back to his own room as she closed the door.

Maura lay in the bed they shared, apparently sound asleep. Lenora stripped off her gown and slid into the unoccupied side. She was startled a few moments later by Maura's quiet voice.

"Hasn't it been a wonderful evening? Sleep well, Lenora."

Chapter Twenty-Six

The morning brought changes. Lenora was barely dressed when two elderly women appeared at the bedroom door, followed by the arrival of a young servant girl, reeling under a heavy load of brilliant fabrics and glittering trimmings. An irritated Eirena finished off this odd procession.

"I don't understand it at all," Eirena fumed. "Basil woke me at dawn to insist that Maura must have new clothes. He says my old gowns are too small for her."

"And so they are," Lenora observed.

"What does that matter? They are perfectly good material." Eirena tugged at the light green silk dress Maura had hastily donned. "This will last for years."

"Then give it to a servant to wear," Lenora said

pertly. "Maura should be decently covered."

"For what?" Eirena regarded the two women with a suspicious expression.

"Perhaps she will want to go to church."

"Could I? That would be lovely. I know it's different from the church I am accustomed to, but at least it is Christian. May I go with you, Eirena?" Maura's pale gray eyes were wide and innocent.

"Oh. Well, yes, once you have a respectable dress and a cloak. I hadn't thought of that." And that was the end of Eirena's protests for the moment.

It was later in the morning when Lenora, bored with the chatter of the seamstresses who had cluttered every corner of the room with their work, went looking for Erik. She found him with Eirena in a chamber off the inner courtyard.

Lenora had quickly learned that in the Panopoulos house information was usually gained by eavesdropping on the conversations of others rather than from an open exchange of facts or plans. She had been repeatedly shocked at finding servants—and on several occasions Eirena herself—listening at partly closed doors or behind pillars. Lenora had done this for the first time the evening before, with Maura, as almost by accident they had overheard Basil and Erik. Now, more deliberately, Lenora stood in the empty courtyard and listened to Eirena and Erik. They were discussing her.

"Shameful," Eirena was saying. "If my personal maid is talking about it, you may be certain all the other servants know. Lenora does not set a good example."

"Then neither do I, for I was with her, and she was in my room. She has been my slave for well over a year now, and we have—"

"Lenora is a slave?" Eirena was horrified. "But she is a Christian. Not Orthodox, but Christian nonetheless. It is only acceptable to have heathen slaves. You must free her at once."

"Must I?" Erik sounded amused.

Eirena changed the subject abruptly.

"I have a plan, Erik. I know how you can stay in Constantinople and go into partnership with Basil as you wanted. It is very simple."

"I'm surprised to hear that. I would expect any plan you concocted to be intricate and totally clandestine."

"Erik, be serious."

"I am. I know you. I have been here before, remember?"

"I remember. I remember an evening at our villa on the Bosporus, when the moon was dark." Eirena paused suggestively.

"Tell me your simple plan." Erik's voice was businesslike.

"You will become an Orthodox Christian. Then you and I will marry. Once you are the husband of a respectable woman of Constantinople and the brother-in-law of Basil Panopoulos, it will not be difficult for you to become a citizen. After that, you may stay in Constantinople for the rest of your life."

Lenora, listening outside the door, was livid

with anger. Instead of bursting into the room and confronting Eirena, however, she clamped her hands over her mouth to smother any sound she might make and forced herself to listen as Erik made his calm reply.

"You make it sound very easy. I doubt matters could be arranged as smoothly as you suggest."

"In the past," Eirena said, "prisoners of war have been baptized and granted citizenship. If our former enemies can do it, why not an honest trader from the northlands who comes in friendship? Once you are his brother by marriage, Basil will admit you to all of his business secrets. He is much richer than you imagine."

"Indeed? This is all very interesting."

"And you will have me." Eirena said this as though it were the final, irresistible inducement to Erik's joining her scheme.

Lenora peered around the edge of the doorway. She saw Eirena's hand snake out in a graceful motion and rest on Erik's arm as she gazed at him with her face upturned.

"You will find me a compliant wife, Erik."

"Compliant? You?"

"We have kissed, and although we never went beyond that, you know I can be warm."

"A warm and compliant wife," Erik mused, looking down at her with a half-smile.

"And," Eirena went on, "I know a lot more about Basil's business than he suspects. With my help you could take the business from him and make yourself a wealthy man. We would do it slowly, so he wouldn't notice, but in a few years it would all be ours."

"You are an amazing woman, Eirena."

"Thank you. I do make one condition to this plan, however. Lenora must leave Constantinople. I do not want your cast-off mistress making trouble or causing me any embarrassment."

"What do you suggest I do with her?"

"Free her and give her a little gold. She could go back to Kiev with your friend Harald the merchant, or take passage by ship to Venice and from there return to her homeland. But from the day we are betrothed, you are never to see her again."

"And what of Maura?"

"Maura is of no importance. It is obvious she has never been your mistress. Maura is free to do whatever she wants."

"That's very generous of you."

"Are we agreed then? We can tell Basil at once."

"I think we should wait."

"Wait? Why? Is this not a good plan?"

"It is a remarkable plan, Eirena. I compliment you on your cleverness. But you must see it would not be wise to be too hasty. There is the matter of my conversion. Surely you don't want me to accept your faith without thought, without careful contemplation of what such a step means?"

"Of course not, but—"

"And then there is Basil. We should tread cautiously where he is concerned. I have already talked with him about a partnership and he has refused. I must not seem too eager or he may become suspicious and forbid you to marry me."

"I have thought of that. I can handle Basil."

"Before we say anything to anyone let me think over everything you have said. In a few days we will talk again and decide exactly what to do."

"Very well, if that is what you want. I'll do whatever will please you. Kiss me, Erik. I want you to kiss me. I have waited for you for five long years." Eirena strained upward, reaching for Erik's mouth.

He did not embrace her. He took her hands instead, and kissed each one. Then, dropping them, he moved apart from her.

"I dare not do more," he said softly. "If I were to touch you now, I might not be able to control myself. Who knows what I might do?"

Eirena bowed her head in agreement. "I understand," she said.

"Do you? I wonder. Excuse me now, Eirena." And with that, he was gone.

Eirena drew a deep breath. "Good," she said, so softly that Lenora, still watching and listening outside the courtyard door, had to strain to hear her. "It won't be long now and he will be mine, and that miserable slave-girl will be gone."

Lenora saw Eirena spin around as Basil entered the room.

"Where is Maura?" he demanded. "I want to speak with her."

"She is still with the seamstresses. What are you going to do, Basil, make her your mistress? I have never known you to waste money on a woman before."

"Mistress? Certainly not. I feel sorry for her. The poor woman has had a dreadful time. Her husband and child slaughtered before her very eyes, herself half-starved and forced to make a long journey through a dangerous wilderness; it's a miracle she survived. She deserves a few pretty things after all that."

Eirena wasn't really listening. "I have some news for you," she said. "Erik has asked me to marry him."

"What? How dare he? I forbid it. I won't have my sister marrying a barbarian."

"It's not such a bad idea, you know. If—I say only if—I were to accept him, you could use his connections with the Rus to make even more money. And use them as a political lever. Imagine having a monopoly on furs and amber."

"Too much prominence is a danger. The government would keep an even closer watch on my activities than it does now."

"You could find ways around that problem. Basil, consider the possibilities."

"I am considering them. What did you tell Erik?"

"That I needed time to think about his proposal. I wanted to talk to you first."

"How do you feel about Erik? About being his wife?"

"I will do whatever I must. Like most northerners, he is transparently open and honest. I'll be able to manipulate him easily."

"Hmm. Well, I must think about this. If he

presses you for an answer, make some excuse to delay."

"Basil, don't tell him I've reported this to you. His feelings might be hurt. He was very emotional when he proposed."

Brother and sister left the room together, and Lenora, deep in thought and appalled at Eirena's lies, made her way back to the chamber she shared with Maura.

The seamstresses had left. Maura sat in a carved chair, idly turning a scrap of brocaded fabric over and over, her face serious.

"Basil is very kind to me," she said.

"Be careful, Maura. In this house people are not always what they appear to be."

"I am certain he would never hurt me." Maura's pale gray eyes were soft. "Basil is a good man."

"All the same," Lenora cautioned, "be careful."

Lenora was not sure what excuses Erik had made, but there was no objection when she announced she was going for a walk with him. She met him in the entrance hall at midday and together they left the Panopoulos house.

The late September day was cool, with gray clouds scudding across the wind-whipped sky, but Lenora did not care about the weather. She pulled her borrowed cloak about her and looked around, trying to absorb as many details of the city as she possibly could. Erik kept his hand firmly on her elbow, guiding her through narrow, crowded streets to a tiny brick church.

As they entered Lenora blinked several times, trying to adjust to the dim light inside. Except for one black-robed priest kneeling in prayer before the altar, the building was deserted. A deep silence filled the little church, the more noticeable for its contrast with the noisy street outside. Painted figures of saints, highlighted with gold, lined the walls, and a red glass lamp suspended from a gold chain glowed before the iconostasis at the far end of the nave. Incense hung heavy in the still air.

"Remember it well," Erik told her softly. "Eirena is sure to question you about it, just to be certain you really were here." He led her to one side, where they stood sheltered under a rounded Roman arch, hidden from the view of anyone entering the church but able to see who came and went.

"I must warn you," Erik began, "not to trust anyone in Basil's house."

"Are you going to marry Eirena?"

He looked astonished. "Have you been spying?" he said. "How much do you know?"

"Enough to be certain Eirena will betray you." And she told Erik what she had heard that morning.

"I thought so," he muttered. He slapped one hand against the plastered arch, then leaned his forehead on his hand.

Lenora watched him, knowing he was making an important decision, waiting patiently until at last he straightened and faced her again.

"We cannot stay in this city," he said. "I

thought we could. I thought we would all be safe here, and that I could work with Basil. But I hate the rules and restrictions on merchants, I loathe their mean-minded intrigues, I despise their corrupt officials. What a fool I've been. How I long to breathe clean northern air again!"

"Then you won't marry Eirena?"

"Marry a woman who would plot against her own brother, then turn around and betray her husband? I'm a fool, but not a madman. I never intended to marry her, and never gave her reason to think I would. One kiss five years ago is hardly a proposal. Besides," he looked deep into Lenora's eyes, "how could I agree never to see you again?"

Her heart pounding hard in response to his words and the tender tone he used, Lenora raised one hand to brush his cheek. He pressed his lips against her fingers.

"What shall we do?" she asked. "Can we go back to Kiev with Harald? If we did, we would be going to meet Snorri, I think."

"Kiev isn't the only place in the world."

"I know that look, Erik. What are you planning?"

He grinned at her with a touch of his old humor. "I'll tell you later. Trust me."

"I do. You are the only person in this entire city I do trust. Even Maura is behaving strangely."

"Maura." Erik chuckled. "I don't think we will have to worry about her too much longer. Basil asked me about her this morning, wanting to confirm what she has said about her recent past. I told him she is a free woman of good family and a Christian widow. I think he plans to marry her in time.''

"Marry Maura? But she's so timid, and so afraid of men.''

"Not of Basil. You saw them last night. He is wooing her in the cleverest way possible. He makes her feel safe, and pampers her with new clothes and attention.''

"A few baubles and clothes wouldn't win me,'' Lenora stated.

"You, my sweet, are made of stronger stuff than Maura. We should both remember how harshly she was been treated since she was taken from her home, and how completely her spirit was broken. Basil is repairing that damage, and I am happy to see it.''

As Erik smiled down at her, Lenora realized again, with a sudden constriction of her heart, just how handsome he was, and how precious to her. He towered above her, his black, smoothly brushed hair shadowing his tanned face. That streak of white, toward which her eyes were always drawn, caught a shaft of light from a window set high in the church wall. His emerald eyes watched her with an expression of great tenderness. She swayed toward him. His hands took her shoulders and pulled her to him. His lips brushed hers as he folded her against his chest.

"This is not the right place,'' he whispered, "but how I want you, Lenora. How good it is to know that you are an honest woman.''

She knew he was thinking of Eirena.

Erik released her as they heard a step behind them, and a priest came into view. Under his disapproving eye they hastily left the church.

"There is one matter on which I do agree with Eirena," Lenora said as they walked along. "You should free me, Erik."

"I will do so as soon as it is safe," he replied. "For the moment it is better for you to be my slave. No one thinks it strange for a man to take his property with him when he travels."

She slipped her hand into his, feeling the strength of his long fingers as they closed around her softer ones.

"Are we going to travel?" she asked.

"What do you think?" he teased.

A few days later Maura was given her own room.

"It's lovely," Lenora said, admiring the marble floor and the view of the Sea of Marmora from the three tall windows along one wall. A mural covering two walls depicted a lush garden with trees and flowers in brilliant greens, yellows, and reds. A large, comfortable bed was draped in deep green silk. There were carved wooden chairs inlaid with ivory, and several low tables adorned with enamel plaques of bright-colored design. Many of the furnishings, and the silks, were obviously new.

A servant was busily putting away the first of Maura's new gowns, which had arrived from the seamstress that afternoon. After the woman had finished and left the room, Lenora spoke more freely.

"Basil is growing fond of you if he gives you a chamber as rich as this."

"He is so kind. You know how frightened I have been, Lenora, but here with Basil I feel safe. Basil says that is right and proper, that women shouldn't flaunt themselves in public, that it is good I want to stay inside the house. He says he will always protect me."

"Will you marry him?"

Maura blushed a deep red.

"I don't know. Perhaps, if he asks me. When I came here I wanted nothing more to do with men, not after Snorri and Sven treated me so badly. But Basil is different." Maura blushed again.

"He kissed me last night," she confessed, "and I liked it. Yes, I may marry him in time."

The amazing thing, Lenora thought, was not that Maura had so quickly learned to care for Basil, but that Eirena seemed to have no idea what was going on between her brother and Maura. Eirena was only interested in Erik and in her own plans. She complained briefly at dinner about Maura having her own room, made a sarcastic comment about Maura's new blue-and-gold brocade gown, and then dropped the entire subject. Lenora, catching Erik's glance across the table, imagined she saw a thoughtful twinkle in his green eyes.

Late that night, as Lenora lay alone in the bed she had previously shared with Maura, there was a light knock at her door and Erik slipped inside.

She sat up in surprise and would have gotten out of bed.

"Hush," he warned, a finger over his lips.

In an instant he was beside her, his mouth stopping her exclamation of joy at his presence. He pushed her down onto the silken sheets, pressing his hard, passionately erect body over hers. She responded to his touch with a sudden, fiery desire that would not wait. She clutched at him, pulling aside the short tunic he wore.

"Hurry," she moaned, now tearing at her own sheer linen nightgown with her free hand, pulling him toward her with the other. "Oh, please, my darling, hurry."

He answered with a triumphant laugh just before his mouth seared hers with a passion that answered her own. She felt him enter her and move once, twice, and then she was plunged into a blinding white heat of sensual delirium that exploded with such force, it threatened to destroy her. Her nails raked at his back as she pushed upward against him, consumed by urgent need.

It was over too quickly.

"I never get enough of you," she whispered, nuzzling at his neck, satisfied but still longing for something else. She did not know what it was, yet a strange wanting gnawed at her.

"You will get more than enough of me tonight." He laughed. "How glad I am that Basil gave Maura her own room."

It was only now, with the passion between them in momentary abeyance, that he finally removed his clothing and slipped Lenora's crumpled nightgown over her head, letting his hands slide along the soft, curving length of her body as he did so.

He stretched out beside her, playing idly with one of her full, rounded breasts, rubbing it gently until the nipple stood up proud and hard. He leaned over, teasing it with his tongue, then sucking boldly, drawing more and more of the tender flesh into his mouth. She moaned, gritting her teeth. He raised his head.

"Shall I stop?" he asked.

For answer, she pulled his head back, to the other breast this time, and he served it as he had the first. Her breath came more quickly as her volatile emotions were rekindled.

As he bent over her, she ran her flattened palms along the firm muscles of his shoulders and upper arms, then briefly tangled her fingers in the silky black hair on his chest before her hands slid around to cup his smooth, tight buttocks.

He moved lower to concentrate on her softly rounded belly, stroking and caressing. Her warming flesh seemed to rise to meet his hands and lips.

Then his hands slipped down over hips and thighs, lingering on their silky smoothness. He kissed and gently teased at the backs of her knees before moving upward again, this time along her inner thighs, separating her legs as he went, until he reached the red-brown hair of the soft-curving mound between them. And there he lingered, exploring with slow, gentle, but determined probing, tracing concentric circles with one finger, round and round, moving ever closer to the pulsating, painfully sensitive spot now aching for his touch.

She felt his mouth on her and she cried out at the hot, moist pressure of his tongue. At first she tried to wriggle away, then, as he continued, she caught his head and held it there, reveling in the exquisite new sensations that spread, pulsing deliciously, throughout her body. With hands and lips and tongue he drove her to near-frenzy. When finally he pulled away from her she cried out and tried to draw him back. She saw his manhood, hard and throbbing with barely contained eagerness, and the sight nearly drove her mad with longing to hold him within her.

Now he was covering her breasts and throat and face with hurried, burning kisses, while that place between her thighs where lately he had lingered tormented her with an unbearable need.

At last, at long, long last, when she was nearly screaming in an agony of frantic, clamoring erotic hunger, he took pity on her. Slowly, deliberately, he moved deeply into her eager, welcoming warmth.

A long sigh of pleasure escaped her parted lips as she wrapped her arms about him, her eyes half-closed in ecstasy. He moved deeper still, and now a warm sweetness overpowered her, spreading outward in waves from the taut center of her body to her fingers and toes and to the very hair on her head. She was intensely aware of the full length of his body against hers, from his hard, demanding mouth covering her own and his tongue thrusting against hers in a sensual rhythm to his hair-covered chest bruising her tender, sensitive breasts to his firm-muscled thighs, scratchy with hair, that rubbed against her own smoother flesh. At the center of his being was that part of his body that now gave her such intense, exquisite pleasure, surging into her and withdrawing, then returning again, generating unbearable heat with each movement, sucking her into a whirlpool, holding her captive, leaving her empty and yearning for more, then filling her with joy and lifting her up into the heavens.

On and on it went, unending, hot, honey-sweet and head-spinning as the strongest mead, until he gathered her even more closely into his arms, and blindly she clutched at him to pull him even farther into her. At the same instant they both whirled into another plane of existence where together they became one whole and complete being in a passionate culmination that united them with a life-generating force that shook them to their very souls.

When at last Lenora came back to herself Erik was kissing her reverently. He began with her forehead and her eyes and continued until he had kissed every inch of her body. He lingered on her lips, and at that place where their bodies had joined, and ended at the tips of her toes. Then he stared at her face as though she were something more than human, something miraculous, until she pulled him down into her arms again, and their lips met in a deep kiss of infinite tenderness.

Finally he slept, and Lenora lay beneath his

protective arm in a contented daze, still too sensitively alert to his presence to be able to sleep. In the deep fulfillment she now felt, Lenora had found the elusive something for which she had been longing. She knew, although how she could not have said, that from the sublime act of love just completed she and Erik had conceived a child.

"It will be a son," she told herself, "and he will have black hair and sea-green eyes."

Chapter Twenty-Seven

Lenora was brushing her hair in a peaceful, deeply satisfied mood when Eirena swept into her room without knocking.

"You disgusting creature," Eirena hissed. "I gave you shelter and food and clothing—my own beautiful clothes—and how have you repaid me?"

Lenora put down the hairbrush and faced her visitor. Her movements were slow and languourous, in contrast to Eirena's rapid, nervous pacing as she prowled about the room.

"What are you talking about, Eirena? I have done nothing to harm you."

"Nothing?" Eirena stared at her from hate-filled eyes. "Nothing? My servingwoman tells me Erik spent last night in this room. How dare you say you have done nothing to me?"

Lenora realized there was no point in denying what was undoubtedly household gossip by now. She tried to speak calmly.

"Erik came to me because he wanted me. You know perfectly well that we have lived together."

"You vile, filthy woman!" Vainly Eirena struggled to regain her self-control. "You will not see Erik again. He has gone out, and you will be taken from this house today, before he returns. I know just the place for you, and it is far enough away to keep you from ever returning to Constantinople. There is a strict convent outside Alexandroupolis. Once you are locked inside, out of his sight, Erik will soon forget all about you."

Lenora felt a chill settle about her heart. For the first time she was really afraid of Eirena. She knew the jealous, violently angry woman before her would find the means to do what she threatened, and to keep Erik from learning what had happened until it was too late. If she were taken from Basil's house and Erik could not find her, what would happen to her? And what would happen to the babe that, illogical though the idea was, she felt certain sheltered even now within her womb?

Eirena continued her tirade, scarcely pausing for breath.

"Erik and I will be married soon," Eirena said. "I have waited for his return for five years. He belongs to me, not you. My guard will remain outside your door. You will see no one, nor will you leave this room until I have completed the arrangements for you." With this, Eirena tried to

411

leave the bedchamber. She found Maura blocking her exit.

"Get out of my way," Eirena screeched, losing her self-control for a second time. "You stupid nonentity, let me pass."

"Certainly." Maura moved aside. As Eirena whisked past her, nose in the air, Maura spoke again. "If you send Lenora to the convent of which you were just speaking, I will go with her."

"That is perfectly agreeable to me," Eirena commented acidly. She would have continued on her way, but Maura's next words stopped her.

"I don't think you are aware of it, Eirena, but Basil has become extremely fond of me. I think, were I to enter a convent, he would miss me terribly. Unlike Erik, who is a stranger in this country, Basil would have the means to quickly discover where I had gone. He might even follow me to inquire why I had done such an odd thing. I would naturally feel obligated to tell him the truth, how I would not leave my friend Lenora, who was being forcibly detained at your order. I don't think Basil would care much for that news, do you?"

"You—!" Eirena raised a small, heavily beringed hand as if to strike Maura.

"Do be careful," Maura said calmly. "I have such fair skin that any injury leaves a clear imprint for all to see. I would hate to have to explain a bruise in the shape of your hand to Basil."

Lenora thought Eirena would fling herself upon Maura and tear her to pieces. She could almost feel the strength of will Eirena was exerting to control herself.

"There will be another time," Eirena said at last, between clenched teeth, "and I will not forget you, Maura." With a last, baleful glare, Eirena left the room.

The two friends fell into each others' arms in relief.

"Thank you," Lenora said, half laughing, half crying. "I thought you claimed once or twice in the past to have no courage."

"It is Basil's doing," Maura replied. "He gives me strength. I will tell him what Eirena threatened. He'll see to it that she doesn't harm you. Now, I have something much nicer than Eirena to talk about. Basil has agreed you shall have a new dress too. Come to my room; the seamstress is waiting."

In the manner Lenora had learned was characteristic of this peculiar household Eirena ruled, no further mention was made of the morning's threats. It was as if the confrontation between Eirena and Lenora, and the shorter altercation between Eirena and Maura, had never occurred. Eirena showed no trace of dislike or anger when they met the men for the evening meal. She was perfectly polite and apparently eager to attend to her guests' needs and slightest desires. Lenora, knowing Eirena's kindness was false, felt certain she was plotting something new.

"Erik and I have some final arrangements to make with his friend Harald the merchant," Basil said over honey tarts and dried fruits. "We will go to our villa on the Bosporus and meet with him there."

"How long will you be gone?" asked Eirena with sudden intense interest.

"Only a few days. Why do you ask?"

"I have an idea," Erik said, speaking into the silence while Eirena fumbled for an answer. "Why don't we all go? I have talked about your lovely house so much, I'm sure Lenora would like to see it, especially the gardens."

"No, no," said Eirena, too quickly. "In mid-autumn? It is much too chilly at this time of year. We women will all stay here, where it is warm and comfortable."

"I would love to see the gardens." Lenora was suddenly anxious not to spend time in Basil's house with the men gone. "I don't mind the cold. Wouldn't you like to go, Maura? I have a feeling you will miss Basil if he goes away for even a short time."

"I would miss him," Maura agreed, "but I'm not sure I want to go outside the city walls."

"Very wise of you." Eirena shot a triumphant look at Lenora. "We will remain here at home."

"But this is a splendid idea of Erik's." Basil was enthusiastic. "We will go tomorrow. You will enjoy my villa, Maura. I'll make it warm enough for you. We will have charcoal braziers lit in every room. We can take long walks in the gardens. Your new cloak is ready, isn't it?"

"Yes, but I'm not sure I should go." Maura hesitated, torn between fear and her desire to please Basil. "Are you certain we will be safe?"

Basil reached across the table to take her thin hand. Eirena looked away in disgust at this open sign of emotion.

"There is nothing to worry about, my dear little bird. Leave everything to me. I will take good care of you, I promise."

Maura allowed herself to be won over.

"If you promise, Basil, then I believe you."

When Lenora returned to her room at bedtime she found a tall, armed man posted outside her door.

"What are you doing here?" she demanded.

"I am here on order of the lady Eirena," the guard informed her. "She is concerned for your safety. Once you enter your bedroom, no one may go in or come out until morning."

"I don't need a sentry."

The man made no reply, but opened the door and motioned her in. Lenora bolted the door on the inside and moved a low table in front of it, piling a collection of small objects on the table, so anyone trying to get in during the night would knock it over and make a warning noise.

She slept not at all that night, nor did she rest well the following night at Basil's waterside villa, where the same guard stood outside her chamber.

It was cold, as Eirena had warned it would be, and a wind off the Euxine Sea rattled through the shuttered windows. The villa was a smaller, more open version of the Panopoulos house in Constantinople. In the hot Greek summer its constant breezes must be delightful, Lenora thought, but in mid-autumn it was distinctly uncomfortable.

Because it was outside the protection of Constantinople's impregnable walls, the villa was guarded by Basil's personal force of armed men. Basil took care to mention this to Maura as evidence of their safety.

Around the villa, wide, terraced gardens swept down to the water's edge. Erik pointed out a tiny, curving beach.

"It was there Eirena found me, washed up by the sea."

Maura, muffled in her new saffron-yellow cloak, had been walking with Lenora when Erik appeared. She shivered in the chill wind.

"You must have been terrified," she said.

"I don't remember a thing." Erik laughed. "But that is where I first came to Miklagard."

"And now you are going to leave it forever, aren't you? You and Lenora will go away." Maura blinked back tears. "I will be sorry to see you go, but I know it's best for you. Neither of you could live for long in that city, enclosed behind walls, with a thousand rules to tell you what to do and not do."

"You may come with us."

"Not I. I'm happy here. The very things that you dislike about Byzantium are the things that make me feel safe. I will marry Basil eventually. After I do, I think perhaps Eirena should retire to a convent." Maura laughed, then looked directly at Erik. "I won't say a word to anyone about your plans, not even to Basil."

"We have no plans."

"Erik, you always have a plan. Sometimes more than one." Maura stood on tiptoe and kissed Erik on the cheek. "I have neglected to thank you properly for saving my life. I will never forget you. Or you, Lenora. I just wanted to tell you now, in case you have to leave suddenly and there is no time for good-byes."

A rich, deep chuckle sounded behind them as Harald the merchant strode into view, followed by Basil.

"What a tender scene." Harald laughed, even white teeth showing through his blond beard and droopy mustache. "Erik and the two prettiest women in Miklagard. What's your secret, my friend? I never have such good luck."

"Maura is not Erik's woman." Basil was plainly annoyed by Harald's assumption.

"Oh-ho, is she yours, then?"

Basil scowled. Before he could answer, Erik intervened.

"There is no insult intended, Basil. Harald was only joking. Let us go inside where it is warmer and talk about this agreement for next year's merchandise."

"Erik, why don't you travel back to Kiev with me and my friends once the agreement is signed?" Harald asked as they moved along the path, the women following close behind.

"Perhaps I should leave Constantinople," Erik replied, as though the idea had never occurred to him before.

Basil was astonished.

"Leave? You told me a few weeks ago that you wanted to live here. Why would anyone ever want to leave the Holy City? Everything a man could possibly want is here. All the merchandise of the world comes to us. The city contains all of the pleasures, and, if you want them, all of the vices known to man. It is the world's most beautiful city. And Eirena is here. Erik is very fond of my sister Eirena," Basil informed Harald.

"Is he? I didn't know that." Harald glanced at Lenora and raised an eyebrow. When she shook her head behind Basil's back Harald gave her a comical look and followed the other men into Basil's study.

It was later in the afternoon when Erik found Lenora sitting alone by a charcoal brazier in an upper room, trying to warm her hands. He bent to kiss her, then drew up a wooden chair to sit beside her.

"I'll come to you tonight," he murmured, taking her hands in his and holding them against his heart to warm them.

"My door is well guarded. Eirena wants to keep you away from me."

"Nothing will keep us apart, Lenora. You belong to me."

That was just the problem, she thought. She was his possession, and sometimes, try as she might, it was hard to trust him as he wanted her to do. She reminded herself he had not failed her yet, and then she stopped thinking as his lips met hers in a sweet, lingering kiss.

Eirena glided into the room, her stiff, ornately trimmed robes barely moving as she walked.

"Erik," she said, her voice sharp, "I have told you I do not want you to meet with this lascivious, despicable woman. Tell her to leave."

Erik rose and stood by Lenora, one hand on her shoulder, holding her firmly in her chair by the glowing brazier as he addressed Eirena.

"Lenora and I were speaking privately. You have no right to interrupt us. Furthermore, I insist you treat her with respect."

Eirena's lip curled, her eyes flashing angry fire, but she kept her voice level.

"When I came in you were not speaking. When we are married I will no longer tolerate this—this—*diversion*."

"I assure you, once I am wed, my only diversion will be my wife."

"Is that a promise, Erik?"

"It is a solemn vow."

"Then tell Lenora to go."

"No."

"Erik?" Lenora shook off his restraining hand and rose, looking from Erik to Eirena, with a frightened question in her eyes. Eirena had said *when* they were married, not *if*. Had something happened, something Erik had not told her?

"Lenora will stay here with me for as long as I want," Erik insisted.

"You will pay dearly for this insult," Eirena hissed. "Both of you will pay." She stalked out of the room, her tiny figure stiff with anger.

"She frightens me," Lenora said. "She is de-

419

termined to marry you and to do me harm."

Erik gathered her into his arms, his face buried in her fragrant curls.

"She won't succeed," he whispered.

Chapter
Twenty-Eight

They sat through another evening meal during which Eirena was a charming hostess, hiding what Lenora knew was bitter anger under a smooth, placid manner. When the main course of roast lamb with garlic had been cleared away and trays of fresh apples and grapes, dishes of sweetmeats, and small silver bowls of raisins, almonds, and pistachios had been placed on the table, Eirena leaned back in her chair and smiled sweetly at Erik.

"Did you not tell me once that you have a brother?" she inquired.

Maura set her wine goblet down so hard the ruby liquid splashed across the table. She began to tremble. Lenora sat unmoving, sure Eirena was plotting something but uncertain what it could be.

"Snorri," Maura whispered.

"Yes, that was the name. Thank you, my dear." Eirena transferred her smile to Maura. "You look frightened. Is anything wrong?"

"What about Snorri?" Erik's voice was harsh, cutting across Eirena's honeyed tones.

"One of my servants brought me news late this afternoon that a man calling himself Snorri Thorkellsson has landed at St. Mamas not far from here and is looking for you. Shall we invite him to the villa, Erik?"

"No!" Maura burst into tears. "Eirena, how could you? Basil, don't let him come here. Oh, I knew we should never have left the city. We were safe behind the walls."

Lenora leapt from her seat and hurried to comfort Maura, who clung to her in desperate fear.

"You know what Snorri will do to me," Maura wept. "Don't let him hurt me again."

Basil, too, attempted to calm Maura.

"You saw all the guards I have here," he told her. "No one can enter the villa grounds without my permission. You are perfectly safe, *poulaki mou*. I won't let anyone harm you."

"What in the world is the matter with her?" Eirena was the picture of baffled innocence. "All I suggested was a simple family meeting. I thought your brother might like to come to our wedding."

Lenora had had her fill of Eirena. "You bitch," she spat, "you vicious, contemptible, troublemaking bitch!"

Barely concealing her boredom, Eirena headed for the door.

"Really, Erik, I wish you would make your mistress watch her tongue. This unnecessary display of emotion is dreadfully tiresome. I am going to bed."

"Just a moment." Erik stood between Eirena and the door. "Who informed you Snorri had arrived in Grikkland?"

"I told you, one of my servants." Eirena did not meet Erik's eyes.

"Which servant?"

"I don't remember. There are so many of them, and they all chatter so. It's not important."

"Did you see Snorri yourself?"

"I? Of course not."

"I don't believe you."

"You had better believe me, Erik. I am going to be your wife." With that, Eirena left the room.

"No," Erik said after her, "you are not."

He turned back to the others, who were still attempting to calm the terrified Maura.

"Do you think she did that deliberately?" a furious Lenora asked him.

"I am certain of it." He bent over Maura. "Are you better?"

"A little. I'm sorry to make a scene and anger Eirena, but Erik, you know how much I fear Snorri."

"I understand, Maura. It was a cruel thing for Eirena to do. Basil," Erik looked his friend in the eye, "I must speak plainly. If you plan to marry Maura, you should beware of Eirena. She will do

423

everything she can to make both of you unhappy. She may even betray you."

"I understand more than you think, Erik. Maura will be safe with me. I have learned some surprising things about my sister since you returned to us. You are not going to marry her, are you? You never even asked her, did you?"

"No."

"Then you had best leave Greece at once."

"I plan to do just that, after I have seen your new agreement with the Rus completed to your satisfaction."

"Thank you. For a barbarian, you are a remarkably honorable man, my friend. And you are almost subtle enough to be a Greek." Basil allowed himself a half-smile at his own joke. "As you know, tomorrow morning we meet with Harald and his fellow traders for the last time before they return to Kiev. Once our business is completed and the agreement is signed, I will take Maura back to the city, where she will feel safer. Three days later, I will return to this villa. If you are still here, I will do what I can to help you, but I suggest you take my advice and leave before Eirena can do you harm."

"Agreed." Solemnly, the two men clasped hands.

Lenora stayed in Maura's room all night. Maura could not stop trembling.

"I will never leave Constantinople again," Maura said. "I will just stay there with Basil, forever. Come back with me, Lenora, and make Erik come too. You are my only friends. I want to know you are safe from Snorri."

"I can't do that. I think Erik wants to resolve this feud with Snorri now, to have it over at last, whatever happens."

"Then you come with me. Erik will join you after he has met Snorri."

"I can't leave. I have my own quarrel to settle with Snorri."

Their farewell the next afternoon was tearful. Maura, halfway out the door, ran back to embrace Lenora one last time.

"Take care of yourself, and Erik too. Be safe and happy," she said in a choked voice.

"That is disgusting." Eirena had come into the entrance hall in time to see Maura's tears. She had insisted on remaining at the villa, saying she could not leave her guests. "Maura is a coward and has absolutely no sense of dignity."

Lenora, so upset she was beyond words, hurried to the gardens to get away from Eirena. She paced along the terraces, glad of the icy wind from the Bosporus that dried the tears on her cheeks. Looking down the hill from the topmost terrace, she was momentarily diverted from her sorrow at parting with Maura by the sight of Harald pushing a small sailing craft into the water.

She watched Erik wave good-bye to the merchant and begin to ascend the winding path to the house. A few moments later he appeared beside her. He opened his arms and she went into them wordlessly, feeling the strong beat of his heart under her cheek, knowing he understood her anguish at parting from Maura.

He bent his head and kissed her. Enclosed in their own private world, in the sweet rapture of that embrace, neither of them noticed Eirena, standing in the open door of the villa, watching them.

In late afternoon Eirena let Snorri into the house.

"Leave your men outside," she said. "That is what we agreed upon."

"And let your guards slaughter them?"

"So long as their swords remain in their sheaths, my men will not strike."

Snorri squinted at her, hating the strong southern sunshine that bounced off the white walls of the villa and hurt his eyes.

"I don't like taking orders from women," he said.

"If you follow my plan, you will have what you want," Eirena told him. "Erik is here, and he is unarmed."

"All right. You win. For now." Snorri motioned to his men to remain behind and followed Eirena into the soothing dimness of the entrance hall.

Erik and Lenora were sitting in an upper room that overlooked the Bosporus. They had been talking intently, huddled over a brazier for warmth, and at first they did not notice Snorri. Then Lenora gasped.

"A pretty sight," Snorri drawled. "I thought

you would have tired of that wench by now, cripple."

"You let him in, didn't you, Eirena?" Lenora's
face was white, her dark gray eyes wide. "Don't
you know he wants to kill Erik?"

"No, he doesn't." Eirena was completely assured. "He wants Erik to give him back the silver
he stole from their father, and he wants you. In
return for my help, Erik is mine."

"You talk about Erik as though he were a bolt
of silk," Lenora said contemptuously.

Eirena looked at Erik, who had risen from his
chair and now stood, halfway across the room
from her, with an easy grace that did not mask
his readiness to deal with whatever happened
next. Eirena's eyes lingered over every detail of
Erik's body, while Snorri chuckled beside her.

"I want him," Eirena said, her voice low and
throbbing with barely restrained passion, her
painted face clearly revealing the obsession that
motivated her.

"I don't think much of your choice in men,"
Snorri told her.

Eirena ignored him and spoke directly to Erik.
"Give Snorri the silver hoard you stole from
your father," she said.

While Erik's attention was focused on Eirena,
Snorri lunged at Lenora, catching her by the
wrist. Lenora cried out as he pulled her back
against him, but ceased her struggles when she
felt Snorri's sharp dagger pricking at her throat.
The rancid smell of his hot body nearly choked
her. She thought she would faint from terror.

"Let her go," Erik demanded.

"Give me the silver."

"Give me Lenora first."

There followed a tense silence during which Erik and Snorri faced each other across the brazier while Lenora held her breath. Snorri's muscular arm encircled her waist, pressing her tightly against him. Her every nerve revolted at his touch. She tried to pull away and she felt a trickle of blood as his dagger pushed deeper into her throat.

There was something else, something worse than the threat of having her throat cut. She could feel Snorri rubbing himself against her with obvious, obscene intent. His hand slid down across her abdomen and pushed her back harder against him. Unable to control her reaction, she felt her stomach heave. She retched, bending away from him.

Suddenly Snorri twisted her arm cruelly and thrust her at Erik. Lenora stumbled and nearly fell against the red-hot brazier. Erik caught her and steadied her.

"Tie them to the chairs," Snorri ordered.

"What?" Eirena clearly had not expected this.

"I said, tie them up, woman!" Snorri roared at her.

"How?"

"With the cords from those draperies, idiot. Put their arms behind them. Do it!"

Eirena, visibly shaken, bound Erik and Lenora to two heavy wooden chairs while Snorri stood threatening them with his sword. At last, satisfied the knots were secure, he poked at Erik with the point of his sword.

"Now the silver, cripple. Where is it?"

"The silver is safe at Limfjord. Freydis has it. Your long journey was for nothing, brother."

"You lie."

Erik shrugged beneath the cords holding him. "Believe what you will, Snorri."

Snorri looked at the brazier with a reflective air.

"Perhaps a few hot coals applied to a sensitive place will open your mouth."

"No!" The cry was wrung from Lenora. "He's telling the truth. Don't hurt him."

"I do what I please," Snorri told her. "You there." With his free hand, Snorri motioned to Eirena. "How many bundles did he have when he arrived?"

"Erik came to my brother's house with only the clothes he wore and the two women," Eirena said. "I believe he has left the silver with Harald the merchant, or else buried it somewhere."

"You told me the silver was in this house." Snorri was growing angry.

"I told you Erik was here, and that he could tell you where the silver is hidden."

"I don't like women lying to me."

"I haven't lied. I brought you to Erik."

"And no silver." Snorri regarded Eirena thoughtfully. "Your brother is a wealthy man."

"There is no gold in this house."

"You are mistaken. There is a fortune here. You." Snorri walked around Eirena, appraising her in much the same way she had looked at Erik earlier. "You don't look like you'd give a man much pleasure, but we'll see about that later."

"What are you going to do?" Eirena's carefully composed veneer had begun to crack in the face of Snorri's menacing attitude. Her voice trembled.

"I'll hold you for ransom. Your rich brother will pay well to get you back. In the meantime, you can share my blanket."

"This is treachery!" Eirena was outraged.

"You dare to speak of treachery?" Erik accused her. "You let him in here, betraying me."

"I wanted you for my own. I wanted to be rid of Lenora."

Erik's voice was bitter.

"A woman of your accomplishments should have known better than to trust Snorri."

"I should have known better than to trust any Norseman."

"Be quiet, all of you," Snorri growled, brandishing his sword. "I could kill you right now, Erik, but I have other plans for you. You will die slowly and painfully, and as you die, you will watch me using your precious Lenora. I'll have her over and over again before your eyes, and you won't be able to do anything to stop me. Then I'll give her to my men. If she's still alive when you die, she'll join you soon enough."

"You told me I could have Erik," Eirena said angrily. "You said you wouldn't hurt him."

"And you said my silver hoard was in this house."

Eirena stared at him, unable to speak for rage.

"Now, woman," Snorri went on, "you must call off your guards so we can all leave here. And we will send a message to your brother demanding gold for your release."

"I won't do it."

"Oh, you'll do it." Snorri advanced on Eirena with a threatening gesture. She stood her ground.

"I have a better idea. We needn't hurry, Snorri."

"I don't trust you, woman."

"I have never known a man with a beard." Eirena's voice was suddenly seductive. She moved closer to Snorri. "Must we leave at once?"

"What are you up to?" Snorri stepped back, looking at her suspiciously.

Eirena laughed, spreading her arms wide as though to prove she was no danger to the guarded man before her.

"What could I, a tiny, helpless woman, do against someone so large and strong as yourself?" she asked. "You wondered whether I would give you pleasure. Let me show you how I will receive you."

"I don't trust you," Snorri repeated. "Get away from me."

"If you won't touch me, how will you take me to your bed?"

Snorri did not answer.

"You are so clever," Eirena cooed. "You have tricked us all. I admire cleverness in a man."

"I am known for my crafty ways," Snorri told

her, flattered in spite of his reservations about this devious woman.

"I am sure you are. And you are so handsome too."

Snorri pulled himself up, puffing out his chest.

Eirena drew nearer. She put out her little hand and stroked Snorri's sword arm, and this time he did not draw away from her.

"How strong you are, Snorri." Her hand slid up his arm, squeezing at his bulging biceps.

"Oh-h-h, Snorri." Eirena's voice was a carefully modulated moan of naked desire. "How could I ever have imagined I wanted Erik?"

Snorri grinned down at her, completely distracted by her open admiration.

"I will show you the most intimate secrets of Greek women," Eirena promised.

"I'll show you a few secrets too," Snorri told her.

Eirena's small, clawlike left hand caressed Snorri's blond beard, then moved to tangle in his long hair.

"I have never kissed a bearded man."

"Never kissed a man at all, I'll wager."

"You will be the first."

"Good. I like virgins. They always scream."

"I promise to scream for you, my beautiful Snorri."

"I'll see to it that you do." Snorri grabbed at Eirena's hips, pulling her hard against him.

"Kiss me, Snorri," she whispered.

He lowered his head and Eirena reached up to

him. Their lips met, as Lenora and Erik watched, frozen in astonishment.

Lenora saw Eirena's right hand slide between the folds of her dress and emerge with a long, wicked-looking knife. She slid her arm around Snorri's waist.

"Again, please," she murmured, and Snorri kissed her once more.

Eirena's arm moved suddenly, like a snake striking its victim, and her knife found its target between Snorri's ribs.

He knew something had happened, but he wasn't sure what. He released Eirena and staggered backward, staring at her with disbelief in his rapidly glazing eyes. She stabbed him again.

He tried to speak, but no sound came from his lips. He raised his sword arm to strike her, but the sword slipped out of his numb fingers and fell to the marble floor with a loud clatter. It was the last sound Snorri ever heard.

He crashed face-forward onto the floor, falling into the brazier and sending red-hot charcoal scattering across the polished surface.

Lenora, gaping at the scene before her, heard echoing through her mind the words of a long-ago prophecy: "Treachery and double treachery ... death at the hands of a woman."

Eirena stepped back with a dainty little movement, just in time to avoid having her gown splattered with Snorri's blood.

"Filth," she muttered, wiping her mouth as if to erase Snorri's imprint. "How dirty he was. An evil-smelling man."

433

She turned to Erik and Lenora, still bound to their chairs.

"I should kill you two and blame it on him," she said in a conversational tone.

"Release me, Eirena." Erik's voice was quiet but commanding.

"Not yet."

Eirena approached Erik, smiling. Suddenly she sat on his lap, wound her arms around his neck, and kissed him. It was a long kiss, and, on Eirena's part, a passionate one. At last she drew away and smoothed down his hair. Her fingers traced the outline of his mouth.

"That will take away part of the stain Snorri put on me," she said, "even though I finally know you don't want me. You never did."

"Let me go."

"Now I will."

Eirena worked at the knots in the heavy cord until Erik's hands were free. Then, while he rubbed at his wrists, she went to Lenora and loosened her ropes.

"Thank you," Lenora said.

"Don't thank me. Just go. I have had enough of you Rus barbarians."

Erik's steel-strong hands caught Eirena by the wrists.

"You betrayed me twice, Eirena. First to your brother and then to Snorri. Now it's time for you to pay."

"What do you want of me?"

"Gold."

Eirena bared her teeth in an angry grimace.

"You Norse are all alike. All you think about is gold."

"Are you Greeks any different? We will go away and you will never be bothered by us again, but we need money for the trip."

"I don't have any gold."

"Basil keeps money here. I want it."

"No."

Erik twisted her arm behind her back. Eirena cried out in pain, and then screamed in real fear as she saw Lenora.

Lenora had pounced on Snorri's sword. Holding it before her with both hands, she advanced toward Erik and Eirena.

"You witch," Lenora said slowly. "You terrified Maura, and you were going to give me to that monster. I should slice you into little pieces."

"I did you a favor," Eirena snarled back at her. "I killed him for you."

Lenora lowered the sword a bit.

"Yes, you did." She looked at Erik. "Now only you are left. You are the last unpunished member of the family on whom I once swore vengeance."

Erik thrust Eirena aside and stood still before Lenora, his arms down at his sides.

"Kill me if you want," he said. "It is your right. Exact your revenge."

"I—I—Erik?" The sword in Lenora's hand wavered. Did he truly believe she could want to harm him after all they had endured together?

"I love you, Lenora. I did not want to, and I have never said it before, but I do. I love you with

435

all my heart and soul. Now do what you will. I'll not fight you."

Lenora swayed, the weight of Snorri's great sword pulling at her. Her lips parted, but no words passed them. *Love.* He had said *love.* She cast the sword away, and with it the last traces of old hatreds and the desire for vengeance.

"Oh, *Erik.*" She fell into his arms. She rested there only a moment before he pushed her away and sprang after Eirena, who had pulled open the door into the hall.

"Not so fast." He slammed the door shut again, holding it with one shoulder. He caught Eirena by the elbow, spun her around, and shoved her into the middle of the room.

"The gold," he said. "Where is it?"

"I don't know."

"You're lying, as usual. Give me the sword, Lenora."

He took the heavy blade and tucked it neatly under Eirena's chin.

"The gold, please." There could be no doubt Erik meant business.

"It's in Basil's room."

"Good. Lenora?"

"I'm here."

"Go to your room and pack a few warm clothes, then go to my room and do the same. We are going to Kiev, and it is cold there in the winter.

"To Kiev again? Is that safe? Won't Snorri's people follow us?" Lenora sounded as doubtful as she felt.

"Kiev will be safer than here. Meet us back in

this room. Eirena and I are going to get our passage money."

Eirena laughed at them.

"Don't think you are going to St. Mamas to find your barbarian friends," she told them. "Ten of Snorri's men are waiting by the front gate. If you step outside they will kill you."

Erik smiled at her. "Thank you for the warning, Eirena. You really are very helpful."

When Lenora returned to the room where Snorri's body lay, she found Erik and Eirena already awaiting her.

"Here." Erik tossed her a pouch of gold bezants, the coins of the Eastern Roman Empire. "In case we are separated. These are good anywhere in the world."

Lenora tucked them into the bundle of clothes she had prepared.

"Sit down, Eirena," Erik said. "We are going to tie you up and gag you so you can't betray us again before we escape. You won't be uncomfortable for too long. One of your guards or servants will come looking for you soon."

"You can't leave me in the same room with him." Eirena looked with loathing at Snorri's body.

"Why not? You can spend your time thinking of a good explanation for having a dead Norseman in your sitting room. You might also decide on an acceptable apology for the men who are waiting at your front gate."

He bound her securely and turned the chair away from the windows.

"I hope you don't mind the lack of a view," he said. "I don't want you to watch us sail away."

"I already know you are going to Kiev." Eirena glared at him. "You aren't as clever as you think, Erik. You let that information slip a little while ago."

"Did I? Foolish of me, but by the time you're found, it won't matter. Anything you'd like to say before I put this in?" Erik held up a wad of cloth.

"I hate you."

"From my point of view, that is a great improvement." He gagged her with apparent pleasure.

"There is just one more thing to do. Since you have suggested it several times, Eirena, I think you should be the witness."

Erik took Lenora's hand.

"Before this witness," he said, reciting the formula slowly and clearly, "I declare this woman has been my slave. Lenora, I hereby set you free."

"Thank you." Lenora could barely whisper the words around the sudden lump in her throat.

"If you want to rejoin Maura in the city," Erik told her, "I can arrange for that, or you may go with me. You are free now, and the choice is yours."

"There is no choice. I am going with you. I love you."

She had a glimpse of his moist eyes before he turned and picked up their bundles. When he spoke again his voice was a bit rough. "Are you ready, Lenora?"

"I'm ready."

They slipped out of the room, crept down the back stairs, and, after a careful reconnaissance, went out a garden door. The wind tugged at Lenora's cloak. Erik caught her hand and pulled her along the terrace toward the path leading to the beach.

"We are going this way," he said, "to avoid Snorri's men."

They hurried down the path, twisting and turning among bushes and trees, until at last they came out on the narrow, sandy beach.

"What shall we do now?" Lenora asked.

"Give me your scarf."

She unwrapped the long piece of white silk from her head. Erik took it, and holding it high in one hand, waved it back and forth. A few moments later Lenora saw a movement on the water as a tiny boat drew steadily closer. At last she could see the blond, bearded figure at the oars.

"Harald," she breathed. "So, we are going with Harald."

When the boat approached the beach, Erik swept Lenora into his arms and deposited her on the nearest seat. Then he dumped in their scanty baggage and jumped in beside her.

"Your sword is there, wrapped in silk," Harald said. "I thought you might need it."

"My brother came to see me." Erik buckled the belt around his waist and adjusted the sword as he spoke.

"I had heard there was someone looking for you. Did he get what he came for?"

"I think so. Let me help you."

Erik took an oar, and together the men rowed, heading straight out into the Bosporus. They had nearly reached the opposite shore before Lenora noticed Harald's knarr. It had been painted black and was almost invisible in the rapidly deepening dusk. As they pulled alongside, friendly hands reached down to help them aboard. The rowboat was quickly hauled onto the deck and secured, the anchor raised, and then the sail was let out.

Lenora stared open-mouthed. The sail was black. They began to move toward the setting sun.

"Erik," she protested, "We're going west. Kiev lies east of Constantinople."

His strong arm was around her shoulders. "We aren't going to Kiev, my love."

"But you told Eirena—" She stopped and began to laugh.

"When Eirena gives the alarm," Erik told her, "if Snorri's men go after us, they will start looking in the wrong direction. Meanwhile, hidden in the dark, with black hull and sail and no lamps lit, we will smuggle Harald's ship and its cargo past Miklagard, past the Greek guards and watchtowers, through the little ocean they call the Marmora, past the Byzantine outposts guarding the straits at the far end of the Marmora, and into the great Middle Sea that lies beyond Grikkland."

"Maura was right. She said you always have a plan." She glanced up at his handsome face, just

440

discernable in the fading light. "Where are we really going?"

"Where would you like to go?"

She considered that a while.

"It doesn't matter," she said at last, "so long as we are together."

He pulled her into his arms, ignoring the humorous comments of nearby crew members.

"We will sail as far as Harald is going. We have a full cargo of silk and ivory, on which we have paid no taxes, since we neglected to inform the customs authorities just when we were planning to leave Constantinople. Harald and I will make a handsome profit from this voyage." His lips brushed her forehead, and they stood quietly for a while.

"I knew you would never kill me," he told her later. "You are too tender-hearted to take the revenge you said you wanted."

"I killed Hrolf and Bjarni," she reminded him.

"Hrolf to save me, and Bjarni for Halfdan's sake. You have never hurt anyone for your own sake." He sighed happily. "I am glad you are finally finished with hating, and with your foolish idea of revenge."

"I'm not finished. I have only begun." Her eyes were dancing with mischief, but he could not see them in the dark. He only heard her serious voice, and she felt his body tense. She smothered laughter, but only for a moment. It wasn't fair to tease him into doubting her. "I have chosen to go with you. You will have to live with me for the rest of

441

your life. That is my final revenge, Erik the Far-traveler."

He let out a great shout of laughter. "I think I can bear it," he said. And then he kissed her.

Epilogue

In mid-December of the Year of Our Lord 868, a black-hulled, black-sailed vessel dropped anchor at the ancient port of Marseilles in southern Frankland. The cargo of rich silks and fine ivory from the Eastern Empire was immediately sold to eager merchants. The ship's captain then found a priest to marry his two passengers.

It was said by the local gossips, who always know about such things, that the wedding ring was a gold circle that the bridegroom took from his own finger and slipped onto his new wife's hand, while the lady openly wept for joy.

The next day passengers and crew reassembled, and the ship sailed toward the Western Sea. No one in Marseilles had been told where they were going.